BERTOLT BRECHT

THREEPENNY NOVEL

–

Translated by Desmond I. Vesey
Verses translated by
Christopher Isherwood

PENGUIN BOOKS

Penguin Books Ltd, Harmondsworth, Middlesex, England
Penguin Books Australia Ltd, Ringwood, Victoria, Australia

—

Der Dreigroschenroman first published 1934
This translation first published under the title *A Penny for the Poor*
by Robert Hale 1937
Published as *Threepenny Novel* by Bernard Harrison 1958
Published in Penguin Books 1961
Reprinted 1962
Reprinted in Penguin Modern Classics 1965, 1967

—

Made and printed in Great Britain
by Hazell Watson & Viney, Ltd,
Aylesbury, Bucks
Set in Linotype Granjon

THE SURVIVOR

THE SURVIVOR

A SOLDIER by the name of George Fewkoombey was shot in
the leg in the Boer War, so that the lower half of his leg had
to be amputated in a hospital in Cape Town. When he came
back to London, he received £75, in return for which he signed
a paper stating that he had no more claims on the State. The
£75 he invested in a small ale-house in Newgate, which, as he
could see from the books (small, beer-stained notebooks written
in pencil), made a comfortable profit of £2 a week.

When he had moved into the tiny back room and had sold
beer with the help of an old woman for a few weeks, he knew
that the loss of his leg had not been particularly worth while;
the takings had remained considerably under £2, although the
soldier was always a model of politeness towards his customers.
He learned that there had recently been some building going on
in those parts and that the builders had been good customers at
the ale-house. But now the building was finished and all the
custom was gone. As people said to him, he could easily have
seen from the books that business had been brisker on weekdays
than on holidays, which is contrary to the expectations of all experienced public-house keepers; but then the man had always
been the customer at such places and never the owner. He was
able to keep going for just four months. It might have been
longer, only he wasted so much time looking for the previous
owner. And then he found himself penniless on the streets.

For a time he found shelter with a soldier's wife, to whose
children he told stories of the war while she looked after her
little shop. Then her husband wrote to her that he was coming
home on leave and she told the soldier, with whom in the mean-

time, as does happen in these small houses, she had been sleeping, that he must leave as quickly as possible. He waited a few more days, then had to go. He visited her once or twice after her husband had returned home and was given something to eat. But he sank lower and lower until he finally joined the endless line of wretches whom hunger drives day and night through the streets of the greatest city in the world.

One morning he stood on one of the Thames bridges. For two days he had had nothing proper to eat, for the people in public houses whom he had approached in his uniform had given him drinks but no food. Without the uniform they wouldn't even have given him drinks, and that was why he had put it on.

Now he was again in the ordinary clothes which he had worn as landlord. For he was intending to beg, and he was ashamed. He was not ashamed of having had a bullet in the leg, nor of having bought a public house that didn't pay, but because he was reduced to asking complete strangers for money. In his opinion no one owed him anything.

Begging came hard to him. It is the profession for those who have learned nothing; only it seemed that even this business had to be learned. He spoke to several people one after another, but with a courageous expression on his face, and taking care not to stand in people's way so that they should not feel that they were being pestered. Also, he chose rather long sentences that were only completed when the person was a long way past; neither did he hold out his hand. And so, by the fifth time that he had humiliated himself, scarcely anyone had noticed that he was begging.

But someone had noticed it, for he suddenly heard a hoarse voice behind him say: 'Get out of here!' Because he felt so guilty, he did not even look round. He simply moved on, shoulders drooping. Only after a hundred yards did he dare turn his head, and then he saw two ragged beggars of the lowest sort standing beside one another and looking after him. They followed him, too, as he limped on.

It was not until he had crossed several streets that he saw that they were not following him any more.

On the next day, as he loitered around the neighbourhood of

the docks, now and again astonishing people of the lower classes by his attempts to speak to them, he was suddenly struck in the back. At the same time his attacker pushed something into his pocket. When he turned round he saw no one, but out of his pocket he drew a piece of card, much crumpled and exceedingly dirty. On it was printed the name of a firm: *J. J. Peachum, 7 Old Oak Street*; and underneath was written in smudged pencil: 'If you dont want no boanes broke come to the above address.' This was twice underlined.

Slowly it dawned on Fewkoombey that the attacks were connected with his begging. But he felt no special desire to visit Old Oak Street.

That afternoon, as he stood outside a public house, he was spoken to by a beggar whom he recognized as one of those of the previous day. He was quite a young man and did not look really bad. He grasped Fewkoombey by the sleeve and drew him away.

'You dirty swine,' he began in a friendly voice, 'show me your number!'

'What number?' asked the soldier.

Slouching along beside him, still friendly but never for a moment letting go of him, the young man explained in the language of his kind that this new profession was just as well organized as any other, perhaps even better; and that he, the soldier, was not in a wild, uncivilized corner of the globe but in a great city, the hub of the world. For the carrying on of his new trade he must have a number, a sort of permit which he could obtain – at a price – from a union with headquarters in Old Oak Street, to which union he must belong.

Fewkoombey listened without asking a single question. Then he answered, just as pleasantly – they were passing along a crowded street – that he was glad to hear they had a union, just like the bricklayers and hairdressers, but for his part he preferred to do just as he liked. He had had too many orders in his life rather than too few, as his wooden leg proved.

With that he held out his hand to his companion, who had been listening with the expression of one hearing an exceptionally interesting discourse by a clever speaker with whom, however, he cannot quite agree. The latter laughed and clapped him on the back like an old friend and departed across the street. Fewkoombey did not like the sound of his laugh.

The next few days he fared even worse than before.

It appeared that in order to receive a fairly regular supply of alms, one had to remain sitting in one particular spot (and there were good spots and bad spots), and he was unable to do that. He was always driven away. He didn't know how the others managed. Somehow they all looked wretcheder than he. Their clothes were genuine rags through which one could see their bones. (Later he learned that in certain circles a suit of clothes without such flesh-revealing peepholes was regarded as equivalent to a shop-window which has paper pasted over it.) Also their physical appearance was more repulsive; they had more and direr infirmities. Many of them sat on the cold pavement without anything under them so that the passers-by could be really sure that the supplicant would get ill. Fewkoombey would gladly have sat on the cold ground if only he had been allowed to. Apparently however, this detestable and pitiable position was not permitted to everyone. Policemen and beggars continually disturbed him.

Because of what he had gone through, he caught a cold which settled on his chest, so that he had to walk round with shooting pains and a high fever.

One evening he again met the young beggar, who immediately began to follow him. Two streets further on a second beggar joined the first. He began to run; they ran too.

He turned into a smaller alley in order to escape them. He already thought that he had succeeded when he suddenly saw them in front of him on a street corner, and before he could turn round they hit at him with their sticks. One of them even pushed him over on to the pavement and pulled at his wooden leg so that he fell backwards on his head. At this point, however, they let go of him and ran away; a policeman was coming round the corner.

Fewkoombey was already hoping that the policeman would help him up, when, from out of a passage between the houses just beside him, came a third beggar on a little truck, who pointed excitedly at the two men running away and tried to say something to the policeman in a guttural voice. When Fewkoombey, after being jerked up by the policeman and pushed off with a kick, tramped on, the beggar remained close beside him, propelling his iron trolley with both hands.

His legs seemed to be missing.

At the next street corner the legless one grasped Fewkoombey by the trousers. They were now in the dirtiest quarter of the slums; the alleys were no wider than the average man's height, and off one of them opened a low passage leading into a dark courtyard. 'In there!' commanded the cripple hoarsely. At the same time he drove forward with his truck against Fewkoombey's shinbone, and the soldier, being already weak with hunger, was forced into the tiny court, which was little more than three yards square. And before the astonished man could look round, the cripple, an elderly person with an enormous jawbone, climbed like a monkey out of his truck, suddenly became possessed of two healthy legs, and sprang on him.

He was a good head taller than Fewkoombey and had arms like an orang-outang.

'*Take off your coat,*' he growled, '*and show in an open, honest fight whether you're a worthier man than me to have a good, profitable pitch. "Make way for the fittest and damnation to the conquered" is my motto. In that way the whole of mankind is benefited; for the fittest rise to the top and possess the good things on earth. But don't try any dirty tricks, don't hit below the belt, and don't use knees. If the fight is to be decisive, it must be fought under Queensberry Rules!*'

The fight was short. Physically and spiritually broken, Fewkoombey slunk behind the old man.

Old Oak Street was not mentioned.

For a week the soldier remained under the rule of his new master. The latter installed him on a certain corner, once more in uniform; and in the evening, when he had paid in his earnings, the old man fed him.

His takings still remained at a very low level. He had to give it all to his employer, so never knew whether his few pennies paid for the herrings and cheap gin which formed his chief meal of the day. The old man, whose infirmities seemed so much worse than the soldier's but in reality did not exist at all, did immeasurably better trade.

After a time, the soldier came to the conviction that his master had only wanted the site on the bridge occupied for his own benefit. The main sources of profit were the people who came by the place every morning, or if they were going to work, every morning and evening. They only gave once and generally always walked on the same side of the road; but sometimes they changed over. One could never rely on them completely.

Fewkoombey felt that this situation was a step forward, but it was not yet the right one.

After a week had elapsed, the old man received attentions, apparently on his own behalf, from the secret society in Old Oak Street. One morning early, as they were leaving their sleeping-place in a boat-house, they were attacked by four or five beggars and carried along several streets until they reached a small, dirty shop whose sign said INSTRUMENTS.

Behind a worm-eaten counter stood two men. The one, who was small and dried up, with an unpleasant face, stood in shirt-sleeves, with a greasy hat perched on the back of his head, and his hands in his pockets, staring out of the shop-window at the dreary morning outside. He did not turn round and showed no sign of interest in the new arrivals. The other was fat and very red in the face and looked, if possible, even more unpleasant than the first.

'Good morning, Mr Smithy,' he said to the old man – scornfully, so it seemed – and went through an iron-covered door into a back room. The old man looked round uncertainly before he followed in the wake of the men who had fetched him. His face had grown grey.

Fewkoombey, apparently forgotten, remained standing in the shop. On the walls hung a few musical instruments, battered old trumpets, violins without any strings, some weather-beaten hurdy-gurdies. Business did not seem to be brisk, for the instruments were covered with a thick layer of dust.

Fewkoombey was to learn that these seven or eight antiques played no part in the business whose service he had just entered. Even the narrow, two-windowed front of the house gave a very incomplete idea of the extent of its rambling interior. Even the counter with its rickety cash-drawer revealed nothing.

In the house, which was actually three houses in one and

enclosed two back-yards, were a workshop with a half a dozen girls sewing in it and a shoemaking establishment occupied by the same number of expert workmen. And, most important of all, somewhere in the building was a records room which contained at least 6,000 names belonging to all those who had the honour to be associated with the firm.

The soldier had no idea how this unique and disreputable business functioned; he took a whole week to learn that. But he was too desperate not to realize that it was a piece of good fortune to be allowed to come here and join such a mighty and secret organization.

Mr Smithy, Fewkoombey's first employer, did not appear again that morning, and Fewkoombey saw him at the most only two or three times more – and then from a distance.

After a time, the fat man opened the iron door slightly and called into the shop:

'He's got a real wooden leg.'

The small man, who nevertheless seemed to be the chief, walked across to Fewkoombey and with a rapid movement lifted up his trousers to see his wooden leg. Then, hands in pockets, he went back to the window, looked out, and said softly:

'What can you do?'

'Nothing,' said the soldier, just as softly. 'I beg.'

'That's what everyone would like to do,' said the small man scornfully, never even looking around. *'You've got a wooden leg. And because you've got a wooden leg, you want to beg? But you lost your leg in the service of your country? So much the worse. That can happen to anyone. (Unless he's in the War Office.) When a person loses his leg he's thrown upon the mercy of others? Of course he is! But it's equally certain that people don't like giving away money. Wars – they're exceptional cases. If an earthquake happens, no one can help that. As if everyone doesn't know the profit that is made out of the patriotism of patriots. At first they all enlist voluntarily, and then, when their legs are shot away, they won't accept the situation. Quite apart from those innumerable cases, such as where the driver of a brewer's dray loses a leg in the course of his duties and then coins money out of the Battle of Something-or-other. And there's one*

thing more, the chief thing: why is it so profitable to go to war for one's country, why are these brave men so loaded with honour and glory? — simply because there's a chance of losing a leg? If there wasn't this small risk — well, this big risk if you like — why should they have the heartfelt gratitude of the nation? Actually you are an anti-war demonstrator. No, there's no use denying it. When you stand about, making no effort to hide your stump, you're saying to everyone: Look what a terrible thing war is; it takes off a man's leg! You should be ashamed of yourself. Wars are as necessary as they are terrible. Do you want everything taken away from us? Do you want to see Great Britain full of foreigners? Would you like to live in the midst of enemies? In short, you ought not to hawk your misery around. You haven't the talent for that. . . .'

When he had finished speaking, he went, without looking at the soldier, through the iron door into his office. But the fat man came out and took Fewkoombey, because of his leg, he said, through one back-yard into a second yard, where he put him in charge of a dog-kennel.

As a result of this, the soldier walked round and round the yard every morning and evening, exercising and looking after the blind men's dogs. There were quite a number of these dogs; they were not selected for their ability to lead blind men (there were less than five such unfortunates in the place), but for other points, namely whether they would arouse enough pity from passers-by, i.e. look cheap enough, which, indeed, partly depended on their feeding. They all looked very cheap.

If Fewkoombey had been asked by a welfare worker what his profession was, he would have found difficulty in answering; quite apart from his fears of falling foul of the police. He could hardly have called himself a beggar. He was an employee in a concern that sold the accessories for street-begging.

No more attempts were made to make an even tolerably competent beggar out of him. The experts here had recognized at first glance that he would never be a success. He had had luck. He possessed none of the qualifications which make a beggar, but he had one thing which not everyone here could boast of — a wooden leg; and that was sufficient to secure him a job.

Now and again he was called into the shop and had to show

a constable from the nearby police-station his wooden leg. For this purpose there was really no need for the leg to be as genuine as it really was. The man scarcely glanced at it. It nearly always happened that Polly Peachum, the daughter of the head of the firm, was present at these visits, and she knew how to manage the constable.

Generally speaking, however, it was among the dogs that the former soldier spent the last six months of life that were still left to him. After that time he ended his meagre existence in an unusual way, with a rope around his neck and amid the approval of a great multitude of people.

The small man, whom he had seen standing at the window of the shop on the morning of his arrival at this interesting house, was Mr Jonathan Jeremiah Peachum.

Book One

LOVE AND MARRIAGE OF POLLY PEACHUM

—

When I was only a simple little girl –
For I once was simple just like you –
I thought: perhaps some day there'll come someone
And then I'll have to know what to do.
And if he's got money
And if he's a nice boy
And if his workday collar's white as snow
And if he knows how a lady should be treated
Then I shall tell him: 'No.'
For you must talk about the weather
And never let your feelings show.
The moon will shine all night, as before;
Certainly the boat will be tied to the shore.
But that's as far as it may go.
O, a girl can't afford to make herself too cheap!
O, a girl must keep her man well in tow.
Or else all sorts of things might happen!
Ah, the only answer is: No.

The first one who came, he was a man from Kent
And all that a man should be.
The second owned three steamers in the harbour
And the third was wild about me.
And as they'd got money
And as they were nice boys
With their workday collars white as snow
And as they knew how a lady should be treated
I said to all three: 'No.'
So I talked about the weather,
Never let my feelings show.
And the moon shone all night, as before;
Certainly the boat was tied to the shore,
But that was as far as it could go.

O, a girl can't afford to make herself too cheap!
O, I had to keep my man well in tow.
Or else all sorts of things might have happened!
Ah, the only answer was: No.

But then one fine morning, when the sky was blue,
Came a man who did not sigh
But just hung his hat up on the peg in my bedroom
And I let him, and didn't know why.
And as he had no money
And as he wasn't a nice boy
And even his Sunday collar wasn't white as snow
And as he didn't know how a lady should be treated
To him I couldn't say No.
Then I didn't talk about the weather
And I let my feelings show.
Ah, the moon shone all night, as before;
But the boat was cast loose and put out from the shore,
It all had to be just so!
O, sometimes a girl must make herself cheap!
O, sometimes she can't keep her man in tow.
But then, ah, anything may happen!
And there's no such word as No.

(POLLY PEACHUM'S SONG)

The Beggar's Friend

In order to combat the increasing tight-fistedness of mankind, Mr Peachum had opened a shop in which the meanest beggar could hire accessories guaranteed to soften the stoniest of hearts.

At first engaged in the sale of second-hand musical instruments which he sold or hired to beggars and street-singers, and then, since the profits were not sufficient, acting as relieving officer for the parish, he had had ample opportunity to study the conditions of the poor. The use of his instruments by beggars was the first thing that gave him food for thought.

Everyone knows that these men use musical instruments to soften people's hearts, which is not at all easy. For the better off a person is, the more difficult it is for him to feel sympathy, although he is quite ready to pay a high price for a seat at a concert where he hopes to receive his necessary spiritual nourishment. But in the case of a man less well-off, he always has a penny to spare, and so can afford to allow his heart, hardened by the fight for existence, to be softened by this or that little melody.

Yet Jonathan Jeremiah Peachum found again and again that his clients who hired the barrel organs and trumpets were always behindhand with their payments. There are, as has already been said, a few things which can soften the hearts of people today, but the trouble is that after these things have been used a few times they cease to be effective, for man has the terrible ability of being able to make himself hard-hearted at will when he discovers the disastrous results of his soft-heartedness. And so it happens, for example, that if a person sees a man without an arm for the first time, the shock will make him give twopence, but the second time he will only give a halfpenny, and if he sees him for the third time he will most likely hand him cold-bloodedly over to the police.

Peachum had begun in quite a small way.

For a time he had helped with his advice a few beggars, one-armed, blind, or very aged. He sought out situations for them, places where people gave; for people do not give everywhere and at any time. For example, instead of making music in June, it was better to go round the parks at night disturbing couples; they paid more willingly.

The beggars who came to Peachum soon found that their takings were increasing. So they agreed to give him, for his trouble, a part of the money they earned.

Now sure of his vocation, he carried his investigations further.

Fairly soon he discovered that a miserable appearance which was genuine was far less effective than an artificially assumed misery. It often happened that people with only one arm were not, also, possessed of the gift of giving an impression of misery. On the other hand, more gifted people were often lacking a stump. Here was an opportunity for initiative.

Peachum prepared a few artificial limbs, maimed arms and legs which showed plainly that they had been brutally muti-lated. These had a staggering success.

After a short time he was able to set up a studio for the manu-facture of such limbs.

Certain shopkeepers, especially delicatessen dealers and owners of beauty parlours, and also ordinary butchers, willingly paid a small sum to any beggar with such disgusting deformities as an inducement to move on. It was but a short step from this humble beginning to higher payments, in return for which the beggar allowed himself to be sent on to rival establishments. The busi-ness fought hard for its existence.

As the records room grew, Peachum, the 'beggar's friend' as he called himself, began monopolizing special districts for certain beggars. Intruders were kept away, in some cases by force. This new experiment gave Peachum's enterprise its real start on the road to success.

But he did not rest on these laurels. He worked tirelessly to equip his people for their profession. In certain rooms of his business premises, now considerably enlarged, the beggars, who more and more were assuming the status of employees, were instructed, after eliminating tests, in the arts of twitching, walk-ing blind, etc. Mr Peachum allowed no stagnation in the busi-ness.

Various fundamental types of human misery were perfected; victims of progress, victims of war, victims of industrial prosperity. They learned to soften hearts, to attract attention, to pester. Naturally people cannot be expected to give up a lucrative business, but they are often weak enough to wish to cover up the results of it.

After nearly twenty-five years of unceasing activity, Peachum owned three houses and a flourishing concern.

Peach-Blossom

The houses in which Mr Jonathan Jeremiah Peachum ran his unusual factory had many rooms. Amongst them was a little pink-distempered room belonging to Miss Polly Peachum. Two of the four tiny rooms in Mr Peachum's private house looked out over the street in front; the other two looked over the yard. But outside these latter ran a wooden balcony, so their windows had to have linen curtains to prevent people looking in. And these windows were only opened on the hottest of nights so that a draught could come in when the room became stuffy. Polly's room was on the second floor, right underneath the roof.

Throughout the neighbourhood, Miss Peachum was known as 'the Peach'. She had a very beautiful skin.

When she was fourteen years old, she had been given her own room on the second floor; people said that this was so that she shouldn't see too much of her mother, who was unable to control her weakness for spirits. From this age, too, she was addressed as 'Miss', and appeared at certain times in the front shop, especially when Constable Mitchgin was there. At first she was, perhaps, too young for this; but as has been said, she was very beautiful.

Into the other rooms, the sewing-room and the leather-room, she went very seldom. Her father disapproved of her going into his workshops. All the same, she knew them and found nothing of interest there.

Meanwhile the instrument shop flourished greatly, and everyone said that the fat Mitchgin would have taken far more interest in her father's business had it not been for Polly. A tremendous amount of people went in and out just because of those few instruments.

Jonathan Jeremiah Peachum was, indeed, relieving officer for three parishes, but the poor did not like going to him; they were really too poor for that. Peachum would have nothing to do with begging unless it was conducted under his own direction and according to rules.

It was, actually, only natural that the Peach should take some trouble to be nice to the fat Mitchgin, because, after all, everything was being done for her sake alone. Often enough she had heard her father say: 'If it wasn't for the child, I wouldn't lead this dog's life for a day longer; certainly not for you, Emma. Anyway, not so that you could drink yourself into your grave!'

Emma was Mrs Peachum, and when her husband thus expressed his dislike of her little habits, she always said: 'Had I had certain other comforts in my married life, not a drop would have passed my lips. Besides, I could stop today if I wanted to.'

Children hear a great many conversations like this, and it makes a certain impression on them.

One might think, by the way, that with regard to the favours (small, as stated) shown by Polly to Mitchgin and others, she had been brought up that way. Quite the opposite. She could remember no time in her young life when she had bathed in the tub in the wash-house (the windows were always curtained) without wearing a night-dress. Mr Peachum did not approve of her seeing her beautiful skin.

Mr Peachum, also, never dreamed of allowing her to be alone outside the parental home, even for five minutes. Of course she went to school like all other children. But she was always fetched back by Sam.

'Your daughter is a mass of sensuality, nothing more,' said Mr Peachum to his wife after he had once discovered Polly hanging on the wall of her room a photograph of an actor which she had cut out of the newspaper. And for years that remained his opinion of her.

Mrs Peachum had other ideas of sensuality; they were mainly bitter ones. When her daughter had passed her eighteenth year, she took her along on her Sunday afternoon visits to the

'Octopus'. This was a public house of a respectable kind which had a little garden behind with three stunted chestnut trees in it. On Sunday afternoons and evenings a brass band played there. And there was dancing, highly respectable, of course, while the mothers sat beside the garden fence knitting.

Here, a girl like Polly could not remain long unnoticed. Soon she had many suitors, of which two were worthy of serious consideration. Of these two, Mr Beckett was the first and Mr Smiles the pleasanter. Nevertheless, Mr Beckett's prospects began to improve because of, and with the advent of, Mr Smiles.

Mr Beckett was a short, thick-set man, with a head shaped like a radish. He wore spats over his shoes and carried an extraordinarily thick stick, which he scarcely ever let out of his plump hands. His complexion was not of the healthiest; he was not to be compared with Mr Smiles, who was much younger and had the healthy colour of young people who go rowing on the Thames. But Beckett was a business man and Smiles was a clerk in a solicitor's office, and because of that Mr Beckett inspired Mrs Peachum with far greater confidence than his rival. Young people like Smiles have no sense of responsibility; they mostly live only for the day, given over entirely to their own enjoyment. What would have been the use of insisting that such a good-for-nothing young fellow should try to consolidate himself in his profession; what was a profession to him?

In the spring the Peach went to evening classes in housekeeping. One night, on the way home, Mr Smiles suddenly appeared beside her. He pushed her against a doorway and talked to her, with his arms outstretched to right and left of her, and the palms of his hands pressed against the wall. For the most part he contented himself with enjoying her fragrance. He himself did little more.

Since Mrs Peachum guessed something of this, she went thoroughly through her daughter's washing once a month and showed her preference in every way for Mr Beckett. Mr Beckett was a timber merchant, a gentleman of sound principles. Energetically patronized by Mrs Peachum, he came well to the fore – and not only outwardly. The attraction of a good-looking man was counterbalanced by the no lesser attraction of a prosperous merchant.

23

His grip about the hips at dancing was, also, astonishing for a timber merchant. It was just these little tendernesses, winked at by the mother, that seemed to promise bigger and better things to come. And yet Mr Beckett never got far beyond such innocent intimacies.

He was at a disadvantage with Mr Smiles because he was an extremely busy man, and so did not have as much time to spare as the latter. He could not always get away.

All the same, he soon noticed that the Peach was inclined to take him seriously. Fortunately he had less reason for objecting to a genuine marriage than most people. He invited Mrs Peachum and her daughter to a picnic by the Thames, which took place one Sunday morning. It nearly fell through, how-ever, because Mr Peachum came home at five o'clock on the Saturday evening in a state of great distress. In a pitiable voice he demanded camomile tea, before going to bed and got his wife to lay a brick wrapped in hot damp cloths on his stomach.

For some time past he had been involved in a transaction which lay outside his usual range of activities; it had to do with some sort of transport-ships. The business did not seem to be progressing favourably, and any worry always upset his stomach. But on Sunday morning he went, although still very weak, to church with his wife and daughter, and then straight on to a conference. The ladies were lucky; he seemed to be in serious difficulties.

For the expedition, Mr Beckett, who arrived dressed in a white suit, had hired a hansom. He had had considerable diffi-culty in securing a vehicle with such a narrow seat.

On the drive out, Mrs Peachum squeezed herself in between Beckett and Polly; but when they reached their destination, the basket, which had been wedged in between the three pairs of feet, revealed, in addition to hard-boiled eggs, ham sandwiches, and a cold chicken, three bottles of gin; and so it happened that Mr Beckett was happily seated beside Polly on the home-ward journey.

It was raining a little; the rug in which they were wrapped was not quite large enough; and Mrs Peachum, in a bass voice, urged on the driver, for it was getting on towards two o'clock.

The parting from the two ladies in front of the 'Octopus'

was short, and no further meeting was arranged. Except for the rain on his square head, the timber merchant stood, at the parting, in exactly the same posture as at the beginning of the little expedition; but he was no longer the same man. During the following week he, to whom time meant money, sat every evening with the exception of Thursday in the 'Octopus'; one evening he even came there twice. Mrs Peachum alone saw him three times at different hours of the day, standing in Old Oak Street and supporting himself on his heavy stick which he propped against his back with both hands. Actually, he stared most of the time at the sign with 'INSTRUMENTS' on it.

He was studying the house.

While he waited for the Peach, he observed closely the activities of this remarkable shop. He saw normal, healthy men enter the door, and others emerge propelling little cripple trucks. He soon saw that they were not others at all. They had been changed into cripples. The nature of the business gradually dawned on him. He realized that it must be a gold mine.

Mrs Peachum, who watched him from behind a window on the first floor, had her own thoughts about the persistent suitor.

He appeared to be expecting some move from the Peach's side which was not forthcoming. His view, that something had happened on the picnic which must have certain results, was apparently not shared by a certain person. When Miss Peachum came home from her evening classes in housekeeping, she used an entrance which lay in another street.

Quite often she hurried away to meet Smiles. It was fun sauntering with him through the park in the evening when the benches were full of couples. He said nice things to her and took a great interest in her appearance. There was a particular place on her neck which he liked to be able to see, otherwise the dress was 'unsuitable'. He said she would drive him mad.

He always came very punctually to their rendezvous, and rather hastily. That gave the impression that he had a great deal of business to attend to.

In those days the Peach really blossomed out for the first time. It was spring. Polly used to go into the workrooms in a light blue dress with white spots and watch the candle-grease being ironed into clothes so that they would look dirty; and while

25

overworked girls in the narrow, tumbledown room with its two skylights made disrespectful remarks, she would lift up her skirts and show a little white behind.

She played around with the dogs in the yard and laughing gaily, gave them funny names. One of them, a fox terrier, she called Smiles. The miserable plum-tree in the yard she suddenly discovered to be beautiful. She sang when she washed in the morning, and she was in love, but not with anyone special.

With her full-moon face propped on her hands, she lay every evening on her window-seat and read novels.

'Oh!' she sighed, 'how dreadful is this scene with Elvira – the pure, beautiful girl, fighting against her sinful thoughts. She loves her lover, the brave, athletic man; she loves him from the depths of her heart, with the strongest and noblest feelings, and yet there are passions deep within her, dark, sensual passions, that are not far different from sinful desires! "What will happen to me with this handsome man?" she often sighs. "And where will it happen to me?" And my case is like Elvira's, only far worse. For I am not in love and yet I have these desires. Can I say that my lover has aroused them in me? I cannot say so. I have not been swept away by his handsomeness – one could hardly speak of handsomeness in connexion with Mr Beckett – nor by the bravery of Mr Smiles. I get up from my feather bed in the morning, and when I'm washing, such desires come over me – and they are wicked desires – that even Mr Beckett and Mr Smiles seem handsome to me! If it goes on much longer, when I lie in my innocent pink-distempered room with the sheets drawn right up under my chin and I imagine such scenes – I dare not even mention my dreams – then I fear that my fleshly desires will drag me down to the gutter where, as I have been told, so many wretches end. A few more such nights and it will have to be old one-legged George in the yard! But after all, Mr Beckett cannot be such a bad match. Yet what can I do to keep up that appearance of pure affection which he will expect from his future wife? How can I meet his eyes with a clear gaze which will quell any base desires he may have had, desires which can never, never be fulfilled before one's marriage?'

The decision of the Peach to marry the timber merchant had been arrived at without any great deliberations. The extremely practical common sense of the daughter of Mr Peachum had selected from her suitors the steadier and more dependable of the two.

All the same, the charming Mr Smiles managed again and again to meet Miss Peachum. He even tried to persuade her to live with him in a furnished room; which gave her the definite impression that he was not economically capable of supporting a wife. When she came for the second time and left the house with him, she was seen by Mr Beckett.

The next day Mrs Peachum opened a very interesting letter from the latter in which he entreated Polly to arrange a meeting with him, and openly reminded her of a certain occurrence at the picnic. The tone of the letter was extremely unpleasant.

Mrs Peachum arranged things so that Mr Beckett should meet her daughter again in the 'Octopus' on the next Sunday. She knew nothing much about Smiles and would not have believed the truth had anyone told her; she only kept on trying to think how she could warn her daughter in a delicate way against submitting too soon to the timber merchant, whom she had chosen as her son-in-law. During the night, and especially towards morning as she lay in bed beside her undersized husband, she would picture to herself with pleasure the marital embraces between her daughter and Beckett – or rather Jimmy, as she now called the timber merchant.

Her worries were unnecessary.

At the round iron table under the chestnut trees the guests sat tightly packed together, except when there was dancing, and then Polly and Mr Beckett danced too. This made conversation difficult. Nevertheless Mr Beckett succeeded in drawing the two ladies apart.

The timber merchant ordered himself a portion of sheep's liver with oil and vinegar. While he was skilfully preparing his dish, he brought the conversation round to Stanford Sills, the murderer, to whom the newspapers had attributed several recent murders in the neighbourhood of the West India Docks. The two ladies knew the name and exchanged surmises with Mr Beckett as to what this man looked like.

Mr Beckett spoke very knowledgeably about this gentleman for whose murders the police had never found a satisfactory motive and whom, so it was said, the underworld held in almost supernatural awe. It had actually happened that certain criminals whom the police were after had surrendered themselves voluntarily at Scotland Yard because they felt that they were being followed by the 'Knife', as Stanford Sills was nicknamed by the dregs of the docks.

Polly knew exactly what he looked like and described him to the timber merchant.

He was fair and slim as a lath, and so elegant that even in dock-labourer's clothes he looked like a gentleman in disguise. He was kind to women.

Polly conversed brilliantly. Mr Beckett had made a deep impression on her.

The two danced energetically and Mrs Peachum only heard parts of their conversation. To her surprise her daughter spoke solely of Mr Smiles and how charming he was. She could plainly see how Mr Beckett was sweating through his collar.

Polly seemed to have him well hooked.

On the next morning, he was again standing in the street opposite the shop. In the afternoon he permitted himself a call on Mrs Peachum – to her great embarrassment for she was afraid of Mr Peachum, who had no idea of the affair and to whom it would have to be broken carefully.

Mr Beckett sat on the edge of the red plush sofa in the drawing-room and warned Mrs Peachum against Smiles who was not a nice young man, rather debauched, and always running after women. He asked whether Smiles had been pestering Polly with letters, and seemed anxious to rake out the stove in search of charred *billets doux*.

As he was leaving, he met Polly on the steps and accompanied her to her class. She chattered of her home, of the great number of people always going in and out, and of the young gentlemen in the costumes department with whom she was very popular because she was never horrid to them.

It seemed to the timber merchant that she had blue circles round her eyes. That depressed him very much.

He saw her now, in his mind's eye, in a huge house like a dovecote, with innumerable doors out of which young men were always coming – in fact, a rather unsuitable house for a young girl. At the back of his mind rankled the remembrance of the occurrence at the picnic, or, to be more precise, on the way back from the picnic. This was an occurrence of which he never spoke, either now – or later, when a series of heavy and successive blows of fate kept him from any lengthy conversation with his wife; but it weighed upon him heavily. It had injected him with a doubt as to her innocence and with a peculiar interest in the same.

He had seldom been so smitten by any woman as he was by the Peach. There were several circumstances which contributed to this happy state.

'It is quite wrong,' he said to himself, as he examined his feelings, *'to ask oneself whether one is marrying a girl for her money or for herself. It often happens that both are the case. There are few things about a girl so attractive as a dowry. Without her money, I should naturally still want her, but not perhaps with quite the same passion.'*

The timber merchant was no novice in affairs of the heart. He had already had several wives – often simultaneously. But he had little time for adventures, for he was mixed up with extremely dangerous company and had serious worries. A fresh marriage was essential for him; his shops were not prospering.

At this time he had several newspaper-cuttings in his breast-pocket, describing an interview that a journalist had had with the Commissioner of Police about the murderer Stanford Sills, whom people called the 'Knife'. These cuttings had been sent to him anonymously and he had been very disturbed by them. For that reason he left the words, which had been on his lips, unspoken.

About a week later, through the machinations of a certain Mr Coax, Mr Jonathan Jeremiah Peachum became involved in desperate financial difficulties, and his thoughts automatically turned to his charming daughter.

2

And now they're off to the war
And they all need cartridges badly
And of course there are plenty of nice kind people
Who'll find them the cartridges gladly
'No ammunition, no war!
Leave that to us, my sons!
You go to the front and fight,
We'll make you munitions and guns.'

And they made munitions in piles
And there wasn't a war to be found
And of course there were plenty of nice kind people
Who conjured one out of the ground.
'Off you go, dear boy, to the front!
For they threaten your native sod
March, for your mothers and sisters,
For your King and for your God!'

(WAR SONG)

The Need of Her Majesty's Government

WILLIAM COAX was a broker by profession. According to his visiting-card he had an office somewhere in the City; but scarcely anyone went there, and he himself very seldom used it. He had really no reason to, for only a pale, ineffectual girl sat there with an old typewriter with battered keys, and she did nothing because there was never anything to type. The girl only sat there to wait for the post, and that was delivered to the office so that Mr Coax never need tell anyone his home-address. He never received anyone at home and conducted all his business in a restaurant.

He used to say: 'I don't need any organization. I only handle big business!' He never touched anything dirty; he always wore gloves. Also he wore a striking light grey ready-made suit, and violet socks, and a scarlet tie. He believed that people took him for an officer in mufti; so he always walked very erect.

But even if he had no expensive staff to keep up, he was not without helpers. In certain Government offices there sat various people who were just as useful to him as a lot of impertinent and lazy clerks.

One such helper he had, for example, in the Admiralty.

From him, he learned one day that Her Majesty's Government was in great need. It was in need of transport-ships to transport troops to Cape Town. Coax immediately decided to do his best to supply that need.

Since this was to be a marine transaction, he went to a public house which seamen of an inferior quality – ready-made seamen – frequented, and he inquired round for a few of the *oldest possible ships*. He soon heard of some. They belonged to the shipping firm of Brookley & Brookley, who carried on a sort of ready-made shipping business.

In London at this time there were a great many people who were not very conscientious in complying with the Government's request that the business world should give its support to the war against the Boers. They were quite ready to sell jam to the Government: but they were not prepared to eat it themselves. Mr Coax did not belong to this company. He had no desire to enrich himself at the expense of his country's misfortune and thereby become involved in harmless but tiresome investigations which would necessitate a show of offices and typewriters. Anyone else with a friend at the Admiralty would have offered to the Government the ships which Mr Coax had heard of in the public house. They were spacious and, as a tactful inquiry at Brookley & Brookley confirmed, cheap.

In the short interview which the broker had with Brookley & Brookley about the ships which were for sale, nothing else was discussed except the tonnage and the price. Neither did Coax ask any further question, nor did the shippers say anything about the condition of the ships. All three gentlemen could have sworn that at any time and before any court.

There was never any suggestion of Mr Coax buying the ships of Messrs Brookley & Brookley, in spite of their cheapness and capaciousness. He knew a great number of people who would be willing to pay a good price for cargo-boats. Freights were very high on account of the war. There were very few ships for sale and these few were very expensive. But of course no one who wanted decent ships would have thought of applying to a firm of shippers like Brookley & Brookley.

Mr Coax was urgently looking for decent ships, not actually for the Government but for private firms. The need of the Government for transports was purely a side-line for him and was only of interest to him in connexion with certain private undertakings of his own. He spent a whole week on a further search.

He discovered three more ships suitable for transports, which were newer and in every way more reliable than the others. To achieve this, he had to make several journeys, one being to Southampton, and when he did find these vessels, they all belonged to different owners and were not at all cheap; but they looked quite like ships.

Mr Coax made a note of these ships and travelled back to London.

There he again took up the question of how he could satisfy the Government's need. But, as we shall see, he did not neglect his own interests in so doing. His interests were, and remained, solely concerned with obtaining at the cheapest possible price a few good cargo-boats like those he had seen at Southampton.

In connexion with the Government affair, Mr Coax spoke in London before several business men whom he had called together for that purpose. It was not difficult to find such people. London was seething with initiative. The City was afire to stand by the country in its fight with the Boers. The Government was an absolutely ideal customer.

Mr Peachum learned of the need of Her Majesty's Government in the company of four or five other gentlemen who were as eager as himself to read a command in the Government's every wish.

They all met in a good middle-class restaurant in Kensington. They found that they had amongst them a real baronet, a bookmaker, a director of a cotton-mill in Lancashire, a restaurant-keeper, an owner of house property, a sheep-farmer, and the proprietor of a large business which dealt in second-hand musical instruments.

They each gave their orders and Mr William Coax made a little speech.

'*The position of our country,*' he began, '*is a serious one. As you all know, the war in South Africa began because* peaceful British citizens *were suddenly attacked without provocation. The troops of Her Majesty which immediately marched to their defence have everywhere been attacked* in the most underhand manner *and have been bloodily insulted in their attempt to protect British possessions. You have all read of the counter-attacks which our Government, because of their exaggerated forebearance and love of peace – an attitude now no longer understandable – have kept deferring. Today, some time after the beginning of the war, England is fighting against a mob of mad farmers for no less a prize than the possession of her overseas dominions. In the town of Mafeking, English troops are besieged by a huge army of Boers and are fighting for their lives. Whoever of you is on the Stock Exchange will know what that means. Gentlemen, the object of this meeting is the relief and liberation of the town of Mafeking!* (Applause.) *Gentlemen, the hour has arrived when British business men must have* sangfroid, courage, and initiative! *Must the heroism of our young men go unrewarded because you show yourselves lacking in these qualities? Who wages a war? The soldier and the business man! Each in his own place. The Government understands nothing about business. The Government says: We need transports. We say: Very well, here are the transports. The Government says: You know about such things, how much do transports cost? We can soon find out, we say: They cost so-and-so much. The Government does not bargain, they know that the money stays in the country.* There should be no bargaining among friends. *It's all the same whether one person has the money or another. The Government and their business representatives are friends. There is a bond between them and they* trust *one another. "You can't do that," says the one to the other, "let me do it. If ever I can't do anything, you shall do it." Thus arises trust, thus arise equal interests. "Look here, Billy," says the Secretary of State for such-and-such to me over a cigarette, "my wife can't manage with her twelve rooms, what shall I do?" "Don't worry about little things*

33

*like that," I say, "you look after your work." And I arrange the
matter for him! Then you read in the papers that the Secretary
of State has made such-and-such a speech for the welfare of the
country, which has advanced us a little in the world, and in
Africa or India or somewhere something great happens which
has enormously enhanced the prestige of our country. "You
must be free from all worries, Charles," I say, "in the interests
of the country. No petty troubles or money bothers. I am a
homely, simple business man, I don't want to have my name in
the newspapers, I don't want any public recognition, I only want
to help you, quietly and unrecognized, in your great work for
the advancement of our country. I want to do my bit!" And just
like me, gentlemen, thousands of other business men are working, quietly and unknown, but, may I be allowed to say, tenaci-
ously and resourcefully. The business man supplies the ship, the
soldier embarks on it. The business man is resourceful, the
soldier brave. Gentlemen, without long-winded discussion, let
us found a Marine Transport Company.'*

Mr Coax's speech met with instant success. The restaurant-
keeper thanked him in the names of the others and in the name
of England for showing them the way their duty lay; and after
discussing a few practical details, a preliminary contract was
drawn up. The waiter brought pens and ink, and the bookmaker
wrote. The three ships belonging to Brookley & Brookley, which
Mr Coax had mentioned, were to be bought as quickly as possible and put into proper order. The purchase price was to be
divided into Eight (8) equal portions and was to be paid over in
cash immediately on completion of the deal.

When they had got as far as this, a deep silence fell on the
table. Now came the question of allotting the share of the profits, more especially Coax's share, he having brought the business to them. They ordered a further supply of cigars and
beer.

Then the textile manufacturer spoke casually, gazing at the
blue smoke of his Corona:

'It seems to me that the net profits should be divided by eight
because we're eight, aren't we? And our friend Coax should
receive in addition a commission of, shall we say – ten per cent
of the price the Government pay.'

The other gentlemen looked at Coax, though not all of them. Coax tilted back in his chair and said, smiling:

'That's a good joke.'

His demands were, as the astonishment of his audience testified, considerable. It took two hours to discuss them. Even then they were not appreciably less, and all had the feeling that two years' discussion would make no difference. The commission was to be twenty-five per cent.

When the gentlemen, with many sighs and with an expression as though they were signing the death-sentence of their nearest and dearest, had set their names to the document, they parted quickly and each went home.

Peachum had received a very favourable impression of the whole transaction, and especially of Mr Coax's resourcefulness with regards to the division of the profits. Such bargaining could only be because the business was a sound one.

Troubles of Which the Man in the Street Never Dreams

On a foggy morning, and in one of the numerous small, bare, yellow-furnished offices that abound in the City, a conference took place between five gentlemen. The frosted-glass door which gave entrance to the office bore in gold letters the legend: BROOKLEY & BROOKLEY, SHIPPERS.

Two of the gentlemen present were Brookley and Brookley, colourless, indecisive creatures, who showed an almost exaggerated fear of taking the responsibility for any decision affecting both of them. For they each had the other's welfare at heart, and each seemed to be oppressed by the conviction that he was too weak to bear his reciprocal responsibility.

Anyone who knew what was what in the City handled these two brothers like raw eggs. Mr Coax knew what was what in the City. A contract was being drawn up whereby the freighters, *Lovely Anna, Young Sailorboy,* and *Optimist,* passed into the hands of the new company for a total consideration of Eight thousand two hundred pounds (£8,200). The inspection of the ships was arranged for the next Thursday. Immediately after it, the contract was to be signed and the purchase price paid over.

'I should be glad to see you all there,' said one Mr Brookley, 'but I hardly think that is necessary in the case of these ships.'

So everything was satisfactorily arranged.

Therefore, Brookley and Brookley were astonished when on the following morning Mr Coax called at the office again. After securing a pledge of the strictest secrecy, he made, on his own behalf, another offer for the ships, in case the deal discussed yesterday did *not* come to fruition. The brothers were in a state of considerable excitement.

On Wednesday afternoon one of the Mr Brookleys spoke to Eastman, the owner of housing estates, because his was the only address he knew, and inquired hopefully whether the contract could not be cancelled; they had had a new offer and he could not take it upon himself to commit his brother to adhere to the old price.

Eastman expressed his regret on behalf of the Company, and Brookley murmured something about Thursday six o'clock, when he would again be free to negotiate if everything should not prove satisfactory. Eastman immediately informed the others and exhorted them to be punctual. But on Thursday morning Mr Coax invited Eastman to coffee in a restaurant and informed him that he could not pay in his money until Saturday morning.

As a result of this, an excited meeting took place in another restaurant at two o'clock, just before the inspection, in which the textile manufacturer heatedly demanded that either Mr Coax should produce his money or a completely new arrangement should be made. At the same time he offered to take over Coax's commitments and share of the profits.

Eastman, in giving his criticism, dealt with these suggestions in two parts; with the one, the ultimatum to Coax, he thoroughly agreed, with the other – the offer – he disagreed. He declared himself ready to take over Coax's share.

Several others of the seven declared themselves equally ready. That Coax, if he did not produce his eighth, should lose his share in the Company, was clear to all – except Coax. He expressed some doubts, though weak ones. At last they were all agreed that the business should simply be divided into seven parts instead of eight, and Coax should only receive his commission.

This decision seemed to hit Coax hard, for he was taken suddenly ill and went home *to go to bed*. He declared that he could not accompany them on the inspection.

For the inspection, Eastman had engaged an ex-ship's engineer, a tall, haggard man by the name of Bile, who had drunk himself out of every job he had ever had. They met him near the docks and then, on Eastman's advice, gave him some more drinks so that he would be in a good mood and report the old hulks thoroughly worm-eaten.

They met the brothers Brookley in their counting-house, and it was not far from there to the ships.

These were huge gloomy hulks, dating back to the days of Nelson. There are always people who hoard old things: hats, cigar-boxes, cradles, etc., either from pure sentiment or from mere stupidity. Some such people must have taken a fancy to these ships. The astonishing thing was that they still floated on the dirty water, in spite of the saying that all things pass away.

Apparently they had been left undisturbed for years, or for decades. But now several thousand Tommies were waiting somewhere in the Transvaal to be relieved; so they would have to be moved. They would probably be glad of it.

The *Young Sailorboy* lay nearest to the shore and the commission boarded her.

The gangway was of wood, there was no doubt about that. The deck did not look very inviting, but was also of wood, just as in a proper ship.

Not one of the visitors was a sailor. If any of them had been, nothing would have induced him to go down the companion. He would have been afraid of breaking his neck.

Inside the ship, rats were skipping about like lambs on the Welsh mountains. They were enormous fat beasts who, in spite of their great age, had never seen a man, and so were unaware of any danger.

Engineer Bile had been prepared to expose, with cynical frankness, the various tricks by which unscrupulous ship-owners are wont to disguise a floating coffin as a luxurious pleasure yacht. 'And what is this, gentlemen?' he had been intending to say, tearing down this contraption or that. But now he just stood around, helpless and exhausted, and kept opening his mouth. A child could have seen what was the matter here.

That from which the *Young Sailorboy* was suffering could no longer, with the best will in the world, be described as a temporary affliction.

Of the ten men, not one moved so much as a step away from the iron companion ladder. For not one of them would have dared to support himself against the ship's side had he tripped over any of the rotting objects that lay all around. He would have been afraid of his hand simply going through the wood.

Eastman suddenly said, loudly and gaily, 'Yes, yes.' It echoed as in a disused attic.

And then one of the Mr Brookleys said quite calmly:

'After all, one must not go by externals. The chief thing is, whether the ship is seaworthy and can stand a bit of a sea.'

There are some people who have the capacity for remaining entirely uninfluenced by the feelings of others, who can remain completely immune from actualities and can speak their thoughts, openly and freely, without regard for time and place. Such men are born to be leaders.

The Marine Transport Company returned to land as though in a bad dream. They scarcely gave a glance to the *Lovely Anna* and the *Optimist*, which latter was, perhaps, the most derelict of the three.

When they were all sitting once more in the office of Brookley & Brookley, one of the Mr Brookleys made a short speech.

'Gentlemen,' he said, looking out of the window, 'I have the impression that you were expecting something better, although you knew the price, and that you are somehow disappointed and are not quite satisfied with the transaction.'

He cast a hasty glance round and, since no one contradicted him, continued:

'If that is so, I would advise you under no circumstances to go against the inner voice of yours which says: "Leave well alone!" If the matter is pressed, you will be hard put to it to secure other ships at this time, especially at the price. But if you have time to look round and can wait a few months, you would most certainly find something more likely to suit your requirements. By a happy coincidence Brookley & Brookley can immediately dispose of the ships elsewhere; as I told Mr Eastman yesterday, we have had another offer and would not be at all sorry to see yours withdrawn. Under the circumstances we might even consider a small compensation. It is now half past five; at a quarter past six my brother and I have another conference. We can and must, therefore, come to a quick decision.'

'The ships are worth two hundred pounds at the most, and they are certainly not seaworthy,' said Bile calmly.

Mr Brookley glanced at his watch.

'You hear what your advisor says. We have no reason to contradict him. We wouldn't think of forcing the ships on you. We are not in the position to accept any responsibility for them. Perhaps, from the point of view of an expert, it would be best to sell them as firewood. In which case the two hundred pounds of which your advisor speaks would be about right. And so, gentlemen, if I were you, I would not waste any more time deliberating.'

And he left the room with his brother.

As soon as the two were outside, Eastman said in an undertone:

'These are the only ships obtainable. We mustn't forget that. Even so I would withdraw, were it not for the fact that I am convinced that this other bid comes from none other than our friend Coax. We have been too hard on him. And now he is trying to put the deal through with other partners. With stupider ones.'

The eyes of several people in the room were suddenly opened. Five minutes later they stood, pen in hand, round the contract.

On the way home, Eastman said to the engineer:

'As a layman it's difficult to understand how anyone could get out to sea in an old barrel like that. One would naturally think that that rotten stuff would crumple up in the water like paper. These modern methods are marvellous. They always manage to make something out of nothing. I'll bet that when we've painted the ships up and put a few things right, they'll sail just as well as any other ships. Really, the layman has no conception of what can be done nowadays.'

And after a few steps in silence, he continued, half to himself:

'*It's monstrous the way one is always up against competition.*

There is no business, however dirty, which, if one man turns it down, another won't jump at. One has to be prepared to stomach anything to make a decent living. If one weakens, even for a second, one is done for. Only iron discipline and self-control can carry a man through. On the other hand, one can't expect something for nothing. If one wants to be what is popularly called "respectable", one must shovel mud or carry bricks. Yes, as soon as a man gets out of the rut, he has worries which the poorer man in the street never even dreams of.'

All for the Sake of the Child

Mr Peachum was troubled by Mr Coax's absence from the inspection. He was unable to get to sleep and passed a bad night.

He was involved in the purchase of three decaying ships, his share representing about half a ship, and it all depended on Mr Coax as to whether the money was being thrown away or not. To a man like Peachum, 'to be in a person's hands' meant the same as 'to be in a python's toils' does to a rabbit. The question was: would Mr Coax be able to dispose of the ships? Why hadn't he been present at the inspection, or at any rate at the signing of the contract? They had pushed him out of the transaction; he was no longer a partner but only a broker.

Once, Mr Peachum got up, ostensibly to see if all the lights were turned off, but really because of an inward disquiet. He was not in a position to be able to afford the smallest loss. The worst of it was that, at the loss of even the smallest sum of money, he lost all confidence in himself. He trusted no one, so why should he trust himself?

All the lights were turned off, but Polly's window on to the veranda was open. He could see her in the darkness, lying in bed. Angrily he pulled down the window from the outside.

'Why am I doing all this?' he asked himself as he climbed into bed again. 'Only for the sake of the child. I shall have to dismiss two more of the women from the workshop. The place stinks of laziness. I can't afford to keep all these people. They go on sewing and sewing, whether the beggars come or not. They don't have to run any risks. Polly could do a bit of work, too. What

40

does she think she is? This Coax isn't to be trusted an inch. We ought never, never to have listened to him. It's a dirty trick to suggest a business like that and then leave a person in the lurch. I'd twist his neck for him, but what use would that be?'

He sat up suddenly, perspiring:

'Oh, what a damned fool I am. I shall finish up on the Embankment yet. Why ever did I do business with a man whose neck I can't twist?'

The next morning Peachum went to Eastman and the two of them went on to Coax's office in the City. The pale typist actually had the effrontery to say that Coax had gone away. And the office, which Peachum had not seen before, made a depressing impression of him. It was the office of a crook!

The rest of that morning was torture for Peachum.

He had come into this business because the Government was to be swindled. That had endowed him with a blind faith in it. Deals of this sort were usually safe. To swindle other people was, after all, the honest aim of every business man. Only the world was always so much wickeder than one thought. There seemed to be no limit to evilness. That was Peachum's deepest conviction, his only one.

But after lunch Eastman came with the news that everything was quite in order. Coax was already back again or else hadn't been away at all, and that afternoon he was going to inspect the ships with his friend from the Admiralty. The others were to await his return in a certain restaurant.

To inspect the ships! That was a fresh piece of bad news. The seven men who sat waiting in the restaurant looked exactly as though they themselves had been condemned to sail aboard the *Optimist*.

At half past five Coax came into the restaurant, wearing a new flaming red tie and looking as dishonest and shifty as possible, and he pulled out of his breast pocket a signed and stamped contract with the Admiralty and a cheque for five thousand pounds (£5,000) payable immediately to the Marine Transport Company.

The Secretary of State had not had time to inspect the ships.

'Between men of honour, such formalities are unnecessary,' explained Coax lightly. 'Oh! I nearly forgot to tell you. I've spent

41

two thousand pounds of your money. I gave it to Hale for his fund for the distressed families of Government officials. He said that one thousand was enough, but I thought that a well-oiled machine always runs better.'

He was in a capital humour. He had been in Southampton again that day and had secured an option on the freighters there. Everything was going like clockwork. Mr Coax was proposing to teach the gentlemen of the Marine Transport Company a moral lesson. He already saw the Southampton ships bowling along under full sail.

The procedure, Mr Coax explained to the partners, was to be as follows: the ships were to be officially handed over to the Government as soon as possible; reconstruction and repairs could be started on after the handing over. The final payment would only be made by the Government when everything was in perfect order.

They all agreed willingly.

It was decided to start on the renovation of the *Lovely Anna*, the *Young Sailorboy*, and the *Optimist* forthwith. A small amount of repairing, painting, and so forth was unavoidable. 'After all, they've got to last for a voyage of several thousand sea miles,' said Coax seriously.

That part of the business was allotted to Eastman. It would cost a few hundred pounds, or perhaps a few thousand. As it transpired, they had all been somewhat worried and were now inclined to countenance a certain extravagance, even Peachum.

So far all was well, so well that Peachum was surprised when the sheep farmer visited him a few days later and declared that he could not carry on with the business because he needed all his available money for army supplies. After a long discussion Peachum agreed to take over his share, so that now he owned two-sevenths of the company. That was an unexpected stroke of luck.

But then came disturbing news from the Admiralty.

The bearer of the news was Eastman, who had spoken to Coax in a restaurant. Apparently there had arisen subsequent difficulties about the contract with the Government. The Secretary of State had been approached from certain quarters with a suggestion that a commission of engineers should be appointed to inspect the ships. So far the Secretary of State had resisted this suggestion, but he had now decided that he would at least like to see the vessels himself. Everything depended on this not happening until the repairs were sufficiently advanced.

This piece of news was the cause of Peachum returning before the picnic with every sign of physical collapse and retiring to bed with hot-water bottles and camomile tea.

A week of breath-taking negotiations followed. Everything was made more difficult by Coax refusing to give any address. When asked, he said that he was just in the process of moving.

All the partners of the Company spent their time travelling backwards and forwards between their homes and the docks. The renovations were proceeding extremely slowly. Discoveries were made in the hold of the *Lovely Anna* which made the carpenters' hair stand on end. And the *Young Sailorboy* concealed an interior that sent shivers down their backs. While the condition of the *Optimist* was such that the contractors were still unable to come to a decision as to whether ladders could be placed against her sides without danger to the workers.

In addition to all this, there were rumours and reports going round in the neighbourhood of the docks. The carpenters made no secret of their discoveries when they sat at their meals; and hints from Eastman that such talk was treasonable merely evoked laughter. The carpenters were all soaked in socialism.

It was already plain that the cost of repairs would amount to a good five or six thousand pounds.

During that week Peachum met Coax at Eastman's. Peachum invited him to dinner at his house. Now, more than ever, everything depended upon Coax. Coax wore an expression of complete confidence. During the dinner, at which Eastman was also present, Coax met Polly for the first time. He was a skirt-hunter of the worst sort, and one of those, too, who strongly disapprove of that failing in others.

Peachum had begun to hear all sorts of things about his affairs, which were all confined to women of the lowest type and which always narrowly escaped the attentions of the law. This, too, if he had heard it in time, would have deterred Peachum from doing business with Coax. Business people whose hearts are not always in their work, are heading for a fall. But as things stood, the only thing to do now was to humour Coax.

Polly showed her best side. She conversed with Coax like a lady. After the coffee she even went so far as to sit down at the piano and sing a patriotic song in her pretty, rather tinny voice. Later Coax did not want to go home and he persuaded Eastman, and even Peachum, to make a tour of a few night haunts with him. He set his grey velour hat at a rakish angle, and on his haggard grey cheeks stood two unhealthy patches of red. Mr Peachum went out beside him as though to a funeral. He would rather have gone to the docks where, at a considerably increased cost, they were working night-shifts as well.

In the night clubs, Coax behaved like a libertine and not like a business man. He also paid for everything.

On the next day, he brought the news that Hale of the Admiralty had officially accepted the ships, *Lovely Anna, Young Sailorboy*, and *Optimist*, without an inspection and on a further payment by the M.T.C. of £3,000.

3

How does Man live? By throttling, grinding, sweating
His fellows, and devouring all he can!
His one chance of survival's in forgetting
Most thoroughly that he himself's a man.
No, gentlemen, this truth we cannot shirk:
Man lives exclusively by dirty work.

(DREIGROSCHEN-FINALE)

The B. Shops

At that time there were, in London, a great many shops of similar appearance where goods were cheaper than elsewhere. They were called B. shops. That was supposed to mean 'Bargain Shops'; though a few people, mostly other shopkeepers, thought it meant 'Bilge Shops'. One could buy anything from razor-blades to furniture in them, and for the most part the businesses were honest. The poorer people shopped in them gladly, but the owners of other shops and small craftsmen were very angry about them.

These shops belonged to Mr MacHeath. He had several other names. As proprietor of the B. shops he called himself Mac-Heath.

At first there were only a few branches; two or three in the neighbourhood of Waterloo Bridge and half a dozen farther eastwards. They all did very well because they were really un-rivalled in cheapness. But goods as cheap as that were not easy to procure and Mr MacHeath had first to establish a difficult and dangerous organization before he could think of expand-ing.

And what was more, this work had to be carried out with the greatest secrecy. No one knew where Mr MacHeath got his goods from or how he got them so cheap.

To people whose curiosity insisted on being satisfied, he could easily point out that in London and elsewhere there were always small shops going bankrupt who had bought good stuff at the usual prices and who, when they failed, were glad to be able to dispose of their wares at any price. *'Life is hard,'* Mr MacHeath would then say, *'and we must not be weak.'*

He had a partiality for high-sounding talk. But he could not produce such circumstantial receipts for all his goods. Besides, these irregular and uncertain sources of supply would scarcely have kept all his shops continually stocked with wares of such astonishing cheapness.

Scattered about the town were other shops, run on the lines of B. shops; in them one could buy antiques, jewellery, and rare books, at higher prices but well worth the money. And people said of these shops that they too belonged to Mr MacHeath and that he financed the B. shops from their profits. This was even less likely, and there still remained the question of how he supplied *these* shops with goods.

In the summer of 19— Mr MacHeath, to the satisfaction of other shopkeepers, found himself in serious difficulties and had to ask a bank, the *National Credit Bank*, for help.

However, investigation by the bank proved the firm of Mac-Heath to be sound. Especially sound was the system whereby the individual shops all stood on their own feet and could only be conditionally described as belonging to Mr MacHeath. Mac-Heath had realized that *independence* was of paramount importance to a great many small traders. They had a dislike of hiring themselves out wholesale like ordinary workmen or employees; they wanted to be dependent on their *own ability*. They wanted no *empty equalization*. They were quite prepared to work more than others, but then they wanted also to be able to earn more. Besides, they wanted no one to have the right of ordering them about or talking a lot of nonsense to them.

Mr MacHeath had spoken about his important discovery of the urge towards individual independence in several newspaper interviews.

He called this urge an *atavistic urge of human nature*, but he expressed the opinion that it was especially the modern man, the man of the technical age, fired by the universal and unexampled triumph of man over nature, who desired to prove to himself and others his surpassing excellence. Mr MacHeath considered this ambition to be absolutely and ethically correct, for it benefited all men equally in the form of price-cutting competition. In this competitive battle of the great the small man now wished to take part. It was now up to the business world to encourage this tendency of the times and to profit by it. We must not work against human nature, proclaimed Mr MacHeath in his sensational articles, but with it! As far as their organization went, the B. shops were a result of this discovery. Instead of employees and mere salesmen, the firm of MacHeath had for its sales organization self-supporting shopkeepers. These (carefully chosen) shopkeepers had been enabled by the firm to open B. shops. The firm had stocked the shops for them and arranged credit for the goods. Every week they received a consignment of goods which they had to dispose of. They were absolutely free to do what they liked with the goods. As long as they paid the price of the rent and their wares, there was no one to examine their book-keeping. They were only pledged to keep their prices low. The system was purely for the benefit of the *small man*.

The shopkeepers mostly did without expensive assistants. The whole family worked in the shop. These people neither grumbled over their working hours nor showed the typical indifference of uninterested employees towards the takings: *it was their business.*

'*In this way,*' wrote Mr MacHeath in another article, '*the disastrous* disintegration of family life, *so much deplored by all philanthropists, is checked. The whole family shares in the work. And because it has one and the same interests, it is once more one heart and one soul. The division between work and private life, in many aspects a dangerous influence, which causes the individuals to forget the family when at work and their work when with the family, vanishes. In this direction, too, the B. shops are examples of what can be done.*'

It was easy for Mr MacHeath to persuade the bank that his difficulties were really no difficulties at all. The money that he needed was needed for the expansion of his business. But the bank hesitated to advance the money, for they were not quite sure about Mr MacHeath himself.

To tell the truth there were certain unpleasant rumours about this gentleman going round the City; these rumours never amounted to an accusation but nevertheless had to be taken into consideration. They were not so much concerned with his methods of buying, although that came into it too.

Once or twice he had been involved in scandals. Each time he had been instantly able to demonstrate his innocence. None of the cases had reached the stage of legal proceedings. But there were always people, neither owning shops nor related to shopkeepers, who asserted, though not exactly openly, that Mr MacHeath was no gentleman, A few would rather have seen a lawsuit than out-of-court settlements, while others had simply found MacHeath's solicitors too clever for them.

The negotiations with the National Credit Bank dragged on for longer than MacHeath thought possible. He was already beginning to regret having approached the bank, for there would now be new food for the old rumours about him. He would have liked to have withdrawn.

For certain reasons he employed several solicitors in the Temple. From one of these he learned that one of the most influential customers of the National Credit Bank was a Mr Jonathan Jeremiah Peachum who had an unmarried daughter. MacHeath soon succeeded in making her acquaintance. As his prospects improved he devoted himself entirely to wooing Polly Peachum, however much time and trouble it might cost him. The only reason for his introducing himself to the ladies as Jimmy Beckett was one of precaution.

He assured himself once more about the state of Peachum's business. It was a widespread organization of beggars, and the methods seemed cleverly thought out and tested. A man who knew Peachum explained why, for example, the beggars did not simply bring their pictures with them and set them up, but instead drew their landscapes and portraits of well-known people on the pavements in brightly coloured chalks. With works of art which were brought and set up, the public never knew whether, in the beggar, they had the artist before them or not; and besides, the pavement pictures were transitory, the footsteps of passers-by defaced them, the rain washed them away, and it rained nearly every day! Every day the pictures had to be drawn anew, so one must pay *today*. Such practices testified to a deep knowledge of human nature.

In the middle of June, MacHeath decided to disregard various

48

subsidiary doubts and press forward his courtship. He must approach the marriage in an aura of complete respectability and be able to point to a steady and unblemished home life.

He inquired of Mrs Peachum by letter when he might call on her. He had correctly interpreted her nervousness at his first visit.

She arranged to meet him in the *Octopus*, in order to 'have the matter out with him'. The remarks which she made there about the waywardness of modern youth got very much on Mr MacHeath's nerves.

'The young people of today,' said Mrs Peachum, wiping the froth from her lips, 'never know what they want. They are like children. I know my Polly as well as the palm of my hand, but where her heart lies I have no idea. Perhaps she is simply too young. She has had no experience with men. She knows perhaps the difference between a he-dog and a she-dog, because she comes into contact with dogs; but I don't suppose she even knows that exactly. She never thinks of such things. You must remember that she has never had a bath except in her night-dress. When an innocent young girl like that sees a man, she probably wonders what he's there for. They are always so romantic! The way that girl devours novels – you'd never *believe* it. Now, it's always Mr Smiles this and Mr Smiles that. And so I know for certain it's you she wants. A mother knows. Oh, Mr Beckett!'

And she gazed deep into his eyes, after making sure that her glass was empty and no one else was in the garden.

When Mr Beckett informed her in due course that he was not Beckett but MacHeath, the proprietor of the well-known B. shops, and that his intentions were entirely honourable, she seemed to take no special notice, as though she had expected *anything* of him, and she only looked at him with a vague glance that was almost evasive.

'Ah, yes,' she sighed, 'but my husband must hear nothing of this; he has his own plans for the girl, as you can well imagine. He always says: everything for the child; and he means it too. The day before yesterday he suddenly brought home a Mr Coax with him. He is supposed to be *very* well off. Do you know Mr Coax?'

MacHeath did know Mr Coax. He was a byword in the City. Personally, MacHeath had heard nothing very favourable about Mr Coax.

He was an unprincipled *skirt-hunter*. Whatever intentions of a material nature MacHeath, whose head was full of business troubles, might have had, at the mention of the name Coax a pang stabbed his heart. He was more in love with the Peach than he had admitted even to himself.

'What can be done about it?' he asked hoarsely.

'That's what I would like to know,' said Mrs Peachum pensively, and surveyed him with such a cold glance that a chill ran down his spine. 'The young girls of today are quite incalculable. Their heads are stuffed full of romantic ideas.'

But then she laid her small podgy hand on his and called the waiter for the bill.

On the short way out between the iron tables, MacHeath was told again that everything must be done with the greatest discretion and without Peachum's knowledge. That same evening he met the Peach herself and received permission to accompany her on her way.

Strangely enough she went from Old Oak Street in the direction of the park by Meath Gardens, although it was her night for housekeeping classes. She looked round a few times on the way, but made no attempt to leave him and finally sat down on a bench among the bushes.

She looked very pretty in her flimsy dress and was completely at her ease. As a matter of fact, she was no doll but a large, well-formed girl. She was a full helping and no half portion.

She was unwilling to speak of Coax and Smiles.

'The evening is too lovely for that,' she said. The fact that he knew of Coax seemed to amuse her; she laughed.

When they walked back again he had learned nothing, but several things had happened. All the same he was not happy, because she had not given way on the most important point and she had had practically nothing on under her dress. That seemed very wrong to Mr MacHeath; as did also the fact that she had so casually missed her housekeeping classes. So they kept no check on the attendance of their students!

Just as after the drive back from the picnic, he could not tell now whether he had really made any progress – and that worried him. What had happened *must* mean something to her. He could no longer doubt her innocence.

Mr Peachum, too, gave his daughter a searching glance that evening.

The affairs of the Marine Transport Company were in desperate straits. On the previous day the bombshell had burst.

The Bombshell

Peachum had been having trouble with Fewkoombey in the yard. The soldier, happy to have a home, had at first punctiliously carried out his duties and kept the blind dogs in condition.

Their feeding was not at all simple; they had to look as miserable as possible and therefore had to be maintained on the verge of starvation. A blind man with a fat dog has very little prospect of exciting real pity. The public naturally reasons quite instinctively. Scarcely anyone looks at a thin dog; but if by any chance the animal is well fed, some sort of inner voice warns the giver that he might just as well throw his money down the drain. It is a fact that these people unconsciously seek for a reason to withhold their money. A good dog must scarcely be able to stand up for weakness.

Because of this, the dogs were continually checked by weight. If their weight went up, Fewkoombey was to blame.

Peachum was in the middle of an investigation to establish whether the one-legged man had gone so far as to make false entries in his notebook simply in order to keep his job, when the restaurant-keeper was announced. He brought the news that Coax had suddenly appeared aboard the *Lovely Anna* and was in a furious rage.

The two gentlemen went immediately to the docks. There, in truth, stood Coax, between ladders and painters. Beside him stood Eastman, pale in the face and staring at the enormous dark sides of the ship with a rigid gaze. Apparently he did not dare look the new-comers in the face.

The icy glance with which Coax greeted him chilled Peachum through and through.

'Is this by any chance one of the ships which you have sold to the British Government?'

Peachum suddenly looked years older.

The shock was not entirely unexpected. Somehow he had always felt that there was something not quite right with the business. As far as Coax was concerned he had had no illusions. But he had not been expecting anything so sudden.

Coax declared the ship *not fit for use*. Peachum felt that no purpose would be served by arguing here to the effect that it was, after all, Mr Coax who had recommended the ships to them. Peachum knew, without further discussion, that Coax would simply say that he had never seen the ships himself. While all the others had inspected them – and before witnesses, too!

A dark suspicion rose within him as to the direction in which Coax's activities (he had always guessed that Coax was working independently) were moving. Not against the Government, but against the Marine Transport Company, like a terrible, irresistible steam-roller!

The details were naturally not yet apparent. Mr Coax did not think the time had yet come to lay down his cards. No one spoke.

Mr Coax turned on his heels and, with a deeply contemptuous look, walked off without a word. Seen from behind, his suit looked more ready-made than ever. Peachum, also, had no desire to discuss with his fellow victims what would happen next. Dimly he heard Eastman say that they must summon immediately, by letter, the manufacturer in Lancashire and the sheep farmer. The sheep farmer! Without another word Peachum walked off.

That evening he developed a high fever and went to bed with an ice-pack. During the night he did not get up. Let the lights burn! The gas-bill would never be paid any more.

The next morning he went off like a sick man, down to the docks. He found no workmen there. Work on the *Lovely Anna* had been suspended by Eastman's order. That showed what *he* thought of the situation.

When he returned home at midday (not to eat) and heard that two gentlemen had been inquiring for him, he thought that the police were after him already. The Company had, after all, accepted the first instalment from the Government.

But closer inquiry revealed that it had only been Eastman and the manufacturer, the latter having hurried up to London. Peachum was glad they had not found him in.

There was no point in going to Coax's office. The pallid girl was as dumb as a fish concerning any inquiry for the broker's address.

But on returning home from a fruitless attempt to get hold of Eastman, Peachum found Coax with his daughter.

Coax had met Polly on the way and had accompanied her, although she had given him no special encouragement. He had been telling her about some interesting pictures which he would like to show her. She had not understood him properly. She did not care for him.

When Peachum entered. Coax behaved as though there had never been the slightest disagreement between them. He held out one gloved hand, clapped him on the shoulder with the other, and quickly took his leave.

All through supper a circular saw was buzzing inside Mr Peachum's head.

Afterwards he sent his wife out and cross-questioned the Peach.

He used no coercion and learned that Mr Coax had told Polly what he had concealed from his business friends – his address. He was careful not to ask why. He went into his dark little office and stared for a time absent-mindedly out of the window. Then, after hastily writing a letter, he returned to the sitting-room and told Polly to take the letter to Mr Coax immediately.

Polly was very astonished. It was already half past nine.

But she put on her hat and went to Mr Coax.

Coax was at home. When the maid announced that a young girl had called with a letter from her father requiring an answer, he laid down his serviette with obvious embarrassment and left the room quickly.

He lived with his sister, a very forceful little person who had by no means such a high opinion of her brother as he would have liked and who made no secret of her suspicions about his moral qualities.

She had a lot to put up with.

Coax had great commercial ability and also his principles in regard to a clean private life were those common to his circle. In his view, shared by many, there is an immense difference between business life and private life. In business it is no less than one's duty to utilize any chance of profit, regardless of others, just as one must never throw away a piece of bread because it is a gift of God; but in private life one has no right to take advantage of another person. Thus far his views were strictly correct.

Unfortunately he did not always possess the strength of mind to live up to his principles. Between his views of the duties of a gentleman towards the gentler sex and those of his sister, there was not the slightest difference; exactly as his sister did, and often with the self-same words, he condemned his lamentably frequent lapses. He often used to say regretfully: 'I am not master of himself.' Thus, figuratively speaking, neither he nor his sister could leave himself alone for a moment.

And his inclinations, socially, were downwards. The commonest women attracted him the most strongly. But he could not resist servant-girls either.

It was exactly the same with his clothes. His taste was terrible. His suits made his sister feel physically sick. He could no more control himself with them than with his staff.

On every possible occasion his sister presented him with tasteful ties. He put them on, too. But in the passage, as if driven by some demon, he would push another into his pocket. And on the steps it would hang, red and aggressive, round his neck.

These were symptoms of illness. He himself attributed them to intestinal trouble. They were attacks of uncontrollable sensuality resulting from constipation.

His sister helped him with all her power in his tragic fight against himself. Sometimes, however, he so far forgot himself that, once started on a 'tour', he seemed to regard her assistance as interference and refused it rudely.

Therefore when Miss Peachum was announced, Miss Coax could do little more than busy herself outside the room where the meeting took place and cough as loudly as possible.

On this evening, Coax was having one of his very worst attacks. His sufferings had been bothering him all day. Under these circumstances there remained nothing else but to show the Peach his collection of photographs, which consisted of all sorts of nudities. He did this under the pretext of their being a new consignment which had just arrived.

The Peach scarcely looked at them and got very red in the face.

They were really filthy pictures.

In the meanwhile Coax read the letter which contained a request for a private interview.

On the writing-table, which had a glass top, lay a large gold brooch. It had come from Coax's dead mother. There was a lot of gold in it; but its chief feature was three large blue stones of negligible value. On the whole, Coax seemed to have inherited his taste from his mother.

When he had finished reading the letter, or perhaps only because he had the impression that the Peach had had enough of looking at photographs, he picked up the brooch, held it out to her, and asked how she liked it.

'Quite nice,' she said in a rather choked voice.

'You can come and fetch it some time for yourself,' said Coax and looked at the corner of the room.

She naturally did not answer. She sat down quite calmly again and smiled at him politely as though he had made a joke. He had to take a strong pull on himself. He was hoping already that he might accompany Polly home, but his sister, thinking things were too quiet in the room, came in and began talking to Polly.

Coax was a little nervous about the photographs which lay face upwards on the table, but the Peach turned them over mechanically as she spoke.

She understood very well how to deal with gentlemen, and this little trait made an excellent impression on Mr Coax.

She left almost immediately and was able to tell her father that Mr Coax would see him on the following day.

She had not much use for the broker. But she did not forget the brooch which had greatly taken her fancy. The next morning she told one-legged George, when she brought him his glass of milk, that she had been given a big brooch by an elderly gentleman and she would show it to him soon. Later, too, she thought about it, especially in the evening just before going to sleep.

Coax actually came the next morning. But he refused to walk

55

through from the shop into the office. He was wearing a brilliant yellow overcoat and spoke very seriously, in a low voice.

He admitted that he had lost his nerve at the sight of the *Lovely Anna*. Those hulks were quite impossible. It was true that he had mentioned the firm of Brookley & Brookley, but he knew nothing about their boats. He couldn't possibly show those floating coffins to his friend, the Secretary of State. The worst part of the business seemed to him to be the fact that the first instalment had already been paid and the Admiralty was counting on the ships. The Company, to which he, thank heaven, no longer belonged, had laid themselves open to a charge of treason, because it was known that they had inspected the ships and had actually rejected the advice of an expert named Bile.

Coax suggested that the only possible way out of the difficulty would be immediately to buy other, really reliable ships. The alteration of the names *Lovely Anna*, *Young Sailorboy*, and *Optimist* he could arrange himself. Whatever happened, his friend could never buy *these* ships.

Peachum looked less upset than yesterday. He knew, of course, that he could never be a match for this man. The sphere in which he was great, even terrible, was another. He had deserted it. Swept away by the patriotic wave which was pouring across the country, he had undertaken something new. Now he was as harmless as a crocodile in Trafalgar Square. But curiously enough the present knowledge, that he had only human vileness to deal with, gave him back a measure of confidence and hope. At any rate, he was among mere men again.

He watched the talkative Coax calmly, even coldly. Then he said that, as far as he knew, there were no other ships.

Indeed there were, said Coax slowly; there was one, for example, at Southampton.

Peachum nodded.

'How much will it cost for you to let me out of this?' he asked drily.

Coax seemed not to understand him and Peachum did not repeat the question. He knew now that it was a very profitable enterprise for Mr Coax.

After a short pause, in which he wandered round the shop and stared at the dusty musical instruments, Coax said that it was absolutely essential for the repairs on the ships to proceed with redoubled energy. The inspection at the official handing-over was certain to be only a superficial one, but at least the surface must look in good condition.

As he was closing the door behind him he called back that he happened to have an appointment on the Wednesday of next week in Southampton.

4

Who wouldn't rather be polite than rough
If only things in general weren't so tough!
(Dreigroschen-finale: On the uncertainty of human affairs)

Serious Discussions

Not everyone knows that wars, as well as giving a spiritual uplift to the nation, also produce a not inconsiderable briskening of trade. They bring much evil in their wake, but business people generally have nothing to complain of.

Peachum had hoped to receive a substantial share of profits when he joined the Marine Transport Company. He was partly influenced by the fact that his daughter had arrived at a marriageable age and an increase in income seemed desirable.

But unsatisfactory developments in this new line of business caused Peachum to hold a number of very serious discussions with his manager, Beery.

Time and again they sat in the office which lay behind the iron-covered door at the back of the shop; Peachum, with the inevitable hat on his head, at an old roll-top desk which had been pushed against the wall directly under the one tiny window, and the heavily built Beery slouching in the corner on a rickety iron chair.

Sitting there in dirty shirt-sleeves, Peachum leaned his arms on the desk and avoided looking at Beery, who chewed incessantly at a cigar stump which he had most likely fished out of a gutter several years before.

'Beery,' Peachum would say at such times, 'I am not satisfied with you. You are too harsh and yet you don't get enough out of our people. On the one hand, I hear complaints that you don't treat the employees politely enough; on the other hand, they are not earning money. The girls in the workroom, for example, say they have to work overtime to keep up with the demand for soldiers' uniforms; and there are fourteen of them – instead of nine at the most. You know that I allow no overtime to be worked here, neither will I have a large and expensive staff. Times are serious, very serious. England is fighting for her existence, the business cannot stand the slightest strain, and you are running it inefficiently. If the apple-cart is upset, every single person who earns his living in and with the help of this organization will be thrown out on the streets. And that may happen any day. I expect some suggestions from you.'

'If I start economizing you'll say that I ill-treat the staff,' said Beery obdurately.

'And so you do. That new man can be heard shouting three houses away. I won't have that.'

'When we hold a cushion against his mouth he suffocates, and then the fuss you make! You know yourself that we shall never get any money out of him if we handle him like a pat of butter. And we only gave him a dressing-down because of the others. The young wretch doesn't even pay regularly. We told him, too, that it was only for the sake of the others and we treated him quite kindly after you went out.'

'Well I shall not warn you many more times. I won't tolerate such things. And the takings from the "soldiers" are going down, too. We are going to the dogs, Beery; I shall have to put the shutters up.'

'Yes, the soldiers aren't drawing, that's true, Mr Peachum. I have gone into the matter carefully. The public have fallen off in that direction, there's nothing to be done about it. I told you that we shouldn't have anything to do with politics.'

Peachum thought for a while. He stared fixedly at a corner of the dusty writing-table and his face had lost all its insignificance.

'The root of the trouble is,' he said, 'that you people have no ideas. Put a few well-written articles on military life and South Africa into the next number of the *Olive Branch* and then your soldiers will at least know half their job.'

In one of the cellars of the house, a newspaper called the *Olive Branch* was printed. It appeared weekly and contained personal announcements, deaths, marriages, christenings. This information was very important for house-to-house begging. The paper also provided in every issue several pathetic little tales, some quotations from the Bible, and a Thought For The Week.

'Besides,' continued Peachum, 'we are making stupid mistakes. We mustn't send our men out when there's been no news from the front for some time. That's all wrong. At the present moment this place Mafeking is being besieged and the whole war is at a standstill; that doesn't say much for our soldiers. People ask, quite rightly: "What do they lose their arms and legs for, if it's not going to get them anywhere?" Incompetence will never be supported. And above all, no one likes to be reminded of the war when it isn't being a success. Quite apart from the fact that people say to themselves: "These beggars ought to be thankful they're at home – the others are far worse off." It was a good idea to dress up some of our younger men, but it's no good sending them on the streets at any old time, especially when there aren't any victories being won. Bring the men in!'

Beery fetched them; at least, those who were there. They were dressed in shabby uniforms and looked sullen. They were earning nothing.

Peachum surveyed them in silence. But his glance was a vague one and took in no details. Years of practice had taught him that glance.

'That's no good!' he said with sudden harshness, while Beery hung on his lips like a faithful dog who knows the infallibility of his master. 'What have you got here? Those men aren't English soldiers. They're tramps! Look at yourself, you!' And he pointed at a tall, thin elderly man of morose appearance. 'That's a discontent, a communist! A creature like that would never die for England! And if he did, it would only be with groans and moans and after he had haggled about the price. Soldiers are attractive young men, smart and cheerful even in misfortune. And these disgusting mutilations! Would *you* like to see them in the streets? An arm in a sling is enough. And the uniforms must be clean. People must think: "He has nothing left except his uniform, but he honours that." That draws people, that softens them! I need gentlemen! A discreet tone of voice, polite, but not obsequious. Besides, a wound is something to be proud of. – That man will carry on. The rest can hand in their uniforms.'

The 'soldiers' went out. Neither the tall man nor any of the others had moved an eyelid; it was a matter of business.

'Well firstly, Beery,' said Mr Peachum when they had gone, 'they must all be attractive, well-grown young men; men who would be of some use if they were sent into the field and whom people would pity if anything happened to them. Secondly, no disgusting mutilations. Thirdly, uniforms spotlessly clean. And fourthly, these beautiful Tommies are only to go out when the official bulletins report some progress in the war, victories or defeats, no matter which – but progress! That of course means that you will have to read the newspapers. I expect my staff to keep alert and know what's going on in the world. Even when the working hours are over the business must still go on. You are becoming slack, Beery. I keep telling you again and again.'

Beery went out very red in the face and displayed great energy during the next few days. There were dismissals from the work-rooms and beatings in the office. But Mr Peachum knew that there was not much more to be rationalized in his business. It was rationalized already. The losses which threatened the Marine Transport Company could not be squeezed out here.

Peachum tried to recall the look which he had seen Coax bestow on his daughter.

£15

With Miss Polly Peachum all was not well. She was compelled to take her washing down to the wash-kitchen herself and was thankful that, because of Mr Peachum's increasing indisposition, her mother had no time to bother about the washing.

She had gone several times to Mr Smiles to ask for advice. But the young man was seldom at home.

When she met him once, he said to her:

'We'll find something. But afterwards we must be more careful. What are preventatives for if one doesn't use them?'

Then he went on to speak of Mr Beckett in a most insulting way. And this affair had really nothing to do with Mr Beckett!

In their house lived an old servant. Polly, in her need, turned to her.

Between them they carried two copper hip-baths into the little room, and Polly sat stewing in them for hours, groaning and pouring great cans of boiling water over herself.

The old servant also brought her mugs of green and brown tea which all had to be drunk; and now and again she stuck her head, which was like a hen's, in at the door and asked if it were already working. But it did not work.

One-legged George had become quite accustomed to his life among the dogs. In his spare time he lay in his little tin hut on a camp bed which he had set up among a clutter of carpentering tools and ash-cans. For his amusement he read an old tattered volume of the *Encyclopaedia Britannica* which he had found in the lavatory. Only about half the volume was there and it was not the first volume. Nevertheless one could learn quite a lot out of it, even if it did not suffice for a complete education. But who had that nowadays?

One day the Peach caught him reading and promised not to tell Mr Peachum anything about it. The soldier had got the impression that Mr Peachum was not the sort of man who feeds his employees so that they can become educated.

Once, when George was not in his hut, Polly took the book away with her into her room to see if she could find anything in it. But she did not know the appropriate words under which doubtless stood the information she sought; and it was possible that this branch of human learning was contained in another volume. At any rate she found nothing.

George was horrified when he discovered that his book was no longer there. He lay dejectedly on his bed for several days and was even unkind to the dogs. It was a bad mistake of the Peach's that she had not returned the book to its place when she had finished with it. When people have the slightest worries they become even more thoughtless towards others than they usually are.

A few days later she spoke to George about the dogs. She was helping him to bandage the sore paw of a Pomeranian. Suddenly she asked him, without looking up, what girls do when they think there is something not quite right with them. She was asking that because a friend in her housekeeping class had spoken to her about it.

For a time George continued to bind the rag round the paw of the whimpering dog in silence; then he gave Polly a piece of sound but not very helpful advice.

62

But in the evening he put on mufti to go for a walk and the next morning he called Polly over to the kennels.

He told her that if she liked she could go with him in the afternoon to a doctor in Kensington who had a large female practice and was said to be clever.

His informant, the woman with whom he had lived when her husband was at the Front and whom he had visited on the previous evening, had given him the address. Actually she had given him two addresses, the doctor's and a midwife's. The latter was more for poor girls. Fewkoombey thought the doctor was the right one for Polly, because he worked in far less dirty surroundings than the midwife.

The Peach did not want to go alone, so the soldier went with her.

The doctor had a flat in a large tenement which reeked of filth and poverty. They had to climb to the second storey, up a narrow staircase, past dwellings whose doors stood open as though unable to contain all the misery within. Then they were astonished to find that the doctor's flat looked very comfortable. Even the waiting room was sumptuous. In the corners stood enormous pots of flowers and on the walls hung foreign-looking carpets. The coats and umbrellas of patients, hanging on the iron hatstand, looked very shabby in comparison.

In the waiting room sat seven or eight women, all of the middle-class type. When the doctor opened the door of his surgery to let in the next patient, he beckoned to Polly out of her turn because she was better dressed than the others. She followed him apprehensively; the soldier remained sitting in the waiting room.

The doctor was what women call a fine figure of a man, with a soft well-trimmed beard and a high forehead. One could see by the way he folded his hands that he was very proud of them. But his face was rather dissipated and he had an unpleasant look in his eyes. His voice was oily.

To Polly's secret horror he began writing down her name and address in a book. She looked round the room. On the walls hung all sorts of weapons such as native spears, bows, quivers, and short knives, and also old-fashioned pistols. In one corner, in a glass cupboard, were shelves of various surgical instruments which looked far more dangerous. On the desk lay a fairly thick coating of dust.

The doctor leaned back and folded his white hands.

'Yes,' he began, before Polly had said anything more than her name and address, *'what you ask of me is quite impossible, my dear young lady. Have you even considered what your re-request means? All life is sacred, quite apart from the fact that such a thing is illegal. A doctor who did what you want would lose his practice and go to prison as well. You will probably say – we doctors hear it often during consulting hours – that these laws are medieval. Well, my dear young lady, I didn't make the laws. So I advise you to go quietly home and tell your mother everything. She is a woman like you and will not be lacking in understanding. She probably has not the money for such an operation. Besides, my conscience would never permit me to do such a thing. No doctor would risk his whole career for a miser- able ten or twenty pounds. We are not insensitive to the suf- ferings of our fellow men. As doctors we have much insight into social distress. Indeed, if it was in any way possible, if you had any sort of symptoms, even of consumption, I'd say: "I can put that right; in five minutes it will all be over and there will be no complications afterwards." But you certainly don't look as though you had consumption. You yourself must admit that. When, in your youthful light-heartedness, you took your plea- sures, you should have thought of the consequences. One should look ahead; one should never give way to one's feelings, however pleasant they may be. Afterwards you run to the doctor and then there's fuss and bother. Doctor this and Doctor that, and Doctor don't let my life be ruined! But you don't worry whether the doctor, who runs the greatest risk, may ruin his own life because his kind-heartedness will not let him refuse your request. Oh egoism! But of course it's an illegal operation and even if, for the patient's sake, no narcotics are used, it still costs fifteen pounds; and that's payable in advance, otherwise you'll say after- wards: "What! I asked you to interfere with me?" And then the doctor, who has got to live, gets nothing for his troubles. For cases like this he can't keep books and send in bills – purely in the interest of the patient. If he's sensible he'll leave the whole business alone. He only ruins himself in the end. An embryo life, my dear young lady, is as sacred as any other form of life. The Church has not made her great pronouncements for nothing. On Saturday afternoon I shall be free for consultation, but think it over again very carefully. Think whether you are prepared to take this grave responsibility upon yourself; if not, much better let things be. And bring the money with you, otherwise you need not come at all. This way out, my dear child.'*

The Peach went away very downcast. Where would the £15 come from?

She and the soldier walked gloomily along, side by side.

'There is another address,' said the soldier after a while. They decided to go there.

The midwife was an old fat woman and did business in the parlour. Polly sat on a red plush sofa.

'It will cost a pound,' began the old woman mistrustfully. 'I can't do it cheaper. And if you start to scream, I shall stop immediately and you can get out. Have you got the money? It will be over in half an hour.'

Polly stood up.

'I'm afraid I haven't got the money with me. I'll come again tomorrow.'

As they went down the steps, she said to Fewkoombey:

'I looked round. It was too dirty.'

'It's more for servant girls,' said the soldier. They went home. Polly's thoughts dwelt on the till in the shop.

She had an ingrained dislike of stealing; since earliest childhood the dislike and the practice had grown up simultaneously within her. When caught she would get fewer pennies (for Turkish Delight) and much good advice. Whenever she stuck her little fingers in the jam pot she had terrible pangs of conscience. The taste of the jam was sweet, the thought of the prohibition was bitter. God, she had been told, could see everywhere and lay in wait day and night. Apparently He saw everything that she did. But to see some things was indelicate. When, in her opinion, He had seen enough wickedness, He had already seen too much to allow any amount of good (but exhausting) behaviour ever to influence Him again in the sinner's favour. The punishment book was already full; there was no more room for new crimes and they could therefore be committed with equanimity. Polly was a Lost Girl, and as such she could permit herself every liberty. Also it was only laziness on the part of the grown-ups that made them delegate God to guard jam jars and money-boxes like a watch-dog.

But between the theft of a few pennies and that of fifteen pounds lay a big difference.

The technical difficulties of stealing proved disappointing to the Peach, for she had once considered them great. She could quite easily have stolen from her father. The till in the shop was always kept securely locked, but Mr Peachum carried a great deal of money around with him in his trouser pocket. He took the money relentlessly, penny by penny, from the beggars, changed it into silver, and stuffed it carelessly into his pocket. In his view, neither this money nor any other could save him in the long run. It was only a sense of conscientiousness that prevented him from simply throwing it away, and that proved his utter hopelessness. Nothing could be spared. With a million pounds he would have thought the same. It was his convinced opinion that neither his money (nor all the money in the world), nor his brains (nor all the brains in the world) could save him from ruin. That was also the reason why he did not work, but walked round his business with his hat on his head and his hands in his pockets, seeing that nothing was left undone.

Within a week his daughter could easily have taken the £15 out of his pockets by going into his bedroom at night; and even if he had caught her, it would not have been as bad as she perhaps imagined. If he had woken up and seen his daughter in the act of emptying his pockets, he would never have moved an eyelid; he would simply have gone to sleep again. His daughter would have been punished, but she would scarcely have fallen in his estimation. There was no one who could fall in his estimation.

Unfortunately people are too little aware of their own capabilities, and so Polly believed that she could never get the necessary £15 from her father.

When she told the soldier of the sum, he made an offer to break up the gentleman who was responsible. There are money-boxes which have to be broken up to get the money out. But unfortunately Mr Smiles was not a money-box. So Polly's thoughts turned more frequently towards Mr Beckett.

But after the soldier had looked at the dogs, he went back and lay on his camp bed. Had he been thinking, his thoughts would have been somwhat as follows:

'£15 wanted again! If the money were always there, it would be inexplicable why anyone was ever born. How could a woman be so inhuman as to bring a child into the world if she had the £15 which suffice to leave the child unborn? Would there ever have been such a monstrous number of human beings to tear each other to bits for the sake of a few breaths of air, a few mouthfuls of ill-tasting food, and a leaking roof, if every time the £15 had been there to stop them being born? Who would there then be to curry on the unwanted wars and for whom are such wars necessary? Who would there be to exploit, if the mother had not been already exploited because she lacked the £15? All the professors say that nothing can alter the distribution of property. The owners can never be got rid of, but why not at least the non-owners? The law forbids abortion and the unhappy girls would soon be happy if they were allowed to be aborted. So they fight against the law. But their wish may not be fulfilled. Of course not! That would be really too disgraceful. Hasn't the Church declared life sacred? So how can these women endanger life by refusing to bring children into this overfilled, stinking world, full of the cries of the starving? They must pull themselves together instead of letting themselves go. They ought to take a gulp of whisky, clench their teeth, and simply give birth! Because anyone can come and say they don't want to give birth! Of course blood is thicker than water and every mother thinks her own child too good for this world. Her child must be made the exception! It's a good thing that abortion costs money. Otherwise there'd be no stopping ...'

That was roughly what the soldier would have thought if he *had* been thinking. But he did not think; he was trained to discipline.

Soon afterwards he got up and went upstairs to the Peach to tell her something. He would take Polly to his friend. She would be sure to know some way out.

When he entered the little pink-distempered room, he saw

the Peach lying on her back on the bed, her hands by her sides, gazing up at the ceiling.

Fewkoombey was just about to speak when his glance fell on a tattered book lying on the seat of a cane chair. It was the volume of the *Encyclopaedia Britannica*, or rather a part of it, which Fewkoombey had studied for so many hours. He already knew a few pages by heart, but how many more still remained to be learned!

The fact that the book which he had missed so much was lying there, shocked the soldier. He was not happy that he could now have it back again. It shocked him that it had ever disappeared. It had an enormous value in his eyes. He could have bought another at a junk shop if he had seen one lying in the window; but why should it be just that volume? That could only happen, at the most, once every ten years. As we know, it was of no great value to the Peach. But there was probably nothing in the world for which he would have exchanged it – except the complete volume. All the same, he could not pick it up and say: Ah, that's my book; how did it get here? Such behaviour would have closed the matter in a most unsuitable way. The sight of the book in this room completely altered Fewkoombey's opinion of Miss Peachum. When she asked him what he wanted, he murmured something about 'Cametoseehowyouwere', and went out of the room without looking at her or the book again. She was very upset to notice his strange behaviour.

With him a friendly being went out of the room, a being indispensable and irreplaceable in such a world, a fund of advice which might have altered her whole life.

During those days Polly went to Smiles again. Since his landlady had already become suspicious, they went into the park. Polly wanted to sit on a bench, but Smiles insisted on a place in the bushes.

She considered that to be blackmail.

With his arms about her hips, he told her that he had been making great efforts to discover something to help her.

'You mustn't think that I don't worry about it night and day,' he said, pressing his cheek against her cheek. 'It's damned unpleasant for me. Besides, you've been so irritable since then. For example, instead of sitting here quietly where it's so nice under the bushes – look at the moon, it's not always so lovely, darling; but you're not looking at it properly – oh, yes, I was saying that instead of taking your mind off it, which might do you good, you always begin about the same old thing. Aren't you fond of me any more? Don't you still like it when I put my hand here, on your breast? You don't trust me. It's my duty to pull you out of the situation I've got you into – even if you did do it with me, which you must admit, darling. But listen, I've found out something which I'm perfectly certain will work. You can do it all alone and it costs nothing. You take an onion ...'

She looked at him in amazement. He continued hastily, removing his arm:

'You take the onion, an ordinary onion like you have in the kitchen ... and then it's all over. Simple, what?'

Polly stood up angrily. She removed a bit of moss from her skirt and put her hat straight without saying anything. When she saw that he was offended, she said shortly: 'No one would pay fifteen pounds if it worked with an onion. Besides, it would hurt.'

They went rather quickly out of the park. When they parted he showed clearly that he felt he had done all that could be expected of him.

Polly knew about Beckett's other name being MacHeath and also about the B. shops. He had told her everything. Since he also dealt in wood, he was entitled to call himself a wood merchant.

Polly met him several times and told him tentatively about her interview with the broker Coax. She said nothing about having visited him in his house and also nothing about her father's letter, but she mentioned some interesting photographs which he had promised to show her. She added that she was going to call on him soon as she had heard that his sister was a very charming woman.

Mr Beckett listened to her gloomily and gave the impression that he was faced with a decision.

In the late afternoon Polly followed her mother down to the little cellar where apples were laid out on racks. She knew that Mrs Peachum did not like being followed in there. But Polly

69

had made up her mind to speak to her there and nowhere else.

When she opened the door, her mother was standing between the shelves with a terrified expression on her face and a glass of whisky in her hand. It was very painful for Mrs Peachum to be driven by her husband to such undignified subterfuges in front of her child just for the sake of an occasional glass of whisky. She was forty-six years old and chafed at her lack of freedom.

Polly spoke sweetly to her because she had a guilty conscience; but at other times she could be very horrid. Polly told her that she wanted to marry Mr Beckett.

'His name is not Beckett,' said Mrs Peachum reluctantly.

'I know. His name is MacHeath – or rather, perhaps it is.'

'And Peachum? What will Peachum say to a man whose name is perhaps this or perhaps that?' asked Mrs Peachum, putting down her glass with a bang on the nearest rack. 'That's no sort of a man to marry. I've got eyes in my head and I can see the way he dances – even if he does think I'm not looking. No man who has a respectable business holds a young girl round the waist like that. And then he thinks that I'm not myself after four or five glasses of that "Octopus" beer. Don't try to deceive me, Polly dear! It cannot be respectable reasons which make you think of such a man; it is something quite different of which I would rather not speak. He has turned your head, that's what it is.'

'Yes, he attracts me.'

'Of course, just what I said,' exclaimed Mrs Peachum triumphantly. 'You've lost your head. You're infatuated with him and you can't even see that two and two make four.'

Polly became angry.

'Don't talk so much!' she said haughtily. 'Tell Papa and then he can talk to Mr Beckett.' And she turned round and went back to her room.

Mrs Peachum sighed and emptied her glass morosely. That night she spoke to her husband. She knew Polly.

During that afternoon Peachum had had a terrible scene with Coax. In the back room of a wine restaurant the broker had openly demanded the purchase of new ships. This had hit the Marine Transport Company like a thunderbolt. Eastman, who for some time past had suspected a good deal, had simply collapsed in his chair; but the bookmaker had jumped up and roared like a bull and then broken down in sobs. Nothing was of any avail. According to Coax, the first steps had already been taken for an investigation of the contract by a Parliamentary Commission. So they had delegated Peachum, who represented two-sevenths of the interests, to accompany Coax to Southampton at the end of the week. He was to commence negotiations for 'respectable' ships.

Nevertheless they all went down to the docks for the official handing over of the old ships to the Government. They had to hand the ships over so as not to arouse suspicion, but later they could be exchanged. The overhauling was not yet finished and work still being continued under the aegis of the M.T.C. The Commission was represented by two gentlemen in lounge suits who went through the formalities quickly. They stood for a short quarter of an hour on a draughty quay. It rained and they all froze.

Just before going to sleep that evening, Mrs Peachum mentioned to her husband the name of MacHeath in connexion with her daughter. Peachum flew into a frenzy.

'*Who* introduced you to him?' he shouted. 'That B. shop crook? What's that? Introduced himself? What sort of places do you go to, where strange men introduce themselves to you? That man's known throughout the whole of the City as a swindler! So that's the way you look after your daughter! Here I am, working night and day for her, and you introduce her to notorious libertines who hang about the waiting rooms of banks all day, trying to get their Bilge shops financed. What's the matter with your daughter? I'll soon settle things in that direction! Exchanging glances with this Coax under the eyes of her parents, the —. Where does she get this sensuality from?'

'Not from you,' said Mrs Peachum, pulling the sheets up under her chin.

'Certainly not from me,' said Mr Peachum, raging in the dark. 'I have no use for such things. I need a clear head in order not to be torn to pieces by these hyenas.' He broke off short:

'I don't want to hear any more. In future I shall decide whom Polly is to meet.'

As far as Polly was concerned, he had made up his mind.

The next morning he spoke to Polly in the office. He questioned her relentlessly about her visit to Mr Coax and even extracted from the weeping girl the story of the pictures. There had been naked ladies on them.

After the interview Peachum told her that he considered most of what she had confessed to be lies. Mr Coax was a highly respectable business man, and she ought to be thankful that he took an interest in her and had heard nothing of her associates. With this intimation, he left the subject.

When she met Mr MacHeath again, she told him that her father would never consent to her marrying him, but that Mr Coax had invited her to a picnic at the end of the week.

The first was true, the second a lie.

When Mr MacHeath learned from the Peach that Mr Coax was the suitor favoured by her parents, it became clear to him that he would have to do something about this Coax.

After some thought he reached a decision and drove in a horse omnibus to one of those dirty two-roomed newspaper offices which are usually inhabited by unwashed, inquisitive gentlemen with unctuous voices.

Some greasy, tattered volumes of old newspapers were brought out and looked through. Then he caught another horse omnibus to Lower Blacksmith Square where he entered a tumble-down house and gave certain orders to an evil-looking man in shirt-sleeves.

Then, although it was still early in the afternoon, he rode in a third omnibus back to his home.

He had a small house in one of the southern suburbs. It lay behind a tiny garden, in a row with other identical houses. He had not had it long; it was scarcely ready for occupation. In one of the bare rooms stood a few pieces of furniture, amongst them a new sofa on which he slept; and in the kitchen was a gas cooker and an ice chest. The house was not a new one. He had taken it over from one of his business friends who had gone bankrupt.

Standing on the steps, he pulled a large bunch of keys out of his pocket and tried several before he found the right one. Then he walked whistling into a completely empty hall where there was not so much as a hook to hang his hat on.

On reaching his room on the first floor, in which great neatness reigned, he took off his boots, lay down on a sofa, and remained lying there until it grew dark.

Towards ten o'clock the bell rang below. He went down and let in a fat man. Without saying a word he took from the man what he had brought and pushed him out again. The man went away grumbling. Apparently he knew the neighbourhood.

After MacHeath (who as a matter of fact lived here under the name of Milburn) had opened the brown paper parcel, he emptied from it on to his washstand a bundle of letters and papers which he proceeded to study for half an hour by the light of a petroleum lamp. Then he made up a bed with some blankets which he fetched from a cupboard and soon fell asleep.

The next morning he had an interview at police headquarters with the Assistant Commissioner.

The two gentlemen bent over the bare desk and studied the contents of the brown paper parcel, especially a ruled exercise book in a red cover which was Mr Coax's diary.

The diary only contained information concerning the broker's private life. The Assistant Commissioner's perusal was preceded by Mr MacHeath's assurance that there were no business notes in the book. If the case had been otherwise Mr Brown would not have been in a position to examine it.

The contents of the book were mostly of a moralizing nature. Indications were not lacking of certain visits and other facts, but mostly there were moral observations and frank self-criticisms, evidence of an incessant fight against overwhelming sensuality. For the most part these observations were beyond the mental capacities of the two readers, for whom indeed they were never intended.

There were also names. They were indicated by initials.

On nearly every second or third day (not a single day was omitted, for the diary was kept with the greatest care and scarcely a word was crossed out) there stood, in red ink and neatly underlined with a ruler, numbers such as: 'Twice' or

'4 times'. Actually, '4 times' was rare and there was nothing higher than '5 times'. Sometimes it was only 'Once', and then it was not underlined but enclosed in a little circle.

There were also two different symbols. What they meant was explained by an entry on the inside of the cover: Evacuation and Laxatives. These symbols, too, were carefully drawn. Mr Coax had a bold, rather flourishing hand.

The remaining contents of the package consisted of extremely questionable photographs. They showed signs of much use.

After a short silent examination, Brown pressed a button and gave an official a slip of paper on which he had scribbled a few words. When the official came back, he laid a bundle of papers on the table. It contained police documents and dossiers.

Brown took out a sheet of closely written paper and compared something with an entry in Coax's diary. Laying a thick index finger on the place, he said in his slow profound way:

'My dear Mac, we can't get the fellow on this. We don't know what sort of business he carries on; and we never stick our noses into the business enterprises of respectable people. Where would that get us? The man pays his taxes – so that's all right. People's private lives are no concern of ours and this man hasn't committed any burglaries. The only thing would be to rake up a charge of two years ago when the gentleman was discovered in a doubtful hotel with the wife of an Admiralty official. But you would do better to put that into the hands of the newspaper people. I'll give you the names of a few reliable men who could make something out of it.'

He again pressed a button and the man brought in another bundle, on the wrapping of which was written in thick lettering: Blackmail.

He looked through the contents carefully as was his way, and finally said:

'Go to Gawn. He's one of the best.'

MacHeath took the address and put it with his own material. Then he clapped his friend on the back and said lightly:

'When I next get married – officially, you understand – will you come to the wedding? I'm worried about the bank people. They're not doing their best.'

'I will if I can,' said Brown without enthusiasm, 'but it really mustn't happen many more times.'

MacHeath went away pensively. Brown was no longer the old Brown as far as his attitude towards his friends was concerned. Of course he was as true as steel, but it seemed lately that he had a great deal of new responsibility. ...

Neither was MacHeath getting anywhere with the bank. They were always making fresh reservations.

His own people were also becoming troublesome. The realization that he was responsible for nearly 120 people, some of them with families, weighed heavily upon him. He took it very seriously.

Something must happen, there was no doubt about that. Once he could get old Peachum's money into his hands, he would be able to breathe freely again.

He drove to one of his shops near Waterloo Bridge. It was not a B. shop but a respectable antique business, and was run by a woman called Fanny Chrysler who knew something about art. He always went there when he had something to ponder over. He would sit in the office, turning over the pages of a book.

Unfortunately Fanny was not there. She was at some auction. Mac thought it important that some of the objects sold there should have proper birth certificates.

The books which lay stacked in the office came from the library of the vicar of Kingshall, as the blue pencil writing on the lid of the packing-case testified. They were volumes of extremely obscene engravings. Mac could not bear such things. He was against art in every form. Disgusted, he laid the valuable tomes aside.

Then he thought of Polly.

Whenever he thought of her lately an indescribable uneasiness had come over him. She was far too sensual.

He got up and went to Old Oak Street.

After he had walked past the house twice, Polly came down. She walked a few times round the block with him.

She was very tender and seemed to be in some sort of trouble. She was also paler than usual. The shadows under her eyes shocked MacHeath. When they parted, she did not look him in the face.

She had mentioned casually that she would not be going to her housekeeping classes for some time, so she would be unable to meet him any more. And on Sunday the picnic with Coax was to take place.

MacHeath went to Tunbridge in a bad temper. He had remembered that it was Thursday.

It was his habit to pass every Thursday evening in a certain house in Tunbridge. He drank a cup of coffee with the girls there and talked to Jenny. This time, because he was depressed, he got her to tell his fortune with cards. But she said nothing interesting. The girls bored him as usual. He had been going there for more than five years.

On the next day he visited Gawn, a journalist who wrote for various unsavoury newspapers, and gave him the evidence against William Coax.

Shortly afterwards Miller of the National Credit Bank dropped a remark in the course of a business conversation which made it seem advisable to Mr MacHeath to put aside all other considerations and take up a respectable domestic life as quickly as possible – which coincided with Polly Peachum's wishes.

The attack on Mr Coax thereby became superfluous and MacHeath troubled no more about the existence of the incriminating material.

5

So they 'found each other' 'twixt the deer and fish
And 'their earthly paths united'
And they had neither bed nor table nor dish
And they had neither venison nor fish
And no names to give to their children.
    But though snow-winds howl, though rain runs wild
    And drowns the prairie plain,
    Beside her husband dear, my child,
    Will Hanna Cash remain.

The Sheriff says he's a lousy thief
And the milkwife says: he goes lame.
But she says: what's all that to me?
For he's my man. And by your leave
She'll stick to him, just the same.
    And that he limps and that he's mad
    And beats her black and blue
    Don't worry Hanna Cash, my child:
    She knows she loves him true.

            (BALLAD OF HANNA CASH)

A Small But Well-Capitalized Business

THE National Credit Bank was a small but well-capitalized business whose activities were concerned mainly with real estate. It belonged to a seven-year-old little girl and was managed by an elderly representative, Mr Miller, who acted under the instructions of an equally elderly lawyer called Hawthorne; Hawthorne was the guardian of the little girl.

MacHeath, in his negotiations with the bank, had had to deal not only with Mr Miller but also with Mr Hawthorne. Together they were more than 150 years old, and when one had to deal with them, one had to deal with one and a half centuries.

MacHeath had come particularly to them, and thereby taken upon himself an almost unendurable trial of patience, because he wished to silence once and for ever the rumours about his B.

shops. For no one in the City could conceive that a business in which the National Credit Bank was interested, could have been founded *after* 1780. And firms as old as that are really sound.

But because of this very circumstance he made no progress.

The bank made evasion after evasion. They wanted to know everything, from the rentals of the shops to the life histories of the shopkeepers. Yet in spite of all this, they seemed remarkably interested. And MacHeath knew why. The real estate business, more especially that which Mr Miller understood the term to cover, was no longer what it had been. New investments were scarce and the old properties had suffered terrible depreciations.

Mr Hawthorne viewed the future with considerable misgivings. He was not wholly pleased with the manager, Mr Miller; although he was older than the latter, he thought him too old to manage the bank. In his pompous way he considered Miller's pompousness responsible for much lost business. He sometimes secretly thought of replacing him by a younger, more energetic person, and Mr Miller sensed that.

In reality, the hostile attitude of both towards the modern age had, some considerable time ago, begun to weaken. Perhaps it was really not advisable to treat everything with such pedantic strictness. Other firms were not so strict; they did business and were regarded as sound. It might be that a certain broad-mindedness lay in the trend of the times.

So when the proposals about the new B. shops had been put forward to them, they were not nearly so averse to the enterprise as one might have imagined. Everything about the business was a little strange and irregular, but that was just its modernity and up-to-dateness. Of course, from their standpoint, they could not so easily distinguish the difference between one new enterprise and another as between a new and an old one. Their investigations were almost a matter of form. Already they had half made up their minds to accept. Hawthorne, in particular, had made up his mind.

Miller had given unmistakable indications that, in the event of an invitation, he would not be unwilling to accept MacHeath's hospitality – which meant a great deal. Unfortunately MacHeath had no hospitality to offer. But when he formally invited Mr

Miller to his impending marriage, the latter accepted with alacrity, and for Mr Hawthorne as well.

MacHeath had the feeling that this invitation might mean more to the realization of his business proposals than all the documents in the world. He was right.

After leaving the bank, he proceeded cheerfully towards the neighbourhood of Waterloo Bridge. In the back office of the shop he had a conference with Fanny Chrysler and then went out with her.

Together they went through the best antique shops in the district, choosing furniture. The finest pieces had to be selected; price was no object.

But when they were eating luncheon in a café, Fanny was silent for a short while and then said suddenly, tapping her spoon on her saucer:

'But this is ridiculous! What do you want this furniture for? For yourself? Of course not! At a pinch you might live with it, although there's no need to pretend to me. A £40 suite, brand new from the factory, would be more suited to you than the stuff I have just chosen. You've got the taste of a furniture packer – admit it, it's nothing to be ashamed of. But the furniture's not for you at all, Mac. It's intended for Messrs Miller and Hawthorne – and what impression do you think it will make on them? You must have a modern house, and it must be an expensive one. It must be the house of a man who moves with the times. You can have a few old things inherited from your mother, standing about. An armchair with a sewing table and so forth. I'll see to that. Leave it all to me. I'll arrange it so that the One and a Half Centuries will have no cause to worry about the money which they will have entrusted to you.'

MacHeath laughed; they went through the shops again and countermanded all their orders. Then Fanny went out alone and bought different furniture.

Polly had lied when she spoke of the picnic to which Mr Coax had invited her. She had not even seen Mr Coax again. Once or twice she had thought of visiting him about the brooch. In her opinion the brooch would have fetched at a jeweller's, or even in a pawn shop, at least £15.

But she was on very good terms with Mac. He attracted her

more. And she had noticed that he had her watched. There were always a few people lounging outside the instrument shop who followed her whenever she went out. At first this had annoyed her, but now it only flattered her. She had a feeling of security with Mac. He wasn't a young prig like Smiles, who had no idea of responsibility. When Mac spoke of a secret marriage, she joyfully conjured up the picture of her father's face when he found out about it.

She was convinced that it had been the mention of the picnic which had driven Mac to this decision. He imagined a picnic as involving something very wicked. She laughed when she thought of it.

On Friday afternoon Mrs Peachum packed a bag with a shirt and a few collars for her husband and he went off to the station with it. Half an hour later Polly also packed.

She had secretly bought herself a pair of silk combinations and a pair of mauve corsets – all from a B. shop so as to surprise Mac. She put them into an old black bag, together with a long, high-necked nightdress, the only one of hers which was not patched.

At the street corner a closed carriage drove up to her; in it sat MacHeath.

MacHeath was not in a very good temper because he had been on his feet since early morning and had missed his usual afternoon's sleep.

First they drove to police headquarters. MacHeath stopped the carriage and ran upstairs to Brown. He found Brown nervous. He had already visited him twice to remind him of their impending arrival.

The search for a suitable house for the reception had, to date, been unsuccessful; and so, in the afternoon, Mac had had to give another address, which had not improved Brown's temper. Now the Chief Inspector showed little eagerness to attend the festivities, but he promised to come. Indeed the whole success of the marriage depended upon his appearing. It was not a question of impressing only Miller and Hawthorne, but also some other of the guests to whom the sight of a police officer would convey a message.

Near Covent Garden MacHeath deposited Polly in a café and

then drove on alone to a house in Kensington. There had been an unpleasant incident at another house that morning, and his people were now preparing this one for the wedding. Mac's own house in South London was out of the question because it was too small.

Mac found everything in wild disorder. The furniture for the ground floor had arrived before that for the first floor and was now in the way. His people were not expert removers; and they had also been drinking. O'Hara, who was in charge of the operations, excused himself by saying that there had been a great deal of quarrelling.

The house was the smaller town residence of the Duke of Dillwater. The larger mansion was also free, for the Duke himself was staying on the Riviera; but that would have been too ostentatious, and besides it was furnished; while the small house was empty down to the butler's room. The butler was under an obligation to MacHeath.

There was not much that MacHeath could do here, and so he soon went away again and drove once more to Brown. But the latter was not to be found at Scotland Yard. So MacHeath drove across Waterloo Bridge, sent Fanny to Polly, and called for Brown at his private house. But neither was he to be found there.

Fanny immediately recognized the Peach from his description of her. She quickly introduced herself. The Peach was a little nervous because Mac had been away so long. She was already drinking her third pot of tea. And she had no money with her.

At first, Fanny's arrival calmed her; but then she began to wonder in what relationship Fanny stood to Mac. She was a little over thirty and not ugly. She laughed suddenly and told the Peach that she ran an antique shop for Mac near Waterloo Bridge, and that she had a sick husband and two children. This soothed Polly noticeably, although not for long.

The worst of it was that it was now too late to go and buy a wedding dress. The fear of having to spend the whole evening in her everyday dress took all the pleasure out of the ceremony for Polly. Mac had told her that there would be a crowd of smart people there.

Mac came rather late, without having found Brown, and he took the two women in his carriage. Polly would not hear of

Fanny being sent away, as Mac had intended. Her excuses that she was not suitably dressed were ignored by an ominous silence on Polly's part.

Mac cursed when he saw the time. Of course all the shops were shut now. He fully understood that Polly did not want to enter her future home in her everyday dress, not even through the back door. Without her having to say a word, he made the coachman stop in the park, a few hundred yards from the house, and went on himself to see about procuring some clothes.

He entrusted this task to one of his people, an expert in fashions, who had good enough taste to have been a buyer at Worth's, but not enough integrity. The next morning five dresses were missing from one of the leading *modiste*'s, and the manageress informed the police they had been some of the best. As a result of this, Bully suffered considerable annoyance during the following weeks, for there was not another man in the underworld with such good taste as his. But Mac was able to bring a first-class wedding dress to Polly in the carriage.

Fanny put on one of the remaining four; so she also was wearing a wedding dress.

In the house Polly met about fifty people who seemed to belong to very different grades of society. Apart from a Lord Bloomsbury, a colonel, two members of Parliament, two well-known barristers, and the vicar of St Margaret's (who performed the ceremony in a back room), she shook hands with a large number of corpulent shopkeepers and also with some of Mac's agents and buyers. Most of them had come with their wives.

A few B. shop owners had been invited too; miserable creatures in respectable suits and with solemn expressions. They stood around as though they had been put out on show.

In the confusion Polly could not see much of the house; but she heard her husband say to the lord that he had rented it from his friend, the Duke of Dillwater.

On the left of the bride sat old Hawthorne. He had known Polly since a child, for she had often come with her father into the bank and had played with cheques while the two gentlemen had talked business. Now she told him that she and Mac had quarrelled with her parents yesterday because Mac had refused to invite anyone from the 'factory' to the wedding. This sounded a bit thin, but the One and a Half Centuries seemed to swallow it.

At first, the seat on the right of the bridegroom remained unoccupied.

Brown had still not arrived. Several times MacHeath went out in the middle of eating to send someone to look for him. The whole marriage would be useless to him without Brown. Mac also believed that the presence of a police official would make a lasting impression upon the One and a Half Centuries.

It was not until they had reached the fowl that Brown appeared. He did not look very cheerful and was not wearing uniform. Secretly, Mac took great offence at that.

To Polly he was charming. She attracted him greatly. She sat very upright with her cheeks a little flushed, and presided. She only ate a very little of everything, as befits a bride. It gives an unpleasant impression when one sees a tender creature stuffing in chicken and fish.

In the eyes of most of the guests at the lower table the seating arrangement was not quite correct, but no one blamed the bride for that. She looked so radiant that she pleased everyone.

MacHeath had been silently worrying about the behaviour of his guests. The B. shop people ate quite politely because they did not feel at home, but the buyers were naturally less embarrassed. MacHeath, who sat with them for dessert, listened involuntarily to the whispering of their wives who all detested one another, and he even reprimanded an undisguised obscenity whose originator he detected.

But on the whole his choice of guests from among his people had been an excellent one. Not one of those present was to be found in any police dossier either at home or abroad – except for Grooch, and all Scotland Yard would not have recognized him now without taking his finger-prints. The majority consisted of shopkeepers who had nothing against them and whose stupid appearance made them look incomparably respectable. The fact that Jenny had been invited was a piece of insolence on O'Hara's part; prostitutes do not belong to the family circle, and besides, the colonel ought to have known her. But people like

Read, 'the Traveller', one of the best black-jackers and conversationalists in the country, raised the social level enormously.

After the coffee Mac retired with Hawthorne and Miller into a neighbouring room where the requisites of the wedding ceremony still lay around on tables and chairs. Brown had pleaded official business and left. The three men discussed, over a glass of liqueur, the financing of the B. shops by the National Credit Bank.

The old gentlemen did not go into details. They never betrayed by a syllable that the absence of Polly's parents in any way disturbed them. MacHeath had of course calculated on this upsetting them. He believed that sooner or later Mr Peachum would come down to hard facts, and the silence of the One and a Half Centuries showed him that they were overlooking the situation and shared his belief.

On returning, they found the company busy dancing. The Peach was dancing with O'Hara. The room had a festive appearance. It was decorated in the most modern style.

Mac sat down for a few minutes at the empty table. His fat chin was sunk in his stiff collar and his bald head was somewhat red, for he had been drinking. He tried to think. In a comparatively short time he succeeded in collecting a few thoughts.

'How sad it is,' he thought, *'that the most beautiful hours of life are streaked with annoyances like beef with gristle. The tenderest scenes are spoiled by trouble and worry. When a man feels himself inwardly exalted and filled with the purest feelings, along come financial difficulties. I cannot sit down here and quietly drink my wine. If I did that my dear guests, the swine, would immediately soil all the clean things here. So I have to be on the watch, and I can't undo my trousers where they're so tight across my stomach. I have to watch myself, too; I'm a swine too. Everything could be so lovely if only these brutes would respect the feelings of a man on the most beautiful day of his life. I'm the best-tempered man in the world, but when Claude goes with Charley's wife into the drawing-room, that makes me mad. I won't have that in my house! Jenny could have kept away too; she's out of place here. I cannot let my wife mix with such people, that's going too far. Polly pleases every-*

84

one. *I wouldn't like to have to tell anyone not to sleep with my wife. Swine! They should be satisfied with their own bitches. Of course, I don't mean that mine is a bitch. I mustn't say that. I mustn't mention mine in the same breath as the others. She stands head and shoulders above them all. I'm not respectable enough for her, not a really decent man. But I'll do my best. When the bank business is completed, then I'll be respectable. It's so nice to be respectable, and it doesn't harm one financially. Or only a little. Or it even helps. Now I've got to stand up again. The most beautiful hours of one's life are full of troubles. It's sad, very sad.'*

MacHeath stood up to summon the carriages. When he went to fetch his bag, he caught Bully, alias Hook-finger Jacob, with Robert the Saw's wife, and he had to create a disturbance and 'forbid such disgustingness in his house'. He was equally displeased to see that Polly was still dancing with the talkative O'Hara. He interrupted the dance rather brusquely. But, all in all, Mac could not complain about the success of the party.

As the bridal pair drove away, the guests stood, as is customary, on the steps and waved to them. But that a number of the guests were treating Fanny as a second bride was observed only by Mac who, being a keen observer of humanity, looked out of the back window of the carriage.

They just caught the train to Liverpool.

The honeymoon had not come very opportunely for Mr MacHeath.

Two weeks ago two ironmongers' shops in the suburbs had been burgled. In the weekly journal, the *Reflector*, so called because the editorial staff held a mirror up to their fellow men until they paid, an article had appeared telling how a member of the staff had bought some razor-blades in a B. shop which should have come from one of these ironmongers' shops. O'Hara had immediately instituted negotiations, but MacHeath was extremely unwilling to pay – so much so that he threw out an editor who tried to hold up a mirror to him. Since then the *Reflector* had been demanding that the B. shops should produce their invoices for the razor-blades. Of course, that was easily arranged, but even then the matter was not at an end.

In the course of procuring table silver there had also been a contretemps; the job had to be done quickly and had resulted in a death. The gang had tried to conceal this from their chief so as not to spoil his happiness, but Mac had got wind of it. Here, too, lack of money had been responsible for indifferent work.

When Mac heard of the death, he would have liked to have put off the honeymoon; but that was impossible. So he thought that he might at least combine his trip with a little business, and had therefore chosen Liverpool.

The Peach looked very pretty in the railway compartment. O'Hara was a dancer above the average, and on the short way between the steps and the coach, under the dark, thick chestnut trees, she had had the distinct feeling that this was the most wonderful day of her life. Never had so many people revolved round her. She was happy. Unseen by the other travellers, Mac squeezed her hot hand.

In Liverpool they had booked a room in a small hotel. Before they went to bed they drank a last bottle of Burgundy in the hall. But that was a mistake. Even as he climbed the stairs, Mac realized that he was rather tired.

He was scarcely able to admire Polly's combinations, and the mauve corsets seemed to be nothing new to him.

But it was only tiredness with him.

They soon went to sleep, but in the middle of the night the alarm clock, which he had carefully set, went off and they had another pleasant hour. After earnest questioning, Mac admitted to some earlier love affairs (not to that with Fanny and rather incompletely to that with Jenny), and the Peach, after a long struggle, admitted to a kiss with Smiles, so that this confession formed the climax of the day and laid the foundation of long and lasting love.

Polly was happy too, and forgave Mac his professional past as a burglar, which he had admitted to her over the bottle of Burgundy in the hall — he had let her draw the dagger a little way out of the thick stick. She even forgave him his past love affairs and, what was more, his somewhat strange little idiosyncrasies, such as scratchingoneschestundertheshirt; and from that she knew that she really loved her husband.

86

Mr Jonathan Jeremiah Peachum had been given a free hand by the baronet, the bookmaker, the housing property owner, the cotton manufacturer, and the restaurant-keeper. He met Coax on the platform at Waterloo.

The journey to Southampton passed without the two gentlemen exchanging more than ten words. Coax, with his pince-nez perched on his thin nose, read *The Times*, and Peachum sat motionless in the corner with his hands clasped in the region of his navel.

Once the broker looked up and said casually:

'Mafeking's still holding out. Tough lads!'

Peachum said nothing.

'It's bad,' he thought in his corner, *'Englishmen fighting against Englishmen. Not only this man here but even the men in Mafeking are against me. They should surrender! Then they would need no relief and no ships and this business, which is likely to cost me my neck, would be at an end. There they are, sitting in that hot climate, waiting day after day for the ships which I am to buy for them with my hard-earned pennies. Hold out! they say to each other every day, flinch not nor weaken; eat less; stand under the hail of bullets until old Jonathan Peachum buys with his last farthings the ships which will bring our relief. If they had their way, the purchase of these damned ships would proceed quickly; if I had my way, it would go slowly; and so we have exactly opposing interests, and we don't even know each other.'*

In the hotel in Southampton they separated quickly; they did not even eat their dinner together. But in the middle of the night there was a horrible noise in Coax's room which was next door to Peachum's.

Peachum put on his trousers and went in. There lay Coax in bed, with the sheets up to his chin, and in the middle of the room stood a youngish person, naked except for a pair of stockings, cursing him like a fishwife.

One could gather from her torrent of words that she was not prepared to accede to the demands which had been made of her. She pointed out that she had had a long career, rich in experience, and she emphasized her absolute freedom from all prejudices; as witnesses to which she cited all kinds of dockers and sailors, widely travelled and exacting gentlemen. But not even a certain elderly magistrate, who was known throughout the town as a profligate, had dared to make such demands for ten shillings.

She understood to perfection the art of disparaging Coax. Without any trouble she found comparisons for him which, if they could be printed, would give this book through their poetic power a near approach to immortality.

Peachum had scarcely entered the room when there came a knocking on the door. He had to repel several excited waiters. Then he turned to the lady, who had artistically draped her shoulders in a plush tablecloth and was beginning to put on her shoes. He soon succeeded in awakening in her a businesslike attitude.

After a lengthy argument she stuffed some notes into her stocking and went – with the words:

'You'd better get two or three ladies for your friend, quick; that is if you want to get him in a suitable state so he can leave the hotel without going on all fours.'

When she was gone the two gentlemen had to pack, for the hotel no longer desired their further presence. They moved into another hotel.

By now it was nearly four o'clock. So they did not go to bed again but ordered a pot of tea and talked together.

Coax showed a strong desire to talk. He did not conceal the fact from Mr Peachum that the recent scene had filled him with uncontrollable disgust. He openly criticized his own weakness for consorting with such scum of the populace.

'These people,' he said sadly and emphatically, 'lose all control directly one takes them out of their accustomed surroundings. They don't understand gentlemanly behaviour. One can't blame them; they don't know any better. They will always use the vulgarest swear-words. The constant self-degradation for money destroys all their finer feelings. They don't want to work. They don't even want to give up the time for the money they earn. They only want an easy life and nothing else. That is what puts me against socialism. This gross materialism is unbearable. The greatest happiness for a creature like that is to be able to live in idleness. These social reformers will never get anywhere. They reckon without human nature, which is utterly depraved.

Of course, if people were as we would like them to be, then one could do all sorts of things with them. So nothing's any good. All one gets in the end is a headache.'

Peachum stood in his accustomed position at the window and gazed down at the square, already growing light, which a man in blue overalls was sluicing with a hydrant. The first vegetable carts rattled by on their way from the harbour.

When Coax had finished speaking, he said drily:

'You ought to marry, Coax.'

Coax grasped at this advice as at a straw.

'Perhaps I ought to really,' he said pensively. 'I need a loving woman beside me. Would you give me your daughter?'

'Yes,' said Peachum without turning round.

'You would entrust her to me?'

'Of course.'

Coax breathed audibly. If Peachum had turned round he would have seen that Coax was not looking very well. The affair had got on his nerves.

'You wouldn't have a bad son-in-law,' Coax said uneasily, 'I know my business. And I am a man of principles. We must discuss this matter seriously. You can see that the business I have in hand is thoroughly sound; it is really good. You have no idea *how* good it is. You yourself are involved and pretty deeply too! I don't think you realize, Peachum, how much I get out of this. You can testify to the way I manage things. Now that there is this understanding between us, I can take you into my confidence; especially as everything is practically fixed up. As far as I can call to mind, you are involved to the extent of at least £7,000. You don't believe me? Whatever do you think the boats that we are going to see today will cost? Between ourselves, I know already. They are all first-class ships. We, or rather you, will never get them under £35,000. Without the option which I have on them, they would be even dearer. At first thought you will say that there is still a considerable margin in the £49,000 which the Government are to pay. But that only seems so. You will buy the new ships and sell the old ones – but for the price which your adviser mentioned. They are really not worth more. Do you still remember? £200.'

Peachum had long since turned round. Now he grasped with

a trembling hand at the curtains beside him. He stared at Coax as at a boa constrictor.

Coax laughed and went on:

'The cost of repairs, the bribes, and my percentage are not very large as long as the ships are cheap and only cost you £11,000. But it's quite a different matter if they cost you £35,000. And in addition to that there'll be new bribes for the exchange of the ships – at least £7,000. What do you think of that?'

In the pale light of dawn Peachum looked very ill. The worst of it was that he had guessed it! He had fallen into the hands of a crook and he had guessed it from the very beginning. Had he been educated, he might have cried out:

'What is Oedipus compared to me? Alone and for centuries he was known as the unhappiest of mortals, the classical example of Olympic vengeance, the most wretched of all men born of woman. Compared to me he is a lucky fellow. He became involved in a bad business without realizing it. At first it seemed good to him; no – it was good. It was pleasant sleeping with that woman. The wanderer found a happy home; for years the husband had no worries or cares and enjoyed universal respect. Then, one day, it came to light that the marriage bonds into which he had entered could not be permanent. They had to be broken, he was again unattached and the marital bed was forbidden him for the future. Fools and enviers attacked him; a great deal of this, nearly all in fact, was unpleasant. But there were other lands; for vagabonds like him there have always been many countries. He had nothing to reproach himself with; he had done nothing that he could have avoided. But I, I knew everything, I myself am the fool, and therefore unfit to live. It is already plain that I can be persuaded into confusing a bluebottle with a thousand pounds. I can no longer cross the street without fearing that I may mistake an omnibus for a leaf driven by the wind. I belong to the company of those who pay too highly for the very weapons which destroy them and include the price of their graves as well!'

Meanwhile the sight of the old man had begun to bore Coax.

'For all these reasons,' he said calmly, 'I am an absolutely ideal son-in-law.'

They breakfasted as relations. Peachum uttered a few cautious words about his instrument business; the broker pictured fleetingly the Peach's beautiful skin. Then they both went to look at the ships.

There were two for sale, very good and very expensive. Together with a third ship which Coax knew of in Plymouth they would cost exactly £38,500, of which Coax's percentage would amount to at least £8,000. Since Peachum had now left the sheep to join the butcher, he raised no particular objections. He was chiefly in a hurry to get home. In the lavatory he had calculated on a piece of paper how much he would have lost without Polly. But it would have been almost worse to have had to have borne Coax's profits. Estimating these roughly he groaned so loudly that a passer-by outside asked if he were ill.

Actually Peachum was henceforth far less concerned with the thought of the ruinous loss that had almost overwhelmed him than with the immense profits to which he would be entitled as a relation of the broker.

The most important thing now was to prepare the Peach. The girl could not have found a better husband. The man was a genius.

MacHeath quickly dispatched his business in Liverpool. For the first time Polly accompanied him into one of his shops.

A huge unshaven man stepped out of a dark back room to meet them. The shop was whitewashed. Arranged in neat rows on counters of rough boards, lay great bales of materials, whole bundles of yellow house-shoes, boxes of pocket watches, toothbrushes, cigarette lighters, pile of lamps, notebooks, pipes – in all about twenty different articles.

When the man learned whom he had before him, he opened a low door at the back and called his wife into the shop. She emerged, with a baby in her arms, from a tiny one-windowed basement, through the open door of which Polly could see a confusion of furniture and children.

The pair gave an unhealthy impression.

They were full of hope. The husband thought that he would make a success of it. He was glad to be standing on his own feet. When he started on a thing he didn't give it up so easily.

'My husband is one of those,' said the woman, who looked rather underfed, 'who never give in.'

As far as Polly could understand they were nevertheless not doing well. The rent was not high, but no delay in payment was allowed. The consignments, which were delivered from Mac-Heath's headquarters, arrived irregularly and in varying quantities, and the unsold remainders turned the place into a junk shop. For there were always too many things there – or else too few. A person who wanted galoshes had no interest in pocket watches, although he might conceivably have bought an umbrella. Other chain shops were strong competitors in spite of their higher prices.

The man said he was finding great difficulty in settling at the end of the month.

MacHeath explained to him, clearly and calmly, that the competition of the larger shops was immoral, for they exploited foreign labour and worked together with Jewish bankers to ruin prices. But he soothed him on the question of the big businesses by saying that in these pretentious shops, especially in those belonging to a certain I. Aaron, things were by no means as prosperous as they seemed. Internally they were thoroughly rotten, even if they glittered outwardly. Now was the time to take up the fight with Aaron and the others with relentless energy. No mercy must be shown.

As far as the rent was concerned, he promised allowances; and also smaller and more varied consignments. He agreed also to ensure that deliveries would be punctual. In return for which he demanded more advertisement on the part of the shop. The couple could draw hand-bills and the children could press them into the hands of workers at the factory gates. Headquarters would supply the paper.

Children there were in plenty. Polly stepped for a moment into the back room. It was all quite clean, but there were only fragments of furniture. On a rickety sofa which seemed in imminent danger of collapse, lay an old woman, the mother of the owner. The children goggled. The old woman stared obstinately at the wall.

They were both relieved when they got out in the fresh air again. Mac expressed his opinion in one sentence:

'Either a man has a B. shop *or* a lot of children!'

At the next B. shop (as yet there were not more than two in Liverpool) Polly waited outside until Mac had finished. Through the shop window, in which hung astonishingly cheap and smart suitings, she saw Mac talking to a young consumptive man who was cutting out suits on a rough wooden table. During the conversation he never stopped working for a moment.

Polly learned later that the man was supplied with stuff; so many yards for so many suits whose prices were fixed – very low of course. He would have been better off if he had had a family, because there would have been more labour. But that was his affair. According to the B. system he need obey no rules or regulations.

MacHeath told her how the man had nailed a newspaper cutting on to the wall opposite his ironing board. On it stood: 'No pains, no gains.'

After MacHeath had gone to a wholesale ironmonger's and ordered a consignment of razor-blades with a pre-dated invoice, he had finished in Liverpool and they could now go back to London.

They had planned to keep the marriage a secret from Mr Peachum at first, so as not to upset him unnecessarily. Polly wanted to arrive home alone, silence her mother (she had a bottle of brandy in her handbag), and then mention Mac when her father returned from Southampton.

But when Polly entered the shop Mr Peachum was already back from Southampton and everything was in a state of feverish agitation because of her overnight absence.

On the very doorstep, her mother tore her bag out of her hand. Out of it she brought to light a bottle of brandy, a night-dress bought in Liverpool, and a wedding dress.

The effect of this apparition was staggering; but who likes family scenes and who would not rather pass over what the old people said to their daughter, the fruit of their bodies? Everything came to light, the 'Octopus' as well as the double-bedded room in the Liverpool hotel. The name of MacHeath in juxtaposition with that of his only daughter was like a knock-out blow to Peachum. To him, who was respectfully known in Soho and Whitechapel as the 'Beggar King', the underworld of the

British Isles and the Dominions was as an open book. He knew who MacHeath was.

Besides, he was not only a disgraced but also a ruined man. Neither the three houses in which he received this merciless blow of fate, nor the worm-eaten table on which he was supporting himself, belonged to him any longer. This morning he had seen in Southampton three ships, for at least one of which he alone would have to pay. And his daughter, his last hope, had laid down in a hotel bed in Liverpool with a dirty burglar!

'I shall end in the mad-house,' he stormed, 'my daughter will drive me into the mad-house. Early this morning in Southampton, after passing a sleepless night, I went out and bought her a new dress, it's lying in the office, it cost two pounds! I thought to myself, I will bring something back for her, she shall see that she is cared for. Other children have to keep themselves from an early age, their legs are bent because milk is scarce. Their souls are warped because they have had to see the shady side of life too soon. My daughter drank milk by the pint, unskimmed! She knew only tenderness and devotion. She learned to play the piano! And now, for the first time, I ask something of her; that she shall marry a respectable business man, a man with principles, who will care for her. She will drive me into a mad-house, because for her sake I entered into a business of which I understood nothing, simply in order to get a dowry for her! What does this depraved creature think she is? If I find one of my sewing girls with my manager, out she goes! – that's the way I look after morals in my house. And my daughter entangles herself with a notorious bigamist and dowry-hunter. Now I shall have to consider how I can get a divorce for her. And even then she has ruined her life. Coax will never forgive her; he has strong views on purity in women and, as things stand, he has a right to be particular!'

The Peach lay weeping in her rose-pink room, not even daring to send a message to Mac who was sitting in the 'Octopus', that cradle of all evil, awaiting the summons for the decisive visit to his father-in-law.

MacHeath waited patiently the whole evening and the next morning he went to the instrument shop.

An enormous surly man of murderous appearance received

94

him, and when Mac announced his name he took him by the shoulders without saying a word and threw him out of the door.

Two days later he got a note from the Peach saying that he should on no account show himself; but in the evening she came, very red about the eyes, to the street corner to tell him that her father insisted on her remaining at home. Otherwise he would disinherit her and turn the police on Mac, about whom he knew quite enough.

Mac listened fairly calmly and said nothing of escaping or any such foolishness. He only wanted her for five minutes in the park, but she did not go.

During the next two weeks they only saw one another for a few seconds at a time.

6

I loathe it; I would not live always: let me alone; for my days are vanity.

What is man that thou shouldest magnify him? and that thou shouldest set thine heart upon him?

And that thou shouldest visit him every morning, and try him every moment?

I have sinned; what should I do unto thee, O thou preserver of men? why hast thou set me as a mark against thee, so that I am a burden to myself?

And why dost thou not pardon my transgression, and take away mine iniquity? for now shall I sleep in the dust; and thou shalt seek me in the morning, but I shall not be.

(THE BOOK OF JOB)

Turkish Baths

IN Battersea, at the corner of Fourney and Dean Street, stood an old bathing establishment, for men only, which was mostly patronized by elderly gentlemen. The arrangements in it were a little primitive. The baths were made of wood and rather weather-worn; the tables on which customers were massaged were inclined to be wobbly, and the towels had holes in them as a result of much use. But there were certain medicinal baths there, made with herbs, which could be obtained nowhere else. They were not recommended by doctors; one customer recommended them to another. The establishment was called 'Feather's Baths'. The prices were very low. The attendants were girls.

William Coax frequented this place; he came at least once a week. The members of the Marine Transport Company had accustomed themselves to coming here whenever they wanted to see him.

The baths were taken in partitioned-off cubicles in which massage was also given. But the steam cabinets and the rest-couches were all in one large room. Here one could converse in comparative comfort, especially, if one occupied all the cabinets.

The establishment was, by now, used to this happening; a board with 'Full up' would then be hung in front of the pay-desk.

Their usual day was Monday. The establishment remained closed over the week-end so that the staff would not be too tired at the beginning of the new week. Coax was great at such computations.

At first, several of the partners had opposed this choice of a meeting-place. But finally no one wanted to stay away. The meetings were especially punctiliously attended when the affairs of the M.T.C. took such an ominous trend.

Even Finney came. He was an elderly dried-up man, always grumbling, who abhorred every form of luxury but who said of the herb-baths that they gave his stomach more relief than anything else he had tried. He suspected that he had cancer and liked talking about his symptoms. The attendant in No. 6 already knew them by heart.

Peachum had, once for all, reserved for himself the solitary male superintendent, a large fat man, much feared for his vigorous massage. The girls were not usually importunate, but they were too lightly clad for Peachum's taste.

Directly after his return from Southampton, he had spoken with Eastman and informed him of the price of the new ships. He gave him to understand that the purchase must be completed without fail and as quickly as possible. To this purpose he expressed himself forcibly about Coax and called him an unprincipled cut-throat. The latter would certainly spread the news about the Company trying to sell the old rotten ships to the Government. From the very beginning he had been engineering the whole business so as to involve them in some criminal proceeding and then blackmail them. The usual certain profit on war supplies was 300 per cent. The Company was aiming at making over 450 per cent and that would raise a horrible stink. Eastman agreed with him that they could only settle with the broker after they had bought the new ships. They decided to let the other partners writhe in anticipation for a few more days and not mention the very high prices until the usual Monday meeting. Coax's presence would then have a beneficial effect rather than otherwise, for he would raise their hopes about an increase in the Government's purchase price.

The discussion among the seven gentlemen which took place in the baths on the following Monday morning did not pass off without a certain amount of tension.

When Eastman began to address them from his steam cabinet, Moon the textile manufacturer, Finney, and the baronet already lay on their couches. Peachum was still being massaged; and Crowl, the restaurant-keeper, who did not wish to take a bath, was sitting in his chair fully dressed. Coax was doing gymnastics.

Eastman began by emphasizing the necessity of getting all ideas out of their heads about selling the old ships. He admitted that the plan was an attractive one, but it had proved impracticable. In return for the £5,000 which they had paid Coax's friend in the Admiralty, the M.T.C. could expect active support, but not connivance, that bordered on fraud. The hushing-up of the Company's first ill-fated attempt with the *Lovely Anna*, the *Young Sailorboy,* and the *Optimist,* and the transfer of these names to new ships would cost a further £7,500, £4,000 down and £3,500 on completion of the deal. They would have to regard that money as the price of experience.

Peachum, in the process of being roughly massaged by the superintendent, watched with interest a silent and terrible contest in sweating between the fat Eastman in his steam cabinet and Crowl who sat, fully clothed, on his wooden chair and stared at the former with an indescribably greedy expression. After the departure of the sheep farmer, the restaurant-keeper was the weakest link in the chain of the M.T.C. From the very beginning he had complained about the bad state of his business and spoken of a sword that hung continually over him. For that very reason he had entered into this new and would-be profitable enterprise with excessive zeal. The first lump of capital that he had paid in had come from his father-in-law, and now, curiously enough, he was having a sweating competition with the property owner. When Eastman, who was still comparatively dry, spoke of the difficulties of finding suitable transport-ships at this time, the beads of sweat began to run down his forehead. And when Eastman came down to actual prices (£38,500 and £7,500) and himself exuded the first small drops of sweat, the restaurant-keeper sat bathed in perspiration.

'So greatly,' thought Peachum, '*do the effects of spiritual in-*

fluences exceed those of purely physical measures. The human body is wholly in the thrall of the mind and the spirit.'

The other gentlemen, too, showed in appearance and behaviour the terrible effects of spiritual distress. Finney, who at the best was a coward, beat his hand despairingly against his body; and Moon whimpered like an old woman. Had the attendants been there, they would have been amazed at the feebleness of these otherwise dominant men. But, of course, as scientific research has proved, a woman is far better equipped to withstand pain than a man.

Peachum himself felt very miserable when he thought of the dreadful blow which had been dealt him by the untimely marriage of his daughter.

When Eastman had finished speaking and came out of his cabinet, the restaurant-keeper said first, in a remarkably hollow voice, that he was then bankrupt and must ask the gentlemen not to count on him any more. All further questions should be addressed to his solicitors.

He added that his father-in-law was 78 years old and had taken the money out of his old-age assurance in the hope of providing a carefree existence for his daughter. His, Crowl's, children were 8 and 12 years old. Eastman, in the act of drying his plump legs, replied that things were not as bad as all that, but Moon contradicted him sharply. Which annoyed him.

Finney drew attention to his serious (in all probability fatal) illness and doubted whether he could raise the necessary sum. Eastman answered angrily that he, too, could think of better uses for three thousand pounds. The baronet said nothing. A lot of money had been spent on his education.

Meanwhile Coax had finished his exercises and could deal his sheep their death-blow. He was wearing a pink bathing-dress and black rubber shoes.

'Gentlemen,' he said, 'we have not yet finished. You have heard the price for which proper ships are obtainable. You will not be surprised to hear that money cannot put everything right. These ships, for example, cannot be had for money alone.'

At this moment Crowl began to grin. Completely ruined, he sat on his wooden chair and nodded his fleshy head and grinned.

The second blow did not affect him, for the first had already laid him out.

Coax looked at him suspiciously and then went on:

'I can well believe that you have partly lost faith in yourselves. But unfortunately it is not only you who have lost faith in the M.T.C. We have, too. My schoolfriend in the Admiralty wishes all further business to be conducted by me.'

The gentlemen, all of whom, except the restaurant-keeper, were naked and therefore in that embarrassing condition in which, according to religious teachings, they would eventually appear before the throne of God, collapsed still further. Peachum pushed the fat superintendent aside and sat up. What Coax was saying was new to him too.

'We thought we might settle the unfortunate business in this way,' said Coax. 'Your Company has already paid out £8,200. With that money certain things were bought, things of which we will rather not speak. As I have been told, you have set aside more than £5,000 for the improvement of your purchases. From the Government you have received £5,000. According to our agreement you have to pay me 25 per cent of the sale price, which comes to £12,250, and to my friend, who has already had £5,000, another £7,500 is due in two instalments as Mr Eastman has already explained to you. In addition to that, there will be a further £38,000 for the new ships. If you add these sums together, you will find that your total expenditure comes to about £75,000. The Government's payment amounts to £49,000 and I am prepared to buy from you for £2,000 the three objects which I will not specify – being no lawyer. In the opinion of your expert they are worth £200, but you have spent £5,000 on repairs and I am always in favour of a just estimate. If you deduct that amount you will see that, provided my calculations are correct, you do not stand to lose more than £26,000 in all. I don't need to tell you that the alternative to that is roughly twenty years' imprisonment, which is no more than you can all expect as a result of such a transaction. Gentlemen, the last way still stands open to you. If you wish to follow it, I can immediately return to you the cheques amounting to £5,000 which you have given me for my friend. I have them with me.'

The shrewder among those present never doubted it. The

whole thing had been brilliantly engineered by Coax. In spite of the return of the cheques and a certain amount of perjury, the man in the Admiralty would still get into serious trouble; for nothing could lessen the fact that he had bought ships which he had never seen. But that would scarcely help the Company. They had bought ships of whose worthlessness they had been warned.

Coax then demanded that the Company should give him full authority, so that he could wind up the business step by step. But until just before the final handing over of the finished ships to the Government, everything was to be done by the Company; only then would he himself enter into the contract with the Government – i.e. when the new ships were ready to be exchanged for the old ones.

Until then, the work on the old ships must be continued in case of unexpected inspections. And thus the sword was to remain hanging over the M.T.C. until the very last moment.

The Company had not strength enough to protest.

When Coax finally invited them all to a small luncheon in a neighbouring restaurant, no one had any desire to answer him. So he said hastily that he could in no circumstances wait longer than eight weeks for the delivery of the ships; and then he went away before the others.

The Company decided to leave the exact calculation of all further expenses to Eastman and Peachum and to meet again as soon as the two were ready, on Monday next at the latest. The situation had reached a stage in which sober offices were to be shunned and it was best to behave as though a chance meeting would be quite sufficient.

Peachum was more worried than ever.

He was now trying to get on to Coax's side. But he had not even his daughter free for him; so what was going to happen now?

Each morning he went down to the docks. The ships were humming like beehives. Everywhere was hammering and sawing and painting. The workmen stood on swaying ladders and hung in frail wire cradles. Peachum stood shivering in the midst of all this industry and activity. All material was being economized to the utmost; wood, iron, and even paint, were of the cheapest. And still this whole business was an enormous and total loss!

Then Peachum hastened back to his factory. Here, too, every-thing was in full swing. In the office the beggars were settling up. Beery was carefully comparing their earnings with a list and receiving their excuses for failure with experienced distrust. He adjusted boundary quarrels and arranged action against in-truders. In the workrooms the girls sat bent over the long tables. When the demands of the factory were covered, they supplied old-clothes stores and second-hand dealers. The instrument-makers were repairing pipes for hurdy-gurdies. A few beggars were trying out new music-rolls and taking a long time to choose before making up their minds. In the school-room, instruction was going on. A dried-up old woman, attendant at a Ladies' convenience during the evening, was teaching a young girl how to sell flowers.

Peachum stood around, sighing. What was the use of it all when one had to listen every minute for steps to come clumping up the stairs to announce that the police were waiting in the office below?

His daughter was to blame for everything.

Through her boundless sensuality, doubtless inherited from her mother, and as a result of culpable inexperience, Polly had thrown herself into the arms of a more than sinister individual. Why she had immediately married her lover was a mystery to him. He suspected something terrible. But his views about keep-ing the necessary distance between relations would not allow him to speak to her about her private affairs. Besides it would only do harm to speak of things which ought, under no circum-stances, to happen; outspokenness only brought these things into the realm of possibility and one lost thereby one's chief weapon, the patent inability to conceive that anything wrong could have happened.

In the middle of the night or towards morning, Peachum usually got up and went upstairs and along the balcony to see that Polly was still there. Then he saw her, indistinctly, through the half-open window, lying in bed. She was quite content to live at home now and seemed scarcely ever to meet her hus-band.

In any case her marriage would have to be annulled as quickly as possible. Peachum needed his daughter.

Peachum never doubted for a moment that Coax would just as soon take Polly after as before. He had noticed his blind eagerness in Southampton. This libertine was all too plainly a slave to his fleshly desires.

And this MacHeath seemed quite willing to tolerate the continued residence of his wife under her parental roof. He made no serious trouble; he allowed himself to be thrown out without taking counter-measures and, as far as Peachum could discover, had not yet revealed the name of his wife to anyone. The threat of disinheritance seemed to have had the desired effect. He was plainly very eager for the money. He was probably in need of it.

His B. shops had been cleverly thought out, and they made ingenious use of the savings of the poor; but they were also very primitive, being really no more than dark, whitewashed holes with heaps of goods piled on rough pine boards and despondent people behind them. The source of these extremely cheap goods was not apparent.

Peachum had tried through his beggars to get into contact with the owners of some of these B. shops. He had not had much success. The people kept a morose silence, hated beggars, and seemed to know nothing about the origin of their wares.

However more success attended his investigations into the past of this MacHeath. These investigations revealed a series of years obscured by that semi-darkness which makes certain portions of the biographies of our great business men so poor in material; 'giants of industry' usually seem to rise, suddenly and astonishingly, 'straight up' out of the darkness after so-and-so many years of 'hard and necessitous life' – but whose life is usually not mentioned.

The lesser competitors of the B. shops averred that MacHeath, in his none too distant youth, had been convicted of fraudulent marriages. They called the girls involved 'B. brides', but were unable to give any addresses. With such vague rumours there was nothing to be done. But this much was clear: somehow or other this man's life led backwards and downwards into the underworld. Not so very long ago the methods of this successful gentleman had been even bolder, crueller, and more openly illegal than they were today.

Amongst others, Peachum visited the *Reflector*, that paper which had once claimed to have had material in its hands proving certain allegations against the owner of the B. shops. The editors could only faintly remember the affair and murmured something about lack of proper proof. So Peachum had to leave without having discovered anything, but he had the distinct impression that the people there still knew something and also had material.

Mrs Peachum, who recently had been left more than ever to herself and the cellar, began vaguely to suspect the danger hanging over the house, and was also racking her brains as to how she could separate Polly from this 'wood merchant'. She could not bear Coax because he was a 'twister'; but he was certainly the better bargain.

She entertained plans of discovering MacHeath in some feminine entanglement. He must have feminine entanglements; she had not forgotten his grip about Polly's hips; and now he was the whole time without a wife.

But later, spiritually enlightened with cognac, she reconsidered the idea and realized that such revelations at this stage, with their tearful reconciliations, must inevitably lead to still deeper attachment between husband and wife. So she gave her plans up again.

Peachum had already considered offering the dowry-hunter money, but this unnatural solution seemed to be really too hard.

He sent Beery after MacHeath. The wood merchant spoke to him at Fanny Chrysler's antique shop.

Beery sat, like a lump of raw meat, on the edge of a fragile Chippendale chair, and let his stiff hat dangle between his broad knees.

'Mr Peachum asked me to tell you,' he announced, 'you're to get Polly out of this mess as quickly as possible, otherwise you'll get into trouble. She's already had enough of you. And what's more, Mr Peachum has had enough of you. If you think you've got on to something easy, you've made a big mistake. There is no dowry! We've scarcely got the ordinary daily money we need. If you've heard different, someone's been pulling your leg. And we've found out a few women who could also call themselves Mrs MacHeath if they wanted to, and who'd like to know your address. And remember we'll do everything we can to get rid of you. But Mr Peachum says he doesn't want to quarrel with you; he wants to arrange everything in peace and friendliness. Why he does, is a mystery to me. I'd go about the thing quite differently, I can tell you!'

MacHeath laughed.

'Tell my father-in-law that if he is ever in trouble I can help him with a small sum of money,' he said affably.

'We're not in trouble,' answered Beery rudely, 'but *you* soon will be. We're in a free country. I tell you again: we haven't got the money you seem to imagine. It's no good. We're poor beggars, and you shouldn't try to tread down such people. Even the worm can turn, and sometimes nastily.'

'But outside,' commanded MacHeath, 'he can turn outside, not here in my shop!'

Beery went away with threatening grunts. Peachum sighed when he received the news.

He had just eight weeks; then he must either have his daughter at his disposal or pay.

Crowl, the restaurant-keeper, had not lied. It appeared that he not only had no more money to pay in, but that he had also been counting on the profits of the Marine Transport Company – and on quick profits. He was completely bankrupt.

In addition to that the baronet, who was still a young man, appeared one day and announced his inability to pay. He owned mortgaged estates in Scotland and was on the verge of being put under tutelage. Peachum and Eastman spoke with him in Peachum's office. They treated him like a sick animal.

There still remained the possibility of him marrying into money. There was a rich independent American woman who was prepared to buy his ancient name and culture. She was attracted by the furniture in his country house, especially by the chairs.

Young Clive called her an old goat and expressed disgust, but Eastman reacted very sourly to that and made a serious and disapproving face and inquired pointedly after the lady. Comparisons of her legs with those of an (ill-bred) horse, he ignored.

The two gentlemen threatened him with the scandal that would ensue if the M.T.C. collapsed and reproached the young man's conscience so long that he finally promised to treat the American nicely.

'*Why do we educate our noblemen so carefully in our colleges?*' said Eastman to Peachum on the way home. '*Why do we train them, keep all unpleasant facts from them, and instil into them such perfect manners that they are able to employ the very best servants? One doesn't hang Gobelins in the attic. Racehorses are made to race. The higher types of mankind, too, are not bred for pleasure. A short time ago the market was slightly glutted with our lords. Today the demand is as great as ever. This daughter of a transatlantic meat king couldn't find anything better than our young man if she really wants something that knows how to yawn correctly and can hold inferior breeds in check. She only has to read the papers to see that the flower of our country behaves perfectly over there and enjoys universal popularity.*'

But Clive still remained, for the time being, a weak link in the M.T.C.

The meeting arranged for Monday was preceded by a conversation between Peachum and Coax.

Coax received the news of the final collapse of Crowl and the temporary embarrassment of the baronet without excitement. He merely commented that he would simply have to deal with the Marine Transport Company as a whole. He advised that the rotten branches should be lopped off from the parent trunk, but added that care should be taken that the expelled members kept quiet; and then he went on to speak of Polly. He admitted that he could not get her out of his mind. The terrible experience in Southampton had changed him inwardly. Certain good traits in him had, so to speak, broken out. He felt in himself an astonishing thirst for purity. Polly was now his idol. She seemed to him like a well of clear water. A talk with her sanctified his whole working week. He said all this very simply and looking Peachum straight in the eyes.

Peachum listened attentively and realized that the final winding up of the ship business between them would present no particular difficulties. He approved of Coax's cautious expressions. The broker knew how to beat about the bush.

Peachum went alone to the baths.

The others were already waiting for him. No one was taking a bath. They all sat on the wooden chairs, fully clothed, although the atmosphere was unbearably warm and moist.

Peachum first informed them of the default of Crowl and the baronet.

Both of these gentlemen looked straight in front of them, the baronet smiling.

The total loss, Peachum went on to explain, was, as Coax had correctly estimated, about £26,000 – which meant a round £3,800 from each of the members. It was in the interest of the M.T.C. that the business should proceed as quietly as possible.

He offered to secure the assistance of his own bank, the National Credit Bank, if they would put the entire control of the business into his hands.

They all nodded, sweating. Even Crowl and the baronet nodded.

Peachum looked pointedly at the two. Then he began to speak again and demanded flatly that Crowl and the baronet should give promissory notes for their share in the losses, and also sign a detailed account of everything that had already happened. They were to sign an admission that they had sold the old ships to the Government after inspecting them and after hearing an expert's opinion on their worth, and that they had received payment for the sale. This document would be returned to the signatories on payment of their commitments; it was worth nothing in itself for it could not be discounted without compromising the whole Company, but it would guard the Company from indiscretions on their part.

The baronet signed with an air of resignation. All *he* understood was that he would now have to marry the 'old goat' without further delay. The restaurant-keeper behaved as though he were out of his senses.

He explained that he could never bring such disgrace on his wife and his seventy-eight-year-old father-in-law. He simply could not have sold unseaworthy ships to the Government. His father-in-law had been a colonel. Neither, after signing such a document, could he ever again look into the clear eyes of his children; they must not have a criminal for a father. He had always withstood any attempt to make money in a dishonest way, otherwise his present situation would have been different. His honour was more important to him even than business losses.

'You have ruined me,' he said, the tears streaming down his face as he signed. 'I am a broken man.'

The scene got on everybody's nerves.

'That Crowl,' said Eastman to Moon on the way home, 'can't lose like a gentleman. Bad breeding! That weakling's got no honour in his miserable body. Look at the baronet! He signed like a man. He is going to marry a horrible creature – like a man. He takes the responsibility for what he does. A man with a family shouldn't enter into such a business. He can't look his children in the eyes! But he can look the *Lovely Anna* in the eyes! And the *Young Sailorboy* is at least as old as his father-in-law. He was quite prepared to send them into the fray again. Why shouldn't his father-in-law do the same? – I don't like paying up either. Finney has cancer of the stomach. Does he grumble? Does he make an excuse of it? Peachum has two shares. Does he complain? This Crowl hasn't had a proper education, that's what's the matter with him. Such people shouldn't be allowed in the City! Before entering into any business a man ought to ask his partner: "Where were you brought up?" After the transaction is over, can you look your children in the eyes? Is your father-in-law still active? – This Crowl isn't an Englishman at all – at any rate he's not my idea of one. Is that specimen a citizen of a great nation?'

Peachum felt very miserable after this meeting. The contract with the Government was to be put into Coax's hands as soon as the M.T.C. had properly financed the business. And he still had no binding agreement with Coax for a share in the colossal profits, nor even a promise to make good his losses. In the nature of things such an agreement was unthinkable until Polly had agreed to marry Coax.

Peachum avoided all thoughts as to what would happen if he

was unable to come to an arrangement with Coax. Already there were now only three people, Finney, Moon, and Eastman, to bear the gigantic losses. If they were not in a position to pay for the new ships, everything might still end in catastrophe.

More than ever he needed Coax.

One evening he spoke to Polly about him and told her that she must be nice to him. On no account must he discover anything about her marriage. Then he explained to her that he and Coax were involved in a deal with some ships and so deeply that 'perhaps the whole house and shop may be sold over our heads'.

When Polly heard this, she gazed in horror round the familiar, friendly room; the unpainted floor-boards scoured clean with sand, the white tiled stove, the mahogany furniture, and the muslin curtains. She loved the old house very much, especially the yards and the wooden balconies; and that night, because the talk had been of ships, she dreamed that the house, which was really three houses, was sinking into the sea, so that the waves came in through the doors.

The next morning she had half decided to make a sacrifice.

'After all I don't want to have the blame for anything that may happen,' she thought, 'and no one will be able to say afterwards that I shrank from making a sacrifice. Of course it's no light matter for a girl to give herself to a man she doesn't love, especially when he looks like Mr Coax. But family is family, and egotism is hateful. One mustn't think only of oneself.'

She lay in bed a little longer and remembered the brooch which she had once seen in Coax's house and which was now inseparably associated in her mind with Coax. Originally she had wanted to have it to sell for the £15 which she then needed so urgently. Now she no longer needed the money, but she would still like to have the brooch.

After dinner she went to Coax with a letter from her father. She put on a cold and distant expression when the letter was handed to her. She no longer believed that it was true what her father had told her yesterday about impending ruin; that was only because he could not bear Mac.

To Coax also she was very cool. She scarcely glanced at the brooch which still lay on the writing-table.

Nevertheless she was very impressed by it.

Coax seated her in a rocking chair some distance away from the writing-table and handed her several books bound in heavy leather. But she did not look at them while he read the letter. So he got up and left the room.

Even then she did not open the books. But she was red in the face when he came in again.

The fact was that she had suddenly made up her mind to get the brooch. 'If he will give it to me,' she thought, 'the whole thing will only last five minutes, if as long. He can't expect it for nothing, looking like he does. The brooch is certainly worth £20 and will go well with an open dress. Of course, anything more than a kiss is unthinkable; at the very most he may put his arm round me. That's not too much to pay for the brooch. Other girls of my age have to do quite different things to be able to pay for their lodgings. Men are quite mad the way they'll give anything for such things. But then they're like that!'

And she sighed.

When the broker returned, he was forced to think that she had been looking in the books and was under their influence. He crossed the room, waving the newly-written reply in the air to dry the ink, and bent over her. She stood up hurriedly when she saw his face.

He had assured himself that his sister was out of the house. So he laid the letter on the writing-table and suddenly embraced Polly.

She made little resistance, although at first she felt a little regretful that she had not got the brooch, but then she submitted, because he was so beside himself with pleasure. All the same she got little out of it, for in the middle she remembered Mac, who would not approve at all.

When she said good-bye, the ink on the letter was dry.

Arriving home, she put the letter on her father's desk and went upstairs where she immediately began to pack. Half an hour later, without taking any special precautions, she went out through the front door with her bag.

She had heard that MacHeath was now spending his whole time with another woman, the Fanny Chrysler who had the antique shop by Waterloo Bridge.

Her father and mother waited up half the night for her. Mr Peachum stood at the window and said:

'*So he came and took her. He thinks he can do that. His type knows no laws. If he wants anything he takes it. If he feels a need to spend the night with my daughter, he takes her away from my house and has her. Her skin attracts him. I've paid for every stitch of clothing she's ever had. As far as I am concerned, she has never seen her own body. She was bathed in a night-dress. The stupidity of her sensual mother and her own foolishness, which comes from novel-reading, have made her what she is today. But what am I talking about; as if it had anything to do with love! As if a man like that would sleep with anything but a dowry! He wants to have my money and he takes it. What has happened to our family that was once a sure refuge in time of trouble? Though the storms of life raged outside, here was peace and quiet. The horrors of the fight for existence were never known here, where a gentle child was reared in the ways of good breeding; the troubles of business and bargaining had no place in this sheltered retreat. When a young man approached the daughter of the house (after he had given proof of his ability to provide for her), the anxious parents could be sure that, except for a few unfortunate cases, it was love that brought the young couple together. But what has happened? Brutal robbery! I amass a modest fortune by hard work and care, surrounded all the time by rogues and by lazy workers who no longer take any pleasure in their work but only think of wages, and now this Coax appears and deceives me with some criminal scheme and robs me! And while I'm fighting to protect my life and property, I have to watch my daughter, too, being snatched from me by a robber. I have worked my fingers to the bone for her. Why do I consort with the scum of humanity? That man's a shark! If I give away my daughter who is my sole support in my old age, then my house will fall in and my last dog will leave me. I couldn't give away the dirt under my fingernails now without having the feeling that I was deliberately courting starvation.*'

But Polly did not come back, neither that night nor later, until her husband was arrested.

And Mr Peachum never found out that Polly, instead of arousing the broker's desire, had satisfied it.

During the next few days Mrs Peachum drank even more than usual; and in this condition she spoke about her troubles to the ex-soldier Fewkoombey who looked after the dogs.

He had not yet forgiven the Peach for taking the encyclopaedia – even though he had got the book back again. At first he had not wanted to fetch it, for his pride forbade him. But then he was defeated in his struggle with himself, and one day during dinner-time he went and took it again.

As a result of his conversation with Mrs Peachum, his peaceful studies were now to receive an interruption.

When the troubled mother told him that her unhappy daughter had married the merchant MacHeath, he was reminded of the worst time of his life when, discharged from the army and robbed of his compensation money, he had lived with a soldier's wife. She was called Mary Sawyer and owned one of those B. shops. Incautiously he let drop a few words about her. That evening Mr Peachum called him into his office and gave him a commission.

In the West India Docks, a few dozen workmen were still doctoring up the three old decaying hulks which, as a result of an idea of William Coax's and before they finally fell to pieces, were to be instrumental in transferring into new pockets a considerable sum of money extracted from a Scottish estate, a prosperous bookmaking business, an almost bankrupt restaurant in Harwich, a block of tenements in Kensington, a textile mill in Lancashire, and *a large concern for the sale of secondhand musical instruments in Old Oak Street*. And of these threatened firms the last mentioned had to be saved at all costs.

Book Two

THE MURDER OF
THE SHOPKEEPER
MARY SAWYER

For the shark, he has his teeth and
You can see them in his face,
And MacHeath, he has his knife but
Hides it in a different place.

Down along by Thames' green waters
Suddenly there's someone falls
Not from plague and not from cholera,
It's MacHeath has paid his calls.

And Sam Meyer still is missing
Many a rich man's been removed
And MacHeath, he has their money
But there's nothing can be proved.

When they found her, Jenny Towler,
With the knife stuck in her breast
Mackie walks along the quayside,
Knows no more than all the rest.

Where is Alfonse Glite, the coachman?
Will that ever see the day?
Some there are, perhaps, who know it –
Mackie really couldn't say.

Burnt alive were seven children
And an old man, in Soho –
Midst the crowd is standing Mackie who
Isn't asked and doesn't know.

For the shark has fins of crimson
When his victim's blood is shed,
But MacHeath, he keeps his gloves on
And you cannot see the red.

(THE CRIMES OF MACKIE THE KNIFE)

7

coelum, non animum mutant,
qui trans mare currunt.

Mr MacHeath

IN the consciousness of the average Londoner, no very great role was played by such figures as 'Jack the Ripper' or that unknown murderer popularly called the 'Knife'. Even though they bobbed up now and again, they could not hope, in those uncertain times, to compete for notoriety with the generals conducting the war in the Transvaal; besides, these latter were a menace to incomparably more people than the most active knife hero. But in Limehouse and Whitechapel the fame of the 'Knife' far exceeded that of the generals who were fighting the Boers. The people in the great stone tenements of Whitechapel were excellent judges of the difference between the accomplishments of a fancy general and those of their own heroes. To them it was plain that the 'Knife' carried out his crimes at a far greater personal risk than the official picture-book heroes did theirs.

Limehouse and Whitechapel have their own history and their own method of teaching it. Instruction begins at babyhood and is given by people of every age. The best teachers are the children; for they know every detail about the local reigning dynasties.

These overlords understand quite as well as the ones in schoolbooks, how to punish those who refuse to pay them tribute. They have a code of right and wrong like other people; but there are fewer weaklings, for the police are set on them, which never happens to the others. Of course, just like the others, they try to appear in a different light to the true one; they falsify history and make up legends.

Sometimes dominant personalities rise like meteors from the darkness. Obstacles which others, equally gifted, take decades to overcome, are cleared by them in weeks. A few daring crimes, executed from the very first with the virtuosity of experienced craftsmen – and they are at the top. The man whom the slums named the 'Knife' could never truthfully lay claim to such a career. But he did nevertheless. His closer associates, the gang, tried to hush up, as much as possible, his mean beginnings and the inglorious drudgery of his apprenticeship.

But it was not certain whether the man who founded the gang was the 'Knife' at all. He maintained obstinately to his people that he was the murderer Stanford Sills; and he only kept his gang together by this belief. But in Dartmoor, in 1895, a man was executed of whom it was said, not indeed by himself but by the police, that *he* was Stanford Sills.

The deeds which had established the 'Knife's' fame had been a sequence of murders, following one another in quick succession, which had taken place in the open streets. For these, the man in Dartmoor had been executed. It is a well-known fact that people will never believe in the death of a popular hero, as can be observed in recent times in the cases of Kitchener and Kruger; and consequently several murders in the winter of 1895 were ascribed to the 'Knife' which certainly could not have been carried out by the dead man in the cemetery at Dartmoor and scarcely by the person who had taken on his nick-name and as such claimed these murders.

The cruelty, mercilessness, and cunning with which this man compelled other criminals to give him the credit for their deeds was perhaps even more terrible than their own treatment of their victims. It was only a little less flagrant than the way in which our university professors set their names to the work of their assistants.

The murders were probably instigated by reasons of pure starvation, for it was an unusually hard winter and the unemployment was very great. But this man, who had used the name of the 'Knife' for the purposes of organizing his gang, had another weakness common to those who move in spheres more familiar to us book-buyers. Like most of our successful industrialists, authors, savants, politicians, etc., he loved to read in the papers that his deeds were not committed for any material profit but rather for *sport* or for the satisfaction of a creative desire, or even because of an inexplicable *demoniacal urge*.

Articles were continually appearing in the yellow press which emphasized the element of sport in the 'Knife's' crimes.

But it is probable that this demon, like our other celebrated friends, in addition to reading the newspapers also read his bank-book. At any rate he had soon realized that one's fellow workers always yield the best profits; and this is the realization which alone can ensure a successful career.

At first the gang was small and its activities modest. There were still robberies with violence, and, more rarely, cold-blooded and brutal burglaries. More originality was shown by some of the methods used for the disposal of captured booty. One of these filled the whole of the world's press.

One day two vigorous-looking gentlemen entered the dining-room of a fashionable restaurant in Hampstead. They stood for a moment looking round the room and then stepped up to a smartly dressed man sitting at one of the tables.

'That's him,' said one of them in a loud voice. 'There he sits and squanders my money! My name is Cooper and his is Hawk. Here, Mr Bailiff, my writ! The judgement is executable immediately. That ring on his middle finger is worth a good two hundred pounds, and he has a carriage standing outside which cost a pretty penny – as will be seen when we auction it!'

At this point the waiters usually had to restrain the gentleman from springing at the throats of his tactless creditors. He would then assert that he did not deny his debt, but that he objected to the way in which they were distraining his goods.

The scene ended with the three men and some of the other guests going out to look at the carriage. The auction then took place in a neighbouring public house.

After that, the debtor and the two duns vanished, and the proceeds which the 'Knife' thus obtained from the stolen carriage and jewels were very much greater than if the goods had been sold to a 'fence'.

That was one new way. But it could not be repeated. The cancer of stealing was the 'fence'. The difficulty of turning the booty into money remained the weakest point of the whole business. All attempts to enlarge the activities of the gang foundered on this snag.

Towards the end of '96 the 'Knife' vanished almost completely from the ken of the underworld, and a peaceful man by the name of *Jimmy Beckett* opened a shop in Soho for the sale of paving stones. He also had a small wood-yard next door. When houses were being demolished, he bought old paving stones and was very strict about the invoices.

Then there occurred in Whitechapel widespread thefts of these stones. A number of small carts came and carried off a pile of new paving stones in broad daylight, when the workmen were at lunch. No one thought of stopping them. The trail led to Jimmy Beckett's shop. But Mr Beckett could produce perfectly conclusive invoices for his stones.

One day a whole street near the docks was stolen; this time it was wooden blocks. Towards evening, when the traffic was at its thickest, some workmen appeared with a cart; they put barriers across the street, tore it up, and loaded the wooden blocks into the cart.

This scandal did not appear in the papers because at that time the County Council was investigating the case of a firm which, with perfect legality and on the grounds of some old and carefully suppressed contracts, had taken over certain streets which had already been repaired by other smaller firms; so that the large firm had to be paid again although the streets needed nothing doing to them. The authorities wanted no parallels to be drawn.

At this time there again occurred several cases of murder and manslaughter, all of which were attributed to the 'Knife' gang, especially the latter. But they were scarcely mentioned by the newspapers, for they were all directed against the lowest class of humanity. The victims were nearly all criminals who had been shot down in organized brawls.

Here there is less doubt that the murders were carried out by the gang.

At this time, too, the gang gave up street robberies entirely and turned their whole attention to burglaries. Their speciality was shop-breaking on a large scale.

Already, in the year '97, the 'Knife' gang had well over 120 permanent members. The organization had been very carefully built up; at the most only two or three members knew the 'Chief' by sight. They numbered amongst them smugglers, 'fences', and lawyers. The 'Knife' (that is, the man who called himself by that name) had been a very indifferent burglar and himself willingly admitted it. But on the other hand, he was an organizer far above the average. And everyone knows that the laurels of the present age go to the organizing class. They seem to be the most indispensable.

Actually the 'Knife' gang succeeded, in an incredibly short time, in bringing under their control practically everything that came into the category of shop-breaking. It became more than dangerous for an independent operator to enter this field. And the gang was not even ashamed of having the police as accomplices. Everyone knew that Mr Beckett had friends at headquarters.

Betrayal to the police was also a means of strengthening the internal discipline of the gang. By the beginning of the year '98 such members as still knew the founder were already all, or nearly all, arrested by the police and sentenced to many years' imprisonment.

One day Mr Beckett sold out to a Mr MacHeath who had just opened several shops in the City, the so-called B. shops, which he wanted to stock with cheap goods.

When Jimmy Beckett, the wood merchant, vanished out of England – ostensibly he had gone to Canada – there appeared, as the underworld immediately knew, a certain *O'Hara*, a young man of great talent, who became the official head of the organization.

Mr Beckett recommended him to Mr MacHeath, and Mr MacHeath apparently valued him highly for he received from him large and frequent consignments of goods. That meant the elimination of the 'fence' fraternity.

The organization had found a regular customer and flourished mightily.

Mr MacHeath was thus able to keep his prices very low, but he never knew exactly what sort of goods he was going to receive. Finally it proved wisest to select such articles as could be altered in appearance by the industry of the B. shopkeepers. So the shops had to change from receivers to consumers.

At this stage in the development there arose the question of obtaining capital. A further extension of the gang in its activities of shop and warehouse breaking demanded more money than was at Mr MacHeath's disposal. His enterprise was now in that dilemma so greatly feared by all our business people.

If the supplying organization were to be enlarged, the present number of shops would be unable to cope with the increased flow of goods, while if the shops were to be increased the first organization would be too small. At the instant of the projected enlargement of supply and demand, both organizations must be increased simultaneously.

There were already other chain shops, big businesses with good bank connexions. They were in sharp competition with one another. It would need far greater resources than Mr MacHeath commanded to win through against them.

This was the position when Mr MacHeath married Miss Polly Peachum.

One fine summer evening, Mr MacHeath drove in an old hansom cab to the western suburb where Mr Miller of the National Credit Bank lived.

He was wearing a light grey suit and the drive through the busy streets was entertaining; but he was not happy. His marriage had been a disappointment.

His wife was prettier than any he had had before, and in his way he was in love with her; but he was no longer twenty and had no sort of feeling for the romantic. He sometimes had to banish the thought that he had, more or less, been sold a pup.

Mr Miller received him on the steps of his little house. Behind him stood his wife, a kindly, talkative person, well past fifty, who immediately treated MacHeath like a son. They had tea and Miller chatted of bygone days. He related a few episodes out of the history of the National Credit Bank.

The founder of the bank had been an employee at Rothschild's when that house had fought its first great battles. His name had been Talk. Miller related a story that old Talk had often told him.

The Rothschilds were already in business on a large scale and counted as one of the most important firms on the Continent, when the head of the London branch, Nathaniel Rothschild, tried out a new idea. Those were war-like times. The original operations of the firm consisted for the most part in the financing of certain Government projects; these were not entirely concerned with war supplies, but that, of course, was included. The banks' accounts with their large customers were mostly very complicated; a certain amount of latitude prevailed. Numerous unforeseen occurrences made everything quite extraordinarily expensive. All transactions were burdened by hundreds of additional expenses, mostly concerning people who wished to remain anonymous. Old Nathaniel, who was then still a young man, had the idea of trying to make contracts that would be carried out exactly as they stipulated. He wanted to calculate the costs beforehand and then keep to that sum, whatever events might intervene.

In this way he hoped to introduce into the world of finance that quality which in private life is called honesty.

It was a bold thought and the other Rothschilds, all bankers as everyone knows, were, from the very beginning, strongly against it. They tried to intimidate the head of the family. But he cared nothing for them and immediately put his revolutionary ideas into practice.

Miller explained the idea as he gazed at the rhododendrons in the tiny garden; it was rather complicated, something to do with a corner in zinc.

The family was almost reduced to desperation during this speculation. The other brothers even went so far as to consult a nerve specialist and once tried to have Nathaniel dragged from his office by force and shut up in a private asylum. But they had an easy time of it compared with the doctor. He had to listen to the idea and face the man. The idea saved him any further diagnosis.

The doctor with two attendants entered Nathaniel's office.

'Don't worry any more, Mr Rothschild. Your brothers tell me that you have lately had some very interesting ideas, but you are a little overworked and run down. You are coming with me now to a nice, quiet house in Wales; you won't need to trouble about anything more for a time and you'll lead a healthy, pleasant life. We'll talk together about your ideas, which are doubtless very profitable. Don't say anything. I agree with you absolutely and I understand you. You are right and your family are wrong; you don't want to have any costs in your accounts, that is only as it should be. Can you tell me offhand what four times thirteen is?'

The doctor had to withdraw, but Nathaniel often found himself in desperate situations. He was betrayed by everyone; no one kept to their agreements, though he himself had to. But at last the enterprise was a success, although the brothers were not so completely in the wrong as everybody afterwards thought. The fate of the family had really hung by a hair. And success came only because the idea was quite unique and unexpected. Everywhere else there were costs; only the Rothschilds charged none. In a certain sense this was unfair competition. The governments naturally all ran to the Rothschilds, at least until the others tried the same scheme. Today absolute honesty in all settlements is a matter of course, but someone was bound to have had the idea sometime. Humanity has had to fight for everything, for every step up the ladder of progress.

MacHeath listened with an effort. He could only understand the drift of Mr Miller's story with difficulty; he never, so to speak, got to the bottom of it.

'It makes one realize,' he said at last, uncertainly, 'that in business *everything* must be tried. Don't you think so? If one wants to progress and show a respectable surplus at the end of the year, one must try everything, even the most unpromising propositions.'

While he drank his tea, during which process he had his thumb deep inside the cup, he did some serious thinking. He had the impression that Miller was rather doubtful about his ideas and wanted to show him what real business acumen was. So when Miller was finished, he endeavoured to put a few of his plans in their right light.

Before he began, he drew carefully out of his breast pocket two folded newspaper cuttings, containing his articles on the theory of B. shops, independence of the smallholder, etc. They were encircled in red pencil. Miller knew them already.

Then MacHeath took a cigar out of his breast pocket, bit the tip off, threw it with two fat fingers out on to the gravel path, and lit the cigar ceremoniously. He had a few more ideas that had not yet been published in the papers.

His chief activity at the moment, he explained, was the study of customers.

The customer usually appears to the shopkeeper as an indecisive, miserly, malevolent, and mistrustful person. He seems wholly antagonistic. In the salesman he sees, not his friend and adviser who is ready to do anything for him, but an evil creature with foul intentions who is trying to deceive and betray him. In return, the salesman, warned by experience, hesitates and gives up any hope of genuinely winning the customer over, of bettering him, of making a personal contact with him, and, in short, of transforming him into a high-class purchaser. He lays his wares on the counter resignedly and places his only hope in the want and naked need which now and again forces a customer to make a purchase.

But in reality the customer is thereby grossly misunderstood. In the depths of his being he is better than he looks. It is just that certain tragic experiences in the bosom of his family, or in his business career, have made him taciturn and suspicious. Deep down within him there still flickers a hope that he may yet be recognized for what he really is: a potential purchaser! Because he wants to buy! There is so much that he needs! And if he doesn't need anything he feels unhappy. Therefore he wants someone to convince him that he needs something! He knows so little.

'To be a salesman,' said MacHeath, tapping with his teaspoon on the mahogany table, 'is to be a teacher. "To sell" means: to fight the ignorance, the terrible ignorance of the public. How few people know how badly they live! They sleep on hard and creaking beds, they sit on uncomfortable and ugly chairs. Their eyes and their hinderparts are incessantly offended; they sense it vaguely, but only when they see something different do they know it. One must tell them like children what they need. They must buy what they need, not what they must have. And to succeed in that object, one must be their friend. Under all circumstances one must be friendly to them, obliging. Of course a person who buys nothing seems to be a despicable creature. A miser! one thinks, involuntarily filled with contempt *and disgust. But as a salesman one must never think that. One must be friendly, always friendly, even if one's heart is breaking.'*

MacHeath had become more excited than he realized. This was a sore point with his small shops. The people were not friendly enough. He had them continually watched by his 'buyers', and he punished all shopkeepers who were unfriendly. But that did not help much. As far as that went, it was easier for the large shops. For the staff to keep smiling, they must feel the whip on their backs. If a customer took too long choosing, the small shopkeepers immediately began thinking about their unpaid rent. Should the customer then leave the shop without having bought anything, they made a face as though their whole world were collapsing. Of course the customer dislikes being made responsible for the misery of the salesman. If the shopkeeper lets him notice that by buying nothing he is dealing him a death blow, he becomes angry. One must learn to smile with death in one's heart! I will teach them to look happy, even if I have to chastise them with scorpions, thought MacHeath and wiped the perspiration from his forehead with an enormous handkerchief.

Not without humour, he continued.

He mentioned a number of methods for awakening the weak and undeveloped appetites of the public. A certain artless confusion of the goods works wonders. In that way the customer can make discoveries. He espies something useful. After a short time his glance becomes noticeably sharper. Looking for one thing, he finds another. Under a heap of materials his eagle eye catches sight of a welcome piece of soap. It has nothing to do with the stuff he needs for aprons, but is it for that reason any the less useful? No! He buys the soap. He never knows when he may need it. Having once got so far, he is a customer.

Of course the prices are a decisive factor. If they differ too much, they weary the customer. He begins to calculate. And that must be prevented in all circumstances. MacHeath wanted to introduce a new system whereby all prices would fall into a few categories. Nothing arouses such an intoxication of self-assurance in a purchaser as a vast prospect of all that he can buy for a certain sum of money. What! this huge piece of garden furniture only costs so much? And this complicated shaving apparatus no more?

But the prices must be very carefully fixed. The public is not so easily frightened by high figures as by high sums. Two shillings is too much for many a woman who would willingly pay one and elevenpence halfpenny.

Miller looked at him curiously with his vague eyes. MacHeath was now in full spate and explained to Miller the idea of his Bargain shops: only a small selection of goods and not more than three or four different prices. It did no harm if some of the articles had to be put together by the public. For instance one could buy garden chairs consisting of deck-chair, foot-rest, and canopy, in separate parts, so that together they were more expensive than the previously agreed top price, and yet they came within the three categories.

The quite small shops with workshops, which sold shoes or underwear or tobacco, should still be conducted as before and only receive limited credit. But the bigger shops were to be stocked as full of goods as possible. Unit prices were to be the basic idea which would overwhelm London. He wanted to start them off with a great sales week.

Miller motioned to his wife.

Mrs Miller rose discreetly and left the room. Miller nodded his white head pensively and looked at his visitor, as if searching for words.

'What is Mr Peachum's attitude with regard to your marriage?' he asked finally. 'Is he in agreement with it?'

'His heart is not made of stone,' answered MacHeath.

'Really?' said Miller astonished.

MacHeath took a gulp from his cup. They were silent for a time. Some children were shouting outside in the street. They were swearing about something.

Miller continued mildly:

'Then everything is quite simple. You can understand that we would like to have your father-in-law with us in this affair. Rather because of the people who might otherwise ask us why your own father-in-law was not in the scheme. After all, he is really the man who ought to have the most understanding for your idea, for he is bound to you by ties of kinship. Bring Mr

Peachum with you, and in five minutes everything will be settled, MacHeath!'

'And if,' asked MacHeath with sudden brusqueness, 'it doesn't suit me to ask my father-in-law a favour?'

'Don't get excited, MacHeath, there's not the slightest cause for that. You must understand that we have to be careful. The bank doesn't belong to us but to the little Talk, an exceptionally charming child. Quite right, you have the shops. But really, it is more your idea which interests us; the shops are of secondary importance, they are fairly simple I should imagine. The chief point is, and remains, your splendid ideas of uniform prices, sales week, and the fructification of the independence of the small owner.'

MacHeath left rather hurriedly.

He went a part of the way on foot. It was already dark. He swung his thick stick and thrust it now and again into the yew hedges of the little front gardens. He was extremely dissatisfied.

On the afternoon of the day before, Polly had been for a walk with him in the park. After two hours she had gone 'home'. He had not dared to prevent her.

Why ever had he married?

The next day he had a further conversation with Miller and Hawthorne in the bank. The position remained unchanged. The date for another meeting was all that they arranged.

MacHeath did everything possible to convince the old gentlemen of the excellence of his ideas. He described with uncommon vividness their effects upon competition.

They listened appreciatively and attentively and then said that all that was still castles in the air. He should get his father-in-law interested and everything would be all right.

During the whole course of these irritating negotiations MacHeath could not rid himself of the impression that it was the evening with Miller that had done the harm. Probably his ideas were too progressive for these old-fashioned people. He was filled again with fury at the stupid Rothschild story of old Talk's.

The obvious possibility that the old and respectable National Credit Bank might be hesitating to associate with him because of his obscure past which corresponded to the equally obscure origin of his wares, was only suggested to him very much later by Fanny Chrysler.

At the appointed meeting MacHeath had naturally nothing new to tell them. He had to admit that he and Mr Peachum were completely 'unreconciled'. Miller and Hawthorne immediately made extremely startled faces. They did not throw him out, but they asked him, quite baldly, some tactless and astonishing questions.

They were genuinely disappointed. They had by now satisfied themselves with regard to the innovation and were actually eager to cast their old nets into new waters.

A few weeks later MacHeath learned that they were negotiating with *Chreston's Chain Stores*.

That was more than bitter. The Chreston chain shops were the very ones which MacHeath had envisaged as his ambitious pattern; great, impressive buildings in good positions with a rich selection of wares. Part of his idea had been the forcing of this organization to its knees. Instead of which he was now informed that the Chreston concern, as well as taking in new capital, was planning *innovations*. It announced a great *sales week* with all sorts of surprises for the public. It was quite obviously a mean theft of his ideas. MacHeath should obviously never have trusted the two old men; and that enraged him greatly.

'*Why*,' he fulminated in front of Fanny, '*does everyone try to cheat me? I do everything possible to become respectable. I desist from any use of violence, I keep slavishly, or at any rate fairly closely, to the law. I deny my past, put on a stand-up collar, rent a five-room house, contract an advantageous marriage, and the first thing that happens to me in this higher sphere is that I am robbed. So* that's *more respectable than what I've always been doing! That's far worse! We simple criminals aren't equal to these people, Fanny. In twice twenty-four hours they take away not only our whole earnings which we have scraped together with the sweat of our brow, but also our house and our shoes; and all that, they take away without having broken any law, probably with the fine feeling that they have only done their duty!*'

He was deeply wounded by the treachery which had been practised on him and he began to doubt his own capabilities.

For hours he rode on horse-omnibuses, backwards and forwards through London, pursuing his dark thoughts. The tumult of people getting on and off soothed him, and the change of surroundings with their poverty and their wealth cheered him. But his lack of education which had allowed a small bank and the Chreston Chain Stores to make a fool of him, oppressed him continuously. It was only with difficulty that he found his equilibrium again.

MacHeath lived through one of the darkest periods of his life.

A Friendly Hand

IN those days Fanny Chrysler became a strong support.

She had a small house in Lambeth with beautiful old furniture and a spare room.

He sat a great deal in her shop and in the evening she took him back with her when he did not want to go home. He always said he got no breakfast at home.

Difficulties with Grooch, with whom she had a permanent affair, were avoided without trouble; she simply told him to keep away for a few weeks.

She never spoke of MacHeath's marriage, for she knew that he regarded it as a disappointment and he scarcely saw Polly now. So she was all the more energetic in helping him reorganize the affairs of the B. shops, which were becoming critical.

The owners paid irregularly or not at all. They were still receiving enormous consignments of the same goods – one time watches and spectacles, another time tobacco and pipes – and they did not know how to get rid of them.

An unpleasant experience with a woman whom he had installed out of kindness in a small shop, showed only too clearly the state of these miserable concerns. The woman was one of his old friends, a certain Mary Sawyer.

She had discovered that he had just married. For some reasons she seemed to think that he had wronged her by doing this. She raised a great outcry and found supporters in some people who were visiting B. shops trying to bring the conversations of the owners round to the subject of Mr MacHeath. These supporters sat in the editorial offices of the *Reflector*. This editorial department had taken a great deal of interest in all the affairs of B. shop owners since the throwing out of one of their colleagues. They were superstitious enough to believe that anyone who broke a mirror would have seven years bad luck. Besides, they had something of a reputation as a socialist paper because they only attacked rich people, although the reason for this was that the others had no money out of which they could be blackmailed. So MacHeath had to be on his guard. Like all well-to-do people, he had to have an irreproachable moral reputation. And he needed it, in order to be able to swindle the B. shop owners without interference.

The negotiations between himself and Mary Sawyer took place in Fanny Chrysler's antique shop and in her presence.

Mrs Sawyer, a pretty, full-bosomed blonde in the late twenties, declared that she was at the end of her resources. Mac had taken her from her own circle and pestered her for years with his jealousy. And for years she had had to look on while he fluttered, so to speak, from flower to flower. Now he had had the impudence to wrong her by getting married in front of everybody. She had only married her husband, who was now at the war, at Mac's instigation and she was in no way attached to him. The shop which Mac had given her was no good. Her husband had landed her with two children. If she couldn't get at least a few pounds with which to hire sewing-girls, she might as well throw herself into the river. Her nerves had gone on strike. Certain utterances which she had made in anger, could only thus be explained.

Fanny tried, before anything else, to discover whether a connexion with the *Reflector* had already been established or not. She asked:

'To whom did you address these utterances? That is important.'

But Mrs Sawyer had enough nerves left not to be caught. She remained vague and generally reproachful. She had given Mac the best years of her life. When she began with him she was a budding young girl; except for an assault at the age of twelve, she had never had anything to do with a man. Now, if Mac threw her over, she would no longer be able to get another. And she pointed out the furrows which the passage of years and worry for Mac had stamped on her face.

When she had finished speaking, Mac spoke.

He emphasized that he was an advocate of complete freedom for women. If they gave themselves to a man, it must be upon their own responsibility and at their own risk. He was entirely against a woman being restricted by any rules or regulations. Love was no old-age policy. Love that lasted must have been enjoyed.

Mary began to scream again. What had her past pleasures with Mac got to do with this? She could have had the same with anyone else; for example with a respectable man who would look after a woman who had given up everything for him. She had been a shop girl and Mac had taken her from her job because he had seen how her manager sent her up a ladder to fetch a box from a shelf and he had been able to see her legs. Now no one wanted to see her legs. The young man who had talked so nicely with her about the whole horrible business had told her so.

MacHeath wanted to answer sharply, but Fanny thought it better to be careful. It was clear that the bad state of business alone was responsible for the behaviour of this otherwise inoffensive woman.

'How can I sell that muck?' asked Mary angrily. 'My customers don't all need watches. I have been trying to start a line in underclothes. If Mrs Scrubb wants a petticoat, must I say: I'm afraid I haven't one in stock, but perhaps you would care for a watch instead? Yes, it's possible that watches are easier to steal – don't interrupt me. I can think for myself even if I wasn't at a boarding-school like Mac's new wife – I can't do all the washing alone, I need two maids and that means I must have money.'

The negotiations were long and exhausting. Mary fought like a tigress. The suggestion of Fanny's that Mac, although he recognized no sort of obligation towards her, would finance the extension of her B. shop for the sale of underwear, if she, in return, would keep silent about her connexion with him, was received by her with a wrinkled forehead and a face feverish with distrust.

She took the cheque greedily, pushed it hastily into her silk purse, and went away without glancing at Mac.

'It's remarkable,' said MacHeath when he was sitting with Fanny that evening in Lambeth, 'how these shops never want to remain what they are. Once upon a time a shop was opened, perhaps as an ironmonger's, and it remained an ironmonger's. Today it always tries to become something else. Whatever one starts, it can never remain as it is. A hosiery shop must become a tailor's or it will go bust. The tailor's must immediately have branches. With the big businesses it's no different. Chreston had chain shops, but now he has to steal my ideas and try something quite new. That is not progress, it's retreat. And it all happens because property isn't property any more. Formerly a man owned a shop or a house and that was a source of profit. Today it can be a source of loss, a cause of ruin. How can that be expected to build character? Suppose a man has courage and enterprise. In past years he has already made some money. Today he opens a business and is lost. Even if he has caution, too, he is lost. Courage has suddenly come to mean the ability to pay debts; caution, the ability to contract debts. A man who for three years has exactly the same outlook, only shows that for three years he has never faced reality.'

Fanny made some tea and put her pyjamas on. Her skin, even on her legs, was brown. Quite different from Polly's, thought MacHeath.

She had her own views about what should be done with the B. shops.

She considered that, after the unsuccessful attempts to secure money either by marriage or from the National Credit Bank, they were finished. She was of the opinion that Mac should abandon them.

'My shop is much better,' she said, leaning back with her legs crossed and her cup in her lap. 'You ought to concentrate on that. Grooch is very clever. He said that if he had up-to-date tools he could do all sorts of things. If that is too slow for you, you could make quite a heap of money on one or two deals and then look further afield. But he will only do it with absolutely modern instruments.'

'So it's burglary again!' said MacHeath darkly.

'Yes, but with modern tools!'

It was nearly morning when they finally agreed.

Before she went to the shop Fanny took away the bedclothes from the spare room, and in the evening Grooch sat with them and dictated his terms.

MacHeath was not happy about the whole business. It oppressed him to see that even Fanny no longer regarded him as a man capable of bringing off a big deal with a bank. He had the feeling that this was a terrible degradation – and also a decisive one.

A few days later he and Grooch went to Liverpool where, at that time, an international exhibition of crime and its prevention was being held.

They saw some marvellous things. There were safe-breaking implements for every type of safe, even for the most modern. No automatic alarm could defeat the modern technique. Locks, however complicated in design, formed only a hindrance for people who had legitimate intentions; for the expert they were child's play.

In the hotel that evening they began to quarrel, because Grooch wanted the French models while MacHeath advocated the English. 'We are in England, Grooch,' he reminded him angrily. 'Englishmen use English instruments! What would it be like if French products were given preference over here? That would be a fine state of affairs! You have no realization of the meaning of the word "patriotism". These instruments are devised by English brains, manufactured by English industry, and therefore good enough for Englishmen. I won't take anything else.'

They waited until two o'clock and then started off.

Once in the building, they worked rapidly and soon overpowered the watchmen. But when steps were heard outside, MacHeath's nerve failed completely. With perspiration starting out of his forehead, he stood there with terrified eyes and was unable to find the right pick-lock. Grooch shook his head and took the bunch out of his hand. The great merchant was apparently no longer equal to this kind of work.

Grooch had to do nearly everything himself. He was successful. The next morning they laid the instruments before Fanny.

During his leisure hours Grooch had already evolved all sorts of plans for further enterprises. He had several schemes to select from.

'That'll bring in a mint of money,' he said pensively, 'it's safer than marrying.'

But when MacHeath drove to Scotland Yard to visit Brown and ask his advice on a certain question, he received an unpleasant surprise.

'So it was Grooch?' stormed Brown. 'That's the limit! Have you read the papers?'

He had reason to be angry. The Press had made a great ado about the burglary of the crime exhibition.

They found it humorous that someone had burgled burgling instruments from the police.

Brown was seriously upset and became very excited.

'I have never let anything be taken away from you,' he complained, 'and I expect you to show the same regard for *my* career. Up till now we have always played fair. I gladly admit that I would not have reached my present position so quickly without the arrests which you have enabled me to make. But our relations, which date from the time when you and I were in India together, are more to me than a mere business arrangement. And now you disregard the most primitive of considerations between old friends. I am attached to my job. If I did not care for my profession I would not continue with it. I'm no brick-layer. My abilities may raise me to the rank of commissioner. It's not the stripes that attract me, even though you may think so. But I cannot bear to see that ass Williams holding a position for which he was never fitted. By this evening I must have the tools – *and* the man who stole them – in my hands.'

MacHeath listened with dismay. He realized that he had trodden on Brown's toes. He could only explain to him what had impelled him to commit the burglary.

'If you must have money,' said Brown, slightly mollified, 'there are other ways of getting it. Why don't you want to go to a bank? There are other banks than the National Credit.'

MacHeath replied that his shops, and also the company which

supplied them, were not in a position to induce banks to finance them. Without a respectable office in the City he could do nothing.

At this stage Brown showed his best side. Without much prompting he offered to advance some of his own money.

'Why take the downward path?' he said, addressing Mac-Heath's conscience. 'No one should do that. A merchant does not burgle. A merchant buys and sells. By that means he reaches the same end. When we lay in that rice-field in front of Peshawar, under a deadly barrage of bullets, did you stand up and rush at the Sikhs with a branch of a tree or any such thing? No! That would have been unworkmanlike and also useless. You say that your business must first be got into a condition that will attract the banks. Well, get them into this condition! Why didn't you come to me? If it's disagreeable to you to take money from a friend, then pay me interest! Pay me more interest than you would to another person – twenty, or even, for all I care, twenty-five per cent. Then the favour would be on your side. I know that you are a sound business man. I don't want you to go crooked like any stupid fool who knows nothing of business and begins to steal. You must never work with people like this Grooch again! Work with the banks, like all other respectable business men! That is quite a different thing!'

MacHeath was deeply moved. As men who had stood together through the storms of life, they could not express their feelings lightly. In such a situation an embarrassed look spoke more than an embrace.

'How like you, Freddy,' said Mac in a choking voice. 'There are some people who will always give one good advice. But you give practical help. That's what friendship is, only that is true friendship. A friendly hand. . . .'

'I only ask one thing in return,' added Brown, gazing earnestly at MacHeath, 'I ask you to give up such people as Grooch and O'Hara completely. If not immediately, then at all events when you have got yourself out of this unfortunate mess. The business that you have in mind should enable you to do this. If I help you up today, it is because I wish to see you in other surroundings in the future. By that I don't mean tomorrow or even the day after. I know that you still need these creatures to help you to success. But sometime there must be an end – I demand it.'

MacHeath nodded speechless; there were tears in his eyes.

He went away happy. They had agreed to leave Grooch unmolested for the time being and arrest another man as the burglar. MacHeath himself delivered the tools that afternoon.

Brown kept his word too. It was not easy for him to raise the money. He first had to arrange raids on several clubs; and MacHeath saw the results of his exertions when he visited Mrs Lexer in Tunbridge on the following Thursday. The girls complained bitterly about the deductions which Mrs Lexer had made from their pay.

But a week later MacHeath held in his hands the means whereby he might once more raise his 'buyers' to the peak of their efficiency.

Together with O'Hara he drew up a detailed plan of campaign.

In addition to the present warehouses several more large sheds were rented. Means of transport were also procured – heavy lorries. For jobs in provincial towns, money was deposited in readiness and lodgings arranged for.

O'Hara showed that, in spite of his youth, he was extremely useful. He had a pronounced aversion to laying his hand on anything, and that is the basis of many a great career. MacHeath had immediately noticed that; the young man resembled him in that respect.

O'Hara's rise to success had started from very obscure beginnings. At the age of sixteen he had been obliging shop-lifters and servant girls who had committed certain crimes, and who, by becoming pregnant, could more easily secure a pardon. But he did not like to be reminded of that time or of that profession.

Fanny did not get on so well with him. In her opinion he had been too spoilt by women. She mistrusted him. He was also Grooch's rival, and the Liverpool affair had lowered Grooch in MacHeath's estimation.

They held their meetings in Lambeth. Afterwards, MacHeath always went away with O'Hara. That proved to her that he did not trust the young man either. Once, O'Hara had come back again to stay with her and she had had to speak her mind very plainly.

But more than anything else, it was O'Hara's unscrupulous attitude towards the division of the spoils which displeased her most. He was a real blood-sucker – insatiable. Even if he got no advantage out of it, he always interfered with her share of the profits.

All night long he lay awake trying to think out new schemes for getting money out of people.

She always reprimanded him for this. It seemed to her financially stupid.

After the Liverpool affair, Robert the Saw was arrested by the police. As a consequence of this, the gang nearly broke into open revolt against their leader. It was rumoured that Robert the Saw had been handed over to the police; and other similar cases were suddenly remembered.

O'Hara announced with a grin the news of the disturbances at Lower Blacksmith Square.

But Fanny shut him up. This, she said excitedly, was nothing to laugh about. If it had really happened, it was a bloody serious occurrence and a most regrettable one too.

'But the chief himself went to Robert in his cell and shook his hand,' said O'Hara derisively, squinting over at MacHeath. The latter actually *had* visited the prison after the arrest of his unfortunate employee and had told him that he would stand by him. In such details he showed his talents as a leader.

Fanny Chrysler considered the gesture merely cynical.

A lengthy dispute arose in the little house. MacHeath sat in silence with a thin black cigar between his teeth. The heated exchange of words amused him. He was still jealous, although he was by no means in love. It pleased him that O'Hara had no luck with Fanny.

She pointed out that, since the arrest of Robert the Saw, disturbances within the gang had not abated; and because of that, several enterprises had gone wrong; and she finally persuaded O'Hara, after many hours' wrangling, that deliveries to the police should cease. She even succeeded in inducing MacHeath, who always favoured generous measures, to engage a reputable firm of solicitors to defend members of the gang who might be arrested.

Mac went further. He promised fixed salaries.

'They want to live securely,' he said thoughtfully, 'a sort of official position appeals to them. They like to sleep peacefully at nights and not have to worry whether there will be money enough in the house to pay the rent at the end of the month. That's quite understandable, even if it is a little different to what I had hoped for. I thought perhaps that our little band might regard me with a sort of sentimental attachment – their leader working with them through good times and bad. The chief draws the reins tighter and the boys come closer, too; or something like that, you know. But they can do what they like. They shall have salaries because I believe they want salaries.'

He foresaw that fixed salaries would be considerably cheaper to him because he would now have to start 'buying' on a very large scale in order to be able to interest a bank in his shops.

The gang regarded the new system of regular payments as a victory, and Fanny was now a popular heroine among the people in Lower Blacksmith Square, for Grooch had sung her praises loud and long, much to the annoyance of O'Hara. She was said to have compelled the chief to take the whole risk on his own shoulders; and he was said to have agreed, whether he liked it or not, because he needed her and had to keep her in a good temper.

After the reorganization, the burglars of the O'Hara gang were no longer small independent operators but employees of a large concern; and only as such, that is working in close co-operation with others of the same standing as themselves, could they succeed in their jobs. For some were specialists in the use of blow-pipes; others, the 'travellers', reconnoitred the ground; while others again perfected a plan of campaign. One man would arrange for the storage of the goods, another saw to the alibis. And then, when the burglary took place, the 'buyer', who chose the goods and had to be an expert, came in with his squad of packers and set them to work on the shelves. That was a pleasant and modern way of working, and a return to primitive methods would have been almost impossible for these highly trained men – for psychological reasons alone, if for no others.

Because of the interdependent nature of their work, it was, of course, essential that they should be punctually and continuously employed, or at least paid. Whether the sale of the goods slumped or not, they still had to be kept busy, for sales problems were no concern of theirs.

'You have them much better in hand now,' said Fanny to MacHeath, when O'Hara had gone off one night to Blacksmith Square. 'Admittedly you can no longer use a revolver or a knife against them, but you have their work tools. You no longer have them arrested by the police, but hunger keeps them at work. Believe me, that's far better. All modern employers manage like that.'

MacHeath nodded pensively. He strode backwards and forwards across the blue Chinese carpet, Fanny's best piece, clinking a few coins in his trouser pocket and now and again taking them out and throwing them into the air and catching them.

He had now almost recovered from the blow dealt him by the One and a Half Centuries and was evolving great plans in his mind.

These plans were gigantic, but yet they did not emanate from a surplus of self-confidence in him. They were very necessary to save him from ruin. The buying side was flourishing now. A stream of goods poured into the shops. The rough shelves were filled to overflowing. The sewing girls at Mary Sawyer's sat until late into the night and worked. Bales of leather were transformed into boots. Wool passed through the industrious hands of whole families to become jumpers. Writing materials and lamps, musical instruments and carpets, crowded out the cheerless holes that were called B. shops.

But MacHeath knew that the money which Brown had lent him would scarcely suffice to keep O'Hara's gang going for six weeks.

In such a situation only plans of Napoleonic dimensions could save him.

8

On s'engage et puis on voit.
(NAPOLEON)

'Oh! But it's raining outside!'
'Oh! But the house is on fire, don't forget!
Rather than be burnt alive
Let's go out and get wet!'
(SONG OF THE YOUNG PIONEERS)

Napoleonic Plans

IN a large building in the City a young man rented a whole floor. He signed the agreement as Lord Bloomsbury and furnished four or five rooms as offices. The furniture he installed was mostly old and shabby, but it gave the rooms an air of time-worn respectability. A young woman with golden brown skin helped him to arrange everything and engage the staff.

'You know,' she said, when the furniture arrived and she saw him eyeing it disapprovingly, 'old firms have a great attraction for people. Their age proves that they have never been in trouble, and that again makes it extremely unlikely that they will be caught in the future.'

The biggest room was arranged as a conference room. On the outer glass door stood in great gold letters: 'C.P.B.' Underneath, written much smaller, was 'Central Purchasing Board'.

The first meeting of the directors of the new company was short. Two solicitors, well known in the City, a Mr O'Hara, a Lord Bloomsbury, and a Mrs Chrysler elected a Mr MacHeath, merchant by profession, to be president. The vice-president was Lord Bloomsbury. MacHeath had met him in a house in Tunbridge where he spent his Thursday evenings. He had easily been able to catch this vapid but pleasant young man, for the latter was in permanent need of money and completely dependent on Jenny Month, Mrs Lexer's star performer. He was very stupid, but said little and had an extremely embarrassed smile which suddenly appeared for no reason at all. He made a good impression and lived on it.

The first business of the company consisted in the drawing up of two agreements. In one of these Mr O'Hara contracted to deliver large consignments of cheap goods to the C.P.B. The other gave Mr MacHeath an option for the B. shops on all goods handled by the C.P.B. Then Mr MacHeath gave up the chair to his friend Lord Bloomsbury and asked those present to keep his presidency a secret until further notice.

Everyone parted on the best of terms and the offices commenced their activities under the management of Mrs Chrysler.

These activities consisted in corresponding with various agents in England and the Continent who bought up for the C.P.B. the stocks of bankrupt businesses and delivered them to the warehouses in Soho. The invoices for the goods received and the receipts for money paid out were carefully filed in two different departments. Also the deliveries to the warehouses were separately entered and were dealt with independently of everything supplied to the B. shops.

The offices had scarcely been opened a fortnight, when two gentlemen, Mr MacHeath and Lord Bloomsbury, appeared in the precincts of the *Commercial Bank* and asked to speak to the Chairman.

The Commercial Bank was an institution with excellent connexions in the Dominions and newish and extremely ornate premises in Great Russell Street. It financed all sorts of commercial enterprises, amongst others Aaron's chain shops (B. Chreston's great rivals) and a whole string of smaller firms of this type in the provinces.

The people of the Commercial Bank were very respectable and well versed in the retail trade. Their reception of MacHeath was more than reserved. As it turned out, they knew the organization and the position of the B. shops astonishingly well.

MacHeath had a carefully prepared line of approach.

'The old National refused to advance anything on my new warehouses because they hadn't got a first-class pedigree,' he said to Bloomsbury before they went to Great Russell Street. 'Now they have got a pedigree; and besides there's sharp competition now; that will weaken considerably any curiosity as to the origin of our cheap goods. I shall have to say that the warehouses are very cheap, otherwise they won't believe that the money they are going to lend me will be profitably employed. But in order to be able to offer the shameless rate of interest which they are sure to ask, I shall either have to describe the warehouses *as* so cheap that they will be bound to ask about their origin, or I shall have to appear as a fool who has ruined himself. They love people in desperate straits. Believe me, Bloomsbury, it won't be hard for me, in my position, to appear as a desperate man: I am lost.'

So MacHeath did not appear as a cold business man but as a ruined supplicant. With a pale face and beads of sweat on his forehead he admitted that he was at the end of his resources. He had gone trustfully to the National Credit Bank with a detailed proposition and his confidence had been disgracefully misused. These people had cold-bloodedly stolen his ideas and gone with them to the Chreston concern. Now he was landed with enormous warehouses, which he was pledged to take over and for which the C.P.B. were demanding extortionate rents and rates of interest.

He was lacking the necessary money which would enable him to expand his shops and arrange for credit. The warehouses could be viewed on application to the C.P.B.

The inspection took place in Lower Blacksmith Square and yielded remarkably encouraging results. Receipts and invoices for purchases were produced, among them those of Danish and French firms.

The faces of the directors of the Commercial cleared up noticeably during the inspection.

But when MacHeath and Bloomsbury came to the bank on the next day, they suddenly saw, sitting next to Messrs Jacques and Henry Opper, a fat gentleman of extremely Jewish appearance. It was Mr I. Aaron, owner of Aaron's chain shops, who, as Jacques explained, worked in conjunction with the Messrs Opper.

'Mr Aaron,' said the younger Opper courteously, 'whose name is doubtless not unknown to you, is very interested in your ideas, gentlemen.'

MacHeath was somewhat taken aback.

I. Aaron owned at least eighteen large shops in the best neighbourhoods, and in comparison to them the B. shops were like a lousy street cur beside a gigantic, thoroughbred Newfoundland.

For some minutes, MacHeath considered whether it would not be better to leave the room immediately. He only needed to cast one glance at the two Oppers to see that they would never enter into any negotiations without Aaron's support. He had a strong feeling that he had again been sold a pup, a feeling that later he was to remember often. But his position permitted no retreat. He needed money.

MacHeath repeated his story and the great Aaron said hoarsely that that was exactly what he would have expected of Chreston. In his opinion, which he expressed with many a witty turn of phrase, Chreston, a comparatively young man, was absolutely unscrupulous and only bent on making money. In spite of his youth, or perhaps because of it, he was a typical example of those rather old-fashioned business men who do everything in their power to swindle the public. He, Aaron, was in no way a moralist, immorality even amused him, but he would have nothing to do with it in business. It wasn't worth the risk.

'Your idea of unit prices isn't a bad one,' he said benignly, tapping MacHeath on the knee, 'but your warehouses,' and he turned to Bloomsbury who represented the C.P.B., 'are almost better. How was it that you went to Mr MacHeath? You should have come straight to me. But I understand that your way is now via Mr MacHeath. Our small B. shop brothers are to be included.'

MacHeath listened to him with little amusement. He found his witticisms poor. He felt no desire to share the warehouses with Aaron. Only by the greatest self-control did he manage to continue to play his role as the small man whom Chreston had insulted.

Aaron seemed to be very amused, but MacHeath noticed that every time the name Chreston was mentioned a gentle flush spread over his temples. He had some score to settle with Chreston.

The fact was that Chreston was too much on the ascendant. Even the gentlemen in the Commercial Bank had their own ideas about that. The National Credit Bank was to them what

Chreston was to Aaron. The One and a Half Centuries dealt in real estate, what did they want with retail trading? A small, unenterprising concern with a few mildewed strong-boxes. The Commercial was too big to feel competitive jealousy, but it had a very high opinion of its influence in the retail trade. It considered itself *the* authority on everything to do with this branch of commerce. It had no consciousness of having to partake in rapid and unscrupulous deals. Its mission was to watch over the *morals of the retail trade.*

It was clear to them that men of the stamp of MacHeath could only be handled with tongs; but in this case a somewhat doubtful character seemed, to put it mildly, to have been treated unfairly. Anyone could see that his nerves were on edge. He gave the impression of a broken man.

He showed plainly that he was filled with thoughts of vengeance against the National Credit Bank and Chreston's. He would do anything to be able to pay these gentlemen back in their own coin, even at the cost of personal sacrifice. Apparently swept away by his own eloquence, he offered to present I. Aaron with his warehouses at a knock-out price in order to crush Chreston, and in return he only asked that his B. shops, towards which he had certain obligations, should be brought into the business too, an additional reason being that they were small independent people who had put their trust in him.

The opportunity of exploiting the revengefulness of the B. shop Napoleon, which, by the way, was a weakness which seemed to point to his murky past, decided the gentlemen of the Commercial Bank, and Mr Aaron too, to investigate the project more closely.

Mr MacHeath received from Mr Jacques Opper, the chairman of the Commercial Bank, an invitation to spend a week-end at Warborn Castle.

Warborn Castle was, to the retail trade, what Downing Street is to politics and Wall Street to another branch of commerce. All 'strings' were pulled from there.

MacHeath came very excited into the offices of the C.P.B. and Fanny sent someone to fetch Bloomsbury immediately. MacHeath declared that he had no idea how one ate fish at Warborn Castle. The Oppers had not been there very long.

Fanny solved the difficulty by a frank talk with Jacques Opper. She went to the Commercial Bank with a portfolio full of details under one arm and destroyed any illusions Opper might have had about the manners of her chief. She said that people who were accustomed to scoop in money with their hands, also used their hands to scoop meat from their plates. If he would invite Bloomsbury as well, he would then have someone who was not so talented as MacHeath. So Opper invited Bloomsbury.

But even then the whole thing was nearly wrecked by this young man. He had not nearly such a high opinion of the Oppers as MacHeath, because he understood little about money and wanted at all costs to bring Jenny with him. He thought it would be a great joke. He would say that Jenny was his sister and then give an exhibition of the latest dances with her. This would, he anticipated, produce startling results.

Fanny dissuaded him with the greatest difficulty.

She carefully supervised MacHeath's clothes and took his sword-stick away from him.

'You don't need it any more,' she said.

But at the last moment he bought himself a pair of natural-coloured calfskin gloves with thick black stitching which she did not see. Bloomsbury noticed them with pleasure.

On the journey to Warborn Castle, Bloomsbury convinced MacHeath that it was absolutely essential for him to keep to his accustomed mannerisms; otherwise the Oppers would no longer consider MacHeath an upstart. This little harangue to which Bloomsbury gave utterance was his only contribution to the business about to be inaugurated by MacHeath's intrusion into Warborn Castle.

The week-end was much pleasanter than MacHeath had expected.

They strolled over well-kept lawns and ate game and venison and drank glasses of vintage port. The library smelt of old leather and MacHeath was able to make good use of Fanny's lessons in the appreciation of pornographic *éditions de luxe*.

Mr Jacques Opper was unmarried and occupied himself with aesthetic things, chiefly with a biography of Lycurgus. The driving force of the business was Henry Opper.

Bloomsbury was rather superfluous. The fish problem did not arise.

MacHeath was amazed at the way in which business affairs were treated at the Castle. Money was never mentioned at all. Bloomsbury discovered that the great Aaron had only been excluded from the invitation because he talked too much about money for Jacques Opper's taste. Jacques Opper could not bear money. He said: these things must be arranged somehow, so that life can be made bearable. That evening after an excellent dinner he returned to the subject.

'*Admittedly a man must eat to live. But a man who has eaten has not necessarily lived. The real motive power of humanity is the necessity of self-expression, that is, the perpetuation of personality. How that happens, is entirely beside the point. The born rider expresses himself by riding. Whether the horse belongs to him or not, is of no consequence. He wants to ride. Another person wants to make tables. He is happy when he has his beloved wood in his hand and can shut himself up in a room with his tools. That is the whole secret of living. A man who wants nothing, whose every action is impelled by a desire to earn money, is always a poor man, even if he gets his money. He is lacking in actuality. He is nothing and therefore wishes to create nothing.*'

Without Henry Opper, MacHeath would have been hard put to it to bring the conversation round to chain stores and credit.

Not until long after the coffee was he able to develop his thesis of independence for the small holder. When he got into his stride, he explained how he would like to introduce his principles, partly at least, into larger shops such as Aaron's.

With great persistence and with much reiteration, he assured everybody that it was, of course, only a superstition to think that most trade came from the customers. The real source of profit was, and would always be, the employees.

After all, the customers were only there to enable the business man to make use of his employees and workmen.

But the mainspring of the employees was common self-interest. What did the salesman care, cried MacHeath, for the welfare of his form? With complete indifference he will watch the customers stay outside as long as he receives his wages. The only solution was to give him an interest in the business. To put it briefly, one must give him a sop.

'Are you thinking of profit-sharing?' asked Opper in horror.

'Of nothing else.'

'But that's terribly expensive,' said Opper.

'There I cannot agree with you,' replied MacHeath. 'The share-out will naturally be in the form of credit notes on the firm. Thereby the salesmen are enrolled as customers.'

Henry Opper growled something. But Jacques, the bookworm, looked at MacHeath attentively and searchingly.

Taken all in all, the evening was a success. They went to bed fairly early, but Mac was unable to sleep. He delivered a discourse to Bloomsbury on the decadence of the upper classes.

'These people,' he said, walking about with his braces dangling at his side, 'are lacking in seriousness. Listening to them one would think that they made their money only for the sake of the excitements that go with it. That's just like a dog that falls into the river and then says it's only swimming to the bank for fun. They think I don't know that the entry of the One and a Half Centuries into retail is going to give them sleepless nights. Chreston has got money; that means that Aaron will need money. They bring me down here as though they wanted to investigate my character, but of course it's really my warehouses that interest them. If they don't know that, so much the worse for them. Without my warehouses, Aaron could never reduce his high prices. And for all that twaddle about Lycurgus, or whatever that old Greek was called, Jacques was listening pretty closely to the prices of my goods. In my opinion, these people won't ask any more questions. The old saying about "some things can't be got without stealing" is out of date now that stealing costs so much money. You'll see if I don't get this money from them, the money which they despise so.'

MacHeath condemned Jacques far more than he did Henry, he called him 'dense'; but at the same time, as he expounded to his confederate, it was Jacques Opper who imbued his still doubting brother with a favourable impression of him.

'This simple man has ideas,' he said, 'and, what is more, he has instinct. His perception of the value of the salesman's contest with the purchaser is absolutely Grecian. He doesn't simply see ordinary sales-drives, like Aaron; in his mind's eye he sees chariot races. His profit is the laurel which crowns the victor's brow. He doesn't know all that, but he feels it. He demands, quite rightly, the fully developed, harmonious *personality* of the salesman. Collocacadia, as he put it, I saw Alcibiades before me. That's not bad!'

Before he fell asleep, the younger Opper envisaged Aaron's salesmen dragging vanquished customers to the pay-desk, like Achilles once dragged Hector.

During the week following this week-end, the arrangement between Aaron's chain shops, the Commercial Bank, and the C.P.B. was ratified. Henceforth Aaron was to purchase goods from the C.P.B. at the same prices as the B. shops.

The contracts which Bloomsbury had to sign for the C.B.P. were terrible.

MacHeath did not dare look Bloomsbury in the eyes.

Then, in the street, he had hysterics. Bloomsbury, embarrassed and not a little surprised, took him into a nearby tea-shop. There they ordered bread and butter. It was some time before Mac-Heath regained his self-control.

'At those prices which Aaron is to pay,' said MacHeath to Bloomsbury as they left the tea-shop, 'we can't even steal the goods. It will be impossible to hold out for long. The most we can do is to have a sales week like Chreston, and that's just what the Oppers want. They want to have to deal with us for the shortest possible time. They are too good for us. Look at their offices, Bloomsbury! Marble and bronze! I have never understood why the public brings its money to buildings which cost so much and will always go on costing a lot. Apparently people think that firms which can afford marble and bronze don't need any more money and therefore *their* money is safe there.'

The old National Credit was more to his taste. Its dingy offices seemed to say: We don't earn much from our customers.

He thought regretfully of the National Credit Bank, that treacherous old amphibian. *Without* the National meant *against* the National. But the National held his wife's dowry. MacHeath had bitter feelings when he thought of that. It was plain to him that his fight was now directed against this dowry; in fact, so

147

strange was his present position, he must make every effort to destroy it if he wished to win through. The fight allowed no quarter; he could only win by the annihilation of his opponents.

MacHeath saw a period of hard work before him.

The inauguration of the C.P.B. as a decoy duck for the Commercial had been a great expense; but had he now been allowed to expand his needy B. shops, they would have been plentifully supplied and become a flourishing success. Instead of which, the worst had happened; he had been forced to include Aaron, his rival – his superior rival – in his scheme! He had expanded his warehouses only to have them stolen! Once more, he was really no further forward than he was before. If no stroke of luck came to MacHeath's aid, he would still, now as before, be lost. He was like a man who stands barefooted on red-hot coals. He never stops jumping into the air, even though he only changes one hot spot for another equally unbearable. His happier moments are those when his feet are in the air.

For the present, MacHeath had a certain amount of capital in hand for the improvement of his B. shops. They were now able to be increased and restocked. The arrears of wages owing to O'Hara's 'buyers' were paid off.

MacHeath delivered an exhortatory oration in Newgate before the assembled B. shop owners.

First he announced that he had decided from now on to give his undivided attention to them, the B. shops. To leave himself free for this purpose, he had as good as disposed of the purchasing side, which was being taken over by a very influential firm called the Central Purchasing Board. This company offered excellent goods which, however, were only cheap if taken in large quantities. There had also been the question of preventing the C.P.B. offering equally advantageous terms to other shops, although the B. shops alone would never be able to handle all their wares.

He continued:

'As you may have heard, the united B. shops entered yesterday into a close business association with Aaron's chain shops. The Central Purchasing Board will also supply Aaron's shops. What does this sensational step on the part of the mighty Aaron *combine mean? Gentlemen, it means a victory,* an overwhelming victory *for the B. shops. And, what is more important, for the* B. shop ideal. *What is that ideal? Gentlemen, it is the ideal which brings the gifts of modern industry to the aid of the poorest classes of the people.* A man of the people, one of the masses — *you may think that these are not very inspiring phrases. But, gentlemen, you are mistaken. It is the masses that count. The business man who ignores the penny, the hard-earned penny of the worker, makes a great mistake. That penny is as good as any other. And a dozen is twelve times as much as one. That is the ideal of the B. shops. And this ideal of the B. shops, your ideal, has won a decisive victory over the mighty Aaron concern with its dozens of great branches. In the future, Aaron's shops too will open their doors to the poorer people and thus serve the ideal of cheapness and of* social progress. *Some among you are unbelieving — for everywhere there are weaklings and grumblers — and I can hear them saying to themselves: Why should the mighty Aaron combine want to work together with us small shopkeepers? And to that we must admit: not because of the blue eyes of the Bargain shops! Wherever we look in nature,* nothing *is done* except for material profit! *Whenever one person says to another: I want to help you, let's start together and . . . etc., that means, Look out! For men are only human beings and not angels, and they think first of all of themselves. Nothing is ever done from kindness alone! The stronger overcome the weaker, and so, in our mutual work with Aaron's, the question will be, in all friendliness, who is* the stronger? *A fight? Yes, gentlemen, a fight! But a peaceful fight. A fight in the service of an ideal! The healthy,* thinking *business man is not afraid of fighting. Only the weakling is afraid, and over him the* wheel of destiny *will pass to crush and to destroy! Aaron's have joined us, not because our blue eyes attract them, but because they must; because they respect the tough, enduring, and* self-sacrificing work *of the B. shops. And these qualities must be still further strengthened. Our power depends upon our* industry and our contentedness. *Everyone knows that each of us does his bit! And therefore I, too, have decided to dedicate in the future all my powers to you and to the B. shops. Not for reasons of material gain, but because I believe in the ideal and because I know that inde-*

pendent retail is the very life-blood of trade and also a gold-mine!'

The speech was listened to by about fifty people, men and women, and a few journalists, and it made a strong impression. There were quite a number of weakly, or weak-looking people among the crowd, but, as everyone knows, an appeal to individual effort seldom goes unheard.

MacHeath could well be satisfied with his success, but he left the assembly with Fanny Chrysler and somehow or other Polly got to hear of it.

He found her rather late one evening, standing in front of his house in Nunhead. She had asked for his address in a B. shop and had already been sitting on the doorstep for several hours. She was in rather low spirits and said immediately that she could not live longer without him.

As he unlocked the door, he warned her of the condition of the new house which was temporarily only furnished in one room. The reason for leaving the big house he explained to her upstairs, when she was seated in the only chair, her bag at her feet.

He told her seriously that the attitude of her father towards him had made things very difficult for him. He admitted openly that he had counted on her dowry, or at least on an improvement in his credit.

'I hope', he said, 'that you are not disappointed to find that you have a husband who reckons in pennies. My whole life long I have worked hard; and now that success is in sight, I need a little extra money to settle everything up. A man of my calibre must not marry blindly. He must be careful. His wife must be a help to him. When I realized my feelings towards you, I still kept a clear head and asked myself coolly: Is this the right wife for you? My instinct said: Yes. And my inquiries, which I made with the greatest discretion, proved that my instinct had not been wrong. Why even Kipling says: The sick man dies and the strong man fights.'

Therefore he could now face the present situation with equanimity.

Well then. He had sold the house. They could live here, if she did not wish to return to her father whose hostility at the present time would be most unwelcome for reasons already specified.

She cried a little and then spoke of the importunity of Mr Coax, to whom she was defencelessly exposed. He understood this immediately, and when she also told him that she was going to have a child, that a little MacHeath was growing under her heart, he showed his best side.

His tone was different from before. He treated her now with a certain abrupt embarrassment which pleased her very well.

Happily she admitted that she had been waiting for him to come to her one night. It was not difficult to climb up to her balcony. Unpleasantly astonished, he replied that he could not climb up a balcony at dead of night in order to sleep with his own wife. That seemed to him thoroughly improper.

She agreed.

For a long time he lay awake beside her, his hands folded under his head, staring at the uncertain glimmer through the curtains.

'I shall call him Dick,' he dreamed. *'I shall instruct him in everything, tell him all I know. I know a lot. Much that I have had to work out for myself, he will be able to learn direct from me without any effort. I shall take him by his little hand and tell him how to conduct a business and get something out of other people, out of his shifty, unreliable, despicable brother-men. If someone tries to steal the porridge off your plate, hit him with your spoon, I shall tell him; and again and again until he lets go. Wherever you see a door ajar, push your foot in and then shoulder your way into the house. Only never stand around despondently and wait for something to fall into your lap. I shall teach him with great patience, but I shall also be very strict. Your father was an uneducated man, but no professor of history could teach him how to pull wool over people's eyes! You can go to a university, but never forget who made that possible for you. Your father has had to drag the money for your education, penny by penny, from the pockets of his brutal adversaries. Increase this capital! Widen your knowledge. But also strengthen the foundations!'*

He went to sleep with a deep furrow in his forehead, but well pleased with Polly.

The next morning she fetched the milk from the dairy, learned to cook liver for him as he liked it, and helped him to arrange the other rooms.

She never mentioned Fanny Chrysler, either that night or later.

Recently MacHeath's relations with Fanny Chrysler had become more intimate and he was afraid that she might make difficulties. But to his relief she showed no change in her attitude when he now began going home again at nights. He would have been sorry to offend her, for she was a great help to him in the C.P.B. He had brought her in because he believed that she was attached to him for physical reasons.

Also he needed her.

Chreston's sales week was proclaimed with much blowing of trumpets.

At a meeting which took place in the great mahogany-furnished board-room of the Commercial Bank, it was decided that Aaron's chain stores and the B. shops should engage Chreston's in decisive battle, with a monster sales week to begin three weeks later.

9

For Man lives by his head;
He needs a larger size;
You try it for yourself. Your head
Won't feed a pair of lice.
>   *Why, for this existence*
>   *There's no man who's smart enough,*
>   *Life's too short for learning*
>   *Every trick and bluff.*

So make your little plan
And think you're mighty smart,
Then make another little plan —
They'll land you in the cart.
>   *Why, for this existence*
>   *There's no man who's bad enough,*
>   *Still it's nice to watch them*
>   *Trying to be tough.*

So run and catch your luck
But don't you run too fast,
For all of them run after luck
And luck is running last.
>   *Why, for this existence*
>   *There's no man who's meek and mild enough.*
>   *All his high endeavour*
>   *Is just one more bluff.*

(SONG OF THE FUTILITY OF HUMAN ENDEAVOUR)

Fighting All Round

MR PEACHUM, too, was engaged in a desperate battle.

He was fighting day and night to shift the responsibility for the shipping business off his shoulders. With all his might he struggled to return to his own profession of wholesale begging.

His fear of finishing in the gutter and his feeling of having been tricked by one craftier, crueller, and cleverer than himself, filled him with thoughts of expanding his own business, which itself flourished on oppression and deceit. He was accustomed to making capital, even out of his own troubles.

Sometimes he stood by the dog-kennel in the yard and talked to Fewkoombey as though he were a friend. The one-legged man wondered at this until he realized that Mr Peachum was probably addressing himself to the dogs, for he never looked at him at all.

'I've been reading in the newspapers,' he said one day, 'that there has been too much begging lately. That's ridiculous! At the very most, one sees a beggar every few miles and that's always the same one. To go by the number of beggars one would think that there was no poverty. I have often asked myself: Where are the poor? The answer is: Everywhere. They hide themselves behind their own multitude. There are great cities entirely inhabited by them, but they too are hidden in the same way. They are never seen in any place that is pleasant. They shun the open streets. They mostly work. That is the best way of hiding themselves. No one notices that they are unable to buy food to satisfy their hunger, because they never come into the shops to buy anything. Whole nations languish away in back-yard houses. The process of their destruction is almost imperceptible (quite apart from the fact that it is anonymous!). They are destroyed, but the destruction lasts years. Adulterated food and too little of it, infected dwellings, repression of the natural instincts, all that takes a long time to destroy a man. Man has unbelievable powers of endurance. He only dies quite slowly, bit by bit. And all the time he looks like a man. Only at the very last does he admit defeat and give in completely. This strange process of decay makes it difficult to perceive its widespread and incalculable effects. I have often tried to think how one could do anything about this poverty – real poverty. It would be a wonderful business. But it's impossible. How could one make use of the pitiful glance of a mother who holds her sick child in her arms and watches the water seep down the walls of her room? There are such mothers, hundreds of thousands of them, but what can one do with them? One can't take conducted tours round the poorer quarters, like one can round a battlefield! Or the sight of a man who realizes that he is being eliminated from the struggle for life because he is worn out –

and it is not he, but the world around that has wasted his strength; admittedly, such a sight is heart-rending, but the man won't give it the necessary publicity. From a business point of view he is useless. Those are only two examples from thousands.'

Mr Peachum appeared suddenly to lose interest in the subject. With a vague gesture he waved Fewkoombey back to his work and went away with a worried, restless expression on his face.

Or he said:

'There is something extraordinary about the begging business. Even for me it was difficult at the beginning to believe in it. But I soon noticed that people are driven to give by the same fear which drives them to take. There is no lack of sympathy in the world; only with sympathy one can't earn a warm meal as easily as without sympathy. It's plain to me now why people don't examine the injuries of beggars more closely before they give. They are convinced that the wounds are there, because they themselves have dealt them. When a man does business, isn't there another man somewhere else who is being ruined? When a man supports his family, aren't other families being forced into the gutter? All these people are already convinced that, because of their own way of living, there must be dirty, poverty-stricken wretches creeping about everywhere. Why, therefore, should they take the trouble to make sure of that? For the sake of the few pennies which they are willing to give?'

Another time he only said:

'Don't think that I starve my blind dogs because I'm cruel; it's only because it injures trade if they look well-fed.'

And one day he furrowed Fewkoombey's happy face with the words:

'You look much too contented. I tell all my people they must look degraded and unhappy; people pay gladly to escape from such a hateful sight.'

He would certainly have been deeply horrified had he known that such soliloquies in front of inferiors are a symptom of serious psychological disorders; for he knew that sick people can expect no consideration.

The raising of the money for the purchase of the Southampton ships was proving extremely difficult.

Miller of the National Credit Bank rejected with uplifted hands the suggestion that he should advance £50,000. He did not want to offend his client and therefore referred to his responsibility towards the little seven-year-old owner of the bank. He was up to his eyes in big business deals, more especially, he might add in confidence, in one with the Chreston concern. He seemed very shocked at Peachum's lack of capital and he was even more so than he seemed.

Peachum had about £10,000 on deposit at the National. But he did not want to touch that in any circumstances. Besides, it would not have been enough.

Finney declared that now, at last, it was essential for him to have his operation, and threatened to go into hospital the next day. Only Eastman fought on, but his efforts seemed unavailing.

And then the news reached them that Hale of the Admiralty was threatened with a scandal.

Coax himself came to Peachum and waited in the little office behind the iron-clad door until Eastman had been fetched.

He informed them of the situation.

Some days ago Hale had received a blackmailing letter. His wife had been caught in a police raid two years ago. She had been found in a doubtful hotel in company with a friend of her husband's. The blackmailer declared that he held the diary of this friend and this diary revealed that Hale had known of the affair – and had done nothing about it. In fact he was now engaged in business with this friend. . . .

The broker looked pointedly at Eastman, to whom he was chiefly addressing himself. The latter turned his tortured face towards Peachum.

Peachum looked very ill again.

'What will the diary cost?' he asked painfully, avoiding Coax's glance.

'A thousand,' said Coax casually.

'He's got that. The M.T.C. paid him £9,000.'

It was Eastman who spoke.

And Coax said patiently:

'He has nothing. His wife must have dresses, otherwise she would have no friends, not even in hotels. The rest of the money which he received from the M.T.C. will have to be used for the suppression of the investigations. This man's case is a tragic one.'

'What will happen if he doesn't pay?' asked Peachum.

'Then he will have to resign. It's terrible that people with whom one has business dealings should also have private affairs. In his hour of need, Hale immediately turned to me because I am his best friend. He wanted no help. Your trouble is my trouble, I said to him. Gentlemen, we must think of something. A man like Hale must not be ruined for such a trifle. In all humanity, we must not let ourselves be responsible for such a disaster! But also for purely selfish reasons, we must help Hale.'

When Coax said good-bye in the shop, he hesitated for a moment.

'Miss Polly is not yet back from Chamonix?' he asked, twisting his moustache into shape – a bold, impertinent shape.

'No,' said Peachum hoarsely.

Coax had been told that Polly was in Switzerland, finishing her education. Peachum had already considered whether, in order to strengthen the illusion, he should not arrange for false picture postcards to be sent from Chamonix. But that was not advisable. Sooner or later the whole awful story would have to be confessed to Coax; although that would not be until every- thing was satisfactorily arranged.

Coax never forgot to inquire after Polly.

Peachum was to meet Coax and Hale next Monday in the baths. Coax now did all his business with the M.T.C. in Feather's Baths, and always on a Monday, irrespective of how much time might be lost thereby.

Half an hour before the time appointed with Peachum, Coax and Hale met there.

They undressed slowly, without the girls. Hale, a fat man in his forties, spoke:

'I was always against your affair with Evelyn, and you knew it, William. You have caused nothing but trouble between her and Ranch. I could tell you some fine stories about the terrible scenes she's had with Ranch, all because of you. Any psycho- logical worry upsets her for days. And I'm never happy when there's anything wrong with her. I'm fond of her. And then that hotel! You must have been mad! I wonder she didn't get nettle-rash! In a hotel like that where the sheets are changed every two hours and therefore bound to be damp! And above all the idea of a *hotel*! Evelyn is the most sensitive soul I know. Those sheets must have had a purely perverse fascination for her. And otherwise she is quite normal. That's one of the sweetest things about her. I can never forgive you for this; and by God, it's not the consequences I'm worrying about. But now I've got to humble myself and beg for £1,000 from these tradesmen. I hate doing that. What have my private affairs got to do with them? They can say with perfect right: We are doing business with you, we're not going to pay for washing your dirty linen. – I would much rather go now. After all, I am a Government official.'

Coax looked at him and said:

'Yes, after all you are a Government official.'

'I'd like to know how this Gawn got hold of your diary,' grumbled Hale, arranging his socks on a stool.

They climbed into the wooden tubs.

Hale was taking a mud bath. Coax had certain vitalizing herbs in his tub.

'*Just think,*' continued Hale sadly as he lay, '*think how closely we in office must observe the dictates of honesty. We may not take part in any other transactions. I will not speak of recent occurrences in the Admiralty. I prefer to leave Great Britain out of it. I know nothing about such things and, as an Englishman, I wish to know nothing about them. But look what Herr von Bismarck has done in Germany! He's a great man. He has already acquired vast estates, and his country has benefited by it. People don't always judge our statesmen rightly. They only see this action or that, and they criticize it. But what do they understand about such things? They say: Such and such a diplomatic action was wrong. But only because they go by the outward results. An absolutely ridiculous viewpoint! Do they know what the real purpose of the action was? When the German Kaiser telegraphed to President Kruger, do you know which stocks rose and which fell? No! Of course, only the communists ask that. But between ourselves, it is not only the communists; the diplomats want to know too. That's rather a blunt example, but the idea is very near the reality. The chief thing is*

158

to learn to think bluntly. Blunt thinking is great thinking. Politics is the pursuit of business by unbusiness-like methods. And for that very reason we must be careful that no stain falls on our personal honour. If this affair in the hotel comes out, I shall be hounded from the Admiralty with contumely and curses. No record of faithful service, however long, can survive such a suspicion. But after all, I am inherently honest and that makes it incompatible for me to associate with these tradesmen.'

At this point he was interrupted by Peachum's entry. The three gentlemen took a Turkish bath together.

They were lying on the couches to cool off, their heads resting on their damp towels, when Peachum began. He spoke softly, like a sick man; which indeed he was.

'Our transactions with you, Mr Hale, have not been remarkable for their success. Contrary to our expectations, you are not, we are informed, in a position to purchase our ships for the Government, which of course means an enormous loss for us.'

Hale growled something. He lay stretched at full length and kept patting himself on his spongy breast with his little fat hands.

Peachum went on, still speaking very softly and laboriously.

'We are only small business men. Our money has been hard earned. I hope you have tried everything?'

Peachum turned his face to the side and looked at the Secretary of State. The latter was now silent. He did not look particularly imposing. Coax had made a mistake in presenting him without any clothes. He looked like an obese, unintelligent middle-aged man, and not at all like a high Government official. And something about him caught the attention of the Beggar's Friend.

An almost imperceptible change was now apparent in Peachum's voice.

'We hear from Mr Coax that you have private troubles which are hindering you in your work? We much regret this. Would it be of help to your work if we removed the cause of these troubles?'

Hale growled something again. He would have liked to have looked at Coax. The interview was not proceeding along the lines they had anticipated.

'You probably know,' continued Peachum, 'that we have had bad luck in procuring transport-ships. The ones we have bought have subsequently proved to be not quite so satisfactory as their description led us to believe. We also hear that you fear unpleasantness on account of these ships. We can well imagine that private troubles make it more difficult for you to give your whole attention to these unpleasantnesses. At this point I must also mention something personal. I see in Mr Coax my future son-in-law.'

Coax turned round lazily. He looked at Peachum in mild astonishment. He suddenly remembered a moment in Peachum's shop when the latter had asked him how much he wanted to let him out of this transport business. At that time he had received a remarkable impression of Peachum which he had since forgotten.

Meanwhile Peachum had resumed his monologue.

'We shall *still* try', he said calmly, 'to use these old ships.'

The two other gentlemen remained silent. Peachum knew now what he had not known in Southampton. They had always intended to use the old ships!

Coax laughed harshly.

'I see,' he said, 'for the sake of a few thousand pounds you still want to palm off your old hulks on the Government?'

Now Peachum was silent.

'Is that the decision of the M.T.C.?' asked Coax with sudden brusqueness.

Peachum turned his head towards him.

'No,' he said. 'It is mine.'

A few minutes later Hale began to grumble about the fog. Peachum agreed with him. They went into the cubicles. Then, outside the baths, they arranged for another meeting. Coax had never uttered another word.

At last, after months of blind fumbling, Jonathan Jeremiah Peachum saw his way clearly.

When he began his conversation with the Secretary of State, he had, of course, never thought for a moment that he would be ready to grant concessions on quite unwarranted claims or that he could demand anything in return. It was only his long training as a business man who, in the course of years, had learned never to give away something for nothing, which had compelled him to try, if only for form's sake, to think of something which *he* could ask for in return. The humiliation of having to give away money for *nothing* had seemed intolerable to him. So the business man in him made him demand of his ruined brother, whose ruin he must at all costs prevent, that he should surrender his life insurance to him; or, to put it another way, he ordered a beggar to dig a hole in the garden for old bread crusts, which hole he immediately made the next beggar fill in. Hale's silence had then filled Peachum with boundless excitement. He suddenly saw.

But he saw only to suffer.

It was not the new Southampton ships, the ones which had brought him to the verge of ruin, that were to be delivered to the Government, but the old, unseaworthy ones. Coax and this miserable Hale were relentlessly squeezing out of the weak, sick, good-natured Marine Transport Company every penny that still remained in it. They would either buy or not buy the new ships, that had nothing to do with the Government; but whatever happened, the M.T.C. would have to pay for them. And all this had been planned from the very beginning!

That Coax had not initiated him into the plan, shocked him deeply. In all other ways Coax had treated him as his future father-in-law.

But now Peachum had nothing more to fear than that Coax might become impatient about Polly. But Coax showed no impatience.

When Peachum handed over to him the agreed sum of money for Hale, he nervously turned the conversation to the subject of his daughter. At first Coax was silent, then he said that he was not disposed to press Polly. He wanted to be loved for himself. There was no need for Peachum to worry either. However Miss Polly might feel towards him, he, Peachum, would always remain her father in his eyes. It was a pleasure to him that for once in his life, a life that had had many ugly sides to it, he could make a sacrifice for a deeper and purer cause.

Mr Coax belonged to the widespread genus *Spellbinder*.

Peachum listened with an impassive face and made up his

mind, for the thousandth time, to hurry on as quickly as possible the marriage between Coax and his daughter. It seemed to him that Coax's talk was too ethereal and his motives too beautiful to possess any lasting quality. And Coax had already said, in the presence of the Marine Transport Company, that he would not hesitate to take Mr Peachum's money.

After an exhaustive discussion in Old Oak Street, it was decided to make another attempt to free Polly. Perhaps it would be possible to arrange business difficulties for Mr MacHeath.

One day, in the middle of the great sales-campaign, Mac-Heath was informed that large crowds of beggars had suddenly collected in and in front of his shops. They were rummaging through the goods and were not sparing their criticisms. With loud complaints they were turning everything upside-down. They stood in twos and threes in front of the doors of the shops and talked loudly to one another about the junk that was being sold inside. Since the customers, in order to get into the shops, had to push their way between these beggars, and since the latter were uncommonly dirty, a great many purchasers simply turned away to go elsewhere. MacHeath recognized the minions of his father-in-law in front of several of his shops. At first he contemplated calling in the police. But then he thought of a better way. On the next Friday, when the crowds were at their thickest, he made his shopkeepers hang hand-painted notices in their windows. These notices said:

EVEN BEGGARS CAN BUY FIRST-CLASS GOODS HERE

The affair got into the newspapers and the B. shops were more popular than ever.

Mr Peachum had once more suffered defeat.

But though his son-in-law saw many difficulties ahead of him, he saw one too few. Mr Peachum's expensive meeting in Feather's Baths with a high official in the Admiralty was to have a far-reaching effect on Mr MacHeath's ambitious schemes. From now on there was one picture incessantly before Mr Peachum's eyes. The picture of three decaying ships, full of soldiers, sailing along on the high seas. A horrid business!

MacHeath divided his time between O'Hara and Fanny Chrysler. He usually met the former in a barber's saloon, together with two other people from Lower Blacksmith Square, Father and Grooch, old burglars. They planned the more important burglaries in a nearby public house.

MacHeath still had good ideas and he was unequalled as an organizer, but the conferences with Fanny Chrysler in the offices of the C.P.B. gave him a far greater spiritual satisfaction. The purchasing of the stocks of bankrupt shops demanded no less ingenuity and was, taken all in all, more profitable.

He would have felt like a fish in water with this business, had there not been the contract with Aaron hanging round his neck like a mill-stone.

Several intimate conversations between MacHeath, Fanny Chrysler, and O'Hara in the conference room of the C.P.B. ended in ominous silence.

A cautious beginning had already been made with the introduction of C.P.B. goods into Aaron's shops. The salaried buyers were electrified by O'Hara into a state of feverish activity. But it was already apparent that, although the C.P.B. had been an almost inexhaustible source of supply for the B. shops, it was not nearly potent enough to deal with the sudden immense increase in deliveries required simultaneously by the sales week and by the arrival on the scene of Aaron's chain stores.

After a very short time the supplies of marketable goods began to dwindle.

For several days MacHeath went around more depressed than ever. He had a horrible fear that he might have to admit to Messrs Aaron and Opper that the imminent and decisive battle against Chreston's could not take place. Then he suddenly thought of an unusually dangerous plan.

Every night he pondered in bed for many hours about his perilous position. He could see and think more clearly when he heard Polly's calm, untroubled breathing at his side. His boldest decisions were made then.

One morning, without telling Fanny or O'Hara, he went to Aaron and spoke to him as follows.

'We must not allow everything to depend on our sales week. We must try to take the wind out of Chreston's sails before he has even started on his campaign. It would be best if we began to lower our prices already. The C.P.B. can just as well deliver the goods now as later. But Chreston's cheap goods are not yet ready.'

Aaron gazed at him dreamily. There was something about MacHeath that he did not like. For a robber he was rather too respectable, for an honest citizen he was obviously too dishonest. Also he had too few hairs on his radish head. Aaron was influenced by such trifles.

But he agreed nevertheless. During the last few days his wife had gone shopping with Mrs MacHeath and she had nothing but good to say about the newly married couple. By this means Aaron learned that they had been economizing. MacHeath kept the household accounts. In his view, it was the extra penny that counted in the end.

Moreover MacHeath found a supporter in the elder of the two Oppers. The latter had taken a personal interest in the reorganization of the house of Aaron and its policy. He was obsessed with the idea of a Greek contest and unselfishly praised MacHeath as the originator of the idea. The sales staff now had a share in the profits and so took just as much interest in the business as the owner of the shops. The contest flourished.

Advertisements multiplied like rabbits. The shops were plentifully supplied; the number and variations of goods increased enormously. Even the tiny cellars of the B. shops were filled to the ceilings. The public bought one thing and saw another equally desirable. It took away all it could carry, fascinated by the low prices. Gigantic inscriptions, written in coloured chalks on brown paper, informed the public that this was their one and only and never-to-be-repeated opportunity to buy superfluous things. The purchasers crept out of the shops like thieves, filled with a secret fear that the shopkeeper might suddenly notice that he had charged pennies instead of shillings.

MacHeath was frantically busy. He went from one shop to another and helped the owners with good advice and with ticketing the goods. But his chief occupation was the procuring of immense quantities of the cheapest wares, some even coming from Denmark, Holland, and France. His Central Purchasing Board under O'Hara was working night and day.

One or two consignments were recognized as being the proceeds of burglaries. Information was laid against a B. shop in Mulberry Street whose owner was a woman called Mary Sawyer. The suspected goods had been denounced by beggars.

MacHeath withdrew the articles in question, handed them over to the police as coming from other shops, and had a few of the lesser burglars arrested.

Nevertheless MacHeath remained for a time in a considerable state of disquietude. He suspected that his father-in-law had not yet spoken his last word. Up till now he had only lacked the opportunity.

'Your father's hatred for me', said MacHeath to Polly, 'is unnatural. His dependence on this Coax must have increased again. He never stops persecuting me. I have an unpleasant feeling when I think of him. I thought he would one day come down to reality. After all, I only earn a bare subsistence for us two.'

In the stormy developments which soon overtook his business, he completely forgot this worry.

Aaron's stores and the B. shops announced in the leading dailies that they gave a rebate to all relatives of soldiers in active service. Also that they gave special preference to war-widows when considering the applications for new B. shops. This step received great applause.

The prices were forced down by every possible means.

Chreston's chain shops soon began to feel the ruinous competition, and they too found themselves compelled to lower their prices. The National Credit Bank made astonishing exertions. All night long Miller and Hawthorne sat with Chreston, poring over the books. The campaign was swallowing up enormous sums of money. The One and a Half Centuries scarcely dared look each other in the eyes. They felt their responsibility very strongly.

To spur them on to the utmost, MacHeath got into touch with them again through intermediaries. They were to conclude from this move that the Commercial Bank, together with

Aaron's stores and the B. shops, were slowly collapsing, and that the Brothers Opper were unobtrusively trying to get in with Chreston's.

They did draw these conclusions and lowered the prices of their goods still further.

As a result of this, Aaron and MacHeath, too, had to reduce their prices again. And at this stage the two concerns were on the verge of their great sales weeks!

The public had long since realized that this was a battle to the death between Aaron and Chreston. It also realized that it could now buy cheaply. Some bold housewives had already begun to buy, but the great majority were waiting for still lower prices. They wandered greedily through the shops, comparing the prices.

Aaron had already started on the preliminary work for the new scaled prices. In doing this, he came to realize the worth of his companion. Whenever he saw MacHeath's radish head he doubted whether this man could write even a short letter without a misspelt word; but there was no doubt that he could reckon up money. It was soon to become apparent that he could do more.

The C.P.B. was now preparing for the great sales week which was to eclipse everything previously attempted. Without a pause, Aaron's chain shops swallowed up the great consignments of the C.P.B. as fast as they could be delivered, and scarcely said thank you for them. The profits were certainly not very large, for the prices were already below an economic level. But the whole scheme was really only a means of eliminating competition. For the great sales week Aaron relied completely on the wonderful C.P.B. They seemed to have an unlimited capacity.

Unforunately they had nothing of the sort.

When the stocks in the warehouses began dwindling more and more, MacHeath had a severe nervous breakdown in Fanny's shop. He screamed, weeping, that he was being ruined, that he had fallen among brigands. He was doing what he could, but they wanted the skin off his back. He couldn't endure this living on a volcano any longer. They couldn't expect more from him than one man could endure.

The immediate result of this seizure was a conversation with Jacques Opper in which the great sales week was likened to an Olympic, and Henry Opper agreed to an advertising appropriation of fantastic proportions.

Fanny made cold compresses and rubbed Mac's chest with arnica. He cried half the night through and accused her, too, of regarding him as a prize fighter who was to ruin his health for her sake.

Like many great men he shrank from his decisions when it came to carrying them out. Even Napoleon fell unconscious at the moment when his long-planned empire became a reality.

This mood alternated with other moods.

Sometimes he was in a better temper and took Fanny out to smart restaurants in Soho where he laughed with her over the faces Aaron and the Oppers would make if his *great* plan were a success.

Fanny laughed too, but she did not know what he meant by the great plan. He had told no one of his intentions, not even her.

But usually his darker moods predominated. O'Hara's people began to take advantage of the situation and make demands.

One day in September MacHeath was summoned to Lower Blacksmith Square by a messenger of O'Hara's.

That was most irregular. MacHeath never appeared in the warehouses in Lower Blacksmith Square. Of the whole gang, only O'Hara, Father, and Grooch knew him as the erstwhile Mr Beckett.

Nevertheless MacHeath drove down there. Something unusual must have occurred. He met O'Hara in the barber's shop.

They said nothing and went into a neighbouring public house.

O'Hara apologized for the summons and explained that he wanted to speak to MacHeath without Mrs Chrysler knowing anything about it. All sorts of extraordinary things had been happening in the gang, and Fanny played a dark role in these occurrences.

The gang was dissatisfied with the new arrangements. The fixed salaries were too low for them. He, O'Hara, had immediately taken steps in the matter, but Fanny had opposed him wherever she could and had thwarted all his measures. Probably she was working together with Grooch, who was certainly helping her to incite the gang to mutiny. He was also living with her again in Lambeth.

MacHeath was very upset. He had considered Fanny absolutely faithful.

Now, according to O'Hara, she had been compensating the reductions in wages, which had been introduced since the beginning of the campaign against Chreston's, by paying percentages from the C.P.B. But that had not satisfied the gang. During the last week they had not been working as well as usual. Various acts of sabotage had taken place and several members had not turned up to work. O'Hara asked whether the B. shops had not been complaining about the decrease in deliveries.

MacHeath had heard nothing about complaints. On the contrary, the B. shop people seemed very optimistic.

'Then she's buying the goods somewhere else,' said O'Hara excitedly. 'And she's told you nothing about what's been happening down here?'

MacHeath dabbled his fingers in a puddle of beer on the table and glanced sideways at O'Hara out of his watery eyes. He ordered some strong cigars and sent the young man off to Ride Lane where the gang, so he said, were at the moment having a meeting.

O'Hara knew nothing about the regular buying of the C.P.B. In MacHeath's opinion it had nothing to do with him whether the C.P.B. was procuring goods with invoices.

When O'Hara came back, he reported that there was nothing to be done. The gang had told him that Mrs Chrysler knew their demands.

He complained, for the hundredth time, that MacHeath had taken away all his authority when he gave up surrendering recalcitrant members to the police.

They drove together to Waterloo Bridge, but Fanny's shop was already shut. They found her in Lambeth. Grooch was with her.

An excited quarrel arose during which MacHeath again kept silence. Then, with an oblique glance at Grooch, whom he had greeted very coldly, he went into the next room and rummaged through the drawers of an Empire desk until he found a cigarette-box. This gave an impression of great familiarity with the house and seemed to embarrass Fanny somewhat.

It finally appeared that Fanny really did consider the demands of the gang reasonable. They wanted to change their status again. It was to be as before; they would work at their own risk and receive payment for the goods.

'The wages have been depressed too much,' concluded Fanny, 'that's the only trouble.'

'It's only for a short time,' argued MacHeath, 'the goods must be cheap now. When Chreston is out of the running, we can put the prices and the wages up again.'

O'Hara banged his fist on the table.

'They're taking advantage of the situation. That's what it is!'

'One can't explain the campaign against Chreston to them,' persisted Fanny. 'Besides, that has nothing to do with them. They don't know what they are working for and they're not told when the job will be over.'

'It's not nice,' said MacHeath, apparently lost in thought. 'First they wanted fixed salaries, like officials, now they want an independent income again. That's no way to show the mutual attachment between a leader and his followers. They are always changing from one side to another. Yesterday fixed salaries, today profit-sharing. That leads to no good. That's not sticking together through good times and bad.'

'Don't keep talking about sticking together through good times and bad, Mac!' said Fanny angrily. 'It's too likely to be your good times and their bad.'

'But there may be bad times coming,' argued MacHeath, 'and who will have to bear the responsibility then?'

'They'll bear the responsibility themselves. Don't let your finer feelings run away with you!'

'All right,' said MacHeath with sudden abruptness. 'They can have what they want. Tell them they have you to thank for it, Fanny.'

And he stood up.

Fanny looked at him searchingly.

'So they can work on their own again?'

'Yes. But I shall do the ordering.'

He took O'Hara's and Grooch's hats from their pegs on the hat-stand and handed them to them with an absent glance. Grooch seemed somewhat astonished.

'I've got something else to discuss with you,' said MacHeath to Fanny carelessly, and the two men went out disgruntled.

Fanny took them downstairs. When she came back again MacHeath was standing by the window with an indefinite expression on his face. He had pushed the curtains aside and was looking down on the street.

'Grooch may come back again to see if the lights are still on,' he said calmly. 'We'd better go into the bedroom.'

He went on ahead. The bedroom was next to the sitting-room and also looked on to the street. MacHeath waited until Fanny was inside and then turned out the light in the sitting-room.

'One light in here will be enough,' he said. 'You'll have to economize now. The percentages that went to the gang will be deducted from your salary.'

He sat down on the bed and pointed to a chintz-covered armchair. Fanny sat down with an injured air. She was plainly uneasy. He was not in the habit of displaying his rights of ownership so brutally.

'Are you jealous?' he asked suddenly.

She looked at him in amazement. Then she laughed.

'I was going to ask you that, Mac. You are funny.'

'Then tell me what you know about the plan,' he growled angrily. 'Everything!'

She was rather astonished, for she knew nothing at all about his plan. She was simply interested in seeing that the work people were treated properly. She was not out to make trouble. Her standpoint was, live and let live. Perhaps she took this standpoint because Grooch belonged to the gang.

When he began to explain his plan to her, she was genuinely astonished.

He now believed her assertion that she had known nothing, but he was in full spate and explained the whole scheme to her. She could listen better than anyone else he knew.

There were all sorts of weak points in the position of Chreston and the National Credit Bank. And here he saw enormous possibilities. One of the chief clients of the One and a Half Centuries was still Mr Peachum, and Mr Peachum was still his father-in-law. But first he wanted to 'come into the open' with his allies, Aaron and the Commercial Bank.

'I cannot fight side by side with him as whole-heartedly and relentlessly as I would like, as long as I have the feeling that he has defrauded me. That feeling stands between us. As soon as I have given him a lesson, it will be easier for us to come to a proper understanding.'

He was proposing to cut off, in the near future, all supplies to Aaron's stores and also to his own B. shops. By this manoeuvre he hoped to corner Aaron and the Commercial Bank in a desperate situation, so that, just before they had Chreston on his knees with 'the bit, so to speak, half in his mouth', they would run short of supplies for the carrying on of the struggle and would therefore realize how deeply they were in his power. The C.P.B. could then renew the contracts and dictate fresh terms. Aaron would not wish to be left with empty warehouses in the middle of the contest and immediately before the great sales week. But if Aaron agreed to pay other, more reasonable prices, the questionable methods of buying could then be dispensed with. For that reason the new arrangement with O'Hara's people was a completely unhoped for stroke of luck. In certain circumstances such a scheme was highly desirable.

'I must found a family,' he said simply. 'I have reached the age when a man ought to have a banking account.'

During his speech he had become jovial and stumped aggressively up and down the room, puffing at his cigar.

In the excitement of telling her everything, he had forgotten his anger against Grooch. He had thought that she must have guessed something of his plan when she demanded the independence of the gang.

Now she was so enthusiastic that he had difficulty in getting away. Only on the way back to Nunhead did he remember Grooch and the fact that he was living with Fanny again. He made up his mind that, in spite of everything, he would treat Fanny a little coldly. Besides, she was getting too independent for his liking.

A few days later, a meeting of the C.P.B. took place in Mac-Heath's presence.

MacHeath opened the proceedings by inviting the gentlemen to help themselves to cigars. Whisky and soda stood on a side table, for the meeting would probably be an exhausting one.

Then, rolling a new cigar in his mouth and not without a certain evident pleasure, he laid on the green-topped table the dispositions drawn up by him and the great Aaron for the forthcoming sales week. They were extremely comprehensive and complete to the last detail.

'We have worked for four days on these. Last Sunday I submitted them at Warborn Castle. Jacques Opper said that they would make an Olympiad to be remembered in London business circles for many years to come.'

MacHeath spoke slowly and clearly. He leaned back in his presidential chair and asked Fanny whether the C.P.B. could procure the necessary quantity of goods in time. The figures which he mentioned were colossal.

Fanny smiled and turned towards Bloomsbury who understood nothing of the proceedings and was looking at the two solicitors with an expression of inane embarrassment. Then she said:

'Impossible. We are at the end of our supplies. At the most, we could deliver a third of what you ask. The campaign has been begun too soon.'

'That's bad,' said MacHeath and looked at the ceiling.

'We could still deliver a third,' suggested Fanny boldly.

'That's no suggestion to make as a contribution to a gigantic plan, about which Jacques Opper says there can never have been anything like it since the Greek Olympic contests,' answered MacHeath profoundly. 'A third! I believe in a person fulfilling his obligations completely or not at all. I mean real obligations in the legal sense, not only moral obligations towards friends, such as we have here of course.'

'We have done everything possible,' said Fanny shortly.

'Bad,' said MacHeath and looked at the ceiling.

'Why don't you say what you mean?' said one of the lawyers,

a man by the name of Rigger who was not so amused as Mac-
Heath by this little comedy. 'So you want to leave Aaron in the
lurch?'

'What do you mean: I want to? I must! After all, it affects
my B. shops too,' said MacHeath sourly. 'They'll be hard hit.
I can't make an exception for them. Chreston will have his sales
week and we shan't, that's bad enough. But we can't do anything about it. It was not for nothing that I advised you to
help yourselves to whisky. We have come to an end and we
shall be lucky if the C.P.B. survives the crisis. Let us get down
to facts. It would be best to avoid telling Aaron openly. The
flow of goods must gradually decrease. That can be arranged.
If we can't organize the supply efficiently, we can at least
organize the stoppage. And one thing more, gentlemen. Never
forget: the sick man dies and the strong man fights. That's
life.'

'Come down to business,' interrupted Rigger abruptly. He
had nothing to say, but he was not very pleased with the whole
affair.

MacHeath had not yet finished.

'It will be a hard trial for our friends in the B. shops,' he
continued slowly, taking his cigar in his left hand so that he
could grasp a pencil in his right, 'but unfortunately it is not
within our power to help them. Many of them are backward
with their rents and payments and now we need every penny
of our money. They must think of repayment. We helped them
when we gave them credit, now they must help us by paying us
back; that's only right. We need reserves to tide over the hard
times ahead. You must remember that they would all be ruined
if we collapsed.'

Now even Fanny was horrified. She had not thought that
that would be necessary. What did Mac want reserves for? How
would he gain if his shops went bankrupt? Aaron would totter
but survive; Chreston, the enemy, would triumph brilliantly,
even if only for a time, as Mac hoped. But the small shops
would die off like mayflies.

MacHeath was already hard at work. He was scribbling on
every piece of paper within reach. O'Hara was in his element.

The five of them arranged precisely how the stream of goods

to the shops was to dry up, and MacHeath insisted that the B. shops were to be kept short exactly the same as Aaron's stores. He could not afford to give Aaron, and with him the Commercial Bank, any just grounds for complaint.

The carrying out of this decision was put in hand immediately. In the middle of the sales campaign the supply of goods began to fail.

In his blind trust in the inexhaustibility of the C.P.B. Aaron had neglected to draw up new and explicit contracts, imposing penalties in the case of non-delivery. Aaron and his bank were thrown into a state of confusion and inquired first of all whether the B. shops were better supplied. They learned that the latter were just as hungry for goods as themselves.

Actually the B. shop owners were already storming the offices of the C.P.B. where Mrs Chrysler, friendly as ever, comforted them from day to day.

On their return home they found letters from Mr MacHeath, politely requesting them to pay their arrears.

MacHeath, summoned by the gentlemen of the Commercial Bank to their office, confessed himself helplessly and painfully astonished.

He took a cigar from his case, then shook his head and put it back again as though he had lost all pleasure in smoking. Then he said:

'I am deeply disappointed. My shops are in desperate straits. The poor people have gone to great trouble in making the announcements. For the most part they have painted the placards themselves. And now their shops are as empty as mouse-holes. Full of people and empty of goods! And just before the end of October when the rents fall due! And in addition to all that, they have engaged assistants for the sale. But I won't speak of that. After all, those are only *material* losses. I am far harder hit by the other side of this tragedy. Bloomsbury was a personal friend of mine. He ought never to have treated me like this. I regard the whole thing, not as a business catastrophe, but as a moral one.'

MacHeath carried off this attitude with determination and success. He in no wise avoided his friends in the B. shops. On the contrary, he visited them exactly as before. With a serious face, he explained why he had to collect his money. He sat in the little back rooms and perched the children on his knees and did his best to infuse the desperate shopkeepers with something of his own confidence and optimism.

He talked with the women about their troubles and pointed out to them how there were always new ways of economizing. He dealt with the men separately.

'This business has hit me hard, but I don't show it,' he said. 'You must be a comfort to your wife in these difficult times.'

Thus he proved himself a born leader and proved also that a man can say anything as long as he has unshakeable determination. He knew these people. The dark looks which they gave him at first did not frighten him. They must hold out now and be strong. 'Only the strong survive,' he said, meeting their wavering eyes with a piercing glance. It was a long time before they forgot that glance.

As history shows, it is just this class of people who regard it as only right that the strong should triumph over the weak.

During this time MacHeath spoke to Polly in the same tenor. He demanded the utmost economy from her. He wished to starve with his people, he told her seriously. He bought cheaper cigars and smoked less. He even cancelled one of his daily papers.

'Keep faith!' he said. 'I expect much from them – everything. As the Spartan mother said to her son when he went out to battle: Either with your shield or on your shield; so I say to my friends in the B. shops: Either with your signs or on your signs! But then I too must keep faith with them in these dark hours. Now you see the reason why I am cutting down your house-keeping money!'

He tried to explain himself to Jacques Opper. But Opper was strangely abrupt. He said drily that he classed those who had no luck with those who had no intelligence. Pity for the vanquished was only a sign of weakness.

MacHeath found Greek philosophy rather too inhuman for his taste.

MacHeath still had large quantities of linen and wool in his warehouses. Shortly before the decision of the C.P.B. to cut off the flow of goods to the shops, several consignments of linen, the results of a burglary in a textile factory in Lancashire, had been received. He did not know what to do with them.

The papers were again writing a great deal about the war in South Africa.

Not only in London were desperate battles taking place, but also in South Africa. And not only because of the conflict of interests in London were the poorer classes in distress – think of the Tom Smiths and the Mary Sawyers of the B. shops – but also because of the conflict of interests in South Africa.

Something must be done to help in that direction.

Welfare committees were formed. The women of the upper classes sprang into the breach. Old and young competed. In aristocratic houses and exclusive schools well-bred hands tore up linen rags into bandages for the wounded. And shirts, too, were made for the brave soldiers, and stockings knitted. The word *sacrifice* took on a new meaning.

MacHeath sent Polly to one of these committees. He saw a good market for his linen – and for his wool.

Polly spent her afternoons in improvised sewing-rooms, where the ladies sewed shirts over a cup of tea. They all had serious faces and the conversations were pregnant with the theme of *sacrifice*.

'They will be glad to get such beautiful white shirts,' said the ladies.

Smoothing the seams flat with their thumb-nails, they spoke of England's greatness.

The older the ladies were, the more blood-thirsty their natures.

'We're much too merciful with those brutes who shoot our brave men down in ambushes,' said an aristocratic old lady sitting beside Polly. 'We ought simply to attack them and shoot them all, so that they know what it means to quarrel with England. They aren't men at all! They're wild beasts! Have you heard how they're poisoning the wells? Our people are the only ones that fight fairly, but they oughtn't to when it comes to dealing with such riff-raff. Don't you think so, my dear?'

'I'm told,' sighed a still older lady with enormous gold-rimmed spectacles, 'that our men advance under fire with unheard-of gallantry. They march through a hail of bullets just as though they were going across a parade ground. It's all the same to them whether they fall or not. One newspaper correspondent made inquiries. They all said the same thing: Nothing matters to us as long as England remembers us with pride.'

'They are only doing their duty,' said the first sternly. 'Are we doing ours?'

And they sewed faster.

Two young girls began to giggle. They got very red in the face and tried not to look at one another, otherwise they would have burst out again. Their mothers angrily signalled them to be quiet.

Another girl, aged about twenty, said calmly:

'When one reads in the papers what's happening out there and then thinks of the handsome young men in their soldiers' uniforms, it makes one sad.'

The two young girls burst out laughing. But not for a moment did they give up the fight against their lower natures; they gulped furiously, made deadly earnest faces while their bodies were shaking with laughter, and completely doubled up in their efforts to keep serious.

A young lady came to their assistance.

'Do you know,' she said, beginning a new conversation, 'when I see our brave men in their sweat-soiled, threadbare tunics and when I think of the dangers and hardships they have been through, I could kiss them, just as they are, all perspiring and unwashed and covered with blood. I could really.'

Polly threw a fleeting glance at her.

'How right my father is,' she thought as she bent her round face still lower over her sewing. 'After a victory one must send out mutilated, dirty, miserable soldiers begging; but after a defeat they must be smart and clean and spruce. That's the whole art.'

The conversation turned to the subject of comforts for the soldiers.

The ladies were sending out packets of cigarettes and tobacco, chocolate, and little notes of encouragement, all tied up in pink and mauve ribbons.

'You get more tobacco for a shilling at Aaron's in Miller Street,' said one of the girls brightly. 'It's not perhaps quite so good, but then they want quantity rather than quality, they all say that.'

The soldiers thanked their benefactresses in letters which the girls passed round. The letters had the sweetest spelling mistakes and were much treasured.

'It's a pity we can't send the shirts and socks ourselves with our little notes,' said the girl who shopped in Miller Street. 'That would be much more fun.'

Suddenly the old lady with the glasses turned to Polly and said in a voice trembling with rage:

'When I think that this clean English linen will soon perhaps be stained with the blood of a British soldier, I could kill such murderers with my own hands.'

Polly stared at the old woman in horror. Her withered hand, clutching a needle, quivered in mid-air and her lower jaw hung open in a blood-thirsty grimace.

Polly suddenly felt sick and had to go out.

There was momentary consternation among the ladies.

'She's in a blessed condition,' they whispered one to another.

When Polly came back into the room again, still a little pale, and sat down silently among the chorus of stitching bloodsuckers, a woman with great, soft cow's eyes, said:

'I hope it will be a boy. England needs men!'

Then the conversation turned to other questions. A fat woman in a flowered silk dress, whose husband, as everyone knew, was an admiral, began to speak:

'The behaviour of our lower classes is really wonderful. I am on another committee where we tear bandages. You should come and see it. We have such a charming lot of people. Well, last Thursday quite a simple woman came in. One could see straight away that she was one of the working classes. And she brought in a clean and very patched shirt. "My husband has two more," she said, "and I've read there are a terrible lot of wounded out there." When I told that to my husband, he said: "That's a true British mother! There's many a duchess who could learn something from her!"'

She looked round proudly.

'Each in his place and each according to his means,' said the aristocratic old lady beside Polly sententiously.

Polly was able to inform her husband that she had received a whole heap of invitations to smart houses. He was very pleased that he had disposed of his stocks, and he encouraged her to persevere industriously at her great welfare work for the British soldiers.

Mr X

Whenever he met Messrs Aaron and Opper, MacHeath complained of the faithlessness of his one-time friend Bloomsbury; but he had the feeling that he ought to emphasize still more strongly his absolute dependence on the Central Purchasing Board. The suspicions of the Commercial Bank were especially difficult to allay. By the manoeuvre of stopping supplies, the bank had been delivered wholly into the hands of the C.P.B., and the firm's hands must under no circumstances be identified with those of Mr MacHeath.

So he summoned a second and strictly confidential meeting of the C.P.B. He was entered in the minutes as Mr X. He drew up a skilfully worded, legally watertight letter to Mr MacHeath, Nunhead, in which the C.P.B. politely and firmly pointed out that the original agreement between them stipulated prices which were only intended for temporary advertisement. The resources of the C.P.B. were, at the moment, somewhat exhausted, but as soon as possible they would resume deliveries in greater quantities. Contingent, of course, on a basis of new prices.

Then, to everybody's astonishment, just as the business was finished and it was getting on towards nine o'clock, Bloomsbury stood up, and asked in a stuttering voice whether this measure would not harm the B. shop owners.

Bloomsbury's objection was totally unexpected.

It was a still evening. They were all sitting quietly round the heavy table. The windows were open because it was warm and they could see the green of the chestnut-trees across the road shining dully in the gas-light.

MacHeath immediately put his cigar down and delivered a short address, principally directed at his friend Bloomsbury, in which he emphasized the fact that this measure naturally meant for the B. shop owners a short period of self-denial, but all business, and indeed all mortal success, depended on the ability to make sacrifices at the right time. The sick man dies and the strong man fights. It always had been and always would be so. The B. shop owners must now show *what they were made of*. He also recommended Fanny Chrysler to note exactly who collapsed and who survived. He added that O'Hara, too, was having to face this *vital question*.

He, for his part, would take full responsibility. Every B. shop owner whom Fanny turned on to the streets, was turned on to the streets by *him*. A man who did not believe in him, could not work with him.

But then Fanny stood up, without looking at MacHeath, and drily related a few facts about the distressed conditions of the B. shop owners. What was happening to them was nothing less than cold-blooded murder. The majority of them couldn't last out another month. They were asking themselves and each other whether the company could be held responsible if the B. shops went bankrupt.

She finished with the words:

'If we cannot decide on some relief measures here and now, catastrophe will be inevitable.'

MacHeath said quite coolly and with apparent astonishment: Firstly, at the very worst it would only be the B. shop owners that went bankrupt and not the B. shops, which was a very different thing; and secondly, the Company was not in a position to start supporting widows and orphans. Besides, he took the viewpoint: Let fall what is falling – and further, what is falling should be given a push.

With that the meeting ended. It was a Saturday evening. The date was the 20th of September.

O'Hara went away angrily. He always grew angry at Mac's

love of posing. Why, just because of this Bloomsbury, should he behave as though he believed his own words?

But not even when they were talking among themselves did Mac let the mask fall. He hated cynical talk and discussed the most doubtful subjects in a completely dispassionate voice. O'Hara's sense of decency was deeply offended by this behaviour.

But he did everything exactly as agreed and he stood up like a man to the buyers and told them that they were to take another few weeks' holiday, this time at their own expense. The flow of goods now dried up completely. And the letter from the C.P.B., which MacHeath handed to the Commercial Bank without a word, made a very strong impression.

Within a few days the poorer owners of the B. shops were reduced to a state of utter desperation. They were all in debt to their landlords and they also owed money in other directions, partly for their stocks and partly for their household expenses. Quite recently half a dozen new B. shops had opened and they had hardly had time to get properly started. Now they naturally believed that they had been betrayed to the big chain stores. Their confusion was complete.

From this time on, Mr Peachum's employees were continually coming across B. shop owners or their relatives who were trying to beg in the streets.

Since they had been turned out of their houses by the agents of Mr MacHeath, their *independence* had been increased. In fact, their *independence* had grown to absolutely intolerable proportions, for they had not even a roof over their heads. By their *own ability* they had reduced their weight to eight stone.

Peachum had no use for them, for it would take at least two months until they lost their *pride*.

Aaron and the Oppers were faced with a problem. At first their attitude towards Bloomsbury had been very violent, but just before the sales week it became unusually mild. Aaron's shops had become as accustomed to the C.P.B.'s cheap goods as a drug-addict to cocaine. They *had* to have them.

MacHeath was not at the Commercial when Bloomsbury called there. He adhered strictly to his assertion to Aaron that he had completely broken with Bloomsbury and had not entered the offices of the C.P.B. for several weeks. Aaron and the two Oppers, who, by the way, no longer seemed as friendly with Aaron as they had been some time ago, made a great fuss of Bloomsbury, who sat with a fat Corona in his mouth and thought of Jenny and promised to do everything possible to smooth over the 'differences' between them. They decided not to postpone the Great Sales week. Bloomsbury held out hopes that the C.P.B. would soon be ready to recommence deliveries. They all parted with cordial hand-shakes. Each side had the feeling of having contributed towards a mutual *rapprochement*. Higher prices had also been mentioned.

Moreover Jacques Opper even invited MacHeath to another week-end at Warborn Castle.

This time MacHeath took Polly with him. Fanny had to use all her powers of persuasion to keep Polly's wardrobe within the limits of mediocrity. MacHeath wanted to deck her out like a duchess; and that would have been worse than Bloomsbury's plan of taking Jenny with him. Mrs Opper received Polly most charmingly.

Polly spoke neither too much nor too little. But she was surprised that the Oppers smacked their lips so loudly when they ate. With Jacques Opper she had her usual success which she always had with gentlemen of that age.

When Jacques Opper and MacHeath were walking round the park, the banker pointed to the ancient gnarled oaks, each growing in solitary dignity, and he said:

'Look at those, my dear MacHeath. They stand alone, far apart from each other. They are lucky, eh? Do you know, I like people who are lucky. Those trees are lucky. No one says about them that they couldn't help the gardeners planting them carefully. They look magnificent.'

MacHeath walked beside him in silence and made up his mind to be lucky.

Unfortunately there came a discordant note into this peaceful scene. MacHeath received an urgent message from Brown to the effect that the latter could no longer delay the execution of a warrant for the arrest of his friend. On asking why he was to be arrested, MacHeath received the answer: For being suspected of the murder of the B. shopkeeper, Mary Sawyer.

10

My fine gentlemen, today you may see me wash the glasses
And see me make the beds each morning.
And I thank you for your penny and you think I'm pleased as hell
For you only see my ragged frock and this dirty old hotel
And there's no one to give you a warning.
But one fine night there'll be yelling in the harbour
And they'll ask: Who is making all the row?
And they'll see me smiling as I wash my glasses
And they'll say: What's she smiling at, now?
 And a ship with eight sails
 And with fifty big cannon
 Will be moored to the quay.

Someone'll say: Go and dry your glasses, child.
He'll give me a penny, like the rest.
And the penny will be taken
And the bed be made, all right,
But nobody's going to sleep in it that night
And who I really am they still won't have guessed.
And that evening there'll be a din in the harbour
And they'll ask: What is making all that din?
And they'll see me standing watching at the window
And say: Why has she got that nasty grin?
 And the ship with eight sails
 And with fifty big cannon,
 Will shoot at the town.

My fine gentlemen, that'll wipe the smile off your faces,
For the walls will open gaping wide
And the town will tumble down flat to the ground
But a dirty old hotel will stay standing safe and sound
And they'll ask: What big swell lives inside?
All night long there'll be a yelling round about that hotel
And they'll ask: Why is it treated with such care?
And then they'll see me stepping from the door in the morning
And they'll say: What! Did she live there?
 And the ship with eight sails
 And with fifty big cannon
 Will beflag her masts.

And at midday there'll be coming a hundred men on land
And the hunt in dark corners will begin
And they'll enter every house, take every soul they see
And throw them into irons and bring them straight to me
And ask: Which of these shall we do in?
And that midday it will be quiet down by the harbour
When they ask who has got to die.
And then they'll hear me answer: All of them!
And as the heads fall I shall cry: Hoppla!
    And the ship with eight sails
    And with fifty big cannon
    Will vanish with me.

                     (DREAMS OF A KITCHEN-MAID)

Once Again September the 20th

MARY SAWYER'S B. shop was in Mulberry Street, near Waterloo Bridge. Whenever Fewkoombey went to visit her, he found her, like most of the B. shop owners, living with her two children in a tiny room behind the shop. The shop itself was somewhat larger than most, and was divided by a curtain into two parts. In the front part, facing the street entrance, ran the counter; behind the curtain sat two half-grown girls, sewing by gas-light. The living room received its light from a tiny window looking into a back-yard. This amount of light was not sufficient for the workroom, although, for the sake of warmth, the door between the two rooms was always left open.

Things were not going well with Mary. Her husband in Mafeking was sending her practically nothing. He had already been married once before, and therefore she only received half his pay.

The shop was considerably in debt. Mac's cheque had not lasted very long. Mary was also rather slovenly and knew very little about running a business. She scarcely paid the sewing-girls anything, but then the profits on their work were not worth much. And Mary was too anxious to please, for she always gave them something to eat whenever they took out their slices of bread and margarine, and they chewed for hours while they

184

worked. Mary always wanted to please people and be admired for her generosity. She even lent money.

Across her shop window was pasted a strip of paper; on it was written: THIS SHOP IS RUN BY A SOLDIER'S WIFE. She liked telling the customers about her husband in Mafeking and she showed them strategical sketches, cut out of *The Times*, which explained the position of the beleaguered town. She looked very pretty behind her counter, but the unfortunate thing was that now she had opened an underwear department her wares were mostly bought by women and not by men. Otherwise, perhaps, she would have done better business. But then she ought never to have given a customer two pairs of combinations instead of one because she forgot or because she was indifferent. That sort of thing undermines a customer's confidence.

Fewkoombey came several times in the evenings, when the shop was shut, and sat and watched her clear up after the children had been put to bed.

She told him that the announcement in the window had caused her a great deal of unpleasantness. The neighbouring shops had complained of unfair competition. They said that the fact that her husband was a soldier had nothing to do with the disgracefully cheap prices of her stockings. For patriotic reasons, too, such notices were unsuitable. It didn't look well that the wives of English soldiers should have to appeal to public sympathy. Fewkoombey agreed with the latter argument.

About Mac she had little to say. And she scarcely inquired after Polly at all. After all, she had scarcely seen MacHeath for years.

Since she had installed the sewing-girls, she had been doing somewhat better. Business was looking up.

But then came the days when the supply of goods stopped. Already after the gathering at which MacHeath had announced the union of the B. shops with Aaron's chain stores, she had gone home very worried. But that would only mean that the prices were to be lowered again and that goods would be delivered at even cheaper rates than to the great Aaron concern. She took no interest in the necessitous state of London's population. Mac's powers of oratory meant about the same to her as the power of the clouds to snow in winter; but in reality it threatened her as the destructive power of the storm threatens a ship at sea.

All the shops immediately reduced their prices. Chreston's, also, were selling their goods below cost price. And now, in the autumn, at the very time when people were buying wool and yarn, her supply of wool and yarn ran out! She received a printed notice telling her to economize with her wares, very soon there would be no more to come. From the very beginning she lost her head completely.

She had no more powers of resistance left. Continuous troubles and an unhealthy life had weakened her. She had also started earning her keep too early in life. Numerous interruptions of pregnancy, inexpertly carried out, had injured her. In the normal way, people in their thirties have the best part of life before them; but not if they have owned a B. shop in the slums.

At first she tried to get hold of Mac. But of course she never reached him. Fanny comforted her from time to time. At last she threatened to go to the people on the *Reflector* if Mac would not at least speak with her.

But he refused to speak with her, so one evening she went with Fewkoombey to the offices of the *Reflector*.

The people there were very nice to her. They promised her money in return for material against the B. shop Napoleon. They wanted to know something about the origin of his goods. But she knew nothing about that. The goods just came from the Central Purchasing Board. Then she told them that Mac-Heath was the *Knife*. The editors looked at her with open mouths and then burst out laughing. When she became confused and told them that he had killed Eddy Black, they patted her good-naturedly on the back and invited her out to dinner.

She went away in despair. Fewkoombey told Peachum everything. It was the first piece of information he had been able to give him.

Peachum stood in his little dark office, with his bowler hat tilted back on his head, and stared at the soldier meditatively. He had sent out his fat Cerberus. But MacHeath was still his son-in-law.

The information was absolutely useless. The rumour that

MacHeath was the *Knife* had already been brought to him by his beggars. He had naturally not been so stupid as to go to the police about it. They would simply have laughed at him. That this man had risen from the lowest stratum of humanity was certainly true. But that he was also the *Knife* – that was too much to believe, even for Peachum. But even if it were true, such information was wholly uninteresting. Others could waste their time investigating truths that were *improbable*. Truth itself was nothing, probability everything.

'*Everyone knows*', Peachum used to say, '*that nothing safeguards the crimes of the moneyed classes so much as their improbability. Politicians can only take money because people picture their corruption as being altogether finer and nobler than it really is. Should anyone portray them as they are, that is, quite unscrupulous, then the whole world would cry out: What an unscrupulous rascal! and, by that, mean the portrayer. Mr Gladstone could quite easily have set fire to Westminster Abbey and said the Conservatives had done it. Of course, no one would have believed that, because the Conservatives think they have much better ways of getting what they want; but it is equally certain that no one would have ever dreamt of putting the blame on Mr Gladstone. A cabinet minister does not run round with cans of paraffin! Of course, say the poorer people, the rich don't just take their money out of other people's pockets. Admittedly. There is a great difference between Rothschild's methods of getting control of a bank and an ordinary bank robbery. Everybody knows that. But I've learned this much: only those who go in for really big crimes can commit lesser ones without being caught. And people take full advantage of the fact.*'

But Fewkoombey was told to continue visiting Mrs Sawyer in order to extract further information from her.

So in those days the soldier sat with her a great deal. He spent many evenings talking to her. She had a dark feeling that things were happening beyond her control which must eventually ruin her.

MacHeath had induced her to put her little store of money into the shop and now he would help her no further. The fact that she was receiving no more stock seemed unimportant to her. There was no more to be had, and that was that. But then Mac-

Heath must help her to pay the rent when her money gave out.

'That man has me on his conscience,' she said. 'No one can do anything against fate, Fewkoombey. My fate is called Mr Mac-Heath and lives in Nunhead. Sometimes I think I would like to hammer my fists against his face. That would be *so* nice. At least I would like to dream that I was punishing him for his meanness. I always want to dream that, but I never do. I'm too tired at night.'

Another time she complained:

'I count every penny. People say I give too much credit. That I am too kind-hearted. But that's an unfair accusation. If I don't give credit, the customers stay away. I only have quite poor customers. The others go to the big shops where there's more choice. And the worst of it is that he's opened a new B. shop in Clithe Street. That has broken me. It's too much for me.'

She always kept harking back to this new shop. She saw it before her, day and night. More and more she talked of going-into-the-river.

Fewkoombey sat with her while she cleared away the boxes and put them back on the shelves. She always had to strain a little to reach the top shelf. He sat on the edge of a chair that had a tattered cane seat and only three legs. Between his back and the back of the chair were wedged some cardboard boxes. He smoked his cutty pipe which he had saved from the place where he left his leg. And he talked thoughtfully.

'*You have no talent,*' he said slowly. '*You've got nothing to sell. The little bit of breast and fresh skin that you once possessed was soon sold out. And you gave it away too cheaply; or perhaps it wasn't worth more. One gets so little nowadays. And there are some people who come along loaded over with talent, all good, saleable stuff, so much that they can scarcely hold it; you've only got to put up four walls around them, and a shop is ready. But you don't belong to them — and neither do I. People like you and I go selling salt water on the sea-shore. We have no talents, even fewer than a hen has teeth. I have found a home, but I can't stay there always. It's more of a temporary place. I still don't really know why they keep me there. I'm always looking for something that will make me indispensable. Perhaps it*

188

could be something to do with the dogs I thought. But anyone can look after them. It must be something that will make them say: Where's Fewkoombey? Fetch him immediately, we can't do without him. The whole business is at a standstill – thank heavens, there he is! – I've been looking for something like that for a long time, but I haven't found anything. If one has no talent, one must do something else. Then it's a case of: Make yourself twice and three times as useful as anyone else!'

When he had got so far, he became uneasy in his chair and began to question her about MacHeath, concerning whom he would have to find out something more or lose his job.

But he only made her suspicious and she told him nothing.

She nearly always spoke quite generally.

Once she visited an old woman who also owned a B. shop and whom she had met at the gathering where MacHeath had announced the alliance with Aaron's. They went together to a fortune-teller. She told Fewkoombey several times about her experiences there.

It had not been one of those expensive fortune-tellers.

'Probably,' said Mary, 'she was not quite so good as an expensive one.'

The woman lived on the fifth floor of a tenement and laid out her cards in the kitchen. She did not even sit down to them. Then, 'as though she had learnt it by heart', she gabbled something about 'the cards not falling quite right'; but perhaps, she said, she would have more success with their hands.

'You are a strong character, untouched by the storms of life,' she said to the old woman, who had come because she was worried about her shop. 'You are accustomed to having your own way. You are a Capricorn. You face life firmly and energetically and you will triumph in the end. You have two weaknesses, which you must watch. Beware of a woman whose name begins with B. Don't put too much trust in her; she may stand in the way of your luck. In June of next year you must be careful, for then Sirius moves into the sign of the Scales. That is unfavourable to you. But that is the only danger I can see. That will cost a shilling.'

Mary knew it by heart and laughed a little over it. But she would have had her fortune told, too, had not the old woman suddenly become ill because she had no proper food inside her.

'It would be nice to *know*,' she said, 'and where else can one find out?'

On the Friday morning after her unsuccessful visit to the *Reflector*, Mary called on Fanny Chrysler in her antique shop. Fanny was horrified at her appearance and kept her there the whole morning because she thought that Mac would be coming. But Mac did not come and so the two of them went out to Mac's house in Nunhead, although Fanny knew how much Mac would dislike this.

Polly received them quite kindly. She took them into the best sitting-room and then ran into the kitchen to make tea. She tied an apron round her and prepared everything with the bustling activity common to young housewives who still find something sexual in the handling of a saucepan.

Fanny had expressly forbidden Mary to mention business. It would be far better to wait for Mac. But as soon as the Peach brought in the tea, Mary burst into tears. She was unable to restrain herself any longer.

She told nearly everything there was to tell; but of course nothing about the stupid accusation which had made the editorial staff of the *Reflector* nearly die of laughing. She emphasized all the reasons for Mac's obligations to her.

Polly looked at her curiously. She still stood holding the tea things in her hands.

The whole situation was unpleasantly clear; MacHeath had decoyed this woman into a Bargain shop and was now leaving her to her fate. It would have been kinder of him to have slaughtered her with a pole-axe as soon as he got tired of her.

The crockery shook in Polly's hands when she answered. She spoke somewhat as follows:

As to the conditions of the business, she was in no position to judge. But that her husband (my husband) had 'decoyed' Mary into a B. shop seemed hard to believe. Most probably he had given it to her. That he was going to leave her to her fate was a ridiculous accusation and one which, as Mac's wife, she strongly resented. Mary wasn't the only person who owned a B. shop. And Mac would surely not be leaving them all 'to their fate'.

That was highly improbable. But as to the other accusation, she must say, as woman to woman, that what Mac had done or not done (done or not done) before his marriage, had, in her opinion, nothing to do with her. But she must also add, as a woman, that when a woman gets entangled with a man, she generally knows the reason why. She does it at her own risk. She cannot expect that the man concerned should support her for the rest of her life. If that were the case, a man would have half a dozen families before he was thirty. It's not always the others who are to blame when one gets into difficulties.

When she had said all this, she deposited the tea things rather violently on the table and a silence fell. Mary Sawyer had stopped crying and was looking at the young woman in front of her with an empty expression on her face. Even Fanny was astonished. She stood up suddenly.

Mary straightened up from her crumpled attitude and rose to her feet also, although rather more slowly. With shaking hands she reached for her bag and picked it up from the table.

In the meanwhile Polly had taken up the tea-pot again and begun to pour out. She still had the pot in her hand when the two women went.

Fanny wanted Mary to stay with her. But the latter shook her head and climbed into a passing tram. She had an absent look, and the tram, as Fanny immediately noticed, was not going in the direction of her shop in Mulberry Street. Mary's thoughts were no longer clear enough. She had only twenty-seven (27) more hours to live.

The rest of the day Fanny spent searching for MacHeath. But she did not see him until the next morning, when he called hastily at her shop, alarmed and indignant at what his wife had told him about the visit of the two. He blustered at Fanny and wanted to know what had happened. Fanny told him everything with an expressionless face. Polly's behaviour had disgusted her more than she could say. She had suddenly felt that she herself was no more than an employee. Mac's behaviour also disgusted her.

She spoke of the new shop in Clithe Street and how Mary Sawyer was at the end of her endurance. And how she talked continually of going-into-the-river.

He only looked at her furiously when she said Mary was waiting for him in Mulberry Street. Then he rushed out of the shop. Today was the second meeting of the advisory committee of the C.P.B. He had a lot to do before that.

A few hours later he sent a messenger with a note to Mary Sawyer, saying that she was to wait for him at seven o'clock in a public house near the West India Docks. It had probably occurred to him that she knew a great deal.

When Fanny arrived in Mulberry Street towards five o'clock, she was relieved to find the shop still open. Mary sat behind the counter and nodded when Fanny entered. In the shop was a man with a wooden leg.

At six o'clock punctually Mary shut the shop, sent the sewing-girls home, and put the children quickly to bed. Then she went with Fewkoombey to the West India Docks. Thus, during her last hours, there was still someone with her.

On the way there, the soldier tried to talk to her. But she remained monosyllabic. Outside the public house she sent him away. He had accompanied her in vain. And she could so easily, so he believed, have told him something that would have helped him on in his position with Mr Peachum.

At this time of day the bar was nearly empty and Mary Sawyer waited for nearly two hours, a fact that was later established by the statement of the publican. Then, since MacHeath had not arrived, she went away in the direction of the docks. As she told the landlord, she was hoping to encounter the gentleman whom she was to have met there. But she encountered no one and nothing more.

A few hours later a policeman and two dockers dragged her out of the water.

Mr Peachum Sees a Way Out

Since Mary Sawyer had asked Fewkoombey to look in at the children on his way back and had given him the key of the front door, he spent the night in her house. Otherwise she would not have been able to get in.

In the morning they brought her home. All sorts of people

from the neighbourhood immediately collected in the shop, so the soldier was not noticed and was able to go away. They laid the body on the counter, because the bed was covered with cardboard boxes.

Through Fewkoombey, Peachum learnt early of Mary Sawyer's death and he was able to take steps forthwith. The first thing he did was to confirm the facts.

He sent out no less than thirty beggars who made inquiries at the West India Docks, in Mulberry Street, in Fanny Chrysler's antique shop, and at Nunhead.

Some of Peachum's people were actually present at the first police investigation in Mulberry Street.

He learned that some stevedores, who had been lounging by the docks at about nine o'clock the previous night, had seen a woman walking rapidly towards the water-front. Fewkoombey went to Mulberry Street in the afternoon to take the children to Fanny Chrysler's house and he brought back with him Mac's note which one of the children had been chewing. By the afternoon it was plain to Peachum that this was a case of suicide.

In order to be quite certain, he spent two more days investigating MacHeath's affairs. It was, indeed, impossible to discover where MacHeath had been during the period in question, but it was certain that he had not met Mary Sawyer that evening. That was sufficient grounds for making an accusation.

Absolute certainty that MacHeath had really nothing to do with the death of Mary Sawyer was essential, because otherwise he would, of course, have a perfect alibi. He might still have one; but that risk would have to be taken. At any rate he would not have one ready-made. And a natural alibi is always less convincing than a manufactured one.

So Peachum instructed a good solicitor who was to act on behalf of the orphaned children, and handed over the material to the public prosecutor. Peachum could do that because he was a relieving officer.

The solicitor, Walley, fully agreed with Mr Peachum's reasoning concerning Mr MacHeath's alibi. He said:

'Taking into consideration all we know, I too regard it as impossible that your son-in-law could have had anything to do with the death of this Mary Sawyer. Therefore it is highly improbable that he has an alibi. He will trump up something about "sittinginarestaurant" or "wenttoatheatre" or even "can'tcompromisealady". The last would be ideal for you, things being as they are. Most welcome, eh? An alibi, to be effective, must be arranged, and it only is arranged when a crime is contemplated. That is an integral part of all criminal practice. Look at politics! Whenever, for example, a war is started, there are always alibis. Not to speak of a *coup d'état*! The victim is always responsible. The attacker has an alibi!'

The incriminating material consisted of the hand-written note sent to the dead woman by MacHeath, the evidence of the former soldier, Fewkoombey, and the statements of two beggars who were prepared to swear that they had seen MacHeath in the company of Mary Sawyer at nine o'clock on Saturday evening in the neighbourhood of the West India Docks.

Mr MacHeath Is Unwilling to Leave London

MacHeath was not arrested until the following Thursday. When he received the news from Brown, he sent his wife to a hotel in the East End. O'Hara came and fetched her and they had dinner together. O'Hara had done his best to avert any trouble, but he had learnt of the affair too late. Curiously enough, Fanny Chrysler had said nothing, although she must have heard of Mary Sawyer's death.

O'Hara had also visited Brown. Brown had realized too late that MacHeath was suspected of the crime. The first investigation had been undertaken by one Beecher of Scotland Yard, a veritable bloodhound, who, once on the scent, could never be held back. At first Beecher had considered it a clear case of suicide. And inquiries in other B. shops, together with certain articles in the *Reflector* which described MacHeath's enterprises and exposed the desperate conditions of the B. shops, revealed quite sufficient motive for suicide. But after Peachum's damning accusation through Walley, Beecher produced a half-finished letter of Mary Sawyer's which had been found on the dead woman. In this letter Mary confessed to having sent, anonymously, several newspaper cuttings concerning the *Knife* and asked whether the addressee would not agree to 'be a bit nicer' to her. The letter started: 'Dear Mac'.

O'Hara knew, also, the exact time when Mary must have died: about nine o'clock. When he reported this, MacHeath gave him a sharp glance. Nine o'clock was a very unfortunate time. At nine o'clock MacHeath had been at the meeting of the C.P.B. The gist of that meeting, and also MacHeath's presence on the premises of the C.P.B., might in no circumstances be publicly mentioned; for if this happened, all his elaborate schemes would be ruined. Bloomsbury was a good-natured young fool, but he would certainly not lie in a court of law and say that the gentlemen had been playing bridge.

So MacHeath had, at all costs, to vanish and remain hidden abroad; at least until Brown had suppressed the investigations or the business with the Commercial Bank was completed. O'Hara was in favour of MacHeath going with Grooch and Fanny to Sweden, so that he could, at the same time, organize the 'buying' there.

With regard to the business, O'Hara wanted complete control, but MacHeath wanted to give that to Polly. They quarrelled for a time; then O'Hara left.

Polly had listened wanly without asking any questions. She realized that the whole thing was only a plot of her father's against MacHeath. She was convinced that Mary Sawyer had only jumped into the water to revenge herself on him. But she was determined that MacHeath should not go to Sweden with Fanny Chrysler.

After dinner she went home without saying anything. When she was undressing, she spoke angrily of the proposed journey with Fanny. Mac laughed and promised unconditionally to leave Fanny in London. He said that there was something going on between her and Grooch. But Polly was still mistrustful. She believed everything Mac said – except concerning women.

Late that night he woke up and heard her sobbing. She faltered for a bit and then, after she had made him promise he would not be angry, she confessed that she had had a stupid dream the week before. She had dreamed that she had slept with O'Hara. She burst out sobbing again and asked if that was very wicked, while Mac lay beside her, stiffened into frozen silence.

'There you see,' she said, 'now you're angry with me. I oughtn't to have said anything to you; one ought never to say anything. I can't help it if I dream. It was quite short, too, and not at all clear that it was O'Hara. It only seemed to be so when I woke up, and then I was terrified. I don't want to sleep with anyone but you. But I can't help my dreams. I immediately thought: What shall I do? I'll tell Mac, and then it will be quite all right. But then I thought, you wouldn't understand it and might believe that I liked O'Hara, and that's certainly not true. He doesn't attract me at all. Say it's all right, Mac! I'm so unhappy that I had that dream. If you hadn't got to go away now, I would never have said anything about it. Since then, I haven't had any more stupid dreams, really. Or only about you!'

Mac lay for a long time without answering. Then, taking no notice of her attempts to soothe him and lying there stiff as a ramrod, he questioned her hoarsely with short, abrupt sentences. What had it been like when it happened. Had it happened in bed. Whether they had gone to bed specially for it. Whether he had simply embraced her, or did something else happen. Had she encouraged him. Whether she knew immediately that it was O'Hara. Why she hadn't stopped when she did know. Whether she had felt any pleasure when it occurred. Why, if she didn't feel any particular pleasure, hadn't she stopped immediately when she recognized O'Hara. What did she mean by 'no particular pleasure'. And so on and so on, until Polly was so worn out by crying that she fell asleep.

But finally, of course, they made it all up and MacHeath was pleased when she again stormily demanded a promise from him that he would not go away with Fanny. He also persuaded her to return to her parents. He said that she could be of most help to him there. She could keep him informed about everything that her father was planning against him. They went to sleep completely reconciled.

The next morning they said good-bye to each other. When MacHeath went away, he was once more carrying his calf-skin gloves and his old sword-stick. His train was not due to leave until late in the evening, but he still had a great deal to do. O'Hara's people were not in the best of tempers, and Aaron or one of the Oppers had still to be visited.

But first he went to Gawn, to whom he had given the material against Coax, Peachum's companion. The material had not yet appeared anywhere. Gawn was not at home. They said he was in the 'Correspondent'. There Mac found several journalists sitting round Gawn, trying to get racing tips out of him. When MacHeath entered, a strange silence fell.

'Oho,' said one of the young men, not unkindly, 'our friend MacHeath! I suppose you're wanting to make a protest against your arrest. Is it to take place here? That's very decent of you!'

Gawn, who sat smiling in their midst, chewing half a pound of gum, realized now that MacHeath knew nothing. He drew a newspaper out of his breast pocket.

The police were already searching for MacHeath. His name and photograph were in all the morning editions. Beecher had given an interview and spoken about the unfinished letter found on the victim.

Gawn took MacHeath by the arm and led him away.

They went to a small public house.

The material against Coax, Gawn explained, was really material against Hale of the Admiralty, whose wife it concerned. The campaign would be starting in a day or two.

He concealed the fact that he had been using the material entrusted to him for a bit of profitable blackmail. That had cost Mr Peachum a mint of money. Polly's dowry had not been increased thereby.

MacHeath impressed on him once again that he did not want a public scandal but an effective intimidation of Coax and all his associates. Gawn promised to do his best and asked for an interview.

They concocted one together.

It appeared in the evening edition. The merchant prince MacHeath expressed himself as very astonished at the accusation of the police.

'I am a merchant,' it ran, 'and not a criminal. But I have enemies. The unprecedented success of my B. shops has led such enemies to resort to this plan. My methods are more straightforward than that. I try to vanquish my rivals by tireless work in the service of my customers. All suspicions against myself will, in the course of the next few days, recoil on the heads of those who disseminate them. I hope that none of my business friends in the retail trade, whose welfare lies very close to my heart, will doubt me. This Mary Sawyer is scarcely known to me personally. As far as I recollect, she owned a small B. shop in the neighbourhood of Mulberry Street. I have had no more to do with her than with a dozen other B. shop owners. She seems to have taken her own life. I feel the tragedy as deeply as any other business man. There is cause enough for depression; no one knows that better than business people. Mrs Sawyer seems to have been in exceptionally reduced circumstances.'

After this interview, MacHeath drove to the Commercial Bank where he met Henry Opper.

The morning papers had printed Mac's name in flaring headlines and Opper seemed very astonished to see him. He listened to MacHeath in silence and then said: 'You must in no circumstances go to prison. Guilty or not guilty, you mustn't go to prison. Go abroad! You can manage your business from there. You have friends in the C.P.B. and we, also, can look after your interests if you wish it. But go immediately. Aaron has already been here. He is beside himself with anxiety.'

MacHeath went away very thoughtful. Opper's eagerness to get him away disturbed him. He drove to Lower Blacksmith Square and entered a dirty little shaving saloon. In the low room, which smelt of cold smoke, trade was brisk. Half the London underworld congregated there. There was no other place in London where one could hear so much in so short a time.

The chairs were all occupied. MacHeath sat down on a bench amongst those who were waiting. In front of them on the floor stood a great brass bowl into which cigarette ends and chewing gum were spat.

MacHeath saw no familiar face.

A small weasel-faced man was talking loudly about customs smuggling in a Danish harbour.

'They don't want anything cheap in the country,' he complained. 'The poor man mustn't be allowed to buy himself diamonds. That's dirty! A man *must* have coal and potatoes. But if they make trouble with diamonds too, then he might just as well say good-bye.'

MacHeath noted the speaker; he was a man after his own heart.

The barber was a misshapen colossus of a man with a tiny head, the top of which was a masterpiece of tonsorial art. He had thrown a quick, sideways glance at MacHeath when the latter sat down. He had an arrangement with MacHeath to bring the conversation round to him whenever he arrived, and this he now did. The whole shop began discussing the Sawyer murder.

The general view was that the great merchant could have had nothing to do with the death of Mary Sawyer.

'A man like that wouldn't have done it,' said the smuggler knowingly. 'He's got other things to do. You've no idea of the amount of work he has to get through in a day. They say she was threatening him. What could she threaten him with? Whatever she said, she'd have been immediately arrested for embarrassing the police!'

'And I've heard he hasn't got an alibi. D'you think he's giving away ten pounds to everyone who says he didn't see him during that time? Not him! He just wants to see who laughs loudest when he lets himself be arrested. That's it!'

This seemed to exhaust the subject.

MacHeath did not wait for his turn to come. He went out with his thick stick under one arm. After passing through two or three narrow alleys, he stopped in front of a tumble-down, one-storied house occupied by a coal merchant. Beside the door hung a blackboard on which the prices were chalked up.

MacHeath saw that the number '23' stood against anthracite. He entered a house numbered '23' after he had knocked on the door with his stick. Sometimes anthracite costs 23s., sometimes 27s., or even 29s., according to where the gang had their headquarters at the moment. The real prices of coal, MacHeath had once said to O'Hara, depend on a whole combination of circumstances which have nothing to do with coal. And besides, the coal merchant did not sell anthracite.

MacHeath walked with echoing steps across two large yards filled with sheds. He entered a third and turned into a lighted office on the ground floor.

Grooch and Father were sitting on a mahogany table with beer bottles beside them, and Grooch was dictating letters to a smartly dressed young woman. In the next room, packing-cases were being nailed up.

At the entry of the chief, Grooch stood up. Father remained seated.

'It's a good thing you look in once in a while,' said Father morosely, 'there's no work here. Nothing but trouble and discontent.'

Without answering, MacHeath picked up a thick folio from a roughly carpentered shelf and sat down with it on the arm of an Empire chair. The chair had seen better days and finer company. The C.P.B. had their official premises in the city. Here were their warehouses. Between the two there was no communication except by very devious routes.

So long as Father sat on the table, MacHeath refused to talk. Therefore Grooch began speaking.

This enforced inactivity was having most unfortunate effects. The sheds were still partly filled with goods. O'Hara had given the employees permission to work on their own until the firm needed steady supplies again. But he had not given them the tools. They were the property of the Company. With their old, primitive instruments O'Hara's experts could not, or would not, work any more. And for shop-breaking, lorries, at least, were necessary. And above all, they lacked coordinated schemes for working together. So the men were forced into inactivity. They sat around and quarrelled.

MacHeath laughed.

'I thought they were too good for a life of salaried security,' he said offhandedly. 'They wanted to become independent again, unfettered and free. They are always wanting to make changes and they are never astonished when they get what they want. Whenever *I* get what I want, I always expect the worst.'

'They would be all right if they had their tools,' said Father harshly.

'Yes, if,' said MacHeath.

Father took up the attack again :

'Quite wants to buy our new drills off us. He says he has enough money and no one can use them except himself.'

'I will sell none of my tools,' said MacHeath angrily. 'And my tables are not meant to be sat on.'

He picked up the stock list, which was neatly tabulated on a sheet of cardboard, and dismissed the girl with a nod.

'Why are the sheds still full? It was arranged to clear out everything up to 23.'

Grooch looked at Father who had stood up grumbling.

'O'Hara told us nothing about that,' he said, his gaze still fixed on Father.

MacHeath concealed his astonishment. He turned over the leaves of a catalogue in order to gain time.

Then he continued calmly:

'The sheds in 29 must be cleared. It's possible that O'Hara may have to show, in the very near future, that the place is empty.'

'Where are the things to go to? It's mostly tobacco and shaving material. That lot will have to be warehoused for a time, it's far too new. The Birmingham stuff is here too. The newspapers are still writing articles a mile long about that. And then there's the leather and wool; the B. shops could do with that.'

'It must all be got rid of. None of it's to be sold. You'd better burn the lot. The sheds are insured.'

Grooch was deeply shocked.

'But couldn't the boys use it? There'd be trouble if they had to destroy it all. After all they collected it.'

MacHeath was plainly bored by this discussion.

'I believe they were paid for that. And I shall pay them by the hour for their work in disposing of the stuff. I do not want any of it to be sold. And they should buy their own tobacco – in the B. shops if they like. And another thing: all papers here will be signed by my wife and not by O'Hara. Is that all?'

He stood up and began pulling on his gloves. But Grooch still detained him.

'Honeymaker keeps coming here. He says he's prepared to do any sort of work. The business with the safety lock has turned out badly.'

'Wasn't it safe enough, or was it too safe?'

'Oh, that was all right. But the factory has swindled him over the patent.'

MacHeath laughed again. In his day, Honeymaker had been a leading light in his profession, a first-class burglar. But when he began to degenerate physically – in those days sport was not yet the fashion – he took up inventing, and invented a safety lock. He put all his experience into this lock, the rich experience of an active life full of study and enterprise. And now, in the well-known lock factory to whom he had offered his invention, he had found his master.

'He can have a B. shop,' said MacHeath and went away grinning.

But he felt far from happy.

His orders had not been carried out. Any day now, the idea might occur to Aaron of going to inspect the warehouses. And Fanny, thinking that they had been cleared according to arrangement, would see no reason for refusing him; while all the time they were still crammed full of goods.

When he reached the street, MacHeath considered for a moment whether he should go straight to Fanny Chrysler or else to Mrs Lexer in Tonbridge. It was his Thursday.

Then he realized that he would see Fanny on the station when she came to see him off, and he would probably find Brown in Tonbridge. Like him, Brown was there every Thursday. They usually played a rubber of draughts together.

In MacHeath's view, his association with the ladies of Mrs Lexer's house needed some excusing, although the specialized nature of his business was quite sufficient reason. Here, better than anywhere else, he could gather information about the private affairs of his gang. Thus he utilized purely business connexions for those purposes of incidental amusement to which, as a bachelor, he was entitled in moderation. Concerning this intimate side of his life, he often used to say that he chiefly valued these regular and pedantically punctual visits to the Tonbridge café, because they were *habits*, the cultivation and nourishment of which is perhaps the most important principle of bourgeois existence. After a few youthful indiscretions, MacHeath took to satisfying his sexual needs in directions where he could combine these with either luxury or business, i.e. with women who were not entirely without means or with whom he had business connexions, such as Fanny.

MacHeath fully realized that his marriage had done him considerable harm amongst the buying side of his organization. The death of Mary Sawyer had also displeased certain people. They were probably sitting together now and saying: Mac's getting rich. He thinks he's at the top.

There was scarcely anyone who could honestly swear that he had always been called MacHeath; but there was also no one who could prove that he had such and such a name and had gone to such and such a school, that he had been a rowdy or a clerk, that he had lodged in such and such a house. But every day the rumour might be spreading that he was an ordinary respectable citizen, and then it would need an expensive and dangerous massacre to re-establish that convenient twilight in which a man can grow fat and prosperous. And he was now rather too corpulent for that; he was more fitted for mental labours.

So he went to Tonbridge in search of information and to meet Brown.

He did not go straight into the ground-floor rooms, but climbed a rickety flight of stairs and entered the kitchen. A few girls were sitting round and drinking coffee. A fat woman in petticoats was ironing. Over by the window a game of halma was in progress. A thin, flat-nosed girl was darning a mountain of stockings. They were all lightly dressed; but only one had a flowered night-dress on.

When MacHeath came in, there was a general murmur of astonishment. They had all read the papers, and the interview with Gawn lay on the ironing-board. That he had come, just as on any other Thursday, impressed them all greatly.

Brown was not yet there.

MacHeath received his cup of coffee and stretched out his gloved hand for the paper.

'I'm leaving this evening,' he said as he read. 'I thought to myself: it's silly that today is Thursday. It's terrible when a man becomes such a creature of habit. But I couldn't give up my oldest habit. Otherwise I would have gone this afternoon. Where's Brown got to?'

A bell rang from one of the rooms. The fat woman laid down her iron on its stand, threw on a cotton wrap, and went out to see to a customer. Five minutes later she came back, tested the iron with her moistened finger, and went on working.

'*You* didn't do the Sawyer affair,' she said – contemptuously, so it seemed to him.

'Well?' he said and looked at her.

'We only thought you were too good for suchlike now.'

'Who thought that?' he asked with interest.

The fat woman soothed him:

'Keep calm, Mac. You're not the only person that's talked about.'

Mac had a fine sense of atmosphere. Something was not quite right here. He was seized with a sudden feeling of repugnance.

While he sat there in the dirty kitchen and looked at the woman ironing, he reviewed his position more thoroughly than he had for a long time.

The ground on which he had always stood and fought, was giving way under his feet. These fools who did his buying for him were not content to submit for long to an intelligent leadership. A number of small points which he had scarcely noticed in the last weeks suddenly occurred to him. Several explicit and well-thought-out orders had not been strictly obeyed; afterwards, this negligence had been concealed from him by the heads of the organization. More especially since the great stoppage of supplies had he heard a lot from Grooch about the 'discontent' among the workers. These fools could not appreciate operations on a large scale.

And now he had to discover that O'Hara had simply ignored his most important orders!

O'Hara's behaviour had, for some time past, been extremely unsatisfactory. Today he had wanted to have complete control. When this had been given to Polly, he had not argued for very long. Why not?

Quite suddenly a hot wave of distrust swept over MacHeath.

Polly! he thought. What exactly was there between Polly and O'Hara? Now she had control of the business, what would she do with it? And all at once he knew why the occurrence on the drive back from the picnic by the Thames had always worried him so much.

'*A woman who allows that,*' he said bitterly, '*especially on such superficial acquaintanceship, can never make a really good wife for a man. She is far too sensual. And that is not only an*

204

erotic failing, but also – it seems – a business one. Whatever will she do with the power I've entrusted to her, when she's not even sure of her own self? That's where a woman's faithfulness takes on a deeper meaning!'

How quickly the two had agreed to his departure! There had been no 'I shall miss you so'. She was too sensible. A nice sort of sense that!

MacHeath stood up, full of bitterness, and walked over into the offices. They were all fairly large rooms with bare office-furniture, small tables with writing-pads, and ordinary sofas. There were also rooms without sofas, and then one used the tables with the green blotting-paper. It was one of the special amenities of this house that a customer could also deal with his correspondence here. The girls were all expert shorthand typists.

The house was mostly patronized by business men.

MacHeath would have liked to have dictated a few letters; but only Jenny was entrusted with his correspondence and knew his ways. If necessary she could write a letter with only a few notes.

And Jenny was not there. She was at the seaside with Blooms-bury. Nobody seemed to resent her rise in the world.

MacHeath opened a little shutter in the wall and listened to someone dictating in the next room.

'. . . and we are therefore unable to appreciate your standpoint. Either you deliver the Santos, at 85⅝, free in Antwerp, *or* you must reduce the outrageous price, outrageous underlined, and we will deal with the customs ourselves.'

MacHeath went gloomily back into the kitchen and sat down again.

He was still waiting for Brown. The conversation with him would decide whether he was to leave London or not. Everything was in readiness for his flight. Grooch would be waiting at the station, probably with Fanny. But half an hour passed; it grew dark outside and the street lamps had to be lit; customers began to arrive slowly; and Brown had not yet appeared. No one took any notice of MacHeath. He sat in the kitchen and dozed.

With things as they were, he could not go away.

He must first resume complete control of the C.P.B. and

then wind it up. What a life, when a man with the police after him couldn't even go away in peace!

And surrounded as he was by incompetent fools, he could much better conduct his great business transactions from prison than from abroad.

A real desire for respectability overcame him. A certain modicum of honesty and integrity, or even of trustworthiness, was indispensable to a man who deals in big business. Why, otherwise, was honesty so greatly valued if one could do without it? After all, the whole social structure was founded on it. A man must get as much as he can out of his employees and then go in for decent, respectable transactions. If a man cannot even trust his own companions, how can he be expected to concentrate on his business?

At last, at seven o'clock, Brown arrived.

This had always been the best place for them to meet. No one spied after Brown in this establishment. A Scotland Yard official would have considered it indelicate to come sniffing around here. For, when all's said and done, a man's private life is nobody else's concern.

Brown immediately began reproaching him.

'What are you still doing here?' he shouted, pacing up and down the room like a caged tiger. 'I've told you that there will be trouble. Beecher is conducting investigations and he's the most unreliable man I've got. Once he gets on the trail, nothing can hold him back and he forgets all sense of discipline. He would arrest his own mother. This afternoon the coroner viewed the body. After Beecher had spoken, they brought in a verdict of murder. Suspicion rests on you. And worst of all is this blackmailing letter of Mary Sawyer's which openly threatens you with revelations about the *Knife*. What did she know about that?'

'Nothing,' said MacHeath, sitting down on the sofa with the evening papers. 'She had suspicions.'

'And this Fewkoombey?'

'An employee of my father-in-law's, a discharged soldier. He seems to have made approaches to Mary Sawyer recently.'

Brown noted down something on his cuff.

'O'Hara says you have an alibi but couldn't produce it?'

'Yes. The agenda of a company meeting which ought not to have taken place.'

'The one good point is that the two stevedores who met Mrs Sawyer say that she had no one with her. But as for your note, making an appointment with her for that evening, it's terrible. It's in the dossier of the case.'

Brown began to shout again. MacHeath must go away immediately, now.

MacHeath looked at him reproachfully.

'I had expected something different from you,' he said in a sentimental voice. 'I had hoped that if ever I got into a situation like this, hunted and betrayed by everybody, I could turn to you, Freddy. I thought that because of our friendship you would say to me: Here, Mac, is a sanctuary for you. Stay there. Even if you have lost your honour, you shall at least have the opportunity of saving your money.'

'What do you mean?' demanded Brown.

MacHeath looked at him sadly.

'I cannot conduct my business from abroad. How could you think that? Opper tells me that my reputation will be ruined if I go to prison; but I have heard that they intend to ruin me if I leave the country. I must remain at my post. I must come to you in prison and carry on my work there. I am like a horse that dies in harness, Freddy!'

'That's impossible,' growled Brown, but he seemed to be weakening.

'Just think,' MacHeath reminded him in a subdued voice, 'how many people have entrusted their future to me. And you are one of them. Your money will be gone, too, if I leave London. Of course, you can afford it; but there are others who would be ruined.'

Brown growled again.

'It's my father-in-law,' complained MacHeath. 'He cannot bear me. I have never taken any notice of his enmity. It has always been like a tooth that begins to ache. One ignores it. Thinks, perhaps, it will stop. Refuses to think about it. And then one fine morning one's cheek is swollen up like a doughnut.'

They sat together for more than an hour and Brown related

sorrowfully all he knew about Mr Peachum, the author of all evil.

Mr J. J. Peachum was not unknown to the police. His instrument shop had been the subject of several earnest conversations in the Commissioner's room, the first of which had taken place about twelve years ago. At that time they had wanted to suppress his business. But they had not succeeded. Brown told Mac the story:

'We knew all about his instrument shop, and he knew that we were going to take action against him. So he came to the Yard. There he made a ridiculous and insulting speech about the poor having the right to smell and so forth. Of course we threw him out and went on with the case. We soon noticed that he was up to something. Just at that time a memorial was being unveiled in the worst quarter of Whitechapel in memory of a philanthropist who had started some stupid campaign against the misuse of alcohol. I believe he dispensed glasses of lemonade with the help of a lot of girls who had also been saved somehow. For the unveiling of the memorial, a great white affair, the Queen was supposed to be coming. We cleaned up the neighbourhood a bit. Since it was in a condition that had driven its inhabitants to the misuse of alcohol, it was quite unfit for the Queen to see. But a few gallons of whitewash worked wonders. We transformed the place into a miniature paradise. Rubbish dumps became children's playgrounds. Tumbledown tenements took on a festive appearance; the worst places were covered up with garlands. Out of holes in which twelve to fifteen people lived in a room, were hung great twenty-foot flags; I can still remember how the people complained that the flag-poles took up too much of their space; people like that aren't even ashamed of the squalid dens in which they live! We drove out the inmates from a disreputable house and put up a tablet outside: HOME FOR FALLEN GIRLS – which it was. In short, we did our best to create a homely, attractive appearance. But it was during the preliminary inspection by the Prime Minister that trouble first occurred. Out of the windows of the flower-hung, whitewashed houses peered the well-known, hideous faces of Mr Peachum's professional beggars. There were hundreds and hundreds of them. And when the Prime

Minister drove along below, they howled down the National Anthem! We never even tried to improve the children of that quarter; any attempt at disguise would have been hopeless; no amount of clothes can conceal rickety limbs. And what was the use of substituting police children when a real child might be suddenly smuggled into the ranks of the imported ones, and then, if the fat, rosy-cheeked Prime Minister should ask him his age, instead of answering five, as one would imagine from his size, he says sixteen? All round the memorial were crowded under-grown creatures with all the cares of the world grinning out of their eye-sockets. They came in little troupes with balloons and lollipops. The inspection ended in confusion and we gave up our investigations against Mr Peachum. We wanted to have nothing more to do with him. And *that* man is your father-in-law! It's no joke, Mac.'

Brown was honestly worried. He had prepared himself for a desperate battle. He had many bad qualities, but he was a good friend. He and Mac had served together in India. Mac could rely on his loyalty.

'*Loyalty*,' Brown, the old soldier, often used to say among his most intimate friends, '*loyalty is only to be found among soldiers. Why is that? The answer is simple: because the soldier is taught loyalty. When one has to make a bayonet attack — which happens usually for no reason at all — and when one has to hack and stab and grind, then a man must have a loyal comrade beside him with a bayonet that will also stab and hack and grind. Only under such conditions can this virtue attain its highest form. For the soldier, loyalty is part of his profession. But he is not only loyal to one particular friend. He cannot win his promotion by favour. Therefore he must simply be loyal. The civilian cannot understand that. He cannot understand how a general, for example, can first be loyal to his monarch and then to the republic, like Marshal MacMahon. MacMahon will always be loyal. If the Republic falls, he will be loyal to the King again. And so on to all eternity! Only that is true loyalty!*'

When MacHeath had left him, Brown was reconciled to his friend's decision to go to prison. Considerably relieved, he hastened to dictate a letter to the prison governor.

They had arranged that MacHeath should present himself at

Scotland Yard. But when he got on to the bus, thoughts of Polly were running in his head which had been worrying him for hours. So he changed his plans and drove to Nunhead.

He arrived there about eight o'clock. With amazement he saw that there was light in Polly's room on the first floor. She ought to have been with her parents long ago.

In front of the little garden two police officers were patrolling up and down quite openly.

Now a second window lit up. Polly was probably busy in the kitchen. She had evidently decided to spend the night there.

MacHeath walked determinedly towards the front door. At the garden gate he was stopped. He nodded when a hand was laid on his shoulder from behind. The officers agreed to his going in and speaking with his wife.

Polly was, indeed, standing by the kitchen range. She immediately realized who the men with Mac were, but she was astonished that he had remained in London.

'Haven't you gone home?' he asked crossly, standing in the kitchen door.

'No,' she said calmly, 'I was with Fanny Chrysler.'

'And?' he asked her.

'She's going to Sweden.'

'But I'm not,' he said darkly. 'Pack some clothes for me.'

He went to prison very troubled in mind, and troubled because of Polly.

The next morning Walley visited him on the instructions of Mr Peachum. He spoke to him of divorce and hinted that, in that case, certain advantageous material might come to light.

'Why do you want these proceedings?' asked the solicitor. 'Your business is flourishing. Let yourself be divorced and the prosecution will drop the case. The decisive material is in our hands. Mr Peachum wants his daughter back, that is all.'

But MacHeath repulsed him rudely. He stressed the fact that his marriage had been a love match.

11

O, they are such charming people
If you'll leave them well alone
While they're fighting to recover
What has never been their own.

(SONG OF THE COMMISSIONER OF POLICE)

The Leaves Turn Yellow

ONE early morning Polly Peachum, now Mrs MacHeath, came home again. In spite of the early hour, she had managed to pick up a cab. Driving by the park she saw that the leaves of the oak-trees were already yellow.

As soon as she entered the shop, she was astonished at the hurry and bustle all around. Her mother was standing in the middle of a group of sewing-girls, quarrelling with Beery. They scarcely noticed the Peach. Someone carried her luggage up-stairs and, after a time, her breakfast.

They were expecting a police search and for the last seven hours had been clearing everything possible out of the place. Amongst other things that were removed were crutches which could not be used by one-legged men, little trucks with hidden drawers for the legs, and, above all, soldiers' uniforms. The card-indexes were taken down to a remote cellar.

Since midnight messengers had been going round, warning the beggars not to come to headquarters the next morning.

When the police entered the premises about noon, even the barber's saloon had been transferred to the next-door house.

In particular, they were searching for the soldier Fewkoom-bey, who had not reported at the police station as had been arranged. But the soldier was not to be found. He had been dis-missed the previous evening for insolent behaviour – so Mr Peachum said.

Beecher reported that the house, or rather the three houses, was like a rabbit warren and contained a carpenter's workshop, and a tailoring establishment; all for the beggars and all on an astonishingly large scale.

Fewkoombey had, indeed, moved into a dock-side hotel for a few days. He was forbidden to leave his room, but he had his volume of the *Encyclopaedia Britannica* with him.

His dogs were taken over by the Peach, happy to find something to do. She did not see her father until the next morning. He behaved as though she had never been away.

But after lunch Coax arrived to speak to Mr Peachum and when he stepped out of the office and encountered Polly in the passage, he greeted her with a deep bow.

'Indeed,' he said emphatically, 'the Peach has ripened! That must be the effects of the South!'

He grasped both her hands and demanded a piece on the piano.

Behind him stood Mr Peachum, and Polly caught such an entreating glance from him, that she turned without a word and went upstairs with the broker and played *Annie Laurie*.

When the broker had gone and Polly was also going out, she saw her father sitting in the drawing-room on the first floor, staring at the window.

Coax had informed him that the transport business must be completed within the next two weeks.

For the first time, the broker had condescended to explain how he planned to wind up the transaction. First Peachum must have all the money ready; afterwards the projected marriage contract should decide what settlement was to be made between Peachum and Coax. In this way Peachum would be reimbursed for his losses and Coax would content himself with the profits instead of a dowry.

First have all the money ready! That was terrible!

When Mrs Peachum came home, she had to put her husband to bed. He could scarcely speak and hardly managed to get up the stairs. In the night he thought he was dying. His wife had to rub in half a bottle of arnica over the region of his heart. He even suggested fetching a doctor!

The next morning he walked dejectedly through the yards, every stone of which had been paid for by him and which he would now have to sacrifice for three decaying ships, at present being repaired in the docks at his expense. A wonderful business – for those who had arranged it !

From a distance of five paces he stood, hands in pockets, hat tilted on the back of his head, absently watching his daughter tending the dogs. She was kneeling between two stunted trees whose foliage was already yellow.

Could he not still, through her, make the whole business a success and thus avert the great catastrophe? If only he could get her free for Coax ! Nothing less than the closest of family relationships would induce this depraved, unscrupulous, insatiable broker to admit him into the business. Only his abominable lechery could, perhaps, make him do that. Perhaps !

And this MacHeath would rather go to prison and face a desperate accusation than give up his wife.

Peachum racked his brains for a way of persuading him to give a divorce.

Supposing he went to him and said :

'Do you realize that you have robbed a poor man? You probably think: a poor man, all the better ! I can do what I like with him. But there you are mistaken, sir ! Do not underrate the power of the poor. Perhaps you are unaware that in our country they have the same rights as the rich? The weaker must be protected, otherwise he will succumb. Remember ! he has nothing else but these rights of equality !'

For hours on end he composed speeches of this sort. But he could think of nothing compelling enough. He realized that there was nothing that could persuade a sensible man to give up what he already had – except actual force.

During the whole of that morning Peachum fought with himself. Then, out of all his agony and indecision, grew the resolve to take desperate measures, to offer his son-in-law *money*.

A small oily gentleman, a solicitor from the East End, placed Mr Peachum's proposal before MacHeath.

In the second sentence he uttered, he brusquely offered money in return for MacHeath agreeing to a divorce.

'How much money?' asked MacHeath, smiling incredulously.

The solicitor murmured something about a few hundred pounds.

'You can tell my father-in-law,' said MacHeath, staring at

him as though at an interesting reptile, "that the father of my wife stands too high in my estimation for me to take his offer seriously. I cannot think that my father-in-law really believes that his daughter would give her heart to a man who was capable of selling it again for £500.'

The solicitor bowed in confusion and went away.

A few days later Mr MacHeath found himself in a position in which he would have given an offer of this sort, provided that it could have been doubled, far closer consideration.

But the oily little gentleman did not return. Such opportunities rarely come twice in a lifetime.

One's Thoughts Are Free

MacHeath occupied a cell situated in an otherwise empty corridor. It had formerly served as a sick-room for several patients and was high and spacious. It was also light enough, for it had two proper windows.

Brown had arranged for a thick red carpet to be laid. On the wall hung a picture of Queen Victoria. MacHeath was also allowed to receive newspapers, but he did not like reading them; they were full of pitiful descriptions of Mary Sawyer, who was always presented to readers as being very beautiful. More harmful were the accounts of the shop and the miserable surroundings in which she had spent the last six years of her life.

He himself was only mentioned in the more sensational papers, and direct accusations were avoided. But there were unpleasant insinuations.

MacHeath could have as many books as he wanted, except pornographic ones. They were not allowed because the prison chaplain came round now and again. But the Bible was permitted.

Visitors were few, but not because the rules forbade them. O'Hara had a rooted aversion to appearing in this building. He hated meeting acquaintances. Later in his career he was to spend many years in a similar institution. Fanny Chrysler, too, seldom came there.

Everything concerning the activities of the gang and the

situation of the B. shops was reported to him by Polly. She worked together with O'Hara; and mostly in the afternoons, in Mac's study in Nunhead. But MacHeath's arrest was nevertheless a severe handicap.

What depressed MacHeath chiefly was the fact that no word had come from Aaron. After all, he was his partner. He tried to think what the great Aaron could have against him. It could not be the mere fact that he had been arrested. The business world knows far worse fates than that.

Gradually it became clear to him that he must anticipate great difficulties in his dealings with Aaron and the Oppers. The accusation which his father-in-law had levelled at him might mean the end of his business association with them. Should he be forced to produce his alibi, he would then be revealed, naked and unmasked, as the organizer of the 'neutral' C.P.B.!

All through the silent night in his cell, he pondered over fresh ways and means. His thoughts turned more and more towards Chreston. Could not he get Chreston into his power, or at least form an alliance with him?

'My friend Aaron', he thought, 'evidently does not think it worth the trouble to visit me in my sufferings. I have treated him as my friend – certain small differences between us would have been cleared up in time – and Chreston was my enemy. Now it is an old maxim that when a friendship begins to cool, the clever man always breaks it off *in good time*, so that he is the first. In a fight one should never have a fixed rule as to who is the ally and who is the enemy. That is as dangerous as any preconceived notion. Perhaps my real, natural ally is Chreston and my enemy Aaron? That might prove true at any instant during the course of the business. Of course it is terrible when a man is continually faced with decisions of such far-reaching importance!'

He thought with bitterness of the fact that it was only the lack of Polly's dowry that had driven him to that course which he had since followed with such disastrous results.

Immersed in thought he watched an imaginary Polly in the corner of his cell. Could he not still, through *her*, make the whole business a success?

Slowly he began to evolve a new plan.

Whenever he went to the courts, Polly accompanied him. On one such trip, as they drove through the misty streets in a decrepit cab with two policemen sitting in front, he unburdened himself to her. 'The worst of it is,' he said, 'that O'Hara is no longer pulling his weight. In spite of my express orders, he is not clearing out the warehouses. Do you know what he's up to?'

'No,' she said, a little frightened.

'Couldn't you find out?' he asked, searching her face in the intermittent gleams of light. The memory of another drive with her suddenly occurred to him again. The memory was unpleasant, because he was thinking of O'Hara. It was also unpleasant because she did not answer his question.

MacHeath had his doubts of her faithfulness. He said to himself again and again:

'Of course she's faithful to me; if only because she's with child. She would never do anything like that. It would be too horrible, and also too stupid. I should most certainly find out, and then what would she do? So she wouldn't do it because she's too sensible. She knows that I would kill her – yes, kill her – if the worst happened. I would even go so far as to call her a whore. "What!" I would say, "I'm sitting here in prison and you can't even wait three weeks? You are a whore, nothing more!" She would be sure to break down. "Don't say that," she would cry, "it cannot be that I have sunk so low." "You are a whore," I would say. "A child at heart and yet a whore? That is the limit! Not even a dock-side whore would do that! I retch with physical disgust when I think of you." She would have to hear all that. No woman would risk so much. It's quite true; I really couldn't take it kindly if my wife went with another fellow. As a woman, she is like wax in the hands of a man. Such an act would make a deep impression on a person's psyche. After that she would be totally useless to me. Some fellow might easily ask her to go home with him. She wouldn't hesitate to leave me. And just now I must rely on her. It's a good thing that I've put her with child. She can't run wild like that. She simply can't. She needs me physically. A woman in that condition won't let another man near her, for biological reasons. Biological reasons are always the best!'

Actually, during that week, she was very sweet to him and made no further mention of Fanny Chysler and the Swedish trip. He had her continually watched by Father and fought down the tormenting suspicion that the latter might be in league with O'Hara, whom he chiefly suspected. For he needed Polly and O'Hara now that the great battle was about to be fought. And he would have to deliver his master-strokes from prison.

There was no denying that he was in a difficult position. It was quite clear to him that he would have to put all private considerations aside until the business transactions were completed.

He would have to use Polly as a means of separating the National Credit Bank from Chreston's. Just before he went to prison, he had instructed her quickly in what she had to do.

She was to go to Miller in the National Credit Bank, present her father's compliments, then hesitate as though she didn't know quite how to say what she wanted, then burst into tears and ask the old man what she was to do: in the very near future her husband was going to withdraw her father's deposit (which was her dowry) from the bank and invest the whole of it in his B. shops. Her father would visit the bank in a day or two to confirm this. Miller would then probably suggest that she should ask her father not to part with the dowry. To that she was to answer that her father was completely under the influence of her husband. Then she was to go away weeping.

She was so ready to do this that he was quite affected and even told her the reason for these measures.

He explained to her that the bank would probably approach him forthwith. Then he could demand that they should dissociate themselves from Chreston. In this way Chreston, on the verge of his great sales week, would be forced to come crawling to him.

The way in which Mac spoke of his business made a deep impression on Polly.

She realized clearly that he was bent on making a success of both their lives.

'*I'm not a good wife*,' she thought. '*He works for me and I* do nothing. Even though it is only superficial and has nothing to do with my deeper feelings when I now and again sleep with men because I can't resist it if a man kisses my hand and I take nothing from him either, and then he finds me just as attractive afterwards, and even though it is nice, especially with O'Hara, and it has nothing to do with anyone else, it's still not right and in time people will see that I'm like that because there'll be deep lines in my face.'

She went away sadly and made up her mind to break with O'Hara, for whom, indeed, she felt only a physical attraction, especially since he had been speaking badly of Mac and had hinted at plans for making himself independent.

She told him this on the same evening, in the restaurant where they usually met. He laughed and suggested finishing the day's business at home; there were several orders for her to sign.

'Good,' he said, 'we'll stop it all. You're completely free to decide for yourself. No one can compel you to do what you don't want. I would be the last person to force love on a woman. When the slightest thing crops up to spoil it, it's best to drop the whole thing immediately. But you can still come and finish off the work. What has that got to do with our relationship? Can't two grown-up people be alone in a room together without falling on top of one another? There are psychological and ethical reasons for us not having sexual intercourse, so we will not have sexual intercourse. That's quite simple. Why should we take any notice of other fools, with their dull distrust and their dirty suspicions? We're two free people.'

He was good at talking and had been at a Public School. So she went with him and they finished the work. Then they slept together, because, although there were psychological and ethical reasons against it, there were also sexual ones in its favour. Nevertheless this was to be her last taste of pleasure for a long time.

On the next morning the Peach visited Miller at the National Credit Bank.

She looked fresh and bright and was at her best. She never had qualms of conscience after the fall, but always before.

Miller received her in his private office. She presented her

218

father's compliments, hesitated as though she didn't quite know how to say what she wanted, then burst into tears and said everything that Mac had told her.

'Mac', she sobbed, 'is so ambitious. He always wants to do better than anyone else. And so he needs money and more money. He finances so many people. This Mary Sawyer was financed by him, too. It was only meanness on her part that made her slander him like she did. I can't stop him if he wants to have my dowry, he's so generous.'

Miller was more shocked than she had expected. The old man became quite grey in the face when he heard that Peachum's account was about to be closed. He stammered something about Hawthorne and went into the next room. After a quarter of an hour she went away because he had not come back.

That same afternoon the One and a Half Centuries were sitting in Mac's cell. He was wearing his ordinary suit. He had chairs fetched for them and offered them cigars.

The cell was not a bad meeting place – although the red carpet was no longer there. A paper had published an article on the comforts enjoyed by merchant princes in prison. After which two policemen had rolled up the carpet and carried it away. But the picture of the Queen still hung on the wall.

Brown remained as obliging as possible. He had always received his percentage regularly from MacHeath and was, by nature, grateful. He was no politician; he was accustomed to keeping his promises.

'*A man can be free even within prison walls,*' said MacHeath to old Hawthorne, looking round contentedly. '*Freedom is something spiritual. Whoever has once had it, can never lose it. There are some people who are never free outside a prison. The body can be bound with chains, the spirit never. One's thoughts are free.*'

MacHeath was the first to mention business.

'Gentlemen,' he said, pacing up and down the cell, 'you find me astonished and somewhat embarrassed by your visit. The vagaries of life, its eternal ups and downs, carried us, not so long ago, apart. We parted like companions who say: "We have gone so far together – but here our ways divide. Let us not be sad. Let us wish each other *au revoir*!" You went, so I have

219

heard, to Chreston; I turned to Aaron. Each of us acted in the interests of our own business, each with the same objective, always to serve the public efficiently. – Am I right?'

Miller cleared his throat and Hawthorne, with a hang-dog air, took up the theme.

'Mr MacHeath,' he said softly. 'your grasp of what has happened does you honour. Many people would have misunderstood our motives when, after careful consideration, we decided in favour of Chreston. The National Credit Bank belongs to a child. We are her representatives and cannot follow the voice of our inclinations like other, independent people. We hear that you wish to withdraw certain monies which your worthy father-in-law has entrusted to our institution?'

'Quite right,' answered MacHeath. 'I need this money to carry out one or two business operations which have been forced on my shops by competition.'

Hawthorne and Miller looked at one another.

'Is it the Chreston stores which compel you to undertake these operations?' asked Hawthorne, almost in a whisper.

'Perhaps,' said MacHeath.

'We are very sorry to hear that,' said Hawthorne, and Miller nodded.

'I believe you,' said MacHeath.

Hawthorne was somewhat taken aback.

'Of course, Mr MacHeath,' he said, 'it is almost a matter of course that the stronger business should swallow up the weaker. It is the same in nature. I don't need to tell you that.'

'No,' said MacHeath.

'When, some little while ago, you again commenced negotiations with us, we believed that the moment had come when we could offer you our help.'

MacHeath rejoiced inwardly.

'I know. You redoubled your efforts. You quickly put into Chreston's all the money that you had; and also – all that you did not have.'

MacHeath stopped. He had said the last sentence quite casually, without thinking. Now he expected a protest, and suddenly he saw, to his great astonishment, that this protest was not forthcoming.

One glance at the One and a Half Centuries and he knew everything.

They had drawn on the deposit accounts!

There was scarcely a hesitation in MacHeath's voice when he continued gaily:

'So you staked, in a manner of speaking, your last shirt, and, unfortunately, other people's shirts as well. Am I right?'

Hawthorne had bowed his head. Miller stared blindly at the window.

'What do you want?' stammered Hawthorne hoarsely.

'Everything,' said MacHeath happily. 'Or nearly everything; and therefore not much. But wait! We will see what can be done.'

He carefully chose a fat cigar from the box, bit the top off, spat it out, rolled the brown monster between his thick lips, and lit it. It was one of the most blissful moments of his life. A blue cloud of smoke billowed out of his mouth.

'Wait!' he said. 'You have misappropriated my father-in-law's money. With all your hundred and fifty years, you have been guilty of embezzlement. With this money Chreston has been enabled to hold out, although selling his goods below economic prices. That was supposed to ruin Aaron and my B. shops. Therefore, first robbery and then murder. In the streets, it's the other way about. There, murder comes first. And then, if we had been ruined, you would have swallowed us up! Ugh! Really, Hawthorne, that's too much like nature!'

'What do you want?' repeated Hawthorne, now staring at his opponent with blue, unwavering eyes.

These are the first honest people, thought MacHeath, that I have ever met. The only ones.

'Listen,' he said slowly, 'I could ask a lot; but instead of that, I have decided to offer a lot. That's what I'm like. I don't want to destroy you but to help you. For this purpose it would be best if I entered the bank as, shall we say, Director of Business Investments. And before that, we'll make the following arrangements: we will first withdraw our support from Chreston, for he is by nature the weaker. That insane and indecent waste of goods will cease. We shall demand our money back so that he can feel his weakness properly. He will then probably feel a need for a strong hand to guide him. Is that a good suggestion?'

Miller had stood up. Hawthorne watched him. Miller threw a short and astonished glance down at him, but he still remained seated. That altered many things for Miller. He began to age. He bent, his teeth fell out, his hair turned white, his wisdom grew.

'It will be for the sake of the firm,' he murmured, 'if I resign.'

'So be it,' said MacHeath.

The One and a Half Centuries went sadly away. They had promised to prepare the necessary papers for MacHeath's entry into the National Credit Bank. Also they had agreed to withdraw Chreston's credit.

Every day MacHeath waited for a visit from Chreston, who should have come crawling to him because he could not carry through his impending sales week without the support of the bank. After the fierce competition of the last weeks, his supplies must now be almost exhausted.

But Chreston did not come.

Instead of that, there were dark and mysterious happenings in the C.P.B.

The news that came into the prison from Lower Blacksmith Square was scanty and inaccurate. O'Hara still did not appear. MacHeath's orders were apparently ignored.

Neither could Polly tell him anything very precise. She kept going down to the warehouses, but she never discovered much. O'Hara said he was taking an inventory of stocks. Only the inventory never seemed to be finished.

When Polly, now considerably disturbed, went down there once again, she saw cases of goods being driven off in carts; the horses nearly knocked her down in the dark passage-way leading out of the yards. O'Hara was not there, and Grooch was very embarrassed. He was unable to say where the cases came from. Polly went home in a cold fury. She had long since broken with O'Hara, for she could not tolerate him working against her husband's interests. The next morning she went to Mac and reviled O'Hara, crying that he was dishonest and was stealing the goods in order to sell them secretly, and that he had tried to get the keys for the burgling implements from her because he apparently wanted to set up on his own with some of the boys.

MacHeath calmed her. He told her to go to Miller.

It flattered her that he entrusted his business to her like that. She called in at the bank as though on a chance visit, and while Miller told her the news she wandered about the room, clasping her bag behind her back and looking at the prints on the walls.

She learned that Chreston had, at first, been horrified at the stoppage of credit, but now he said that he hoped to carry on all right without further credit. He had recently received large consignments of goods at astonishingly low prices and was expecting to do excellent business during his sales week.

MacHeath was very disturbed at the news.

Polly made a second visit to the bank and demanded, in MacHeath's name, that Miller should himself see these cheap goods before he took any further steps.

On this inspection Miller was accompanied by Fanny Chrysler, whom MacHeath had decided to make use of again. She immediately recognized that these new and astonishingly cheap consignments with which Chreston was reinforcing his sales week had come from Lower Blacksmith Square.

When she was sitting opposite MacHeath in his cell, she scarcely dared tell him the truth. She talked so long of other matters that he at last shouted at her. Before she had finished her first sentence, he understood everything.

O'Hara had found a lucrative way of clearing the warehouses. He had been supplying their opponents.

MacHeath got into a furious rage.

'That's treachery on the eve of the battle,' he shouted. 'And that, while I sit here fettered hand and foot! And why am I sitting here? Why do I allow this horrible suspicion to rest on me? One word from me, and I could walk out of here a free man. Why don't I speak? Because I feel it my duty to carry through this business and not surrender the flag to the enemy! Because I think of all the people who would be ruined if I did speak. Because I say: Keep faith! And then I'm treated like this! What can I say now to the poor B. shop owner when he asks me what I'm up to? There he stands, in his half-empty shop, . with the rent due, without goods, in the window the placards announcing a great sale, behind him his starving family with no raw materials to work on. But still he stands erect, untiring in the fight, full of hope, trusting in me, inspired by the great ideal! And then this man turns traitor! I'll cut him into mince-meat!'

He paced many miles within the confines of his cell. But on the next morning he took no steps against O'Hara.

'It's his old indecisiveness,' said Fanny to Grooch. 'It's a pity he's such a man of moods. When he is disappointed, it's weeks before he's capable of taking a clear view of the situation. He gives way completely to his disappointment. And then he only returns to his idea gradually.'

'Has he really an idea?' asked Grooch doubtfully. 'I mean real plans, not just vague schemes. Sometimes I'm afraid that if he once lacks an idea, he will be done for.'

'We must believe in him,' said Fanny calmly.

But the delivery of illicit consignments from Ride Lane still continued. MacHeath did nothing to stop them.

Instead of that he summoned a conference with the two solici-tors of the C.P.B. and Fanny, and arranged for the energetic promulgation of the decisions reached on the 20th September, whereby the debts of the B. shops were to be collected immedi-ately. Apparently he had thought of a new plan.

He was endeavouring to get as much hard cash into his hands as possible. Fanny helped him in this by working in the offices of the C.P.B. She had ideas of social welfare and this ruination of the B. shops went against her principles. But she knew that it was now a question of to be or not to be. She squeezed out of the shopkeepers every penny obtainable. Only later did she realize what was happening to the money.

One evening, as she was going home tired from her work in the C.P.B., she decided to visit her antique shop. Although it was after closing time, she found it brightly lit up. In the shop were standing several gentlemen, amongst them Rigger, the solicitor. Her clerk was in the act of showing them the books.

Rigger informed her drily that MacHeath wished to sell the shop. He seemed astonished that she knew nothing of this. She had hysterics.

MacHeath had genuinely forgotten to tell her. He was so certain of her that he would not have hesitated to mention that he needed the money which was tied up in the shop. It was his most profitable reserve. Unfortunately, although she had been with him that afternoon, he had not said a word about it.

She went home very upset.

When, in spite of previous arrangements, several days passed without her coming, MacHeath wrote her a peremptory letter. He could well imagine what was the matter with her, but even then he did not excuse himself. He had other worries. It would be well for her to remember that she was still an *employee*.

MacHeath was now engaged in feverish activity, although his liberty had been restricted still further.

For several days there had been a considerable number of people asking to see him; and these people, when they had received their permission, had made no use of it. Then there appeared a sensational article in the *Reflector* revealing how many people had received this permission. So Brown had to limit the number of visitors. In this way Mr Peachum now and again showed signs of life.

But MacHeath's business operations would allow of no restrictions.

He suddenly had toothache and Brown allowed him to have a dentist. The surgery had two doors. While the police watched in the passage and the waiting-room, MacHeath received a great many people whom it was essential for him to interview.

Sitting in the dentist's chair, with a napkin round his throat in case a policeman should come in, he negotiated with numerous grinning women and girls.

Polly was also there. She sat at a desk while the dentist consumed his breakfast. In a little notebook she wrote down the names of the visitors and the sums of money MacHeath allotted to each of them. She took the money out of a leather bag which she had brought with her. This was the money from the B. shops. Several bailiffs had helped with the collecting.

The women signed little receipt forms before they left. They all laughed; and Polly laughed too. It was very funny.

In the *Reflector* the next day there appeared a front-page headline: THE CITY SHARKS ARE HAVING THEIR TEETH REPAIRED. But everything that had to be done was already done.

MacHeath was very satisfied.

He summoned Grooch from Lower Blacksmith Square and asked him over a cigar – also in the presence of the dentist – how many people in the gang were, in his opinion, tired of the business. He was thinking of giving them a change.

He needed a certain number of people – including some women, if possible – who, on a certain day, would go out shopping for him. Details would be given later. Whoever volunteered could count on receiving a B. shop on especially favourable terms. In a short time the C.P.B. would be dealing with fewer orders and therefore would refuse all goods from doubtful sources. The shops had a great future before them and were an ideal means of beginning a new life. It would be a pleasure for him to be able to start a few able people (he was not interested in any others) in such a socially useful occupation.

Then he made a speech to the astonished Grooch:

'Grooch,' he said, *'you are an old burglar. Your profession is burglary. I wouldn't think of suggesting that your profession, in itself, is out of date. That would be going too far. Only in its form, Grooch, does it lag behind the times. You are an artisan, a hack, and that's all there is to it. That class is on the wane – you can't deny that. What is a pick-lock compared to a debenture share? What is the burgling of a bank compared to the founding of a bank? What, my dear Grooch, is the murder of a man compared to the employment of a man? Take an example. A few years ago we stole a whole street made of wooden blocks; we dug the blocks out, loaded them on to a cart, and drove away with them. We thought we had done something wonderful. In reality, we had only made ourselves unnecessary work and run an unnecessary risk. Shortly afterwards I heard that one only has to be a town councillor in order to be able to arrange the distribution of contracts oneself. Then one gets the contract for such and such a street and also several years' guaranteed profits without running any risks at all. Another time I sold a house which didn't belong to me; it was empty at the time. I put up a notice: For sale. Apply at XX. That was me. Childishness! That was really immoral because it was taking unnecessary advantage of illegal ways and means. That can be done just as easily by putting up a row of jerry-built houses, selling them on the instal-*

ment plan, and waiting until the purchasers run out of money! Then one has the houses as well and can repeat the process as often as one likes. And all that without the police having any excuse to interfere! Take our business for example: we break into shops at night in order to get the goods we want to sell. Why? When the shops go bankrupt through being uneconomically run, we can buy their goods with perfect legality at prices far below the costs of burgling! And then, if you set store on such things, we have just as much stolen the goods as if we had committed a burglary; for after all those goods in the bankrupt shops were taken away from the people who had made or bought them, and who had been told: Work or Live! Nowadays a man must work within the law; it's just as much fun! I, too, have several times come back from Belgium and got past the gentlemen in the soft hats who stand on the gangway, by wearing a bandage across my face. But what's that compared to this scheme of the C.P.B.? Child's-play! In this present age one uses more peaceful methods. Brute force is out of date. Why send out murderers when one can employ bailiffs? We must build up, not pull down; that is, we must build up for profit.'

With half-closed eyes he observed Grooch. He hoped to propitiate Fanny by effecting a reconciliation with Grooch.

'I was thinking,' he continued, 'of closing down my whole buying organization and dismissing all the employees, including yourself. But perhaps the latter course can be avoided. How many of the employees, do you think, could raise enough capital to buy some of the many B. shops which will shortly be vacant? Make out a list for me. In that way I could still make something out of the boys. There's no need to throw them straight on to the streets. You might ask Fanny which ones she considers the most reliable; she always has a soft spot for them. Understand, Grooch, I am turning over a new leaf. I summoned you here because you are a capable fellow; for there are also people who cannot understand the signs of the times and who, therefore, will be crushed by the wheel of progress.'

Grooch listened patiently and made visible efforts to understand the signs of the times. Then he murmured something about O'Hara.

'O'Hara?' said MacHeath regretfully. 'He's always thinking

of women. I'm quite sure the invoices for his goods are not so carefully arranged as they should be. And one fine day the police will come asking him questions – and what then?'

He came to an excellent understanding with Grooch. During the next few years, Grooch managed the buying for the shops in South London with skill and honesty.

Chreston's Sales Week

On a fine autumn day Chreston opened his sales week with the introduction of unit prices.

Already at seven o'clock in the morning, two hours before the shops were due to open, there were large crowds collected in front of the iron grilles outside the doors. There was nothing unusual about these crowds – except, perhaps, for the comparatively large number of men in them.

For the grand opening, Messrs Miller and Hawthorne of the National Credit Bank had condescended to be present. Together with Mr Chreston, tall, dried-up, and wiry, they waited in the luxurious offices of the main establishment. The old people were filled with extreme nervousness. Chreston was completely calm. His preparations had been carefully made. The staff had been working late into the previous night, transposing the prices into their four categories. On the stroke of nine the doors opened and the public surged in.

From the very beginning, there occurred in all the Chreston shops several extremely remarkable and unpleasant incidents. The public behaved strangely.

Scarcely had the people been let in, than they began buying like mad. No one troubled to choose. The buying began at the nearest counters and spread inwards to the further ones. Without hesitation the people swept together great heaps of similar articles, stuffed them into bags or even sacks, paid with coins of fairly large denominations, and departed rapidly – only to return again in several minutes, empty-handed.

Chreston soon noticed what was going on. These were no normal customers; they were not the mistrustful, fastidious, hostile beings who pick and choose for hours before they finally

commit themselves. These people were using their elbows mercilessly, shouldering more captious purchasers brutally away from
the counters, and generally creating a reign of terror.

The sales staff, who were now enjoying the novelty of sharing
in the profits, made perspiring efforts to keep up with the demand. The goods were torn from their hands with curses. Only
at the cash desks were the customers more particular. They insisted on receiving their stamped receipts.

Chreston summoned the police. They came and convinced
themselves of the exceptionally brisk demand on the part of the
public. They also recognized several notorious and undesirable
elements in the crowd. But owing to the unusual situation they
were powerless to interfere. Truncheons could hardly be used to
prevent the public from purchasing for cash.

Then Chreston, who in the meanwhile had visited his other
stores and seen the same things happening there, closed his
doors for a few hours. But when the journalists came asking for
an explanation, he opened up again.

Morning and afternoon and late into the evening, Polly and
Grooch sat in a little public house and received the receipts for
the goods. There were enormous quantities of them.

Chreston read in the evening papers that his sales week had
been a riotous success and that the public had bought up the
whole of his extensive stocks in a single day.

The interiors of his shops looked as though they had been
swept by a hurricane. A gigantic swarm of omnivorous locusts
seemed to have eaten everything bare. He could not understand
this phenomenon.

Towards evening, at the same time as a continuous stream of
hand-carts and lorries, loaded high with goods, were rolling into
certain warehouses in Lower Blacksmith Square, MacHeath
received O'Hara in his cell.

'I like independence and initiative,' he told him calmly. 'It
was an excellent idea of yours to offer that unsaleable stuff to
Chreston. We would never have disposed of it without invoices.
And now we have the invoices. For, as you know, I have bought
the goods back again. Where is the money?'

O'Hara was dumbfounded. He was beyond making evasions.
He had received promissory notes from Chreston which he

handed over to MacHeath. Invoices for the goods had neither been asked for by Chreston nor received.

After MacHeath's little speech O'Hara made no further attempt to explain the position. He was dependent on MacHeath and MacHeath was dependent on him. It was just by chance that MacHeath had come to speak of the matter, otherwise O'Hara might have mentioned it himself. No one could prove the contrary. It would have been horrible to suppose anything else. Really, it would have been very horrible.

When O'Hara had gone – and he stayed a little while longer, sitting in silence – MacHeath sent a message for Brown to come to him.

They drank grog and smoked. MacHeath sat on the couch, rumpling with the tip of his shoe the carpet which Brown had had brought in again. He found it difficult to begin. At last he made the plunge.

'Do you remember what you said to me this summer when we were talking about the Liverpool affair? You said you would show me the right way to go. Since then, I have come to understand what you meant. I must break away entirely from my past; that's becoming more and more obvious to me. When I lie awake at nights, I think of your words and fight against my weaker self.'

He made an emotional pause. Brown looked slightly alarmed.

'Don't forget that I helped you with money which you still have,' he said uncomfortably.

'I would rather,' said MacHeath in a pained voice, 'that we did not mention money now. Yours is safe, as sure as I'm called MacHeath.'

'And I would rather that you stopped joking, Mac,' said Brown angrily.

MacHeath continued unruffled:

'I can remember the words you used, as plainly as though you had only spoken them yesterday. You must give up this O'Hara, you said. You must place yourself in a different environment. You said you would give me time to do that. And now I have got so far.'

He looked at Brown earnestly.

'There have been irregularities in my buying organization.

230

Suspicions seem to point to my employee, O'Hara. Do you know him?'

'Has someone double-crossed you?'

'No, not directly. But there's something very suspicious about the goods which were to have been delivered to my shops and also to Aaron's stores. All the invoices seem to be missing. I must investigate the matter; otherwise Aaron will demand an investigation and then it will be directed against me. Do you see?'

'I see. But this O'Hara is a nasty customer. He will scarcely leave you out of the picture.'

'Perhaps,' said MacHeath dreamily, 'perhaps he *will* leave me out of it. He has invoices for a few things. And those are in the care of the C.P.B. Fanny is looking after them.'

'Ah!' murmured Brown.

'Yes,' said MacHeath, relieved.

'And what am I to do in the meanwhile?' asked Brown.

'Perhaps you could find out something else about him. There must be something which could be brought against him and then dropped, according as to whether he comes to his senses or not.'

'Of course that could be done,' said Brown. 'I don't like traitors either.'

'And his habits are so disgusting,' added MacHeath. 'He's always running after women. I only kept him because of his usefulness. But now my patience is exhausted.'

They sat for a while smoking.

Then Brown went away.

MacHeath went slowly to bed. He was still worried.

12

There's no smoke without fire.

(OLD ADAGE)

Has Mr MacHeath Got Mary Sawyer on His Conscience?

THE excitement about Mary Sawyer's death began to get more and more on Mr MacHeath's nerves.

Peachum's solicitor, Walley, had summoned a meeting of all the B. shop owners. They had met in the back room of a fourth-class restaurant and hatched various mischievous schemes.

The case had given enormous publicity to the conditions of the B. shops. The fat solicitor called for the founding of a union of injured retail traders. He reported that the suspected murderer had a princely room in the prison with Persian carpets.

A lanky, consumptive shoemaker attested to the unusual 'friendship' between MacHeath and the murdered woman, and heatedly demanded an investigation into the relations between employers and female employees. In this direction, he proclaimed, authority was being *misused*!

A few of the more enlightened members advocated moderation.

An old woman suggested that all settlements with MacHeath should be postponed until a verdict had been announced and that they should try to make him pay for the October rents. She found only one supporter who approved these measures because they 'would show Mr MacHeath that we have lost all faith in him'.

But the representatives of the more enlightened section won the day. A decision was reached to leave economic considerations out of the discussion; for they had nothing to do with the matter and would only prejudice the high moral standpoint of those present. This decision was unanimously adopted. Even the old woman agreed.

So economic considerations were not mentioned. Poor people

are very fond of regarding their annihilation from a lofty stand-point.

It was therefore decided to protest against the defencelessness of the small retail trader and to demand relentless prosecution of the murderer 'irrespective of his class or standing'.

Yet in spite of everything, the results of this meeting were unfavourable to MacHeath. The feeling against him increased generally.

Pictures of the children appeared in the newspapers. One photograph reproduced the placard: 'This shop is run by a soldier's wife'.

Peachum excelled himself when he stationed a beggar, a starved miserable creature, in front of every B. shop and hung round his neck the announcement: 'If you buy here, you are buying in *my* shop'. The owners of the shops did nothing against this, and the newspapers photographed it.

In heavy black headlines the question was asked: IS MAC-HEATH RESPONSIBLE FOR MARY SAWYER'S DEATH?

And in addition to all this, MacHeath was faced with the problem of getting the proceedings squashed without having to reveal his alibi.

Everything depended on whether a suggestion that Mary Sawyer had committed suicide could be made credible enough.

He had brought the One and a Half Centuries to their knees and he possessed incriminating material against Chreston. But the formalities necessary for his entry into the bank took time and he could not use the material against Chreston to real effect until he was sitting on the board of directors.

But the disclosure of the alibi could only be avoided if Mary Sawyer's suicide could be proved. On the other hand, a suicide would show up the B. shops in a very unpleasant light.

On the evening prior to the hearing before the magistrate, Brown came into his cell and sorrowfully informed MacHeath that the men who had seen Mary *alone* just before her death, had apparently vanished into thin air. Brown had done everything possible to find them. Someone must have spirited them away. Walley had grinningly suggested to him (Brown) that the two men had lied to the police and were now afraid of having to swear to their statements. So MacHeath could well imagine who was responsible for the disappearance of these witnesses. Probably they were now living in the same hotel as Fewkoombey.

'It's no good,' said MacHeath to Brown, who listened to him dispiritedly, 'what's the use of your loyalty when it becomes a question of taking action. You remind me of dear old Skiller who had the best will in the world and yet never took in a soul simply because he hadn't got the ability. He was always ready to crack his enemies, only he never recognized them before it was too late; four nightwatchmen couldn't scare him away, but unfortunately he always left his tools at home! You're just like that. When you remember our time together in the army, you never hesitate for a moment to come to my help. But I'm unfortunately not sure that you don't forget some things. That's a great failing, Freddy! Of course, your duty lies towards the State, but it's a pity that those who enter the service of the State seem to be mostly those who are incapable of holding their own in the open market. That's why, for example, one finds all these judges who are filled with the best intentions but who are a little lacking in intelligence. They are quite ready to enforce the law with the greatest severity against paupers and communists, but they rarely succeed in cutting their careers short, stopping their mouths properly, and, in short, putting their necks in a halter! On the other hand they realize, quite clearly, that such and such a defendant belongs to their class, and they sympathize with him; but from pure inability to apply the law suitably and to administer it as it was intended, and often also through a pedantic lack of imagination, they are quite incapable of getting him off and even if they do get him off, their inefficiency makes our legal machinery appear thoroughly corrupt and dishonest. Whereas, on the contrary, this machinery is perfect, absolutely ideal for the purpose, and only has to be applied intelligently and logically in order that nobody shall have a hair of his head harmed. For people of our sort who wish to avoid trouble there's no need to pervert the law, it's quite enough to make use of it! Oh, Freddy, you're too good to me; I know it. But you're not very clever!'

They sat late into the night, reviving old memories of the past. And it was not until he was just about to leave, that Brown dared admit to his friend that even his employee, Fanny Chrysler, was going to take the witness-box against him. During the preliminary investigations she had admitted to the conversation in her shop between MacHeath and Mary.

The hearing took place in a pleasant, airy room. The Magistrate was a small, leathery man with wide blue eyes, who harmonized perfectly with the bright, sunny court and its white curtains and whitewashed walls.

The statements of the medical officer and police did not take long. The proceedings quickly centred round MacHeath who stood under strong suspicion of having murdered the shopkeeper, Mary Sawyer.

Walley, subsidized by Peachum, was representing the dead woman's children. MacHeath was being defended by Rigger and Withe. He gave his profession as 'Wholesale Merchant'.

MacHeath made a small mistake when asked about previous convictions. He had a feeling that he had not been punished before and said:

'None.'

Walley immediately caught him up.

'Weren't you convicted three years ago and fined a pound?'

'I can't remember,' said MacHeath, unpleasantly astonished.

'Ah! You can't remember. You can't remember that you infringed the licensing laws? You did infringe them, but you can't remember. So allow me to tell you: You have a previous conviction.'

Rigger laughed ironically.

'Convicted for infringement of the licensing laws! That's the only conviction you'll ever get, MacHeath!'

Walley stood up again:

'It is not the nature of the transgression that is important, but the remarkable fact that the accused has tried to conceal the fact that he was convicted for it and punished. It is just the triviality of the whole affair which proves that the concealment of any such thing as might bring him unwelcome publicity has become a second nature to MacHeath. In the course of the proceedings many similar instances will come to light.'

Rigger was about to protest against this attack, but Withe caught him by the sleeve and pulled him back. He was a fat man and had his own theories about how the defence should be conducted. But he had been unable to come to any agreement with Rigger. He wanted to plead suicide, Rigger preferred murder by person or persons unknown. Whatever happened the alibi was not to be used.

Unfortunately, Walley seemed to have been instructed to handle the case with extreme aggressiveness, as was apparent from his first few words.

The two men who had seen a woman alone at the dock-side about nine o'clock in the evening were, of course, missing, but the beggars who had seen the accused walking with Mary Sawyer were present. One of them, an old fellow called Stone, spoke as follows:

'I can clearly remember the man who was with the girl. He's sitting over there. We look at people very carefully. He's one of those who turn their pockets inside out three times before they give a penny. And they only do that because they have a lady with them. He took so long looking for a small enough coin that I said to him: Perhaps you would rather go home first and turn everything out there, in case a bad halfpenny's slipped behind the sofa, mister. I can remember it as though it was yesterday. He seemed to have only sovereigns in his pocket. But then he found a penny.'

The Court laughed. Rigger produced a newspaper from his brief-case and handed it to the jury. It contained a photograph of the shop window with the placard about the B. shops giving rebate to relatives of soldiers.

'This photograph was published by our adversaries,' said Rigger excitedly. 'I ask you, does a man who is lacking all sense of social responsibility behave like that?'

Walley contented himself with saying that he would later throw some light on Mr MacHeath's sense of social responsibility. It was now established, by the previous little anecdote, that Mr Stone had recognized the accused. Of course, as a millionaire, MacHeath was legally entitled to present beggars with trouser buttons – the only question was, where he got them from.

This was the first blow against MacHeath's business methods, and the latter became very uneasy.

He said sharply: buttons were made in factories.

The question, said Walley with a repressive gesture, was whether the manufacturers had received the full price for their goods.

Now Rigger jumped up and asked whether the Court was prepared to tolerate communistic propaganda.

The Magistrate pacified both parties. The substance of the witness's statement was that he recognized the accused as the man who had been accompanying Mary Sawyer on the evening of the crime.

Rigger promised to return to the witness later and drew attention to the fact that his testimony conflicted with that of the two dock-hands. He called the inspector who had interviewed the two absent men. They had certainly spoken of a woman who had been alone.

'What woman?' Walley wanted to know.

The inspector admitted that the photograph of the victim had not been shown to the two.

Walley raised his arms triumphantly.

'Fine witnesses,' he crowed. 'They saw some woman or other walking alone by the docks! As though there wasn't more than one down there!'

In response to a sign from him, a woman emerged from the witness-room who was plainly of the lowest type. She stated she was a prostitute, her territory the docks. On that very Saturday evening she had walked along the quays. She had found no one free. It was a poor neighbourhood. She herself only worked there because the docks were badly lighted and she had a rash on her face.

Rigger asked whether the neighbourhood were not very unsafe for solitary women because of the unsavoury elements that haunted it.

She said:

'Not for us.'

'The women there', explained Walley, 'do not carry a great deal of money on them.'

But there were also murders, persisted Rigger.

'We run that risk everywhere,' said the witness calmly.

What was the present state of competition among prostitutes? asked Rigger. Was there not a great deal of jealousy among the girls over customers? And finally, whatever sinister intentions the men there might have, the girls regarded them purely in the light of potential customers?

'We have our districts,' said the witness.

'And you also have your protectors?'

'I haven't.'

'Why not?'

'Because I earn too little.'

'Come, come, even asses give milk. Don't try to lie to us here. And these protectors are not only against customers but also against other prostitutes who wander into your "district", isn't that so?'

'Perhaps,' said the witness.

'I suggest,' said Rigger pompously, 'that Mary Sawyer was killed in a way suggested by the statements of this witness.'

Withe nudged him in the back.

'But we know,' he whispered behind his papers, 'how the woman was killed. Leave that alone!'

The witness was dismissed. Everyone had to admit that she might quite well have been 'the woman who had been alone' who had been seen by the two men. So Mary Sawyer might also have been accompanied by MacHeath, as the beggars had stated.

There was considerable excitement among the Press when Fewkoombey, who had remained hidden since his first deposition, was called by Walley.

Rigger immediately asked him where he had been.

Walley answered for him:

'He has been under special protection. We did not want him to share the same fate as Mrs Sawyer.'

Fewkoombey described in a calm voice his experiences with the dead woman. MacHeath had made an appointment with her; she had been expecting him when he, Fewkoombey, left her. She had probably wanted to persuade him to help her financially; she was most likely going to threaten him because she knew something about him.

Rigger stood up.

'Was Mrs Sawyer afraid of the accused?'

'What do you mean by that?'

238

'Whether she was afraid he might do something to her – for instance push her into the water?'

'Hardly, otherwise she wouldn't have met him down there.'

'Quite right, Fewkoombey. Otherwise she wouldn't have met him. So she said nothing about being afraid?'

'No.'

Now the fat Withe stood up. In his squeaky voice he asked whether Mrs Sawyer, then, had nothing at all to fear from Mr MacHeath? Whether, for example, she had not been afraid of his taking financial measures against her?

The ex-soldier hesitated. Then he answered coolly:

'She thought that he might not be willing to help her in her business. In that way she was afraid of him.'

'Quite right,' said Withe and sat down with aplomb.

Walley had listened to this with a grin. Now he said:

'There is a third possibility. Her desire to obtain monetary assistance, her necessity, might have been greater than her fear and therefore driven her to take physical risks. You have just heard how little thought these street-walkers give to the horrible dangers that beset them. Gentlemen, I stand here as the representative of two little waifs. We may take it from Mr Fewkoombey's statement that their mother showed no fear because she was fighting for her children.'

Then, in reply to a question, MacHeath admitted that the note making the appointment with Mary Sawyer had emanated from him. He said he did not know Mary Sawyer's writing. He really didn't know it; otherwise he would have identified in good time the writer of the letter about the *Knife* which he had carried about on him for so long.

The Court adjourned for luncheon. Polly went to her husband who was sitting in a room where, besides himself, there were only the two solicitors. They were quarrelling in a corner about which line the defence should take.

Polly and Mac ate sandwiches. He was very upset by the proceedings. He asked, amongst other things, what Walley had meant by that silly remark: the question was whether the manufacturers had received the full price for their goods.

'That was pure impertinence,' said Mac. 'Of course he meant to imply that my goods are stolen. Supposing I do buy them from bankrupt shops. In effect, that comes to the same thing as if I stole them; their full price is not paid. And even if I did pay these little shops the full price, they're not the manufacturers. The manufacturers, that is the button-makers, have the buttons stolen from them, even if they are paid for their work. *Of course* they are not paid the full price. For where would be the profit then? I must say, it seems to me there's nothing to choose between stealing and 'buying'. And Walley's trying to bring that against me; he's trying to prejudice the Court!'

Polly agreed with him.

During the last few weeks she had grown more beautiful. All through the summer she had gone swimming and sun-bathing, of course in sheltered places because of her condition. Her arms were pale brown, but white above the elbows as could be seen when the short loose sleeves of her blouse fell back. The whole effect was very charming; and she knew it.

When the proceedings continued, Walley called Fanny Chrysler into the witness-box.

She had shadows under her eyes and was nervous. The loss of her antique shop had been a great blow to her.

She only said that the victim had demanded a loan from Mr MacHeath on the strength of their previous friendly relations.

'But at the same time she threatened that she knew something about the accused?'

'She probably meant the circumstances of her marriage,' answered the witness quickly. 'Mr MacHeath had something to do with that and possibly did not wish to be reminded of it.'

'What do you know about the *Knife*?' asked Walley suddenly.

She paled visibly under her veil.

'Nothing,' she said firmly. 'Except what I have read in the papers.'

'But Mrs Sawyer threatened the accused with disclosures and mentioned at the same time the *Knife*.'

But Fanny had recovered herself again. She said offhandedly:

'I can't remember now. She talked a lot of nonsense because she was very excited and thought she had been ill-treated. I'm sure her behaviour only annoyed Mr MacHeath because she tried to take advantage of her past relations with him.'

Withe suddenly wanted to know what were the financial circumstances of the victim.

'She was not doing very well, but she was certainly no worse off than other shopkeepers. Business is very poor at the moment.'

'Are you an employee of the accused?' asked Walley pointedly. 'Yes.'

'Then perhaps the defence would rather produce its own witnesses as to MacHeath's business successes,' said Walley ironically. 'People who are not employed by him.'

Withe became angry.

'My learned friend,' he said pompously, 'appears to believe that there is no one left in England who will speak the truth without first having regard to material considerations. I must say I find that very sad.'

'What do you find sad?' Walley asked, not without a hint of satisfaction. 'That there are no longer such people, or that I believe that?'

But the Magistrate waved the question aside. Walley now called the editor of the *Reflector*.

When this witness went on to relate how the deceased had accused MacHeath of being the *Knife*, Rigger proceeded to make the most of his opportunity.

'To any intelligent person,' he said emphatically, 'that is, to anyone who does not read the newspapers, this last testimony will show on what lamentably weak foundations the prosecution bases its case. So Mr MacHeath is the *Knife*! Our great merchants creep around with dark lanterns and go cracking safes! Gentlemen, we know to what lengths jealousy can drive a person. But everything must have its limit! The whole prosecution is based on the assumption that Mr MacHeath, one of our most prominent business men, is really not a business man at all but a criminal, a murderer! For otherwise the prosecution falls to the ground. If, however, he is *not* a murderer, but simply the well-known owner of the B. shops, then he has no reason to fear the "disclosures" of a person about whose morals we shall say nothing derogatory, for she is dead. It's ridiculous.'

He sat down triumphantly.

Walley turned to the accused :

'Mr MacHeath, how do you explain the threats made against you by the deceased?'

MacHeath stood up slowly. He looked obviously embarrassed.

'I confess,' he said, 'that it is somewhat difficult for me to speak of this matter. In fact, I can only do so as *man* to *men*. As such, I must admit that I do not feel entirely free from blame. You may be able to say of yourselves, we have always been strictly *correct* in our behaviour towards women, we have shirked nothing, caused no pain, even unconsciously. I cannot say that of myself. I had no "relations", as people call it, with this unfortunate creature who was known as Mary Sawyer and who was struck down by the hand of a scoundrel or even, perhaps, by her hand – as my counsel, Mr Withe, suggests. But did she, perhaps, have relations with me? I was her employer and I may have encountered her once or twice and perhaps, unknowingly, awakened all sorts of hopes in her. Which of us might not, under these circumstances, have sinned unconsciously? You know as well as I do how difficult it is for an employer to keep his proper *distance* from his female employees. Who can blame these poor girls, working hard for a living and getting little enough enjoyment out of life, if they become slightly enamoured of their chief who is a member of the upper classes and more cultivated than their ordinary associates? And from this point to secret hopes, and again from these to bitter disappointment, is but a short step! With your permission, I would rather say no more.'

The evening papers printed nearly all this speech in black type. The 'humanitarian' attitude of the owner of the B. shops received universal approbation. Only a proletarian publication slung mud at the B. shop Napoleon. But they could not be taken seriously because, contrary to the sporting spirit, they denied their victim any redeeming qualities and devoted most of their space to an impassioned demand for the forcible liquidation of the existing social order.

Mr MacHeath's little speech did not end the proceedings.

'According to the evidence of Mrs Chrysler, you yourself took these relations so seriously that you gave money to Mrs Sawyer?' asked Walley with a satisfied glance at the Magistrate.

The Magistrate was a dried-up little man and liked to give the impression that speeches left him unmoved.

MacHeath answered immediately:

'I *could* say that, under certain conditions, a man will give away money without being threatened, or even in spite of being threatened, if the supplicant is in distressed circumstances. But I do not say that. I only say that I did my best to prevent such occurrences as the visit of this unfortunate woman to the *Reflector*; although I failed in that. As a business man I must take every precaution to avoid any shadow of suspicion that might fall on me. How much importance I attached to these threats can be gathered from the fact that I left her unwatched and did not go to meet her at the "Waterman's Arms".'

'But you made an appointment with Mary Sawyer there?'

'I did that out of pity. Out of pity I would have gone there too, but a business conference prevented me at the last moment. If I had thought it serious, not even that consideration would have detained me.'

Walley came to life.

'What was the nature of this conference? If you were at a conference, then you have an alibi.'

MacHeath looked at his solicitors. Then he said:

'I would prefer not to discuss this matter if it is not necessary.'

'It may be very necessary,' said the Magistrate drily.

But Rigger and Withe shook their heads and called a witness for the defence, the landlord of the 'Waterman's Arms'.

He stated that the deceased had sat in the public bar, waited there for some time, became more and more restless, and when she finally left, had not put her hat on, but carried it away in her hand. No one had inquired for her, either then or later.

Walley asked if anyone could see into the bar from the street.

The answer was yes.

Then he asked whether a person, on leaving the house, could take a way other than that leading back to the docks where she would be bound to meet any late-comer?

The answer was no.

Walley drew his conclusions: the accused could have met his victim outside the 'Waterman's Arms' or on her way home.

At this point the huge glass globes were lit, for it was already autumn and the evenings were drawing in.

Walley waited until this operation was finished and then went on:

'The question has already been asked, with much humour, how this poor shopkeeper could have threatened the great Mac-Heath. I would now like to call a witness who may be able to elucidate that point.'

A neatly-dressed man with long, pendulous arms, entered the box. He was a shoemaker, living in the house opposite Mary Sawyer's shop. He said that the dead woman had once told him that she knew where her goods came from. And she had said this in such a tone of voice that he had had to suppose that the source of the wares was a mysterious one, one which would not bear investigation.

MacHeath stood up. He wanted to answer immediately. But Rigger tugged his sleeve and whispered something to him. Mac-Heath sat down again and Rigger asked for a short interval. He wished to persuade his client, who was wearied by all this endless talking, to disclose his alibi.

The Magistrate consented.

But in the passage outside MacHeath told his solicitors, very emphatically, that he was not yet in a position to disclose his alibi.

They both told him that his behaviour would then appear exceedingly suspicious and he would probably have to face a charge of murder. Withe still wanted to try to persuade the Court that Mary Sawyer had committed suicide. Rigger had no longer the courage to oppose him.

After a quarter of an hour's pause the proceedings continued.

MacHeath's solicitors informed the Court that their client was unfortunately not in a position to reveal his whereabouts at the time of Mary Sawyer's death. The reason for his silence was a purely business one. The Magistrate received the excuse in unsympathetic silence. Then Withe went on to say that he, for his part, was convinced that Mary Sawyer had not been the victim of a murderer but had died by her own hand. He would now try to prove this to the Court.

Withe called his witnesses and examined them. They were all owners of B. shops. He asked them to describe the state of their business. They unanimously declared that their plight was a desperate one. One of them said it was nothing astonishing if a person hung himself. Especially since the supply of goods had ceased. It was difficult to know which way to turn next. Withe thanked him and called some of Mary's neighbours. He asked them :

'Do you know anything about the business affairs of the late Mrs Sawyer?'

'Yes, as much as a person can know of his neighbour's business.'

'Was she a very capable shopkeeper?'

'She was hard-working.'

'Careful with money?'

'Not very. If a person was a bit short, she would let him have things just the same.'

'So she was not very efficient in the ordinary sense of the word?'

'She would give a man socks if he showed her a torn pair. He only had to come in wet weather.'

'Then she was not what one could call a careful business woman?'

The witness was silent.

Then Withe said : 'If the death of this unhappy woman was, as we believe, a voluntary one, then the testimonies of the preceding witnesses only go to show into what straits generosity and kindness can drive a person.'

The Magistrate smiled.

An old woman entered the witness-box.

'Tell us,' Mr Withe exhorted her, 'what the deceased told you about the manner in which she came to own her shop.'

The old woman blew her nose ceremoniously. Probably she wanted to show off her red handkerchief.

'She was as good as given it.'

'I thought she paid for it.'

'A little. But perhaps she didn't pay anything. Her husband is a soldier.'

'But she had a little money. And she paid that?'

'So she said.'

'Tell me, how much was it?'

245

'Eighteen or nineteen pounds, I believe. She certainly hadn't got more. Never.'

'But she had that. And she invested it in the shop? Isn't that so?'

'She wanted to have the living room cleaner for the children. It was just like her to spend all her money on that, just for show, and she in the state she was!'

'And she would have lost that, the eighteen or nineteen pounds, if she had had to leave because of unpaid rent or unpaid goods?'

'Of course; you can work that out for yourself.'

'What could she have done then?'

'Not much.'

The old woman had been holding her handkerchief in her hand as though at any moment she expected to sneeze. Now she folded it up.

The proceedings continued slowly. Various details were cleared up. Nothing new came to light. When asked what they knew about the cause of the slump in their B. shops, several shop-keepers were all agreed that it was because prices had fallen. It was impossible to give reasons for *that*. One might just as well try to say why it rained more one year than another. It was bad that the supply had dried up, but that was probably because there were no more cheap goods to be obtained. Mr MacHeath had made every effort to procure fresh supplies because it was he who had encouraged them to take in assistants and advertise more widely so that the goods would sell faster. But he had been unsuccessful and his buying organization had let him down.

At last Withe stood up – Rigger had become remarkably taciturn – and recapitulated everything that favoured the theory of suicide.

'Mary Sawyer', proclaimed the solicitor, 'needed no murderer. To those who knew the circumstances in which she was compelled to live, her death was no insoluble mystery. Whoever is familiar with this existence, the existence of the needy, hard-working shopkeeper, must admit that, to anyone who is driven to such a life, there will come a time when he or she will say: Enough! Finis! And to end a life such as hers could have needed no very great determination. Surrounded with debts, faced with* *the complete hopelessness of the situation, this existence, like that of many others, offered her no particular inducement to stay alive. You have only to look at the dwelling-place of this woman. (I purposely avoid using the word "house". You yourselves would not dare to call the place a house.) Look at her children! No, do not look at them, only weigh them! Think of living all your life in such surroundings, and don't imagine that she ever had a holiday! And even in that hovel, she was pursued! Even on that door came the knock of her creditors! No, Mary Sawyer did not need to be murdered by Mr MacHeath – Mary Sawyer took her own life.'*

If it was objected that Mary had always been fond of life, there was still the counter-argument that business worries, and even the private disappointment that help was not forthcoming from Mr MacHeath, might have destroyed this fondness. That she had tried to lay the blame on him, probably convinced that she was right, was not to be wondered at. The smaller business people have no very exact knowledge of the laws governing commerce and trade. They nearly all put the blame on the big men when times of crisis come. But they have no idea that the big men are also at the mercy of definite, preordained, albeit obscurer processes of an economic nature. A crisis had simply developed and the smaller, weaker brethren had succumbed.

Walley interrupted him just as he had reached a point at which he could think of nothing more to say.

Walley felt compelled to repeat his previous question of an hour before, in response to which Mr MacHeath had, for a moment, seemed inclined to divulge his interesting alibi. There were rumours going round the City to the effect that the origin of the goods for the B. shops was somewhat shrouded in mystery. Mr MacHeath had stated that, as far as he knew, these goods came from a certain C.P.B. (Central Purchasing Board). Would Mr MacHeath tell the Court something definite about this Company?

'No,' answered Rigger after a short colloquy with MacHeath, 'Mr MacHeath will not.'

At all events, the C.P.B. was a legally registered company, with a member of the peerage and two solicitors on its board. It was quite correct that, during the last few weeks, they had not fulfilled their obligations towards Mr MacHeath. But that was an affair between himself and the Company and had nothing to do with the Court. He had only mentioned the matter so that the impression should not arise that Mr MacHeath himself was in any way to blame for Mary Sawyer's distressing situation. His colleague, Mr Withe, had demonstrated the extremely unsatisfactory conditions of the B. shops. They had doubtless been in difficulties recently, but not through any fault of Mr MacHeath's; the blame for that must be laid at the door of the C.P.B., who had ceased deliveries.

He called witnesses to testify that during the critical time Mr MacHeath had himself taken off his coat in the shops and helped!

MacHeath, too, had a word to say on the subject.

'It has been said here,' he began, 'that Mrs Sawyer's life was a very hard one. And that therefore suicide did not seem out of question. I would like to add that we in the B. shops are always working to the limits of our strength. In our unceasing endeavour to serve the public, we make demands on ourselves which only the *strongest* can endure for long. We sell too cheaply. Our profits are so small that we have to face privation. Perhaps we are too fanatical in our efforts to supply the poor purchaser with the best articles at reasonable prices. I freely admit that, during the last few days when everything has seemed against me, I have often asked myself whether we can hold out. Perhaps we may have to raise the prices again. Believe me, the death of my employee has upset me deeply.'

The Magistrate glanced coolly at the busily scribbling reporters, asked MacHeath again whether he would disclose his alibi, received a reply in the negative, and retired to consider the evidence.

Exactly ten minutes later he came back and announced his verdict: that the prisoner be committed for trial for the murder of Mary Sawyer.

The evening papers were full of the 'MacHeath Case'. Flaring headlines read: MYSTERY OF MARY SAWYER'S DEATH BEGINS TO CLEAR. And: WHERE WAS RICH MERCHANT WHILE WOMAN FRIEND WAS KILLED?

In the week following, MacHeath received news of Aaron.

Fanny Chrysler came to the prison two days after this investigation. She told him that Aaron and the Commercial Bank had lately been extraordinarily reserved in their dealings with the C.P.B.

Aaron had visited them once and murmured something about 'a connexion between the murder of so-and-so and the stoppage of supplies'. In Ride Lane there had been suspicious individuals, probably emissaries of some detective bureau, inquiring for the warehouses of the C.P.B.

Yesterday Jacques Opper had summoned her to the bank and demanded outright the invoices for the last delivery of goods to Aaron.

MacHeath looked very gloomy. After thinking for a time, he told her to procure new invoices and also to be careful about giving credit for purchases in Belgium.

As she went, she said:

'If your case lasts much longer, we shall be ruined. I hope you realize that.'

Personal matters were not mentioned.

It was the last week in October.

The affairs of Messrs Peachum and MacHeath were moving towards their conclusion.

The *Lovely Anna*, the *Young Sailorboy*, and the *Optimist*, painted and corsetted, were waiting for the time when their ancient hulks were to sail forth once more upon the ocean; the *Optimist* with the feeling that her last weeks had come. Peachum visualized his daughter in a veil and orange-blossoms, walking up to the altar beside Mr Coax. MacHeath visualized her in a different position and other surroundings. The B. shops had given up hope and grown in wisdom and experience. Coax was not to fill many more pages of his diary with strange symbols. The records of the case against the murderer of the shopkeeper Mary Sawyer were transcribed in vain and were not destined to have much more added to them. And the soldier Fewkoombey had another sixty-five days to live.

Book Three

THE GOOD LIFE'S FOUNDED
UPON L.S.D.

Those who from duty's path are never shaken,
Basing their lives upon ideal intentions –
The sentiments which every poet mentions –
Those worthy ones are very much mistaken.
They break their bread and, bathed in honest sweat,
Munch proudly the dry earnings of the just.
Commandment Seven bids them quite forget
That roast meat tastes much better than their crust.
But – admirable though modesty may be –
The Good Life's founded upon L. s. d.

It's no bad plan at all, I think, to stick one's
Eyes on the ground and snap up what you're able,
Then take a hot bath and gulp down some quick ones
And plant yourself before a well-stocked table.
You turn your nose up? That's not Life, you say?
For you, man isn't Man until he toils.
That's an idea from which my soul recoils;
Thank God, I'm not of such a noble clay.
The problem simply solves itself for me:
The Good Life's founded upon L. s. d.

(BALLADE OF THE GOOD LIFE)

Ultima ratio regis.
(INSCRIPTION ON THE PRUSSIAN CANNON)

Weighty Decisions

TOGETHER in a room with five or six other business men Mr
Peachum would scarcely have attracted attention. Since, in his
dealings with his fellow men, he was compelled to work to the
nearest farthing, his face had come to assume a certain set
expression, that of a hard and suspicious business man. But one
who regards the whole world with suspicion is still far from
having confidence in himself. Mr Peachum was in no way a
person of character. A strong, perhaps exaggerated, fear of the
mutability in all human circumstances and a deeply ingrained
conviction of the wickedness and relentlessness of the town in
which he lived (and of all other towns) drove him to make unusually rapid adjustments to every new demand made upon him
by his environments. His fellow citizens could only picture him
as the owner of 'J. J. Peachum, Beggars' Outfitter', but he would
have been ready at any time to open another business which
might prove more lucrative, less dangerous, or even, having
regard to the long run, steadier. He was a small, dried-up man
of miserable appearance; but even that was not, so to speak, conclusive. On finding himself in a situation which held no further
prospects for small, dried-up men of miserable appearance, Mr
Peachum could invariably be seen, sunk deep in thought, considering how he could change himself into a medium-sized,
well-fed, and optimistic man. His smallness, dryness, and misery
were indeed no more than a suggestion on his part, an indefinite
proposal which could be withdrawn at any moment. There was
something pitiful in this; but at the same time it was the reason
for his not inconsiderable success. He traded in misery, even in
his own. And, therefore, such dangers as he was facing at the
present forced him out of himself. Threatened with the loss of
his livelihood on the one hand, and spurred on by the prospect of

enormous profits on the other, he changed in a few weeks into a ravening tiger, even in appearance. During the days when he was winding up the affairs of the M.T.C. for Coax, he wore a fleshy and brutal appearance.

Standing in shirt-sleeves, his hands thrust into his trouser pockets, he received Hale, who came to borrow a hundred pounds which he had lost at cards. Peachum did not give him a penny.

The Company was writhing in open agony.

After his interview with Hale, Peachum summoned yet another meeting. They all came. The otherwise silent Moon protested against holding the meeting in the baths. He arrived before the appointed time and stopped each member on the doorstep. He shouted excitedly down the street that he was sick of this wash-house business. So the last meeting of the Company was held in a nearby restaurant.

Peachum informed them of Hale's blackmailing manoeuvres, emphasized the necessity of giving in to him, and did nothing to hide from them the fact that they must be prepared for further attempts of this kind. He declared that his patience was exhausted. He demanded that an immediate computation should be made of the amounts for which each member was liable and that he should then be given full power to finish up the business in his own way. He guaranteed a successful conclusion if no one interfered with him.

His suggestion was accepted.

The collecting of the various liabilities was effected by Peachum with the utmost severity.

He took enough off the baronet to drive the latter for ever, or at least for many months, into the American heiress's bed. The young man's final excuse, that he was homosexual, was ignored by Peachum. Eastman paid with comparative good-will; he was able to; a little while before he had raised the rents of his housing property in the north, the occupants of which, being mostly working men, were unable to afford a move.

Moon, before he paid, needed, rather astonishingly, special treatment. He was a bookmaker and it was not until a crowd of beggars had forced their way into his offices and lined up before him, some with the placards 'Who bets, has money – who has money can give' and 'I too have betted here', that Moon at last agreed to pay £800 in cash and the rest in securities.

Crowl failed at the last moment.

He came one morning to Old Oak Street and demanded to see Peachum. They reviewed his position together. Crowl said: 'Then I might as well put a bullet through my head.' Peachum gave him Coax's office address. It seemed to him a good thing that Coax should see the results of his machinations.

The restaurateur went that same afternoon to the office in the City and explained to the personnel that he had an appointment with the broker and that he would wait. He waited for over two hours without Coax having arrived; indeed, it turned out later that the latter knew nothing about any appointment. When the girl wanted to lock up the office he murmured something unintelligible, turned to the wall where an umbrella stand stood, and shot a revolver bullet into his mouth. On his desk at home, his wife found a letter in a sealed envelope with the inscription: 'For my wife. To be opened at eight o'clock if I have not returned.' All that the letter said was: 'My dear, I have been ruined by a gang of unscrupulous crooks. Forgive me, I did everything for the best. Albert Crowl, Restaurateur.'

But the greatest difficulties were made at the last moment by Finney.

When he heard of Crowl's suicide, he decided to be operated upon without further delay. But Peachum discovered this in time. He immediately rushed to Finney's house. Finney had already gone into the nursing-home. Peachum had almost to use physical force before he could extract the address of the nursing-home from the housekeeper. He reached Finney half an hour before the operation was due to begin.

His rage was boundless; but Finney, too, turned equally green with fury and immediately resolved to dismiss his housekeeper. Peachum shouted so loudly that all the sisters in the building came running into the room. He said to the matron:

'This man won't even pay for his bed-pan. He's only having himself operated on because he's in debt. In my breast pocket I have a newspaper with the announcement of the suicide of the restaurant-keeper Crowl who wanted to get out of the same trouble in the same way as this fine gentleman here! The newspapers may wonder what your surgeon is up to! Of course, it may be that he does a regular trade in such would-be suicides!'

Finney was not equal to such treachery and paid before he was wheeled into the operating theatre.

Within a week Peachum had a fairly accurate idea of the amount of money that was to be got out of the M.T.C.

Crowl's death was the alarm signal for MacHeath.

It was Fanny who brought him the morning papers with the news of the restaurateur's suicide in the broker's office.

Some time ago MacHeath had set Fanny on Peachum's trail. The transport-ship business between his father-in-law and Coax had proved increasingly interesting to him. Polly had told him of her father's confession that Coax had brought him to the verge of ruin. The suicide of Crowl threw some more light on the background of this business.

From Polly, MacHeath had also learned that Coax had visited her father on the fatal evening, and that he had shouted round the office for at least half an hour. He seemed to have been blaming Peachum for something he had done against him. It was obvious that Peachum and Coax were fighting a battle for life and death, but whether it was against one another, or both of them together against someone else, was not so clear.

Towards midday Fanny came again. She had already been in the suicide's house.

She had learned a great deal. Crowl's widow was an ugly, tear-stained woman without any trace of self-control. Within five minutes she had made God and the world responsible for the late restaurateur's death.

Fanny related with disgust that she had screamed in the presence of her old father, 'What am I to do now with that old wreck there? His insurance is gone and he's more trouble than he's worth!'

MacHeath shook his head over this tactlessness. But he was extremely disturbed.

Fanny had also discovered that the M.T.C., now apparently under Peachum's control, was in a very precarious situation. Coax seemed to have got Peachum completely under his thumb, 'rather like you've got Hawthorne', said Fanny. In the very near future they would be needing large sums of money – in a few weeks in fact. But Peachum seemed to have arranged something which relieved him of this almost insuperable task. This was the only possible explanation of why he had not withdrawn his money from the National Credit Bank.

MacHeath knew that Peachum was hoping to free his daughter for the broker. Since he had not succeeded in this, he would certainly have to pay now. Therefore his visit to the National Credit Bank was to be expectedly hourly.

MacHeath himself was still not yet on the board of the bank. But the formalities were on the point of being completed. Everything now depended on gaining time. He must hold on to the dowry and give up his wife – at least for the moment. That would not mean that Polly was lost to him. She was still pregnant by him and that would keep her faithful.

He *must* complete his task.

On the same evening he summoned Peachum's solicitor, Walley, and agreed to a divorce.

Coax still visited the Peachums. Of late he had even been bringing his sister with him, and the relations between the two families could not have been more intimate. Miss Coax was charmed with Mrs Peachum and her daughter. The older ladies played whist and Polly worked at an embroidery representing Lord Nelson at the Battle of Trafalgar. In the evenings, the broker came to fetch his sister home, and he always sat a few minutes with the ladies. As ever, he would ask the Peach to play a piece on the piano. She did it very well. She also had a pretty voice, and when she played, her tulle sleeves fell back so that one could see the whole of her arms.

When he looked at her playing the piano, he could still understand why he had once thought of marrying her. She had great qualities.

'Should it', he wrote in his diary, '*really make so much difference having already had a girl? What does that first, lamentably incomplete embrace signify? Think of the inner, dominating urge in a man, which finds its chief satisfaction in subjugating the woman, in conquering her! Why otherwise that indifference after complete possession? One feels it even when the subject is not a virgin! Or should purely economic considerations play a role in a man's spiritual life? Should it influence me*

257

inwardly, spiritually, that the Peach can no longer be seriously considered as a wife, now that her father has lost so much money? Of course I was responsible for his losses ... But perhaps instinct has no regard for causes, keeping only to facts. ... At any rate, my feeling now is one of complete estrangement.'

Such feelings had to be concealed from Peachum.

He concealed them. The bouquets of carnations which he sent to the family grew larger and larger.

At the end of September he learned that Mr Peachum's daughter had already been married six months to a certain Mac-Heath. He was extremely astonished, but said nothing and stored the information away for future use.

Then came Crowl's suicide and Coax had a good, official reason for being depressed. It did actually cause him considerable inconvenience. For business purposes, he belonged to a certain extremely respectable club, and on reading the news of the unsavoury occurrence in his office he had felt himself compelled to resign. Still unpleasanter was the fact that, should there be a public scandal over the ships, his name was now inseparably entangled with the whole affair.

Crowl's death gave Coax an excuse for cutting Peachum. But he still continued to visit Mrs Peachum and Polly. That had to suffice to reassure Peachum with regard to Coax's future intentions. But when the dockers' strike broke out, their mutual work brought them together again.

Peachum had several times used various tricks to lower the wages of the workers. And one fine morning only five out of the two hundred employees appeared for duty. The others stood in front of the dock gates to stop other workers offering their services.

This was unpleasant, even dangerous. Of course the final handing over of the ships could be postponed on account of the strike. But, mellowed by the confidential mood engendered by their common difficulties, Coax admitted to Peachum that the Government's desire to buy transport-ships from the M.T.C. was not a very ardent one. They had enough ships. It had been Hale who had discovered that those in higher circles would have no objection to securing further transport accommodation. When the contract had been signed, Hale had then, purely in order to prevent any unwelcome questions, arranged through friends in the War Office for a small convoy of troops to be allotted to the newly purchased ships. These troops could naturally be transported by other means. But Coax's option on the Southampton substitutes, which had to be kept up until the conclusion of this dangerous deal, was due to expire soon. Hale was completely unprincipled and might any day make new attempts at blackmailing.

So Peachum did everything in his power to restart the work on the ships. He began by working behind public bodies, talking about 'Proletarian blackmail at a time when the nation was in distress'.

And then the idea of the military occurred to him.

He started his workshops manufacturing uniforms at high speed. For his next move he planned a great demonstration against the strikers, to be carried out by invalid soldiers. It would create a deep impression, especially in the columns of the newspapers, if the war-wounded soldiers took this step in the interest of the whole nation.

Into the midst of these activities fell Walley's announcement that MacHeath was prepared to agree to a divorce. So Peachum's terrible difficulty – to ensure Coax's support and thereby to give a happy ending to a wretched business which had kept him in suspense for more than three months – seemed now to be resolved.

But when his daughter heard from her father the news of her impending divorce, she replied to him with a furious 'I'm pregnant!' He was beside himself.

'But you're still going to be divorced,' he shouted back at her. 'You're going to be divorced and you're going to a doctor! Do you think I'm going to let myself be ruined by you? After all, I have my feelings too, and I'm not going to let myself be trampled on. If you go on behaving like this I shall go to bed, turn my face to the wall, and let everything go to the devil; and *you* can all go to the poorhouse!'

During those days he looked neither to the right nor to the left. He followed the trail like a bloodhound.

He knew too little.

Had he guessed that the broker had long ago learned of his

daughter's unfortunate marriage, had he only known what had occurred during his daughter's last visit to Mr Coax's house, he would have planned differently.

On that very same evening Polly visited her husband in prison.

Of course, he told her immediately that everything was purely *pro forma*. A divorce took some time. And after all, one only needed insufficient grounds for divorce for the whole thing to fall through at the last moment. But the institution of the proceedings could not be avoided; her father was pressing him too hard and had him completely in his hands.

'He can get me hanged – and he will. You know him!'

Polly immediately said that she must then go to a doctor and have the child removed. In her confusion she had admitted that she was pregnant.

MacHeath was horrified. He had not counted on this. In a husky voice, and not looking at his wife, he said: of course that was not to be thought of, he could not sacrifice his child, at least not unless it was absolutely necessary.

He was really worried about this and lay half the night awake, after Polly had gone away crying. He had the family instinct and was pleased with the idea of having a son. His painful meditations carried him so far that at last, just before he went to sleep, he really began to believe that it was only the thought of his little son which had driven him to embark upon these dangerous business operations.

'*Ah,*' he thought, '*what's the use of all this toil and drudgery when all at once we may be dead and done with, and there is no one left to carry on the work? Why am I sitting here in this cell if it's not for the sake of my son? What else could give me the strength to win through? I shall take his little hand in mine and we shall walk through the shops which will one day be his, and I shall say to him: my son, all this has cost infinite pain and trouble, never forget that! Your father sweated blood so that you could have such an inheritance. He wasn't working for himself alone. But he asks no thanks – no, no. He only tells you all this so that you can see that we, your father and you, are bound together by many ties. Your father will die when his time comes, and then you will work on in memory of him who, for your*

260

sake ... well, who worked for you. – I shall tell him that and he will understand. I shall call him Dick.'

He really meant it. But on the next morning he told Polly she must go to the doctor, it was necessary. He was counting on her putting off her visit as long as possible, at least for two or three days. By then he hoped to have accomplished something which might render the operation superfluous. But she must still be prepared to have it and must on no account give her father any grounds for suspicion.

Indeed, he could afford no diminution of the breathing space which, by his consent to the divorce, he had engineered in order to enable him to carry out his *coup de main* with the National Credit Bank.

He again urged Hawthorne and Miller to hurry on with the reorganization of the bank.

When they next called they had to wait for half an hour in the waiting-room. MacHeath had arranged that. So they sat there, immeasurably depressed, among the relatives of the prison inmates, well-to-do or depraved, or well-to-do and depraved, persons of both sexes.

MacHeath shouted at the two old men that the arrangements were taking too long for his liking; it was incomprehensible to him why he should have to wait so long to enter a thoroughly corrupt business.

Then he discussed Chreston's position with them.

Chreston had finished his sales week without having to borrow further money. He was still astonished at his rival having bought up his whole stock. But of course, the prices had been far below normal.

He was also troubled by the much advertised sales week about to be launched by Aaron and the B. shops; for the public were waiting eagerly for it. Of MacHeath's impending entry into the bank he knew nothing.

Now MacHeath arranged for him to be informed that several of the consignments which he had sold during his sales week were suspect. A description of goods stolen in Manchester fitted them closely. He would like to see the invoices.

At that, Chreston came in person.

He stood six foot two and was a sallow man with an aversion to meat dishes, the clergy, and I. Aaron. He was very upset.

'Mr Chreston,' MacHeath received him with extreme reserve, 'a painful reason brings you here. I must say that I could hardly believe my ears when I heard that, during your sales week, large consignments of goods of suspicious origin were offered to the public. I hope you have the invoices for them?'

Mr Chreston had no invoices.

He had bought the consignments because they were cheap and because he needed goods after the weeks of cut-throat competition. He looked as guilty as though he had been caught consuming a fresh cutlet in direct defiance of his maturest convictions.

MacHeath showed himself relentless. He spoke, in an unctuous voice, of fairness in competition and of the wisdom of the law which punished the fence and the receiver with the same severity as it did the thief. Should he, MacHeath, now sell the goods in question during his sales week, he would have invoices for them; namely, Chreston's receipts. But Chreston had no invoices. Then he informed him, shortly and brutally, that he was about to enter the directorate of the National Credit Bank. And finally, he recited the conditions under which his, Chreston's, shops could join a ring, controlled by MacHeath and supplied by the C.P.B.

The lanky Mr Chreston seemed stunned when he heard that his rival was entering the very bank which held him so completely in its hands. He was not slow in realizing his position.

The warder was summoned to bring pencils and paper. Soon they were writing down innumerable figures and pointing to them with glowing ends of cigars. On the wall of his cell Mac-Heath had hung a blue-green plan of London; with heavy red strokes he encircled certain areas which had a steady consumption of goods; then he underlined place-names and drew a complicated system of lines over the whole town and its suburbs. It was the distribution scheme for the B.C. (Bargain-Chreston) shops.

Several of Chreston's shops would have to be altered, combined, or sold. With his red pencil MacHeath mercilessly dictated their fates. His bank needed 'its' money.

'Don't forget,' said MacHeath to Chreston, 'the bank belongs to a child. Her money has been disgracefully misused. Other people's money, too, has already suffered the same fate. This must stop. I must be in a position to take over all responsibility towards the little owner. I am not a sentimental man, but I will not have it said of me that I robbed children. The children are England's future, we must never forget that for a moment.'

The prices were to be slowly raised. The word 'quality' was to be introduced into advertisements.

MacHeath described to Fanny his conversation with Chreston:

'It was a sort of one-sided dialogue between us. I asked him: will you take the responsibility for what you have done? He answered me quickly: no. – So you don't want to maintain your independence – at any price? I asked him then. Not at any price, he answered. – You would rather admit defeat and bow your neck under my foot? – Certainly, was his answer, it comes cheaper in the end. – He's not what one would call a great character, he is quite sensible. It's really very little use nowadays trying to have personality.'

Miller and Hawthorne had to suffer another indignity at MacHeath's hand. He said he must request Miller to sign a statement that he, Miller, had, on his own responsibility and without Hawthorne's knowledge, embezzled Peachum's deposit for purposes of speculation. The bank itself must remain unsullied.

Miller broke down completely. He laid his old head on the back of his chair and wept. Then he pulled himself together, stood up, and said with quiet dignity:

'I cannot do that, Mr MacHeath. I can never sign a document stating that I have used, for purposes of speculation, money entrusted to the bank. Do you realize what that means: *entrusted*? Supposing you had put your hard-earned money in my hands? You said: Mr Miller, here is my fortune, I put it into your *good hands*, take it and employ it according to the *best of your knowledge and ability*. I trust you. You are a man of honour. – And now I'm expected to say: it is gone. I am still here, but your money is gone. Never! Do you hear, Mr MacHeath, I can never say that.'

'But you *are* still here, Mr Miller, and the money *is* gone!'

'Yes,' said Mr Miller, and sat down with an expression like that of an astonished child.

After they had sat there for more than five minutes without saying another word, he went out, still shaking his head and murmuring something to himself.

Two hours later Hawthorne brought in the signed statement.

Miller's name stood below, clear and plain as though written by a schoolboy.

In a voice trembling with emotion, Hawthorne begged Mac-Heath to leave Miller, for the time being at any rate, at his desk in the bank – of course without any salary – because the old man did not know what he could say to his wife and neighbours.

MacHeath consented to this request.

On the same day MacHeath's entry into the National Credit Bank was ratified.

A ton weight was lifted from his mind. Now Aaron and Opper could learn that the president of the C.P.B. was called MacHeath; for now the director of the National Credit Bank was also called MacHeath. And Chreston's business friend was MacHeath.

After lunch Polly went to Mrs Crowl.

Her father had sent her. Recently she had taken over certain of his duties as a relieving officer.

Mrs Crowl was very touched by the little basket of food with the bottle of cider which Polly brought. She complained loudly about the M.T.C. which had seized all the furniture except what was 'absolutely necessary' to her. She also complained of her father, who listened sadly.

'What can I do with him?' she wailed, 'he's worse than the children, who are at least clean about the house. And now that my husband has speculated away his income, we've got nothing left at all.'

'If one could only raise *some* money,' said Polly sympathetically, 'I might be able to persuade my husband to let you have one of his small B. shops. But even that costs a little capital to start with.'

She was very charming to Mrs Crowl. The comfortless room

was somehow brighter when she sat there, smiling, with the empty basket on her lap.

Mrs Crowl hesitated. Her dull glance passed over the miserable furniture, ignoring the old man. Then she said suddenly:

'There might be one possibility. He's got a sister who might, perhaps, put a little money – she hasn't got more – into such a safe investment. . . .'

And then she turned to the old man.

'What do you think?'

The old man said nothing. He had probably not understood. He seemed no longer quite right in the head.

The two women discussed the possibility for a few minutes longer. When Polly got up to go she had given her solemn promise that she would ask her husband for a B. shop for Mrs Crowl. To be sure, she had forgotten all about it when she reached the front steps. But then it was a weakness of hers that she wanted everyone to like her.

On her return home she was summoned into her father's office. In a few dry words he told her that her husband had agreed to an abortion. He had sent along a certain Grooch who had given the message to him personally. There was a note waiting for her in her room.

Polly read the note and was deeply hurt. Did Mac care so little for his son? Because to him it *was* his son, since he knew nothing of Smiles. It was horrible! She was so angry that she said to her mother that she wanted to go to a doctor that same afternoon, she knew of one too, it cost fifteen pounds.

Mrs Peachum wanted to try it first with quinine.

The first day one took three capsules, the second four, and so on up to seven. It was dangerous to go farther; but it was also forbidden to spit the stuff out and stop when one got roarings in the ears, palpitations, and a feeling of sickness.

Then Mrs Peachum discovered that it was no longer in the first month; so there was only the doctor left.

They went immediately after tea. The doctor seemed not to recognize the Peach; his practice was probably too large. Besides, he had to deal with the mother this time; and for him, those with whom he arranged the price were the patients. He sat in the midst of his gleaming weapons and stroked his beautiful, soft, not-quite-bacteria-free beard and said:

'My dear lady, I would like to point out to you that what you suggest is not in harmony with the law, not in accordance with its dictates.' He modulated his voice in such a way that the suggested harmony became a sort of music of the spheres. But Mrs Peachum interrupted him drily:

'Yes, I know, it costs fifteen pounds.'

Thirty years with her husband and a copious consumption of spirituous drinks had taught her a knowledge of mankind.

'Fifteen pounds cannot accomplish that; indeed I cannot imagine how you came to think of such a sum. The operation is somewhat more expensive than that,' the doctor replied unctuously, 'it is a case of conscience.'

'You say the operation is more expensive? How expensive!' asked Mrs Peachum.

'Well, shall we say twenty-five pounds, my dear lady? But first of all you will have to make the terrible decision as to whether you really wish to destroy a budding life; that is, whether it is really an absolute, imperative necessity, as it is with my poorer patients who simply cannot afford to bring up children – a consideration which, although it does not justify the operation, at least makes it humanly understandable, don't you think so?'

Mrs Peachum looked at him attentively and then said:

'It *is* a question of necessity, doctor.'

'Then, of course, it is different,' said the doctor, since Mrs Peachum and her daughter had now stood up. 'Then, perhaps, you could come at three o'clock tomorrow afternoon. The fee is payable in advance so that no statement need be addressed to your house. Good afternoon.'

The two ladies decided to have an ice. Then, since it was too early to go home, they went into a cinema.

It was one of those wretched little establishments which run continuously. It was in the shape of an oblong box. The screen was tiny. An incessant shower of rain obscured the pictures, and the actors moved as though afflicted with St Vitus's dance.

The film was entitled *'Mother, Your Child Calls!'*

It began with an aristocratic young lady completing her toilet for the ball. With the help of her maid she buckled on a three-foot pair of corsets and hung a few pounds of diamonds on her ears and neck. She admired herself for a moment in the mirror and then went into the next room where her child lay in its cot. It was a little girl of about three years of age, at the moment ill. The doctor, a serious, bearded man, stood beside the cot and felt her pulse. Then he exchanged a few, apparently extremely grave words with the young mother. She, however, only laughed lightly, hastily embraced the child, and went out.

In the middle of the gangway stood the announcer, a fat gentleman. 'Callous frivolity and love of pleasure,' he announced in a rather harsh bass voice, 'lure the young mother to leave the sick-bed of her child for the delights of gilded dissipation.'

The scene changed to an uncommonly elegant and ornate salon in which a large company was surrendering itself to the pleasures of the dance.

'The "Light Fantastic" in full swing,' explained the bass simultaneously.

The young mother entered. A footman in knee-breeches announced her. The gentlemen sprang to their feet. Champagne was ordered. The young mother sat down between two cavaliers on a bulging plush sofa. Now and again she got up to dance and flew from arm to arm.

'The hours fly by unheeded,' the announcer informed the audience.

The nursery reappeared. The child seemed to be considerably worse. She sat up in her cot and stretched out her little arms for her absent mama. Suddenly she fell back.

'Ah,' said the bass, 'she's dying; see, she sinks back! She is gone!'

Once more, the ballroom. Head thrown back, the young mother was gulping down a glass of champagne. Suddenly the wall of the room became transparent; the nursery appeared behind; out of the cot rose the little girl, equally transparent. She stood upright. On her shoulders were two little wings. Then she came fluttering through the wall towards the marble table at which the heartless young mother was sitting. In front of the table she sank to the ground and vanished into nothingness.

'In a vision,' droned the bass, 'the horrified mother sees that her child is already dead. As an angel, the dear little girl says farewell for ever.'

The young mother fell to the floor in a swoon. For a few seconds she was shown in the cloakroom, where she hastily threw a wrap round her.

' "Oh, that it may not be too late!" whispers the unhappy woman, as, with wildly beating pulses, she throws on her wrap.'

Then appeared the nursery again. The mother burst in. She threw herself on to her knees before the cot, embraced her little dead girl, and wrung her hands. The servants came hurrying in and tried to calm her, but apparently they were unable to moderate her agony of self-reproach.

The bass concluded in a choking voice:

> 'Too late, too late! Your child is gone!
> Nor pain nor sorrow can e'er atone!'

The two women sat through the film in a state of fascinated horror. They had bought some chocolate at the desk. But they had finished it just before the beginning of the melodrama. The film gripped them.

When the little girl suffered a solitary death, deserted by her light-hearted mother, Polly felt a stabbing pain in her breast. In the darkness she fumbled for her mother's hand; and both women had tears in their eyes when the little dead girl came fluttering into the ballroom with her arms outstretched. They left the cinema deeply moved by this masterpiece.

'I'm not going to take you there tomorrow afternoon,' said Mrs Peachum determinedly, as they walked down the street. Polly, too, was unable to understand how she could have been willing to sacrifice her child. Wasn't she just like that criminally callous mother in the ballroom?

Not till late that night did the two women recover from the effects of the film. Then Mrs Peachum came up to Polly's room in her cotton stockings and sat on the edge of the bed and said:

'You mustn't eat anything tomorrow morning, otherwise you'll be sick after the anaesthetic.'

Throughout the night Polly saw the doctor's armoury of weapons.

Mr Peachum was very busy.

That evening he received a visit from Withe, MacHeath's solicitor, and Fanny Chrysler. Peachum had insisted that his son-in-law should immediately name the person who was to be cited as co-respondent and who would swear to the adultery. He had to be sure of his step.

MacHeath had suggested a girl from Mrs Lexer's house in Tunbridge, and the fat Withe had brought her with him to Old Oak Street. The girl had spoken extremely frankly, but Mr Peachum had taken offence and refused this witness. He said he would not think of humiliating his daughter to such an extent and before the whole world; although, in reality, he feared that the testimony of a prostitute might not be accepted in court.

This threw MacHeath into a frenzy.

'How many more women am I supposed to have had sexual intercourse with, just for my father-in-law's benefit?' he had shouted.

Nevertheless he had agreed to cite Fanny Chrysler.

True, he was already a director of the bank, but a breach with Peachum was not yet to be desired; he regarded him now as a customer. And it would be much better for the bank if this customer could settle with his opponent in a way which would not compel him to withdraw his money.

At this stage, the possibility of a real divorce from Polly entered MacHeath's head more than once.

To Grooch, with whom, in his usual tactless manner, he discussed Fanny Chrysler's suitability as a witness, he spoke as follows:

'Certain situations may arise necessitating a separation between myself and my wife. For my part, a divorce might be the best thing. But even if I do admit to my relationship with Fanny, there's no reason why that should mean a break with my wife. She is still pregnant by me and therefore cannot simply yield to her inclination and run away on any little trivial pretext. Only the most desperate reasons would drive a woman in that condition to such extremes. That's the advantage of their being pregnant. That's when they realize where their duty lies. Nature is clever, Grooch. She gets what she wants. And why? Because she is clever!'

Grooch squatted on the mattress, smoking and nodding thoughtfully.

'There's only one way in which my wife could get the better of me,' continued MacHeath pensively, *'and that would be if she really got rid of her child. But that would be such a cold-blooded act that it wouldn't matter then if we were divorced. I left it to her conscience. I said nothing for and nothing against it. In that way I wanted to show her that the decision lay entirely in her hands. It will be a heavy trial for her, a trial that will test her to the uttermost. I must frankly admit, I have no idea how she will stand up to it. For all I know, everything may already have been decided. I don't know whether, at this moment, the child is still under her heart or not. I have been careful not to ask. I am apparently indifferent. But the time will come when I shall ask: where is your child? What have you done about him? Was it a case of his meaning so much to you that you would not be separated from him for anything in the world? Or was it otherwise? That second will decide everything.'*

Grooch nodded again, and at that moment MacHeath really believed what he was saying. It was his way to give strict instructions and then to turn round on those who carried them out and hold them responsible. And it was subsequent to this conversation that Withe brought Fanny to Peachum. Peachum received the two in his office.

Fanny behaved herself very naturally and gave, as always, the impression of being a lady. She said she was willing to do Mr MacHeath the favour he was asking of her. She felt in no way bound to do this and not all the persuasion in the world would influence her once her mind was made up.

'Stop!' interrupted Peachum harshly. 'Am I to understand from what you have just said that you are prepared to commit perjury in order to do Mr MacHeath a favour? That would be not the slightest use to us.'

Fanny looked in astonishment at the solicitor who was staring embarrassedly at a corner of the bare room.

'You mean,' she said – she was the only one of three to be sitting down and now lit a cigarette – 'that I am to tell you whether I have really slept with your son-in-law?'

'Certainly,' said Mr Peachum.

She laughed, but not unpleasantly. Then she turned to Withe.

'I don't know, Withe, whether Mr MacHeath would wish me to discuss such a matter.'

She purposely omitted the 'Mr' so as to show that she stood on the same level socially with Withe's clients.

'Whether Mr MacHeath would wish it or not,' said Mr Peachum angrily, 'I must know it. And my wife must know it too, if you have nothing against *that*. It's no joke, this affair.'

And he opened the tin-covered door and shouted for his wife.

She did not seem to have been very far away, for she was there immediately. With her hands folded over her stomach, she stared inquisitively at the visitors. She was no lady.

'This is Miss Chrysler,' said Peachum in introduction. Fanny had put down her cigarette-holder, but she still sat there, with her legs crossed, smiling uncertainly. 'Miss Chrysler has come to inform me that she has had intimate relations with Mr Mac-Heath right up to the present time, even after his marriage. Isn't that so?'

'Quite right,' said Miss Chrysler seriously. And, out of consideration for the newcomer, she added softly:

'I run a business for Mr MacHeath and always work with him.'

Then she stood up, put her cigarette-holder into her bag, nodded shortly, and went out. Withe opened the door with an embarrassed smile.

That night, for the first time in months, Peachum slept soundly.

The next morning he wanted to have the decisive conversation with Coax. He wanted to confess Polly's lapse and at the same time announce MacHeath's agreement to a divorce. There would then be no need to buy the Southampton ships, although the money for them, including Peachum's share, was already collected.

But just as he was shaving for his visit to Coax, the latter burst into the room waving a letter, and shouted at him:

'What sort of a trick are you trying to play on me? For months you've been trying to persuade me to marry your daughter. For months you've been throwing the two of us together on every possible occasion; hoping, I suppose, to secure for your self a special position in this business and so to prevent me from dealing with you as I have with these other crooks to whom you belong. And today I learn that your daughter was married long ago, is now about to be divorced, and that her husband is a criminal who, so I am told, is at this moment in prison. Are you mad?'

Peachum stood motionless, his face covered with lather, his hand still clutching the razor, staring at the little mirror which he had hung on the window handle. His braces trailed behind him on the floor. He groaned hollowly.

'Is that your answer?' continued Coax icily. 'Is that all you have to say to me? A grunt? You've got some nerve!'

Peachum lowered the razor. He had a coarse face, but the pain in it was now so great that it looked almost pleasant.

'Coax,' he said in a hollow voice, 'Coax! How can you say that!'

And the expression of pain was so real that Coax said no more than was absolutely necessary.

'Within two hours, Peachum, *two* hours, you will hand over the money for the M.T.C., and you will hand it over to me in my office; and after that you will keep out of my sight. Alternatively, within five hours, you will find yourself in prison with your fine son-in-law!'

He went out very upright and bumped into Polly and her mother whom the noise had drawn from the back regions. As he passed them, he said cuttingly:

'Good day, Mrs MacHeath!'

Mrs Peachum immediately went into the office. When she saw her husband standing by the window, as pale as a corpse, she knew exactly what had happened.

'We had better put off going to the doctor for a bit,' she said to her daughter a quarter of an hour later.

Peachum was stunned. He had counted so surely on the broker's greed. To him, the puritan, it had seemed so certain because it had seemed so dirty. He had been so sure that Coax would sacrifice his material interests to his carnal appetite, and he had despised him for it. But he had underrated him. . . .

After this checkmate by Mr Coax, affairs developed with bewildering rapidity.

Peachum went to his bank, and, when he said he wished to remove his money, had to listen to a long string of evasions. Becoming suspicious, he demanded to speak to Miller. When they kept him waiting, he pushed his way into the old man's office. At the same moment, and in a great hurry, Hawthorne came in at the other door. One glance at the One and a Half Centuries and Peachum knew everything, or nearly everything.

A short conversation made the whole situation clear.

He had now to deal with Mr MacHeath if he wished to remove his money. Since the day before, Mr MacHeath had been managing director of the bank and was to be found in prison.

Peachum left the two old people and hurried to Coax's office. It was already eleven o'clock.

Coax listened to his news in silence. Then he said drily:

'I will give you until tomorrow midday. By then you will have procured either the money or security for it. According to you, your son-in-law is now your bank manager. Kindly bring me immediately the contract with the Government and also the signed document in which Crowl and the baronet have admitted to their own defaults and to those of the others.'

Peachum went away again and fetched the documents for Coax. He moved as though in a trance. Then he went home again and locked himself into his office. He ate nothing. Towards two o'clock he summoned Fewkoombey from his hotel.

The former soldier looked well-fed, almost fat in the face. Only the colour of his complexion was unhealthy. All the time that Peachum spoke to him, staring as usual at the window in the corner, the one-legged man stood motionless in the doorway, his cap clutched in his great hands.

Peachum spoke to him somewhat as follows:

Of late there had been several attacks made against his factory. He was therefore compelled to reduce the business considerably and to turn out a number of his people on to the streets. Fewkoombey was to be among that number.

For a space Mr Peachum spoke of the terrible problem of unemployment.

'I know well enough what it means, turning people out on the streets like this. Particularly dreadful are the moral consequences of this step. The typical worker usually loses, only too

273

soon, all moral restraint. It is seldom that he is capable of main-
taining his moral standards against the insidious influence of
hunger and cold. His self-respect breaks down. He realizes that
he is a burden to the community. In this state of mind he can
only too easily fall a victim to agitators who wish to make him
an enemy of the established order. I know all that, but what can
I do?'

However, there was a possibility that he might not be compelled to dismiss forthwith a number of his employees, amongst
them Fewkoombey. There was a certain Mr Coax at large in
London, who had in his breast pocket a piece of paper to which
he had no right. This Coax must be removed – and by tomorrow
morning. Anyone who took care of this removal in order to avert
the dismissal of so-and-so-many employees, would be provided
with an alibi. Such a person must, after the deed, go to such-
and-such a place and spend the night there.

'It is a matter of business,' said Mr Peachum philosophically.
'It is the conduct of business by other means. Think of the war.
You are a soldier. When the business people are at the end of
their wits, the soldier steps in. That is quite right. We in business
have other, more peaceable methods. But that is only because to-
day there are other means of getting what one wants than with
a sharp knife. Unfortunately there are still exceptional cases.'

The soldier knew the broker. He had once delivered a letter
to him.

After this conversation, Mrs Peachum saw Fewkoombey in
the yard. It was the last time she set eyes on him and she said
later that he had looked very strange. He stood for a long while
among the washing that had been hung out to dry, and stared
at the dogs. But he did not go over to them, in spite of the fact
that they had not yet had their dinner and were already howling for it.

'God knows what bloodthirsty thoughts he must have had
in his head when he stood there,' she said sighing.

Actually, he probably had no thoughts at all, unless he had
been calculating how much the shelter with the cardboard roof,
which kept out the wet but not the cold and in which he had
found a sanctuary, was worth.

The time which he had spent there had been short. He had

not even been able to finish the half volume of the encyclopaedia.

When he left the instrument shop in Old Oak Street, he had
a knife in his right hip-pocket. But he had not yet made up his
mind.

Almost at the same time, Mrs Polly MacHeath had a conversation with Mr O'Hara. It took place at the latter's house.

Mrs MacHeath related with rapid incoherence how she had
just found in her room a letter from her husband in which he
wrote that she need not worry any more. There would never
be a divorce ('never' was underlined); at the right time, he would
simply accuse the broker, Coax, of adultery with her. He had
conclusive proof against Coax which revealed him as a libertine
of the worst sort. And even if Coax were quite innocent in
this case, the accusation would destroy all his interest in a
divorce.

She showed O'Hara the letter. It was written in great haste in
pencil.

O'Hara did not seem to be very astonished.

'Coax is going to be called as a witness,' repeated Polly in
desperation.

'Well, what then?' asked O'Hara, not even getting up from
the sofa, for it was after lunch and he was reading the sporting
pages of *The Times*.

'What then! I don't want that to happen.'

'Did you commit adultery with him?'

'No, of course not.'

'Then why don't you want him to be a witness?'

'Because I don't. Isn't that enough? I don't want it. So he
must be got rid of before the case begins.'

'If I understand you rightly, you want him to be removed
from this life?'

'No, of course I don't want that.'

A pause ensued. O'Hara picked up the paper again.

'Well, then?' said Polly. 'Put down the paper! Why are you
treating me like this? I asked you a question!'

'Did you?' said O'Hara. 'All right. He shall be got rid of.
But what happens if he refuses to be got rid of?'

'Then I shall produce a witness with whom I *have* committed adultery,' said Polly slowly and pointedly.

'Ah! Then you will produce a witness. . . .'

'There's no need to grin like that. You don't understand. I refuse to appear in a public court with such a ridiculous figure as Coax. If I have committed adultery, then it must be with a passably good-looking man. Have you ever seen this Coax? He's an old goat, but not the sort of man one commits adultery with! *You*'ve got no position either, but at least you're something to look at. At any rate, you'd do for the court.'

O'Hara was more than a little worried. His by no means negligible experience with women told him that there was some reason which made Polly declare that, in an emergency (i.e. in the case of the continued presence of the broker on the scene), she would cite him, O'Hara, as co-respondent, and that reason was, for her, a very cogent one. But for him that would mean a premature break with his chief, the ruin of his plans – and possibly worse. He had known MacHeath from the time when he was still called Beckett. He had not always been fat and easygoing.

O'Hara folded the paper carefully and stood up.

'Shut up,' he said brutally. 'You've talked enough. You can go now.'

He realized that he would have to pay now for what he had done. Polly went away so as not to annoy him. Being in the fashion, she was wearing a hat as big as a cart-wheel, decorated with dyed feathers and a veil. She was also carrying a sunshade and wearing corsets which pushed out her posterior. She had made her toilet very carefully, and as she walked she glanced at herself in every shop window. In this way she could also see which men looked after her or followed her. She went to the prison to visit her husband.

She was charming to Mac. She sat coquettishly on the couch, one leg crossed over the other, boring holes in the air with her parasol; and she praised Mac for wanting to cite Coax so that the whole case would collapse. In the court she would point to the broker with her sunshade and say: so I'm supposed to have gone to bed with this gentleman? And laugh. She laughed a great deal as she described the scene.

276

Mac remained gloomy. Miller of the National Credit Bank had been with him and had told him agitatedly of Peachum's visit to the bank. This Coax was a serious danger to Peachum and his money. He seemed to be unwilling to be foisted off with Polly. But if Peachum could not come to some agreement with Coax, the bank, the directorship of which had cost him so much time and trouble, would simply collapse. He realized with chagrin that his fate was now bound up with that of his father-in-law, and he felt a certain desire to be able to speak with him as other sons-in-law speak with their fathers-in-law when the welfare of the family is in danger.

He was too nervous to be able to talk to Polly and he soon sent her away. But she would not go without being kissed.

Soon after that he had a serious conversation with his man Ready. Ready was his best black-jacker.

The Sick Man Dies

Meanwhile Coax had gone down to the West India Docks. Peachum had told him that his beggars were going to demonstrate against the strike. He had dressed them up in soldiers' uniforms. They were going to express indignation at the avarice of the dockers which prevented the British soldier from being transported to the field of battle.

Placards had been painted in Old Oak Street with the inscriptions: 'You are keeping our comrades away from their duty!' and 'Look what *we* have sacrificed!'

The broker wanted to see the demonstration. Peachum was of the opinion that it would not be anything big; but the chief thing was the papers' promise to make a lot out of it.

On Limehouse pier the broker met Beery who seemed very heated and informed him that Peachum had cancelled the demonstration in the morning and then, after lunch, had cancelled the cancellation; however it had been impossible to reach all the participators in time, so now there would probably be only a ridiculous skeleton demonstration. Beery went away very downcast, intent on saving what was still to be saved.

Coax whistled to himself. So Peachum had gone on strike too, and was now working again.

The nearer he got to the docks the more people he saw. Many of them were only standing on street corners, but a whole crowd was, like him, moving towards the docks. They seemed to be expecting something or to have seen something. On questioning someone, he learned that invalid soldiers were demonstrating by the docks.

The press became thicker.

It was the hour when the shifts were changed. The workers who were still at work had to leave the docks. Since there had been no acts of violence up to the present, it had been decided to give up transporting the strike-breakers to and from their work in boats. So they now had to run the gauntlet through the ranks of the strikers.

There was really a considerable noise coming from the quays.

A few corners further on, the broker met Beery again. He was pushing his way against the stream of people pressing towards the quays.

The two men stood for a few minutes, jammed together.

'It's quite a large demonstration,' said Beery excitedly. 'Only about a third of our people are here, but, believe it or not, a lot of real soldiers have come. All the streets up there are full of genuine wounded soldiers. Of course we couldn't have foreseen that. Our people are paid for the demonstration, so it's natural that they demonstrate. Besides they've seen nothing of the war. But those who have joined in now are real soldiers. They are really blaming the dockers because they're not willing to sacrifice enough for the nation! Just listen to them shouting. That's not the workers against the strike-breakers; it's the soldiers, and the crippled ones at that, against the strikers! At first we wanted to engage proper invalids, because Mr Peachum thought they got so little money and were so wretched that they would do anything for a few pennies, even demonstrate for the war. But then we gave up the idea, because our people seemed more reliable. It only shows now how wrong it would have been to pay them. They do it for nothing! One can never make enough allowance for people's stupidity! These men, without arms and legs and eyes, are still in favour of the war! This cannon-folder

278

really thinks it is the nation! It's fantastic! One could do a lot with them, believe me! We've got a man like that, too; an ex-soldier called Fewkoombey, with only one leg. But we never thought he'd do anything like this. But of course he's learned by now what peace means, while those up there apparently haven't yet! It's amazing! But I always say: one's only got to make a war and then the chances to make money become unlimited; movements come to light which you'd never have expected and you only have to make the right use of them to become a millionaire; and you can run any business you like without capital! It's wonderful!'

They were torn apart.

In rows of eight and ten, filling the narrow streets, with the outside files brushing against the walls of the houses, the demonstrators marched implacably forward, singing patriotic songs. They were all more or less crippled. Some hobbled on crutches – still clumsily, for not so long ago they had been like other men. A trouser-leg flapped emptily. Some had their arms in slings, with their coats laid across their shoulders; in the gathering twilight the dirty white bandages waved like flags. There were even blind men in this mad procession. They were led by such as thought they could see. They were exhibited to the public like captured trophies. Other victims rolled along in little trucks, for they had left their legs on the altar of patriotism. The people on the pavements waved at them and shouted jokes about their injuries; they laughed back. The more mutilated the wrecks were, the more their patriotism enraptured the onlookers. They even argued amongst themselves as to whether, for example, a one-armed man would have a better chance than a man who had lost both legs!

The whole rabble pushed on, through the filth of Poplar, trying with their last access of energy to reach the infamous neighbourhood of Limehouse. They were still singing war-songs and they tainted the air with carbolic and their hunger-thinned breaths.

Among the uniformed demonstrators marched civilians – for the most part young men, neatly dressed, who refused to be left out.

But they all had this in common, that they wanted the ships

to be finished as soon as possible so that they could be laden with new flesh, with healthy men still possessing two arms and two legs and seeing eyes. The wounded, the useless, the outcasts wanted, above all else, to increase their numbers. For misery always possesses an irresistible instinct for self-propagation.

It was rumoured that the demonstrators were now heading for the town hall where they were going to demand active police interference against the strikers.

Coax turned towards home. It was already quite dark. Autumn was in the air.

Everywhere stood groups of people discussing the day's events. For the most part the inhabitants of this quarter were, of course, on the side of the workers. And in their conjectures they came very close to the true state of affairs. They apparently did not belong to the genus 'Londoners', about which the newspapers are so fond of writing.

The broker walked faster. He was somewhat uneasy, with a feeling of uncertainty that always assailed him when he witnessed, or even heard of, a disturbance. He turned into a small, dirty public house and ordered a whisky. It tasted horrible, and he thought: what a frightful taste these people have!

When he stepped out into the street, he bumped into a man who murmured something and ran away. As he ran he made a metallic clacking; he had a wooden leg.

The encounter frightened Coax. It now occurred to him that people might jostle him because of his good clothes.

'Actually,' he thought, 'it's extraordinary why they don't simply knock us down when they see us. After all, there aren't so many of us. Even if I knew that Peachum was looking after me, it wouldn't help me much. I wouldn't exactly shed my heart's blood for him either. The worst of the riff-raff in these parts is that they haven't the slightest respect for human life. They think that every life is worth as little as their own. And they hate anyone who is better situated than themselves; because he's mentally superior to them.'

At the next street corner he heard steps coming up behind him. He turned sharply, received a heavy blow on the head, and crumpled up without a sound.

He collapsed on the pavement, began crawling towards the

blank wall of a house, received a second blow, and remained lying there until a police patrol found him. The policemen picked him up and carried him to the station. Thence he was transported to the mortuary where he was recognized three days later by his sister. She had him buried in the cemetery at Battersea where a headstone, in the form of a broken pillar, bore the inscription 'William Coax, 1850–1902'.

Fewkoombey had followed the broker during the whole of that afternoon. He had seen him leave his house after his midday siesta, as Mr Peachum had told him he would. After a very short time he had noticed that several people were also following the broker.

He had no definite intentions. The job did not appeal to him in the slightest. But he had started, and he must go on with it.

The few months of comparative peace in Old Oak Street had corrupted him, still more so the days spent in the hotel by the docks. He did not want to have to return again to the cold nights on the streets from which he had graduated – especially as it would soon be winter.

Several times he had been quite near to the broker in the crowd, but he had felt no desire to harm him.

While the broker was in the public house, he had even lost his knife. He had been chipping at a wooden railing on which he was leaning and the knife had fallen over into a ditch. He had wanted to climb down after it, but he saw that the broker was no longer at the bar so he ran across the street. When he bumped into the broker outside the public house he was frightened, as though the other were planning an attack on him and not vice versa.

The pursuit began again.

Fewkoombey now saw plainly that at least two other people were on the same trail. They walked at a distance from one another, but they always reappeared again when the streets were empty.

Now that Fewkoombey had lost his knife, he had no prospect of being able to kill the broker; in fact, he gave no further thought to it. As he walked along, he began to talk to himself:

'Fewkoombey, I must dismiss you,' he said to himself. 'I have no further use for you. You ask me: what am I going to do? I must admit to you: I don't know. Your prospects are very limited. Before you came to me, you tried to be a beggar. You said to yourself: I've lost my leg. Without that leg I cannot ply any trade that will bring in enough money to feed me. But do you expect that all the bricklayers, packers, errand-boys, van-drivers, and even the passers-by are worried by the fact that you can no longer lay bricks, pack furniture, or drive a horse, and that they are going to be so sorry for your plight that they will divide their bread with you? Never! Do you know what people would say if they even thought it worth the trouble or worth the unpleasantness of discussing your case? They would say: a man is dying? What does it matter if one dies and a thousand remain? That doesn't make any more room for us. If thousands were to die, that would be a different matter. If our employers had to look round and search everywhere for a man who could pack furniture for them...! – Do you know all that is being done to put people out of work? A great deal, Fewkoombey, in fact nearly everything that's done is done with that object! That is, indeed, the life-work of most men – to put others out of employment. It's not because a man wants to cart furniture that he gets his living, it's because he does not want to and therefore has to be enticed, begged, and even paid. But, for that, we must be too few – definitely. It's when there are enough of us that the trouble and dirty work starts. And now you're the odd man out, my friend. Of course, it's quite right that you should begin to excite sympathy again. But not so much sympathy! – We may therefore assume, Fewkoombey, that you enjoy the general sympathy to such an extent that you are not actually persecuted every time you stand still in the streets. And as things are now, that's a great deal to be thankful for. But you think that you ought to be pitied? The simplicity of the man! The people who walk across Battersea Bridge are to pity you! Those hard-boiled, thick-skinned, miserable (for they have to put up with every misery, including your own) people of Battersea! What do you think it costs to become properly hard-boiled, to become even moderately thick-skinned? That state doesn't come naturally, it's got to be attained! No man is born a butcher. Look at all *those jaws! Look at your own, if you like, in a mirror. I tell you, jaws a quarter of that size would be large enough to masticate the food. But before the mastication comes the bite, and how many of those jaws do you think are strong enough for that decisive, all-important bite which lays low the quarry, secures it, and kills it? Few, my man, very few. You have a foot missing! Have you no more to offer? You are hungry! Is that all? Impertinence! That is just like someone in the street trying to draw everyone's attention to himself because he can stand on one leg. There are thousands of people who can do that! That's not the way things are done. You are unlucky. Well, you are unluckier than most. That makes you unfit for competition. For competition, my man. On which rests the whole structure of our civilization, in case you didn't know that! The selection of the fittest! The extraction of the finest! Of those who excel! But how could they excel if there were no one for them to excel? Therefore, thank God for people like you. You can be excelled. All the development of life on this planet can only be explained by one word — competition! Why, otherwise, should there be any development? Why the apes, if the saurians had not proved themselves incapable of competing? There you see! You lack a leg. Good. If it came to the point, you could prove that; (although a second person is needed who is prepared to admit your proof! Aha, you didn't think of that!) But there is still the other leg. You've got that! And your arms! And your head! But no, my dear chap, it's not so easy as that; that won't qualify you for selection. That assumption is nothing more than indolence, ill-breeding, and obstinacy. In reality you are doing harm. Without helping yourself, you harm, simply by your very existence, everybody else, including those more incapable and more wretched than yourself. What? You say: is there so much unhappiness in the world? But what can one do about it? In what way can one help? This much is clear: the more unhappiness there is, the less one need have to do with it. Unhappiness is practically universal! The natural state of affairs! The world is unhappy, just like a tree is green! Away with you!'*

It grew darker.

During this conversation with himself the soldier had become angry. Arriving at a street corner, he considered again how he could kill the broker. At the same moment he saw from his corner how a thin man in an Inverness cape took a few quick steps up behind the broker and struck him heavily over the head with a sandbag or something similar. Fewkoombey was horrified. But now the victim began suddenly rising from the pavement. On all fours he tried to crawl to the nearest house-wall, apparently so that he could lean against it.

For a moment longer the soldier peered through the darkness. Then he walked rapidly across the street until he stood beside the crawling man.

Slowly he felt in the pocket of his coat, then in the hip-pocket of his trousers. But he found no knife, as he probably expected. With an almost astonished expression he looked at his empty hands. Then, leaning against the wall, with his glance coolly fixed on the writhing figure at his feet which had now turned round and was dragging its retching way towards the gutter, he began to unbuckle his wooden leg. It was fastened on with a strap. At last he had it free. And as he struck the crawling man, again and again on the head and shoulders, hopping all the while beside him on his remaining leg, he burst out, probably still thinking of the trouble it had been to unbuckle: 'My bloody leg!'

14

The Strong Man Fights

POLLY was sitting with her mother in her little rose-pink room, sewing baby-clothes, when Beery came in and said that her father wished to speak to her.

She ran downstairs, with the needle still between her fingers and the thread trailing behind.

Mr Peachum had on his Sunday suit and curtly informed her that she was going visiting B. shops with him.

They walked along Old Oak Street. It was a sunny, late autumn day. The foliage on the trees was yellow, and chestnuts were floating in the canal.

Peachum was silent, for he had nothing to say to his daughter. But she took this walk *à deux* as a good sign; and even the poorest streets became kindly in the thin gold shimmer of autumn. So she felt happier than she had for a long time.

So far she had heard nothing from O'Hara. But Mr Coax had not appeared in Old Oak Street again. Her father seemed to be calmer, too. It was as though the tension had slackened.

In a dismal back-street they entered the first shop. A fat woman was selling kitchen crockery and carpentering-tools. She knew Polly and therefore answered Peachum's questions, though somewhat surlily.

She said that she was only receiving quite small deliveries of goods now. If her husband had not been doing odd tinkering jobs, repairing garden tools and lamps, etc., they would long ago have starved. But now they had been promised a regular supply of materials.

They paid the rent, but it was in arrears. They were not the first people to own the shop; there had been another couple there before them. These had left behind all the fittings, in return for their successors paying the arrears.

'All these shops are just beginning,' explained Polly to her father as they walked on. 'They're scarcely six months old and

Mac's arrest was a great blow to the owners. But now everything is going better. Those who hold out will do well.'

Peachum said nothing.

They walked for a while in silence.

The next shop which they visited was a shoemaker's. There were half a dozen children; the three eldest were helping with the work.

They said they had sufficient leather – even now. And even during the worst time, when for some weeks the other shops had been getting nothing at all, they had still received leather, although in smaller quantities. But a great deal of it was useless and the pieces were measured by area, so that they had to pay for the waste.

The husband was unfortunately ill. Also the light in their workroom was very expensive and it had to be kept burning all day.

'All the same,' said the woman, 'it's better than the factory. You get no chance to increase your earnings there.'

Peachum nodded and asked whether the prices of the shoes were fixed by the firm delivering the leather.

The answer was: yes – and too low.

When they were out in the street again, Peachum asked his daughter:

'Do they ever settle up, then?'

Polly said she thought that the people only got new deliveries when they had paid for the old ones. She was afraid that her father was very displeased with the shops because he said nothing.

In the third shop they had scarcely begun with their questions when the owner began to speak about the disturbances by the docks.

'These communists,' he said, *'are responsible for everything. They break all the window-panes as though we got them free from the makers! They hate us because they have nothing and we have something. Just because they've never made a success of of their lives, they don't want anyone else to. Ability's not to count any more, and the intelligent are to be no better off than the stupid. They're the real anti-Christians! There are some of them in this house, too. They don't drink, but they do some-*

thing worse, eh? If they had their way, they'd take everything
away from a man, even the chair from underneath him. As if
we hadn't got enough to worry about already! But there's one
thing Mr MacHeath shouldn't have done. He ought never to
have gone in with that Jew Aaron. He'll have trouble there!'

During the monologue, Peachum was looking round the shop.
In a rough glass-topped case lay rows of cheap clocks. They
were mostly alarm clocks. But there was also underwear on sale,
and even tobacco. Over the door was written: GENERAL STORE.

The married couple to whom the shop belonged looked very
unhealthy. The man was already the third owner of this shop,
the third person to try to stand on his own feet. To judge by the
appearance of himself and his wife, the effort was rather a strain.

The man had a cringing way about him which accorded ill
with his massive frame. The woman said nothing and looked
gloomy.

'The shops are all rather like that,' said Polly a little sadly
when they regained the street. 'Do you want to see any more?'

They rode a little way in an omnibus and then visited a few
more shops.

In front of one of these Peachum stopped and looked at the
pavement with an enigmatical expression on his face. The owner
of the shop had drawn there, in chalk, a picture of a smartly
dressed gentleman with a top hat on, and underneath he had
written a list of his prices. Peachum knew the technique.

A fair-haired young man was standing behind a counter piled
with suits. In reply to their questions, he said:

'You know, one *can* earn money here. Trade is by no means
slow. As soon as we get cheaper material again and can raise our
prices a bit and get free from the competition of the bigger
shops, there'll be a living in it. After all, we get up at five in
the morning and never go to bed before ten or eleven at night.
And that *must* make a difference in the long run. Don't you
think so?'

In another shop, the people were in the process of moving out
when Peachum entered.

Those who were going had left everything until the last
moment. They were still standing with their children and furniture in the little whitewashed room, while the new tenants were

unloading their goods and chattels from a cart on to the pavement.

The children were crying and receiving angry slaps from the desperate parents. The new tenants came in; large, comfortable people with a well-behaved child. The woman asked a great many questions about the price of gas and whether the room was really dry.

The departing couple began to speak their mind, and it was plain to see that the newcomers were considerably embarrassed. They had made a mistake in asking all those questions and now wanted to hear no more. But the others were in full spate and gave free rein to their tongues.

'Of course, one can't take what they say seriously,' explained the new owner, rather red in the face, to Polly and her father. 'They are embittered. Everything is to blame for their misfortune – except themselves.'

Then the woman said contemptuously:

'They're only labourers. They're going back to Lancashire – to the mills. People like that ought never to start a business on their own. The factory is the right place for them.'

But she still looked anxiously at the large damp patch on the wall which the other woman had triumphantly pointed out. When they had inspected the house before taking it, there had been a wardrobe standing in front. . . .

Polly and her father went away before the confusion had died down. They drove home.

Polly said nothing more, for she felt there was no point in pursuing the subject. But before they got home, she did mention that the people at any rate had their independence and appreciated it. They hated having anybody over them. Rather than that they would work half the night through.

She did not know whether her father had even heard her. But he *was* listening – very closely.

On the next day, Peachum went to the National Credit Bank. He spent several hours there, discussing the situation with Miller. The latter could say little about MacHeath's connexion with Aaron. But Peachum had long since realized that only his son-in-law could save the bank. The way in which he had secured control of it was almost worthy of admiration.

In general, Peachum had received a good impression of the B. shops. Their organization was not at all bad. A lot of money could be got out of people in that way.

Polly had been quite unnecessarily afraid that the wretchedness of the shops might have upset her father. But of course he knew that prosperity was only the reverse side of poverty. What was the prosperity of one man but the poverty of another?

'Don't talk to me about social reformers,' he often used to say. 'I remember once there was a great outcry in the papers about some slums being unfit for human habitation; they were unsanitary and unhygienic. So they pulled down the whole district and moved the inhabitants into a colony of beautiful, solidly built, hygienic houses up in Stockton-on-Tees. They kept very careful statistics and after five years compared the results. It then became apparent that, although the death-rate in the slums had been 2 per cent, in the new houses it had risen to 2·6 per cent. They were very astonished. Well, it was simply due to the fact that the new houses cost four to eight shillings more per week and this money had to be made up by saving on food. Our social reformers and humanitarians had never thought of that!'

His son-in-law's talent made a considerable impression on Peachum. Looking up from the papers spread before him and staring absently at Miller's haggard face, he began to ask himself whether their enmity wasn't just the natural one between two different generations. He had underrated him, treated him as a criminal. Whereas, in reality, he was a hard-working, and doubtless far-sighted, business man.

That same evening Peachum visited his solicitor, Walley, at his private house.

The interview took place in a large luxurious room with richly panelled walls and a great many exotic carpets. In one corner, near an immense writing-table, stood some broad-leaved plants in grey enamel pots.

'You've come to see me about the divorce?' said Walley, rather coolly. 'To be frank, I don't feel quite happy about this case. Mr MacHeath's adultery is proved and will be admitted. But if I have been informed correctly, your business friend, Mr Coax, is to be called as a witness in support of a counter-charge of adultery against your daughter. Of course, that is only a bluff, but I'm afraid it will mean a great deal of dirty linen being washed in public.'

'Who on earth thought of calling Mr Coax as a witness?' asked Peachum, astonished.

'Mr MacHeath. A few days ago.'

'I see,' said Peachum slowly. 'Well, Mr Coax has been missing for two days. The day before yesterday he did not return home. His sister, with whom he lived, seems to be very perturbed about it. Unfortunately, he has certain propensities which bring him into contact with the dregs of humanity; so his continued absence can only make one fear the worst. In other words, I am afraid that we shall never have to worry about Coax again.'

'Ah,' was all that Walley said. He looked searchingly at his visitor, as though something had escaped him.

'I have broken off all business relations with Mr Coax,' continued Peachum. 'I had an experience of him in Southampton which opened my eyes. I hope I may never be called upon to describe the disgusting and revolting scenes to which my eyes were witness. From that day on, I washed my hands of the man.'

Then he dropped the subject of Coax and explained, with an expressionless face, that his daughter had just informed him that she was expecting a child by her husband. This, of course, altered everything. A divorce was out of the question now.

The solicitor seemed very relieved. Peachum went on drily. He inquired about the progress and the probable outcome of the case against his son-in-law. He made it plain that he expected the verdict to be a favourable one.

The solicitor played with a knife-shaped letter-opener.

'Mr Peachum,' he said, 'your son-in-law will walk out of that prison a free man. Not a shadow of suspicion will rest on him, you may depend upon me. After all, he has an alibi.'

'Good,' said Peachum, and was about to stand up.

'It's not good,' said Walley angrily. 'Unless a murderer is found, the acquittal may take some time. The alibi will first have to be investigated. No, Peachum, we must give him a helping hand ourselves.'

He lay back and folded his hands over his stomach.

'My dear Peachum,' he said broadly, 'on you lies, and must lie, the responsibility for elucidating the circumstances which led to Mrs Sawyer's death. I believe it was Withe who, during the proceedings before the Magistrate, propounded the theory that Mary Sawyer, having regard to her economic circumstances, needed no murderer to take her life. She was really in an extremely bad way.'

His words came slower and slower, as though he were seeking some solution for what he wanted to say. He avoided looking at Mr Peachum who sat there calmly with his bony hands between his knees.

With an obvious effort he went on.

'Unfortunately,' he said emphatically, 'this theory becomes untenable in view of certain new facts which have come to light.'

Walley had stood up. With long strides he paced the thick carpet which past eloquence had earned for him.

'Mr Peachum,' he said significantly, still prowling, 'for some time before her death, Mary Sawyer had been seen in the company of a man who was probably in worse straits even than herself. This man was a soldier named Fewkoombey. During the proceedings before the Magistrate, he appeared in the witness-box. He admitted that he had been with Mrs Sawyer on the fatal evening, and that he had even accompanied her to the docks.'

The solicitor paused. He stopped suddenly before Peachum, looked at him sharply, and said calmly:

'He was the last person to see Mary Sawyer alive. And no one who listened to him in that court realized the possible implications of that fact. The eyes of the witnesses, most of them coming from the lower classes, were so blinded by hatred of the prisoner who was so far their social superior, that they missed the most obvious solution! Even the articles in the *Reflector* described how the soldier accompanied the unfortunate Mary Sawyer on her last journey, when, in all probability, she was entirely in his power. There is proof, there *must* be proof – statements by the neighbours, anything – that will testify to the demoniacal domination which the soldier exercised over the unhappy woman. He wormed his way into her peaceful household while her husband, also a soldier, a comrade of his, was at the front. He was a man who took a fiendish pleasure in seducing the wife of his friend, and who did it in a small room, before the eyes of the children! When he learned of the extraordinary friendliness and paternal solicitude with which Mr MacHeath treated even the least of his employees, that man must have importuned the woman day and night to make use of the opportunity which offered. In an access of shame, this respectable and decent-minded woman may have refused to blackmail Mr MacHeath, and that night, who knows? there may have been a quarrel on the wharf. . . . At all events, we have the testimony of a dockyard worker who, while out strolling on the evening in question, saw Fewkoombey at about a quarter past nine, coming from the direction of the wharf. Mr Peachum!' (The solicitor raised his voice.) 'The same logic that will not let us believe that the prosperous banker MacHeath could have murdered Mary Sawyer, that *same* logic convinces us that it must have been the penniless, brutalized ex-soldier, Fewkoombey. It is partly a question of degree of education. Fighting in the war, which raises an educated, intelligent man out of himself and spurs him on to deeds of heroism, arouses in the coarser type nothing but the most brutal impulses. It is gain that lures them on. Gain in every form. Plain lust for murder drives them to murder. For them there is none of that brave spirit of competition to reach the top, no lasting ambition to make the best of themselves, which characterizes our educated classes. The little amount of school-teaching that he receives can have no decisive influence on him; it is only the warm fire that attracts him to the school-house – if it is not the blows and kicks which he receives at home. He never succeeds in earning much money; he is too stupid. Anything he may earn, he immediately squanders. The compensation money which he receives from the Government runs through his fingers like water. Soon he has nothing left. As you know only too well, Mr Peachum, London is not a kindergarten for a man who has nothing in his pockets. He tries to beg. He fails; he is probably not convincing enough. By now he has reached a state of mind in which the slightest chance of making money robs him of all restraint. He *must* kill someone, if, by doing so, he can secure a few shillings! Nature, who distributes her gifts unequally, his education, his environment, are all in part responsible for what happened; that we cannot deny.'

The solicitor gazed for a moment at the chandelier.

'I can hear you objecting,' he continued softly, 'that Mary Sawyer was a poor woman, without means, scarcely likely to have more than a few coppers on her. I have already explained to you that there was probably a scene, an attempt that overreached itself, to compel the unhappy woman to take a course which she had hitherto refused. But it may also have been caused by a few pennies. Even *that* is possible, even that! A human life for the sake of a few pence? Is that possible? Gentlemen!' (The solicitor, carried away by his own eloquence, forgot that he was at home.) 'A mere glance at our city reveals to us the horrible, the incredible! It *can* happen! What, gentlemen, are a few pennies to you? What are a few pounds to you? How much would it have to be, for you to . . . but I will not elaborate the idea further. Do you know what a night under the arches is like? Let me describe it to you!'

The solicitor, with his outstretched hands resting on the back of a chair, stood two paces away from Peachum. Suddenly he seemed to notice him and finished up, a little absent-mindedly as though he were trying to memorize at the back of his mind the highlights of his brilliant extempore speech for the defence:

'I will sum up: the circumstance which might have driven Mary Sawyer to suicide, i.e. her miserable poverty, was the very thing which caused the soldier, George Fewkoombey, who was even worse off than she, to kill her. For whenever I have to find the criminal who committed a crime. I always ask myself: whom could that crime benefit? The person who had the motive, my lord and gentlemen of the jury, was the person who committed the crime!'

The first authority in the land on the subject of misery listened to him in complete agreement.

The Battle of the West India Docks

Stormy the night and the sea runs high
Still the brave ship must fight.
Why sounds the bell with that shuddering clang?
Hold! A reef's in sight!

See each true heart at his own post stand
Fighting the sea for the Fatherland
With death so near, with death so near,
Manful and gallant, they feel no fear.
Out o'er the deck hear the clanging bell speak
Vain is their struggle: the ship's aleak.
Prepare for what must be!
Our course is set for Eternity!
God help us now!
We're away to our peaceful sleep on the deep sea-floor.
God help us now!

(THE SAILOR'S LOT)

It was not until the third day after his murder that Coax was found by his sister in a mortuary in Poplar.

The Press treated William Coax's death as directly connected with the dockers' strike, which was receiving more and more publicity.

'There can be no doubt,' said the newspapers, *'that William Coax has fallen for his country. All the police investigations point to the fact that the strikers have not hesitated to go to the ultimate extreme of committing murder. It is now known that Coax, in conjunction with the Government, was helping to organize transport facilities for the troops. If the Government cannot or will not protect citizens who are working for their country, they will soon find that there are no business men left to support them. It is a tragic coincidence that Coax should have lost his life at the same time as a noble demonstration of wounded soldiers was taking place. For, on last Tuesday, several hundreds of war-crippled men were demonstrating against the iniquitous strike of the dockers, through whose fault those brave men who are shut up in Mafeking, waiting anxiously for relief to arrive, are now doomed to annihilation. As everyone knows, these workmen are striking for the sake of a few extra pence. For a negligible sum of money which will not even buy a pair of boots! The present perilous position of the country must not and shall not be exploited by this type of blackmail which does not even benefit the blackmailers. The best brains in the country are working day and night to keep the cost of living down to a minimum. Only today there comes the news of*

another example which shows how the business world is tire-
lessly striving, even to the detriment of their own profits, to
cheapen the price of goods. Today two great concerns, Chreston's
Chain Stores and Aaron's Stores, together with dozens of small,
independent shopkeepers, have pooled their efforts and joined
the well-known B. Shop System, lowering their prices in accord-
ance with that system. But how can such patriotism be effective
when a section of the people insists so selfishly upon its pound
of flesh? No one will deny that the workers have as much right
to receive a reward commensurate with their labours as any
other class of the community. But the means which have been
employed in this case are means which cannot be justified in
any circumstances, least of all at a time when the Empire is
fighting for its very existence and when every man must be
prepared to make a sacrifice. We may well expect that the Gov-
ernment will now, at last, take energetic action. The murder
of William Coax is a flagrant example of the depths to which
England has sunk.'

As a matter of fact, several more things had to happen before
the Government recognized where its duty lay.

As president of the M.T.C. Peachum gave a series of interviews. He expressed the sorrow of the Company at losing an
irreplaceable business adviser and spoke at length on the high
moral and patriotic standpoint of the departed. During the time
between the discovery of Coax's body and the funeral, Peachum
devoted himself to the purely business side of the M.T.C.'s
transactions.

On Miss Coax's behalf he went through the broker's papers.
After sifting them thoroughly, he informed her that she would
probably receive about £12,250 in payment of her brother's share
in the transaction, and he took away with him a certain document relating to the private affairs of the Company and signed
by two of its members, and an option on the Southampton
ships.

He also unearthed the papers concerning the purchase and sale
of the old ships, which papers he needed for the M.T.C.

Then he made an astounding discovery. He found a *second*
contract with the Government. This concerned the Southampton
ships. The late broker, having bought the three good ships so

cheaply through the M.T.C., had not hesitated to offer them to the Government.

The profits from this transaction would be well over £120,000! Peachum felt dizzy.

For a moment he feared that he was going to have a stroke.

In the next room, the door of which stood open, sat Polly and Miss Coax. The two ladies were sewing mourning clothes. For several minutes Peachum fought the desire to ask for a glass of water. But the danger that Miss Coax would notice something was too great. Those were perhaps the most tragic minutes of his life. He emerged from them a victor. Breathing heavily, one hand pressed on his hammering heart, fearing at any moment a collapse, he decided to go without the sip of water.

When his expression had returned to normal – he readjusted it in the glass front of a book-case – he took his leave of Miss Coax and drove to the Admiralty.

There he forced Hale to transfer both contracts to him. It was sufficient for him to threaten to send the Government a certain receipt for one thousand pounds, drawn up by Coax. Hale was very broken up by the passing of his oldest friend, which, so he said, he would never get over.

The profit for Peachum on the first contract worked out at about £29,000.

His final reckoning-up with the M.T.C. was as follows: The seven partners, one of whom had retired, handing over his share to Peachum, had paid up for the three old ships, for their repair, for the bribes, for Coax's percentage, and for the three new ships (the latter had cost £38,500) a total sum of £77,450. On the credit side stood the £49,000 which the Government had already paid. Peachum also wrote off £2,100 for the old ships which he had ostensibly sold through Brookley and Brookley. And Crowl had paid up nearly four-fifths of his share before he departed for the *eternal* hunting-grounds.

Besides, the Southampton ships would really only cost £30,000 as Peachum found out in the option.

On the way home from Coax's cremation, as he walked through the slums, Peachum surrendered himself, for the first time in those hectic days, to his own thoughts.

'*It's extraordinary,*' he thought, '*how the most complicated business is often put right by the simplest age-old methods. Really, our vaunted civilization is not so very far off from the days when the Neanderthal man had to strike down his enemy with a club. All this business began with contracts and Government stamps, and at the end we had to resort to murder! How I hate murder! What a revolting relic of barbarism! But business makes it a necessity. We cannot do without it. A murderer is punished; but a non-murderer is also punished – and far more terribly. Crowl, for instance, was punished with death for his fatalistic attitude in this ship business. An existence in the slums, such as I and my family were threatened with, is nothing less than imprisonment. That is a life sentence! There's all this talk of better education and improving the people's conscience – no doubt, the picture of this Coax will often appear to me and especially to his murderer, Fewkoombey, in sleep – but conscience, goodness, humanity, these alone are not strong enough, not by a long way, to eliminate murder entirely; the premiums on its commission are too large and the punishments for its omission too heavy! Actually, this Coax died, or was killed, in a perfectly natural way. With him, everything would have gone wrong; without him, everything, or nearly everything, is all right. Admittedly, murder is a last resort, the very last – but it is still useful. And to think that we were only doing business together!'*

The next morning he went down to the docks again. The situation there was bad. There were scarcely a dozen men still at work. The hostility of the workers who stood at the dock gates to see that no one accepted work there, horrified him.

'Brute force everywhere!' he said bitterly to a few of his employees who were standing round, staring at the docks through the dirty windows of a shed. 'I know these people don't want to work for the wages I pay them. But why don't they let others work, who want to? Those who need the money, who must have it, because their families are starving? Why must they use force against these poor creatures and stop them working? After all, everyone must be free to do as he wants.'

He was desperate.

And then came a surprise from his daughter and son-in-law.

The news of Coax's death had created an extraordinary atmosphere in the Peachum family.

Polly was very anxious; she was glad to be able to talk to Miss Coax and help her with all the arrangements for the funeral. It had a very soothing effect on her.

The dramatic news in the papers about the dock strike had opened her eyes to the difficulties with which her father was beset. She sent a message through her mother to ask him whether he wanted people to protect the strike-breakers; her husband would be glad to place such people at his disposal.

'Do you know,' Mrs Peachum said to her husband, 'it's just as though all the suffering which she has had to see during these last few days has taught her to understand the troubles of others. She wants to know if she can help you.'

Peachum growled something about: 'That fellow is the biggest swindler alive!' But then he told Mrs Peachum to tell Polly to speak to Beery about it. She did so.

'One must not listen to the voice of hate when money is at stake,' MacHeath had said when Polly asked him. 'In temperament and theory your father and I are opposed, but circumstances demand that we unite and work together.'

O'Hara sent a few dozen of his people down to the docks. These immediately introduced a system into the strike-breaking. They dealt with the strikers in such a way that even the police were horrified. They displayed a pronounced *sense of order*, broke every bone they could get hold of, and hit out at every face that looked hungry. The engineer, speaking of them to Peachum, said that even in those rough-looking fellows there was a core of goodness; it all depended on *what* they were used for.

The strike-breakers took new courage.

Then O'Hara's people collected a rabble of loafers and stormed a provisions shop in the neighbourhood of the docks.

This attack developed into a pitched battle which went down in the annals of the C.P.B. as the 'Battle of the West India Docks'. It also sealed the fate of the strikers.

Faced with a solid wall of silent workers, Bully and his companions broke all the shop windows. When they got inside the shop, the strikers made no attempt to follow them, for they wanted to have nothing to do with the plundering. The C.P.B.

people then snatched up hams and other pieces of meat and attacked the hungry men with them. A half-starved worker was brought down with a whole leg of beef. Several received pots of pickled meat in their emaciated faces and, being unable to see any more, fell into the hands of the police. Even small rolls were thrown about. A few rickety children were wounded by them. Loaves of bread became formidable weapons. An old woman, carrying an empty market basket, had her arm broken by a five-pound loaf. The broken arm was evidence against her in court.

The newspapers worked themselves into a frenzy over this plundering, and especially over the way in which 'the people' had behaved with foodstuffs.

'These are the horrors of anarchy,' they wrote, 'of the brute instinct unbridled. Our friends the Socialists should take care to avoid such scenes if they wish anyone to believe their hypocritical attacks on the existing order of society!'

From now on the Government took sharp measures against the strikers and their demands.

Two days later the military was called out. The young troops, who were destined for South Africa, threw a cordon round the docks and protected the strike-breakers. During the next few days there were one or two isolated cases of shooting, but the completion of the transport-ships was assured.

The decisive battle had been short and bitter.

The men were nearly all recruits, going into action for the first time. They were better fed than the workers, but had they put on workmen's clothes it would have been difficult to distinguish between the combatants, because they all came from the same class. Indeed, if the young soldiers had been without rifles and uniforms, they would have been fighting among themselves.

But it must not be forgotten that they all spoke the same language with the same accent. The epithets which each side hurled at the other were identical. Should a rifle be torn from the soldier who was swinging it, the workman swung it with no less skill, because he was accustomed to wielding a sledge-hammer. But even if the workers were less practised in this sort of fighting, they had also assimilated with their mother's milk the knowledge that if they did not look after themselves they would never get as much as a crust. And the soldiers knew, from the same source, that they were not paid to loaf about. So, once they came to blows, they fought one another in the same way as they all fought against poverty, hunger, sickness; everything which the town offered them, and with which the country threatened them.

The newspapers gave detailed accounts of the fight. Their descriptions, which more or less tallied, all appeared under some such heading as: 'YOUNG TROOPS, EAGER TO HURRY TO THE HELP OF THEIR COMRADES IN MAFEKING, WIN THEIR TRANSPORTS AT THE POINT OF THE BAYONET!'

The completion of the ships did not take much longer. The chief obstacle now was the mass of formalities designed to guard the nation from being defrauded.

On a Friday the ships were officially taken over by the Government Commission, and a week later they put out to sea.

It was a foggy day. Although this transport was only one of the smaller, weekly ones, the docks were crowded with soldiers, with the relations of those sailing, members of the Goverment, and the Press. It was difficult to see much of the proceedings, for one could scarcely distinguish one's own hand through the fog.

'My friends,' said the Secretary of State in his speech, 'the future of England rests on the bravery and self-sacrifice of her youth. The whole of England rejoices in this moment when two thousand young men, the flower of the nation, step aboard Her Majesty's ships to give an example of bravery and patriotism that will ring down the ages. The blind might of the elements surrounds them, they are threatened by crafty and unscrupulous foes; behind them stands only Britain's greatness. They are in God's hands; and that means everything.'

Among the brazen echoes of a military march and the sobbing of mothers and wives, the three ships, huge, indistinct monsters in the fog, slid away from the quay.

Eleven hours later, while still in the Channel, the *Optimist* went down in the fog, taking every living soul with her.

A National Catastrophe

After the hurricane and the dark
The ship rests, ah, so deep.
Only the dolphin and glutted shark
Swim round that desolate reef.
Of all those spirits so gay and bold
None could break free from death's cruel hold.
Down under on the ocean ground
Pale-mouthed they slumber without a sound.
The sea breathes soft its ancient refrain,
Warning, beats it into the brain:
Sailor beware, sailor beware!
Hark to the voices of wave and air.
Sleep well. Sleep well.
Under the coral a quiet place, too,
Waits one day for you.

(THE SAILOR'S LOT)

Peachum heard the shrill cries of the newspaper boys when he was riding down Oxford Street on an omnibus. He got out and read in the extra edition that the *Optimist* had sunk and that there were rumours going about the City of a plot against the transports. The ships were said to have left the harbour in a condition which could not be described as seaworthy. It was to be hoped that the police would call to account those *irresponsible persons* who had had a hand in this tragedy and had thus menaced the nation's safety.

He went straight home.

The extra edition was already being sold in Old Oak Street. Beery had a copy in his hand when Peachum entered. He was deadly pale and trembling.

Peachum walked past, giving him a terrible sideways glance, and Beery stared after him as though he were an apparition.

Mrs Peachum received him with that cordiality which she always displayed when she had been in the cellar. She had as yet heard nothing.

Peachum went to the room where the reference files were kept and locked himself in. His wife heard him pacing restlessly up and down, hour after hour. When she wanted to fetch him to supper and knocked on the door, she received no reply; the food which she left outside the door was left untouched. He was waiting to be arrested.

Towards eleven o'clock in the evening, about fourteen hours after the publication of the extra edition, he went down to the office and rang for Beery. He sent him to the nearest public house to fetch the papers, for Beery declared that he had bought none.

In the papers were great headlines: 'A NATIONAL DISASTER' and 'FOG RESPONSIBLE FOR SINKING OF THE "OPTIMIST",' together with a description of the disaster according to what was already known. Suggestions as to the cause of the catastrophe, especially of the type which had appeared in the extra edition, were conspicuous by their absence. The announcement only said that the Admiralty were inquiring into the matter.

Peachum read it all, every line. Then he set to work.

Together with Beery, he evolved the exact plans for a complete reorganization of the workshops. Over half the employees were to be dressed up in uniforms and given wounds of various kinds. From the viewpoint of the begging business, a national catastrophe like this was the same as a victory. There was no doubt at all that London, with the description of the disaster still fresh in its memory, would be ready to give. Anybody in uniform with the slightest recognizable injury would be a national hero for the next few days.

Peachum worked for several hours and then slept for a short while. The workshops – saddlery, carpentering, tailoring – started work at six the next morning, manufacturing uniforms and mutilations.

At ten, Peachum visited the Admiralty, where he spoke to Hale for five minutes. Then he went to Scotland Yard.

He had been pleasantly surprised by Hale's behaviour. The latter's military training had taught him to receive the blows of fate with equanimity. The office was a scene of great activity. Hale's orders were brisk and to the point. The official memorial ceremony was to take place on the day after next. With regard to the second Government contract, that guaranteeing the purchase of the Southampton ships, Hale saw no cause for alarm, as long as no scandal broke over the first.

The Assistant Commissioner received Peachum with unconcealed mistrust, and this only disappeared when the latter introduced himself as the president of the Marine Transport Company. And to remove any remaining doubt, he explained that he had come about MacHeath's case which was to come up for trial during the next few days.

Peachum then asked what he was to tell the Press if questioned about the probable cause of the disaster. Brown willingly gave him instructions. The cause of the accident had not yet been ascertained, but it was now known that the *Young Sailorboy* was also seriously damaged. Probably the two ships had collided in the fog.

Peachum left quickly and drove to Eastman. He spent the rest of the morning with him and Moon — Finney was in the nursing-home, having been operated on — making up the final accounts. Neither of the gentlemen was in a mood to go again into the details of the business. They had never seen the Southampton ships which they imagined had sailed, bearing the names of the old derelicts, and they were in mortal terror of an investigation.

On the way home, Peachum made no attempt to hurry. He wandered vaguely through the streets, picking up snatches of conversation. Everybody was discussing the catastrophe.

In front of a tiny B. shop the owner was talking to a few of the passers-by.

'When you're dealing with wind and water,' he said, 'you never know what to expect next. Man is powerless against fog. Such things are the forces of nature, the destructive elements. Everyone's got their own troubles, but simply to sink like that, in the middle of the Channel! It's a terrible disaster! They say there's going to be a memorial service in St Paul's next Friday. I bet you the communists had something to do with it!'

Throughout the afternoon Peachum was working with Beery. The writing-rooms for begging letters were supplied with new texts. With shaking hands, war-widows whose husbands were 'resting in a watery grave', begged for help to open a small business — which, incidentally, was the first time that begging letters from Peachum's factory had mentioned the B. shops.

The addresses were carefully drawn from the reference files, which contained the names of charitable people, together with their various weaknesses.

The Peachum factory showed itself well capable of dealing with a national disaster.

Towards evening Peachum received a summons from Brown.

The latter awaited him with a dark frown on his face. In the room were two other high police officials.

It was a large room. On the desk, on a piece of green blotting-paper, stood a bronze statue of Atlas, carrying on its back a loudly ticking clock. On the face of the clock was written: *ultima multis*. A picture of the Duke of Wellington hung on the wall.

'Mr Peachum,' began the chief inspector, 'according to the reports we have received, it seems that the transport *Optimist* sank as a result of severe internal damage. At the very least, a break-down in the steering-gear is to be assumed. I must inform you that Mr Hale, the Secretary of State at the Admiralty, has been told that he is not to leave his private house until further orders. I presume that you wish to make a statement in regard to this matter.'

Mr Peachum stared blankly at the wall.

'I *do* wish to make a statement,' he said. 'I believe a crime has been committed.'

The chief inspector surveyed him intently, with one of those official glances which are not put on to observe but to be observed.

After a short, impressive silence, Peachum continued:

'*Gentlemen, the steering-gear must have broken; without a storm, without the helmsman being to blame, in calm, though slightly foggy weather, nothing else could have happened. There is no investigation necessary, only a little reflection. Only a little knowledge of our Government and of all the governments of all civilized countries. Only a brief consideration of the way in which we choose our officials whose duty it is to guard the welfare of the State, how we train them, and how and why they put themselves at the service of the nation. Then, in order to come to the conclusion that such ships must sink, it is only necessary to review the purpose for which they were built, the way in which they were sold, and the profits which they must bring.*

304

Once we have made these observations, we must – whether we like it or not – come to the conviction which I previously expressed when I said: I believe a crime has been committed.'

The gentlemen in the room looked at one another. Peachum was sitting. They were now standing, for they had got up. Peachum went on:

'Taking other considerations, I came to other conclusions. Having regard for the excellence of our Government and the honesty of our business men and firms, for the justice of our war and the unselfishness of all our moderately eating, decently living, properly clothed fellow citizens, and faced with the fact that one of our transports sank in a calm sea, I am forced to the conclusion, without any investigation and in spite of any investigation, that a crime is out of the question and that an accident is probable, nay, certain. So I now say: I do not believe that a crime has been committed; I believe that there has been an accident.'

Mr Peachum looked closely at each of his hearers before he continued.

'If you would now permit me to say which of these two conclusions appeals to me the more, I would decide for the second. It is by far the more preferable. In two days, I hear, a memorial service is to take place in honour of those of Her Majesty's soldiers who were drowned in this catastrophe. Would you think it advisable if the selfsame wounded soldiers who not long ago demonstrated in favour of the sailing of those ships, were now to demonstrate against the fact that such ships were ever bought? I am told that there is a notice in the papers announcing their intention of demonstrating in the neighbourhood of the docks.'

Mr Peachum left Scotland Yard unhindered.

Everywhere he saw flags at half-mast. The greatest city in the world was mourning for her sons.

Clean-up

Father was a large bony man, one of the three surviving people who had known MacHeath as Beckett. He worked with O'Hara in Ride Lane and was very friendly with him.

MacHeath had told him to watch Polly and O'Hara, and he had immediately informed his friend of this.

Together they had cleared the warehouses of nearly all the goods which they had been told to destroy, and they sold them for their own profit. During this process, Father kept Grooch away. (Grooch was the third of the trio.)

In addition, Father knew nearly everything about O'Hara's relations with Mrs MacHeath, for he thought it a good thing to be in the picture as much as possible.

He had also been behind the man who had attacked Coax. But his friend O'Hara did not know that he knew anything about that.

One morning anthracite cost 28s. in Ride Lane, and three policemen forced their way into the warehouses behind No. 28 and pulled Father out of his bed there. They asked him most politely to show them where the goods were stored.

There was not much left, but a few things were still lying around. They collected what was left and departed without wasting many words.

Father slowly finished dressing and then, since he was not expecting O'Hara before eleven, went to visit MacHeath in prison.

MacHeath was just having breakfast. He cut Father's long-winded explanation short.

'There's nothing left in 28,' he said calmly, 'they can look there as much as they like.'

'How do you know?' asked Father gloomily, and tried to sit on the table.

'Because I ordered them to be cleared,' replied MacHeath, dipping a piece of toast in his coffee. 'That's why they were emptied. About five weeks ago.'

'But they were not quite empty. We were going to finish the job tomorrow, but today there were still some things left.'

MacHeath went on eating. Then he said:

'Is that so? Then I'd like to know what you've been up to in my warehouses. I sincerely hope it was nothing dishonest and you have invoices for everything.'

Father said nothing. After a while he murmured:

'They came straight to No. 28.'

'That's bad,' said MacHeath, and looked at Father with his watery eyes.

The latter at last pulled himself together. With sudden decision he sat down on the edge of the table, after sweeping away with his huge hand the calendar which MacHeath had carefully laid there, and said loudly:

'You're making a mistake, Beckett, if you really believe that we're going to the Old Bailey just for your sake. We wouldn't think of it! O'Hara's a friend of mine and we're sticking together, even if other people *do* play dirty tricks on their old friends. Do you understand?'

MacHeath went on eating, unperturbed.

'Go on with what you've got to say, Father, but get off my table or I'll have you thrown out of here although you are an old friend.'

Father stood up ungraciously. He was trembling with rage.

'So that's it. You want to clear us out? From the very beginning you've cheated us all with your system; at first, you pay fixed wages because you want your warehouses full; then, when you don't need any more goods, you pay for piece work. Always just what suits you. And now you're going to hand us over to the police! But you're a banker, what? And you don't know anything about what's been happening, eh?'

MacHeath watched him attentively.

'I'm not easily offended,' he said amiably. 'You can speak your mind to me. But you must remember that you had an order from me which you did not carry out. You are a friend of O'Hara's, but I couldn't know that. He's such a treacherous swine that I never thought he'd have friends who would be prepared to go to prison for him.'

'Why ... why ...' Father stuttered with rage. 'You'd better get another spy to watch your fine wife. He'd be able to tell you a whole lot that you don't know! Not everybody seems to find O'Hara as unpleasant as you do! I can tell you *that*!'

He was mad with fury, but he still watched his man all the time he was speaking.

It was no use. MacHeath never moved a muscle.

He only said:

'I can see, Father, that you're not so bad as you're trying to make out. So you kept your eyes open.'

'Yes, I did, Beckett – a little.' Father lowered his head maliciously. 'I also saw what you had done to Coax. That sand-bag didn't fall from the sky!'

MacHeath suddenly put his spoon down. He seemed genuinely interested.

'Father,' he said, in a quite different voice, 'you must tell me about that. I really don't know anything about it. I thought Coax died rather unexpectedly.'

Father had a desperate fight with himself. He knew Mac-Heath, his present tone was genuine. But if he knew nothing of Coax's murder, then it had been a private affair of his friend O'Hara's. In which case he had already said too much.

MacHeath watched him expectantly.

'Listen, Father,' he said, 'you can't save anything by doing this. The only person who works with a sand-bag is Giles. I don't know him personally – and you know that. He's O'Hara's man, isn't he? Now that we've got so far, Father, you had better relieve your conscience completely. And I'll give you a piece of advice. Clear out of Ride Lane and get yourself a passport and some money for the journey! I'm not inhuman. You keep calling me Beckett, but my name is MacHeath. I will even forgive you for having sat on my table. What you said about my wife was said in anger. You have until eleven o'clock to pack your bag; then go to the shaving saloon where you will receive what you need. But if you say a single word to O'Hara, even "Adieu" or "fine weather, I don't think", you'll be in jail by half past eleven. You must understand that.'

Father was too stunned to say another word. And MacHeath wanted to hear no more. Above all, he wanted to hear nothing more about Polly and O'Hara. He did not want to waste another thought on that unpleasant subject. He never wanted to meet anyone again who might wish to speak to him about it.

Father could not know that, but it saved him.

He went back to Ride Lane, very disturbed in mind. There he packed his hand-bag and put on his best suit. It was half past ten when he went through the first gateway. O'Hara was just coming in through the outside door, a cigarette dangling between his lips. Father was in two minds whether to speak to him. After all, they were old friends. And he had known O'Hara's mother well.

He stood undecided behind the door. O'Hara had not yet seen him. Then he made up his mind.

He stepped out from his hiding-place and walked past O'Hara without a word, staring straight in front of him, his lips pressed together like the edges of a knife.

O'Hara stared after him in astonishment.

When Father had turned the next corner, he sighed with relief. O'Hara must have seen the bag and the smart grey suit.

But at half past eleven O'Hara was arrested at his private house.

He arrived at Scotland Yard very self-possessed. When he heard that he was charged with burglary and disposing of stolen goods, he laughed. He declared that he had bought the goods which he had delivered to the C.P.B. The invoices lay in the offices of the C.P.B. in the City.

He was then told that the accusations against him had originated there.

He immediately demanded to be confronted with the banker.

The meeting took place in the afternoon. Also present in Mac-Heath's cell were Lord Bloomsbury and Mr Brown of Scotland Yard.

Before O'Hara could say a word, MacHeath stepped up to him and said: 'And where did you get the goods, my man, which you have been delivering to my shops for the last six months?'

It was not until he was sitting again in his cell that O'Hara began to recover from his astonishment. Then the door was flung open and Sand-bag Giles was pushed in to keep him company.

Father was already on the high seas when the memory of a sentence which he had spoken began to rankle in MacHeath's mind. The sentence had been something like: you watch your fine wife!

It was raining outside. As MacHeath paced his cell, hands in his trouser pockets, he listened to the rain. Sometimes he stopped suddenly, sank his radish head, and listened more attentively. Then he kicked at the thick carpet and thought:

'It's a good thing that he's in prison now. At least I know where he is. I'm told that my people complain about my indecisiveness. But when it comes to the point, I've always been able to make up my mind. I know better than anybody that one must be firm – now and again. One must know everything that's going on in a business, and one must let everything come to a head like an abscess. And one day one must take action, suddenly, like a bolt from the blue – as the chief. The whole trouble is exposed, mercilessly. Everyone is paralysed with fear. The chief has waited long, but at last he has taken action. He has not spared even his oldest friends now that he has discovered that something was wrong. That's what he's like; one can never deceive him.'

He went a few steps further, stopped again, and fell thinking once more.

'The possession of a wife,' he thought, 'has become a very difficult matter. In the old days, a man only had to return from hunting two hours earlier than he was expected and he could probably scare up some fleshy fellow out of his wife's bed. What am I saying, out of her bed? It was enough to find her standing in a room with a man, and everything was clear. Nowadays, the ordinary course of business compels her to expose her calves to the gaze of every man she meets. And in some offices they make love as easily as they wash their hands, chiefly in order to rob us employers of their working-time! Discovery is out of the question when adultery is so frequent and has as little meaning as washing one's hands.'

MacHeath shook his head in amazement, listened again to the heavy autumn rain, and paced on. After a time he sat down at his desk and picked up the documents of his case.

The hearing was due to take place within the next few days.

Uneasy Days

'Work and doubt not.'
(CARLYLE)

The small factory in Old Oak Street was working overtime and night-shifts.

In the girls' workroom, pinned to the wall with a drawing-pin, was a cutting from a newspaper, describing the heroic death of the dressmaker, Mary Anne Walkley.

'Mary Anne Walkley, twenty years old, was employed in a court dressmaker's establishment, making dresses for the ladies of the haute monde *to wear at a ball given in honour of visiting royalty. It was the height of the season. For twenty-six-and-a-half hours she worked without a break, together with sixty other girls, thirty in a room which contained scarcely a third of the normal amount of air necessary for so many people. During the night they slept, two in a bed, in one of the tiny cubicles into which the dormitory had been divided. Sherry, port, and a little coffee restored their flagging strength which, in return for a negligible wage, they had so unselfishly spent in the service of the Queen. Miss Walkley fell sick on Friday, refused to give up, and died on Sunday – no less a heroine than the men of Mafeking.'*

But more effective than this poster with its inspiring message were Beery's methods of speeding up the work. He simply threatened to turn unwilling or weakly workers out on to the streets.

'You're not to blame because you have consumption,' he used to say, 'but neither am I!'

He had made a constructive discovery. He had noticed that the workers were in the habit of smoking an occasional cigarette in the closet. When they had been too long away from their work, he could see, by looking out into the yard, a thin spiral of smoke curling out of the tiny window. So he arranged for a sloping back wall to be built, which forced them to sit doubled up. When Polly returned to her parents and saw this little place, with its view of the old gnarled tree in the yard, she was deeply moved; this was home.

The work was proceeding rapidly. But there appeared in the newspapers, in connexion with the memorial ceremony for the victims of the *Optimist* which was to take place on the same day, a Thursday, as the hearing of the case against the banker MacHeath, all sorts of impudent questions about the progress of the investigations into the cause of the catastrophe.

The Assistant Commissioner preserved an ominous silence. But Peachum knew that the police were investigating round the docks. Several people had already been arrested. Feverishly he scrutinized all the papers, but they still contained no official explanation of the disaster.

And there were several police officers always to be seen outside the house in Old Oak Street.

Peachum suffered greatly during those days.

'I can see that the worst will happen,' he said to himself, especially at night when he walked through the dark passages from one brightly lighted workroom to another and he stopped for a moment in the darkness. 'That's all one can expect in life: the worst. And yet it was conceivable that for once the police might not take action! The Optimist was wrecked, I don't deny it. But must I be wrecked too? Of course, it's a pity for the relatives, no doubt. But would it help them in any way if it were a pity for me, too?'

However, he was also indebted to the disaster for a new commercial idea. So he comforted himself with the following reflections:

'Catastrophes like the sinking of the Optimist are unavoidable. Wars, hurricanes, earthquakes, business enterprises, famines, are all unavoidable. Anyone who knows human nature also knows that all human endeavour is doomed to failure. Even the Bible says that, and it is a consideration which must always be borne in mind. In fact, nine out of ten people are justly afraid of the future. (At the most, one in a thousand is unjustified in his fears.) And one must make allowance for that. A lot of money could be made out of it. Take a few things that everyone fears: sickness, poverty, death. We say to the people who are afraid (because they have a knowledge of life and their fellow men): very well, we will insure you against this inevitable future. You pay us, regularly (so that you will scarcely notice

312

it), a small percentage of your incomes during the time when all goes well with you; and then, when the inevitable catastrophe arrives, we will pay you (or, in the event of your death, your heirs and assigns). Is that a good suggestion? I'm sure that it would be welcomed by everyone. One must help one's fellow men! And help – well, that costs something! If I came out of this business all right – if, for this once, the police do not discover anything – I'll turn this idea into a reality, that's certain. Just think of the soldiers who went down with the Optimist. *They were for the most part young men, but there were also some fathers amongst them. How differently situated their relatives would have been today had they insured themselves against shipwreck! When they received the order to proceed abroad, they would have had no other alternative than to insure themselves as quickly as possible. And then, people who read in the papers about catastrophes like the* Optimist *would have to be insured against such things. And there are so many catastrophes! Old age, for example, is one. Old age in big cities. The last years of a person who is of no more use to the world. Those inevitable and horrible years! Unemployment, too, is such a disaster. For example, there are* my *employees. I profit from the fact that they wouldn't know where to go if I threw them out on to the streets. I work them as hard as I can and draw my profits from them. They must feel a pressing need for help. So perhaps I could make still more profit by helping them? One would have to erect great buildings to house all the money! So long as no demands were made on the insurance money, the scheme would flourish; if, on the other hand, demands were made, it could simply go bankrupt. In any case, if one could insinuate oneself between these people and their employers, and extract a few extra pennies from them, one could always refuse payment by saying they had received the money in the form of assistance already rendered. It would be a marvellous business. Most of the people who would pay die in the sewers, or else they cannot prove their injuries. But perhaps the workers would rather receive such assistance from their fellows, i.e. from former workers. . . . Well, one could always employ a few of them, pro forma. One might even be able to interest the State in the scheme. Laws could be made compelling the workers to pay their subscriptions. The*

State itself would have to fight the improvidence of the masses and their criminal, unpractical optimism. They think everything will come all right, when all the time one knows what is in store for them. One can't stop wars any more than one can stop crises. The men must be turned out on the streets when it's no longer profitable to employ them; houses cannot be built more solidly than the rents allow, etc., etc. – so arrangements must be made for the workers to be provided for. When faced with the incredible improvidence of these ignorant and thoughtless people, who become soldiers and factory workers and so on, one must resort to statutory measures. They must be forced to insure themselves. They cannot do more, but they must do that. It is a question of public interest – and also good business! But to start such an insurance scheme, one would need some capital. If I am successful with this ship business, the capital will be there. Besides, the new ships – the Southampton ones – are absolutely seaworthy! Just this once, everything has got to go right!'

When Wednesday evening came, nine days after the sinking of the *Optimist* and the eve of the official memorial ceremony, and the police had still made no announcement, Peachum was unable to stand the strain any longer.

In a sort of panic, he decided to exert pressure on the police. He sent Beery and two other men to Scotland Yard with various posters on which were written: 'WHAT WAS WRONG WITH THE "OPTIMIST"?', 'HOW MUCH DID THE ADMIRALTY GET IN BRIBES? ASK 200 WOUNDED SOLDIERS', and 'WHY DID THE "OPTIMIST" SINK?' One of these hand-painted placards even bore the inscription: 'WHO IS MR PEACHUM?'

Beery announced at Scotland Yard that he had come from Mr Peachum, president of the M.T.C. The posters had come into his hands by roundabout means; several of the beggars who hired musical instruments from his shop had brought them to him. Apparently a demonstration with such placards had been planned for the next afternoon.

An hour later Peachum himself arrived.

Brown soon disposed of him. His complaints, that he would be ruined if such a demonstration took place and that it was no comfort to him that several high officials would also have their names dragged in the mud, were scarcely listened to.

He went away baffled.

Then, hailing a cab, he drove to the offices of the *Reflector*.

He demanded to see the chief editor and had a long conversation with him, as a result of which the editor promised to hold free, until eight o'clock the next morning, a double column for a sensational explanation by the president of the Marine Transport Company *of the causes which led to the sinking of the* 'Optimist'.

After that, Peachum walked home, arranged the details for the proposed demonstration on the next day, locked himself into his office, and wrote the whole night through.

But Brown, although he had thought it best to give Peachum a cold shoulder, was by no means easy in his mind about the whole affair. That evening he ordered still another (the seventh) raid on the docks, and after he had examined the first twenty workers who had been arrested, he went gloomily to visit Mac-Heath in prison.

MacHeath was alone, reading a book.

Brown sent the warder away and poured himself out a glass of beer from a bottle which was standing in a corner of the cell.

But before he could unload his mind to his friend, the latter began:

'What's happened with O'Hara? I'm damned uneasy about him. Hasn't he agreed yet?'

'No,' said Brown wearily.

'Did you tell him that we can prove murder against him if he doesn't hold his tongue?'

'Yes, I told him all that. He said he would rather hang than get you out of trouble. I think he has rather strong personal feelings about the matter.'

MacHeath paced restlessly up and down the cell. His case was to be heard the next day. If he was going to have to admit that he was the president of the Central Purchasing Board, he could in no wise afford to be involved in a burglary scandal.

At last he sat down again and became somewhat calmer.

'The man has sense,' he said, reaching out for a cigar. 'He doesn't obey blind instinct, he lets himself be guided by common sense. I'll depend on it! If I can't depend on it any longer, I'll let myself be hanged. The towns in which we live, this whole civilization with all its manifold blessings, are proof of the power of common sense. And this man, too, will conquer his thirst for revenge and will choose four years imprisonment – or shall we say three years, for we can afford to forget some of the old scores – in preference to death at a rope's end.'

Brown said he had given O'Hara until two o'clock the next afternoon to make up his mind.

'Yes, I must have the confession by two o'clock at the latest,' said MacHeath. 'Directly after the case, I have a conference with Chreston in the National Credit Bank, at which Aaron and the Oppers may also be present. I should like to be able to lay before them a signed admission that my wholesale supplier is guilty of these burglaries.'

Then, at last, Brown was able to speak of his own troubles.

The case of the *Optimist* looked bad. There was little doubt that this ship – and its two sister ships – had been delivered to the Government in a rather unsatisfactory condition. The Company which had sold these ships had also suffered an 'accident' in the last few days. The broker, William Coax, who had been murdered in the neighbourhood of the docks, had been closely connected with the firm. And the mystery of his death was by no means cleared up. The police had arrested a few unemployed workers who had been dismissed as a result of the strike and who had made some foolish remarks. But nothing conclusive could be proved against them. The sinking of the *Optimist* threatened unpleasant and far-reaching consequences. Brown was not inclined to take too seriously Mr Peachum's threats with regard to the immediate results of the demonstration. At the ceremony there would be police in sufficient numbers to avert any attempt at a disturbance. No. There was something far more serious.

The chief inspector lowered his voice when he spoke of it.

Through some sort of short circuit in the Admiralty, the order recalling the two other ships, of which at least one, the one which had collided with the *Optimist*, must have been damaged, was never sent out. The Admiralty itself was not all clear about the matter. So Brown was extremely uncertain as to what he should do. Perhaps the demonstration ought not to be allowed even to start out? After all, the police were responsible for maintaining order.

Of course, Peachum was not the only trouble, for he could easily be circumvented. But the communists were also planning demonstrations against the memorial ceremony. And these demonstrations could not be stopped.

'Without Peachum they've got no proof,' suggested Mac-Heath, who had just lit a large cigar.

'No, they haven't,' said Brown, slightly reassured. 'They are always making themselves ridiculous with their everlasting suspicions which they can never prove.'

'They'll concoct something about corruption in the Admiralty and probably even suggest that the Secretary of State got a few thousands for himself! It's ridiculous!'

'Do you know,' said Brown, now also picking up a cigar, *'these tub-thumpers infuriate me. They're always attacking us because we don't enforce the laws strictly enough! As if the laws were made for their benefit! They are ridiculously insistent on everything being correct and legal. If there were a law which allowed Hale to receive a percentage for the trouble of winking an eye at what goes on, they would never reproach him with the few thousands he's supposed to have had. They wouldn't have the feeling then of being cheated. It's absolutely extraordinary! Because, of course, in politics and commerce not everything is quite as straightforward as all that; there are really quite a lot of things which, to the ordinary tax-payer, are – well, shall we say, incomprehensible. And those things mean big profits! Not just a few thousands. And then our "apostles of freedom" go howling about pettifogging little things, saying that the local council is corrupt, that the police are not impartial, or God knows what, all of which can never be proved and is mostly quite untrue! All this making black white and white black, like these mud-slingers do, is quite incredible.'*

'If anyone was to write down what you've been saying,' said MacHeath thoughtfully, 'it would also be making black white and white black.'

'Incredible,' grinned Brown, 'absolutely incredible!'

They spoke for a while about politics.

'There is really no party,' confessed MacHeath, *'which wholly represents my interests. I wouldn't go so far as to say that Parliament is a talking-shop. They don't only talk about things, they*

do things. All sorts of things are done there, and everyone who is not hopelessly biased must admit that. But the question is, whether Parliament is equal to its task in an emergency. In my opinion, which is the opinion of a hard-working business man, we haven't got the right men at the head of the country. They all belong to some party or other, and parties are, of necessity, self-seeking and egotistic. Their outlook is one-sided. We need men who stand above all parties, something like us business men. We sell our wares to rich and poor alike. Without regard for his standing, we are ready to sell any man a hundredweight of potatoes, to instal electric light for him, to paint his house. The government of the state is a moral task. Everything must be so organized that the entrepreneur is a good entrepreneur, the worker a good worker, in short, that the rich are good rich and the poor good poor. I am convinced that in time that form of government will come. And it will count me among its supporters.'

Brown sighed.

'Unfortunately we have not yet got a party like that. So what am I to do now?'

'Have you investigated what was happening about the renovations during the strike?'

'Of course. Days ago. That was the first thing I did. But there was nothing happening.'

'How's that? Surely the shipwrights who had just struck so unsuccessfully had every reason to do something in that direction? I can never understand how people can work under such conditions. They must be sub-human.'

'But if they work, they work. They don't think of wrecking a ship once they've started to repair it. They very rarely think, you know. They would never do anything like that.'

'But you had *my* people there just after the strike, or rather Peachum had them.'

'You mean that they . . .'

'Of course. They wouldn't hesitate to do a thing like that. I'll get Bully here.'

'Could you?' asked Brown, somewhat comforted.

'Certainly,' answered MacHeath heartily. 'I'll do that for you. And another thing, without wishing to influence your decisions in any way: Peachum is still my father-in-law. After all, my wife's dowry is in the National Credit Bank. I'm a director there. The deposits have got into a disgraceful muddle through that scandalous price-cutting. Peachum's money is gone, too; and from the family point of view, I can just as well regard it as my own. And then there are a whole host of small investors, and after the *Optimist* catastrophe the fuss which they would kick up when they found their money gone would entirely destroy the wave of patriotic feeling which will result from the sinking of the ship. I have no affection for my father-in-law, but I really think it would be best if you let him out of this business.'

Brown went away half-convinced and cross-examined a few more shipwrights who had been arrested.

But that night he slept badly and towards morning he had a dream.

He was driving over one of the bridges across the Thames. Suddenly he heard something – a gurgling; he got out and leaned over the parapet. But he could see nothing. So he ran back and tried to look down from the embankment. And now he saw the bridge too: he saw it from below. There was a small promontory of bare earth jutting out from the bank, round which the muddy waters swirled. On the bridge hung flags; black and red-white-and-blue. On the little patch of earth under the bridge there were men moving – or beings very like men. Their numbers increased with amazing rapidity, but it was impossible to say where they came from; the river seemed to be very deep just there. At any rate, there were crowds of them, and they now began to move upwards, through the bushes and over the freshly painted parapet, until they were on the bridge itself, directly under the flags. This tiny patch of earth spewed up multitudes; a countless, unending stream, which, once it had begun, would never stop. Of course there were the police; there they stood; they would barricade the bridge; and there stood the troops, they would open fire; and there also were the mounted police, they would ... but *there* was that flood of misery, it was forming up, its ranks were solid, as broad as the road, swamping everything like water, flowing through everything like water, without shape or substance. Of course, the police charged them; of course they struck out with their truncheons; but what use

319

was that? their blows passed through the marching bodies. In a broad wave, straight through the police, Misery advanced on the sleeping town; through the troops, through the barbed wire barricades, silent and soundless amidst the shouts of the police and the stutter of Maxim-guns. And it poured itself like a muddy torrent into the houses. Legions of misery in soundless march, transparent and featureless, marching through the walls, into the barracks, into the restaurants, into the art galleries, into the courts of justice. . . .

This dream tormented Brown for the rest of the night, so he got up and went early to his office. He hated dreaming of the left-wing newspapers. But it had occurred to him that the ceremony would not be improved if several hundred wounded soldiers really did kick up a row.

He turned the charwoman out of his office, sat down, adjusted his green-shaded lamp, and wrote in long-hand a report for the press.

Mr Peachum, too, was standing at his desk. With the ink-pot in front of him, a pen in his hand, and his hat tilted on the back of his head, he had stood the whole night through in front of his high desk, betweenwhiles pacing restlessly round the small, overheated office.

He was writing a newspaper article in which he revealed the machinations of the broker Coax, and the part played by a certain high official in the Admiralty.

Of course, it was inevitable that Peachum would have to face the consequences if the methods of the Marine Transport Company were exposed, but the thinly veiled allusions to corruption at the Admiralty would be sufficient to interest the Government in reducing those consequences to a minimum. But then the new business, the real business, would fall through!

From time to time, Peachum had run from the room and supervised the progress in the workrooms. Placards were being carefully painted, which bore the various legends: 'ARE WE ONLY BEING SENT TO SOUTH AFRICA TO LINE THE POCKETS OF THE TRANSPORT SHARKS?' or 'IF YOU ARE GOING TO SEND US TO HELL, THEN AT LEAST MAKE SURE THAT WE GET THERE!' or 'THE VICTIMS OF THE "OPTIMIST" WERE NOT

DROWNED BY ACCIDENT, THEY WERE MURDERED!' And at five o'clock in the morning, he had gone across to the overnight painters who were kneeling in the passages, working by petroleum lamps, and had given them a further poster 'WORSE THAN STORM AND FOG IS THE GREED OF OUR BUSINESS MEN'.

Now, at eight in the morning his 'confession', lay in an envelope on Beery's worm-eaten desk, and his men had departed, pushing the placards on hand-carts, to various parts of the town, there to start off the demonstration.

An hour later he read in a newspaper that the communists who had sabotaged the *Optimist* had been arrested.

He immediately sent Beery and others to the various rallying points to cancel the demonstration. Then he sat down to a cup of tea.

So the people in Scotland Yard had come to their senses after all. Well, the announcement that socialistically-minded workers had tampered with the ship was far more suited to the patriotic movement which now filled the papers than revelations about corruption in the Admiralty.

Mrs Peachum came to Polly's bedside while it was still dark. She sat on the edge of the bed and astonished her daughter with the news that she had succeeded in reconciling Peachum with Polly's arbitrary marriage.

She gave a moving description of how she had brought this about.

'*Don't tear these two young lovers apart,*' I kept saying to him. '"*Whom God hath joined together, let no man put asunder." Think for a moment; we too were once young and thoughtless, even though we did keep within certain limits. Would you dare to take the responsibility for your daughter pining away for love, let alone for the wicked destruction of a budding life? They desire nothing more than to belong to one another. They have been through terrible times together; but their love has conquered, and that is also a consideration. The ties of such love cannot simply be torn apart. I know you wanted to have Coax as a son-in-law. Of course, he was a handsome man and had attractive ways. You valued him highly for his business capacity. But now he is dead and you can't dig him up again. What have you still got against MacHeath? Everyone* says that he is just as capable and makes a great deal of money. The B. shop owners have nothing to laugh at in him. In his business there is no room for laziness. He will make Polly happy. I have spoken with him, he will be an excellent husband. Such people make the best fathers. You have always done everything for your child's happiness. Why do you slave early and late if it's not for her sake? You have always said that. MacHeath showed a strong sense of family ties when he offered you, in spite of strained relations, the help of his people for the West India Docks. By doing that he has shown that the welfare of the family is more sacred than any personal differences. The family is now the one foundation of all moral living, anyone will tell you that. And the foundation of the family is love. If there were no families, everyone would eat everyone else up, and there would be no more reasonable behaviour amongst men. And apart from anything else, a person cannot always do and be as he would like — and according to religion, the family must be left out of the question. For that reason the family is a sure refuge — and a woman can never forget the first man to whom she has belonged. It was love at first sight, that is plain enough. Do one thing more, Peachum. Our Polly is not the sort of girl who could ever be completely happy without her parents' blessing!'

Deeply moved by what she had said, Mrs Peachum promised to come to the court while the case was being heard.

'You needn't worry about the verdict,' she called back through the door, 'your father has taken care of that.'

At that very moment Peachum had just got up from the breakfast table and was walking across to the window.

It was still dark, but in the street outside swirled a wall of thick white fog. He had a feeling that it would not be easy for Beery to reach the demonstrators with their awful posters in time.

15

And so comes the happy ending,
Quarrels settled, wrongs redressed,
If your capital's sufficient
Things end mostly for the best.

Cox had fished in troubled waters
Cries Box, threatening with the Law.
See them feeding now like brothers
On the last crust of the poor.

Therefore, some are in darkness;
Some are in the light, and these
You may see, but all those others
In the darkness no one sees.

(DREIGROSCHEN FILM)

The Alibi

TOWARDS eight o'clock that morning Polly drove with her mother to the prison. A thick fog lay over the streets.

When they entered the cell where the gas was still burning, MacHeath had not yet had breakfast, but the room was already full of business men. Chreston was there, and Miller and Grooch. With fat cigars in the corners of their mouths, they were discussing the final details of the battle against the Commercial Bank.

The case would have to be brought to a speedy conclusion, for a conference had already been arranged for two o'clock in the National Credit Bank. Hawthorne had written a letter to Messrs I. Aaron and Jacques Opper, inviting them to attend. Mr MacHeath, so the letter ran, had joined the board of directors of the National Credit Bank. He wished to submit to the two gentlemen some suggestions for the elimination of the intolerable epidemic of price-cutting which had recently plagued the retail trade.

MacHeath was counting on being able to reach the National

Credit at two o'clock. He was silently hoping that, so soon after the hearing, the news that he was the president of the Central Purchasing Board would not yet have reached the ears of his opponents.

The arrival of the two ladies put an end to the meeting.

Polly was wearing a simple black dress which she had already worn at the broker's funeral. After the hearing she and her mother wanted to go on to the memorial service for the victims of the *Optimist* catastrophe.

MacHeath was visibly astonished at the appearance of his mother-in-law. He introduced her to the others and they all began talking about London fogs.

Meanwhile MacHeath withdrew with his wife into another corner of the cell, where his breakfast stood waiting.

Polly immediately informed him in an undertone of her father's change of attitude towards him.

MacHeath nodded. He was still not quite clear as to what role Polly had played in the murder of the broker Coax. He had since learned from Ready that it was Giles who had struck Coax down. And what had Coax to do with Giles, who could only have been sent out by O'Hara? Had Polly perhaps been somewhat averse to Coax appearing as a witness in the divorce case? If so, what power had she got over O'Hara?

Actually, MacHeath had no intention of investigating Polly's affairs too closely. Neither did he ask about the abortion. It was she who first mentioned the subject.

With a happy expression on her pink face, which was much enhanced by her black dress, she told how a visit to the cinema had decided herself and her mother against the operation. It had been the profound impression made by a homely story which had prevented her from committing *a sin against a budding life*. The touching sight of the little creature on the screen had overcome her.

'Never,' she said, 'could I have gone to the doctor after that. I would have felt like a criminal. You must understand that, Mac, I simply could not go through with it.'

It was distressing to Polly that she could not tell MacHeath everything. She would much rather have always told him the truth, but that was impossible.

'For example, there's that affair with O'Hara. It would be terrible if he ever found out about it. He would think I had betrayed him. He would never believe that I kept silent for his sake. Really, if I confessed everything to him, he would form an absolutely wrong opinion of me. He would think that he had a wife who could not be trusted. Which would be quite wrong. He is much too mistrustful for me to be able to tell him the truth. And he has a bad opinion of women. It's very difficult.'

MacHeath promised to see the film at the first opportunity, and then began eating his breakfast. He started on a boiled egg. In the pauses, he spoke of the way in which he intended to run his shops in the future. He said a lot of wise things, but Polly was mostly watching the way in which he handled his egg. She had a lot to learn and most of what she knew later as a business woman – and she knew a lot – she learned in those few minutes, while she watched her husband's method of eating an egg. He spoke of the small businesses, the shops in the City, and the egg, too, was small in his fat hands. But how tenderly he held it! It was soft-boiled, four and a half minutes. Cooked for a shorter time, it would have been too runny; cooked for longer, it would have been too hard. With the small shops, too, one must be able to wait, but on no account must the critical moment be missed. The cooking itself was a sort of inaction, which demanded the utmost self-control. But it was also an activity. A clever cook could start doing something else during those four and a half minutes: after all, one egg is not a meal! MacHeath never spoke a syllable about the egg, he simply ate it. Everything was consequent upon the way in which he tapped with the spoon upon the shell before he proceeded to decapitation, and how he then prodded round in the white. Then came the first tentative and yet powerful stroke which filled the spoon: and now the interior economy of the egg lay open to the gaze. One had to be careful that whatever of the yolk would not stay on the spoon after the plunge, at least fell back into the open egg. An agile twist of the spoon, and a little mountain of salt was raised from its cellar and carefully sprinkled inside! Thus the contents of the egg were made more tasty. Together with the yolk, a portion of the white was always simultaneously detached from the shell by the bold sweep of the spoon. The left hand assisted: it turned the egg against the spoon. Such methods *must* lead to success; nothing is left behind! The egg is lifted out, held up, inclined slightly towards the horizontal, and peered into. Then there still remains the top. At the beginning of the enterprise it was laid carefully on the plate beside the egg; now, suddenly emptied, it yields a spoonful.

Polly watched fascinated; such a sight was not to be seen everywhere. From the beginning, MacHeath's face had taken on an expression of deep concentration, almost of worry. It seemed as though he had to nourish himself entirely on this egg, as though this one egg had to supply all his bodily needs, certainly no small task! He continually looked at the egg, and then at his clumsy great limbs, and then back at the egg again. And this was probably the reason for the pensive glance at the empty shell when all was over. He did not complain; not a sigh escaped him; but still, everything was over, and there remained only the worry as to whether it would have the desired effect. ... And two seconds later he threw the shell carelessly on to the plate (although he laid the spoon, that ever necessary implement, slowly and tidily in its place!) and then he turned, without any visible regret, indifferently away from the table.

He was very calm. The impending proceedings were pure formalities. Even in respect of O'Hara he had no more need to worry. He believed in the man's common sense, which would make him take the blame for the burglaries rather than face a trial for incitement to murder. As might be safely anticipated, his private affairs had put an end to his business career.

Rigger came. It was time to drive to the court.

MacHeath got ready. Chreston and Miller went away. They wished to make final arrangements in the National Credit Bank for the conference that afternoon.

MacHeath promised to be punctual.

On the way to the court, Rigger told a few stories about Laughers, the judge who was taking MacHeath's case.

He was not a man like Broothley, the magistrate, who was drunk for eleven months in the year and sober for one, namely when he was on holiday fishing in Scotland. During those four weeks he never touched a drop, for he used to say: fish don't let themselves be caught so easily; they know a thing or two, they don't believe in justice.

Laughers did not need to drink. He was a first-class jurist and had exceptional powers of concentration. Consequently he was never nervous if anyone spoke his mind; his mental training had equipped him not to hear anything. When he came into court, he was thoroughly prepared. He knew the legal aspect of the case exactly and never let himself be confused.

'To the jurist,' explained Rigger, 'the case always appears in a light entirely different from that in which it does to the layman. The layman stands there and talks nonsense and says he is innocent and thinks of such things as: I can't hold out under this arrest; or: what are my starving family doing in the meanwhile? or: if only I had taken a witness with me to my aunt that time! The judge only judges the case. He has nothing but *it* in his head, and so he always has the advantage of the accused layman.'

The court was fairly full. The newspaper attacks had had their effect.

And far back, but so that Rigger saw him immediately, sat the great Aaron. He had secured an outside seat on the middle gangway, had laid his top hat on the floor beside him, and was polishing his pince-nez nervously. Beside him sat his confidential clerk, a Mr Power.

The greater part of the court was occupied by B. shop owners.

Since he had been officially committed for trial on a charge of murder, MacHeath had become very unpopular among them. Grooch, who was sitting with a crowd of them who did not know him, kept continually hearing the following:

'I have heard that he lives quite simply, smokes only a very little, and doesn't drink at all. Someone has even told me that he is a vegetarian. It has been said that, personally, he is impeccable, living entirely for his ideals. Of course that means winking at a good deal that happens in business. It was always said that the people round him were a bad influence. But now, since he's been accused of these things, my eyes have been opened.'

The good people were very excited. It had leaked out that the Court had refused to accept an alibi prior to the proceedings.

Everyone placed great faith in the fat Walley whom they pointed out to one another.

MacHeath appeared in a black suit.

There were others, too, who apparently intended to go straight on to the memorial service afterwards. The black clothes gave the impression that this section of the public had, so to speak, just dropped in on the way.

The proceedings were somewhat late in starting; Laughers had a great many other things to attend to. Meanwhile, one of the solicitors for the defence handed the accused a bundle of papers which he immediately began to study feverishly. The public assumed that they were documents concerning the case, but they were only papers which Miller had sent on, the latest agenda for the conference.

Followed by all eyes, Walley went across to Rigger and Withe and handed them a briefcase. Withe took it with interest and began looking through the documents it contained. Then he and Rigger went to their client to show him the documents. But MacHeath waved them away, he was immersed in his papers. Adding corrections here and there, he listened with one ear to his solicitors, only to shake his head in astonishment when they stopped speaking.

At last Laughers entered the court, complete with wig, ermine, and scarlet robes. A silence fell, as the judge took his seat.

He was plainly treating the whole matter as a pure formality. It seemed almost as though he had only sat down because of his infirmity.

Walley immediately called the accused into the witness stand. The latter answered his few questions shortly and casually. The defence had no questions to put.

When, among other witnesses, the soldier Fewkoombey was called, it turned out that he was not in court. Walley appeared very annoyed. Fewkoombey was the only one who interested him, and he was not there.

Then Withe stood up and embarked on a somewhat longer speech.

'M'Lud and gentlemen of the jury,' he began, 'the prosecution against Mr MacHeath bases its case on his refusal to reveal where he was at the time when the unfortunate Mary Sawyer met her death. Could this alibi be produced – and Mr MacHeath has so far felt compelled to withhold such information – the prosecution would have no case at all. In that event, Mary Sawyer, whether she committed suicide or whether she was murdered, could not have met her death at Mr MacHeath's hands. In itself, the case for the prosecution is not exactly convincing. What benefit would Mr MacHeath, merchant and banker, derive from the death of one of his employees? During the investigations before the Magistrate, mention was made of threats which this woman was said to have uttered against him. She did, actually, make these threats – in the offices of the *Reflector*. And what did the editors do? They laughed at her! And why should Mr MacHeath lift a finger to silence threats which could only make people laugh? But I will not linger over that. Mr MacHeath possesses an absolutely unassailable and irrefutable alibi for the evening of the twentieth of September, which proves that his complicity in a possible murder is totally out of the question. Here, your lordship, I beg to submit the minutes of a meeting of the Central Purchasing Board Limited at which Mr MacHeath took part – in the capacity of president.'

Withe handed the documents to the judge.

'As witness to this I shall call the members of the C.P.B. here present who signed those minutes. They will confirm that Mr MacHeath was the person who, for business reasons, was referred to as "Mr X".'

While the judge was noting the names of the signatories, and while Bloomsbury, Fanny Chrysler, Withe, and Rigger were entering the witness-box, there was a stir in the court. Two gentlemen had stood up and were pushing their way towards the exit.

'I know enough,' said the one gentleman to the other, rather loudly. 'That was the meeting when the letter was written, and after which we received no more razor-blades. And MacHeath is the president.'

Like the rest of those present, MacHeath had noticed the outburst. He was somewhat upset.

'Here is another name,' murmured the judge, 'it looks like "O'Hara". Is that gentleman here?'

MacHeath stood up nervously and said quickly:

'He has been arrested on information laid by me as president of the C.P.B. He is suspected of receiving stolen goods. The proceedings against him took place during my detention.'

Seating himself again, he looked uneasily towards the door through which the great Aaron had vanished.

Fanny Chrysler, Bloomsbury, and the two solicitors then took the oath and testified that the gentleman mentioned in the minutes was the same as Mr MacHeath.

Then Withe stood up again. He held in his hands the brief-case which Walley had given him at the beginning of the proceedings.

'It is not for my client to produce the real murderer,' he said casually. 'But since Mr MacHeath is desirous that the mystery of his employee's death should be finally cleared up, I shall present to the Court certain documents from which can be deduced the probable murderer of Mary Sawyer.'

He threw a bundle of papers on to the table in the centre and sat down again, plainly exhausted.

The public got up noisily and resumed their conversations. MacHeath had, meantime, been glancing repeatedly at his watch. He was doubtless very nervous.

Almost immediately after the jury had retired to decide on his acquittal, he stood up and went out, followed by a police officer. He evidently wished to speak to the reporters in the corridor. After whispering a few words to Polly, he led the group of newspaper men towards an empty room nearby.

The policeman was accustomed to seeing prisoners addressing journalists as their equals and paid no particular attention. When the reporters had all gone into the room, MacHeath shut the door on them and walked on down the passage.

No one took any notice of him. Without a hat, and mopping the perspiration on his forehead, he ran down the steps.

Polly was waiting outside the door at the bottom.

He first had to go to Scotland Yard, and then to the National Credit Bank.

As he climbed into the cab with Polly, Grooch came running after them. They drove off in the direction of Scotland Yard. But they only progressed slowly, for the fog was very thick.

A Victory for Common Sense

While Peachum sat in his little office that morning, writing a new article for the *Reflector* in which he voiced his suspicion that *subversive elements* must have been responsible for the sinking of the *Optimist*, he was also making vain attempts to get into touch with his people in various parts of the City. A few of his messengers came back; they had found no one at all at the meeting-places. The rest disappeared completely.

Towards midday Peachum lost his nerve and drove to Scotland Yard. He found the Chief Inspector already dressed for the memorial service. But he had to be fetched from a cross-examination which he was conducting.

Peachum informed him that a demonstration of several hundred wounded soldiers, with horrible placards and banners, had got beyond his control. Judging by past experience, an enormous crowd would join the demonstrators who were marching to St Paul's.

'You must shoot them!' burst out Peachum. 'They are only riff-raff, the scum of the unemployed! I can give you a list, there are gaolbirds among them! On their placards they are asking what happened to their comrades on the *Optimist* and what use this war is. You *must* shoot them! No one can answer their questions, we must shoot.'

Brown broke out in a cold sweat.

He made a note of all the meeting-places and went away.

Filled with anxiety, Peachum drove to the National Credit Bank.

Shortly after his departure, MacHeath burst into Brown's office.

The Chief Inspector had to be fetched out from a conference. In the interval the banker had a few words with O'Hara, who, with a policeman on either side of him, was squatting in a corner with a hat over his manacled hands. His cross-examination by Brown had been interrupted by Peachum's arrival.

O'Hara seemed calm, almost cheerful. He also spoke cheerfully:

'I'll admit to your crimes now, Mac,' he said. 'I'll take a

load off your mind by doing that. When I've told everything, you'll feel much better.'

The policeman, who knew MacHeath, left the room at a sign from him.

'You are not very sensible, O'Hara. We've got a few minutes left to save you from the gallows and all you do is to talk non-sense. I have asked my friend Brown to let Giles go free, so that he can't say who paid him to kill Coax. Do you under-stand?'

'Quite well. And I'm to disappear into prison.'

'We are trying to find all the invoices we can. *I've* got nothing against you; on the contrary. But it's just that *someone* must take the blame for all this. I am indispensable, everything would collapse without me. But I have been in, too. *For the same thing.*'

'Six years' imprisonment for that? Not on your life! I'm also going to have my little joke. It'll be worth hanging to see you all go west.'

'There won't be so much "going west" as you imagine. No one can prove anything against me, not even you. It's only the business that will suffer if you don't confess. And it won't be six years for you. At the most it may be four. You must confess to ten or twelve burglaries, no more. You will be supplied with invoices for the rest. Our City office has been working hard to help you. You can say that you only went wrong during the last few months.'

'While you were away, eh?'

'Yes, while I was away. And you only did it out of pity. You were sorry for the shops. They were clamouring so miserably for goods. You couldn't bear to witness their distress any longer. You were once one of them. It was a matter of life and death in some cases. And it was a matter of honour with you to deliver cheap goods. The B. shops sell the cheapest goods in London.'

'So I'm to say all that?'

'It won't do you any harm. You must be sensible and see everything in the light of business. But you must make up your mind now, I've got to go.'

Brown came in.

The discussion began anew. It lasted for more than an hour.

O'Hara started to shout again. He said that MacHeath had ruined one of the finest gangs in London – in the world, even. It was now scattered to the four winds. And he, O'Hara, would tear the mask from his face.

But then he became more sensible. The conversation at last came down to earth. O'Hara did not wish to admit to more than two or three burglaries. They compromised on five. MacHeath promised to provide invoices for the rest.

At the end they shook hands.

'Whatever you may feel, O'Hara,' said MacHeath, 'this is a victory for common sense. You couldn't have decided otherwise. But this solution makes me very unhappy. Tonight you will sleep easier than I.'

MacHeath remained for a moment longer with Brown. He handed him a small, sealed envelope.

'I repay my debts,' he said heartily, and then added cheerfully: 'In celebration of today, my dear Freddy, permit me to present you with a small recognition of your kindnesses to me.'

Brown opened the envelope and embraced his old friend and comrade-at-arms, overcome with emotion.

'I accept this,' he said, looking at MacHeath with his clear, honest gaze, 'and I will keep it, because we are friends. It is not the other way about, and I hope you realize that, Mac!'

Stepping out on to the street again with Grooch and Polly, MacHeath perceived that the fog had grown still thicker.

Fog

In the conference room of the National Credit Bank, eight gentlemen were waiting.

In one corner stood a group composed of Mr Peachum, Hawthorne, Miller, and Chreston. In the opposite corner, under a plaster bust of the Prince Consort, stood the two leading lights of the Commercial Bank, and Aaron with his secretary.

The groups avoided looking at one another and conversed among themselves in undertones.

Aaron was telling the two Oppers about the trial.

When they had received Hawthorne's invitation, Aaron had

been the one least astonished at MacHeath's obvious double-dealing. The way in which he accepted the revelation that his friend MacHeath was also president of the hostile C.P.B. and had for some time been conspiring with the opposition, stamped him as a business man of the highest order. He was in favour of suppressing all personal feelings and accepting the new situation as a *fait accompli*. The gentlemen of the Commercial Bank, however, did not share his objective viewpoint and seemed rather astonished at this attitude.

Nevertheless, Aaron confessed that he would be interested to see whether MacHeath could look them in the face today.

MacHeath and Grooch entered.

They stopped in the doorway and bowed. The gentlemen in both corners bowed in return.

A small man with a mean expression on his face detached himself from one of the groups and advanced on the two newcomers.

'Permit me to ask', he said, 'which of you gentlemen is Mr MacHeath?'

MacHeath bowed again.

Peachum saw an undersized, sturdily built man in his forties with a radish-shaped head.

Almost simultaneously they said:

'How do you do? Pleased to meet you.'

Then Peachum went back to the group at the window. His son-in-law and Grooch remained by the door. MacHeath did not think it advisable to involve himself in a conversation with Aaron and the stony-faced Oppers.

So he stood unhappily beside Grooch. Like nearly all the other gentlemen in the room they were both wearing black suits, and both were clearly visible against the milky radiance of the gas-light behind them.

'They are only waiting to be able to make contracts,' thought MacHeath disgustedly. *'All this haggling makes me sick! Here I sit and quibble about percentages. Why don't I simply take out my knife and stick it into them if they won't give me what I want? What a way of doing business – smoking cigarettes and signing agreements! So I've got to smuggle in little sentences and drop suggestive hints! Why can't I say straight off: your*

money or your life! Why make an agreement when one can get the same results by pushing splinters under their finger-nails? Why all this cowardly entrenching oneself behind judges and bailiffs? All that degrades a man. Of course, one cannot get anywhere today with the old, simple, and natural method of street robbery. That bears the same relation to present business practices as sailing ships do to steam ships. But the old days were the best. The old, honest days of landed properties. How they've all come down! Formerly, the big land-owner gave his tenant a smack on the jaw and threw him into the debtors' prison; today, that same land-owner has to go to court and stand there with a statute book in one hand and compel the son of his tenant, who is judging the case, to fill in a scrap of paper which will permit him to eject his tenant. Formerly, an employer could simply dismiss his employees if the wage was not high enough for them, or the profits not big enough for him. He still dismisses them today, of course he still makes profits today, perhaps he makes even bigger profits than formerly, but under what humiliating conditions! He must first stick cigars into his managers' filthy mouths and then drum into their heads what they are to say to the almighty employees so that they may graciously be pleased to work to the greater glory and profit of their master. That's a disgusting state of affairs. Under such conditions, a respectable man can no longer find any pleasure in his profits, however successful he may be! The sacrifice of self-respect is far too great! That affects even the Government. Of course, even today, the masses are brought up to a life of industry and self-sacrifice, but at what a price! The Government are not even ashamed of asking these people to take a ballot-form in their hands and vote for the very police who are supposed to keep them down. Even in this room the universal lack of self-respect is noticeable. These people here ought to be told by me – by me, a former, common-or-garden street-robber – that, in the days when I was still entitled to call myself a street-robber, I would never have dreamed of humiliating myself like they are now!'

They were waiting for Bloomsbury of the C.P.B.

He arrived half an hour after MacHeath and shook the latter by both hands.

'You have been acquitted,' he said heartily. 'But because you ran off you have been given a small punishment for contempt of court.'

With him came Fanny Chrysler. She was now sitting with Polly in the next room. For the sake of his father-in-law Mac-Heath did not wish to have her in the conference room.

The gentlemen took their places at the large round table on which stood a carafe of water, six glasses, and a cigar cabinet. Hawthorne, as notary and host, opened the proceedings.

He welcomed those present and immediately made way for MacHeath with the words:

'Mr MacHeath, known to you all as the founder of the B. shops, wishes, if I have understood his letter correctly, to lay some proposals before you.'

Aaron lifted his fleshy hand.

'Permit me to raise a point which appears to us of extreme urgency and without the satisfactory elucidation of which we could scarcely command the repose necessary to appreciate Mr MacHeath's suggestions. I refer to certain rumours about irregularities in the Central Purchasing Board.'

MacHeath stood up.

'I am fully informed on that point,' he said slowly. 'The rumours were started by the arrest of a certain Mr O'Hara who has been supplying my shops. I myself laid the information which led to that arrest. The origin of some of the goods which he delivered seemed to be extremely obscure. My investigations revealed that they were actually the proceeds of burglaries. Since then, O'Hara has made a full confession to the police. He is now awaiting his trial on a charge of receiving stolen goods.'

Aaron did not seem to be particularly astonished. He nodded in agreement, and not without a hint of admiration.

MacHeath now proceeded to explain his proposals. He spoke as briefly as possible.

The retail business was faced with a crisis. The recent cutthroat competition had lowered the prices to such an extent that a reasonable profit was quite out of the question. The guiding principle of shops with unit prices was 'Service for the Customer'. But in order to succeed in the long run the shops must be *healthy* and be able to build up reserves. The hitherto existing system of more or less blind competition had placed a heavy load on the

336

banks. He would suggest the formation of an A.B.C. syndicate, comprising the Aaron, Chreston, and B. shops organizations, which should study the requirements of the purchasing public, establish a regional system of shops, work out a fixed sales scheme, and thereby aim at a moderately low level of prices.

The great Aaron looked embarrassedly at the gentlemen of the Commercial Bank and then said slowly that a change in the present system of competition seemed to him to be eminently desirable.

A silence fell, and the president of the Commercial Bank cleared his throat.

'I would like to put the question,' he said stiffly, 'as to whether there have already been discussions in the direction just mentioned by Mr MacHeath. So far as I know, the B. shop system of Mr MacHeath's has, up to this moment, belonged to our group and he is therefore bound to discuss with us any decisions affecting our common interests.'

MacHeath chose every word with the greatest care.

Because of certain family connexions – he indicated with a wave of his hand Mr Peachum sitting opposite, who however did not move a muscle – he had been compelled to take a hand in the affairs of the National Credit Bank which was working with Chreston's Chain Stores. The decision as to the future of this concern had, so to speak, been placed in the lap of his family. Consequently, certain discussions of an informal nature had taken place between himself and Mr Chreston personally.

'And what was the outcome of these discussions?' asked Aaron, without looking at his bankers.

'Complete unanimity,' answered Chreston for MacHeath. Aaron laughed.

'At these discussions,' went on the president of the Commercial Bank coolly, 'at these discussions of an informal nature held in the lap of the family, was any mention made of the role allotted to the Central Purchasing Board?'

Whereupon he looked at Bloomsbury who was fidgeting about unhappily on his chair, understanding nothing of what was going on.

With complete calm, MacHeath answered for him:

'You can address that question to me,' he said.

'I am addressing it to the C.P.B.,' replied Jacques Opper.

'That is, to me,' assented MacHeath easily. 'I can no longer conceal the fact that I have been in close connexion with the C.P.B. for some time past.'

'A family connexion?' asked the younger Opper with icy irony.

'No, a friendly one,' answered MacHeath amiably. 'Bloomsbury and I are friends.'

'Very interesting,' said Henry Opper, and looked at Aaron.

A painful silence fell. Hawthorne poured himself out a glass of water and politely begged those present to avoid any bitterness in the discussion.

'Well, MacHeath,' resumed Aaron, in a not unfriendly tone and with a certain gallows humour, 'as I see it, you are the president of the C.P.B. and a director of the National Credit Bank. Am I right?'

MacHeath nodded seriously.

'Then that rather alters the situation, Opper,' said Aaron, addressing his own party. 'If I am not mistaken – and there is no reason why I should be mistaken – Chreston may soon expect to receive fresh deliveries from the C.P.B. I may say, without any bitterness, that family and business connexions, not to speak of friendly ones, have engendered a very harmonious atmosphere amongst the opposite side. That raises the question, Opper, of whether there is really any need to take opposite sides. We could come to an understanding tomorrow, but we can also come to an understanding today. And now is the best time, gentlemen! What is your opinion?'

'The C.P.B.,' interpolated MacHeath, 'is a very powerful organization so long as the prices it receives are not too low—as has unfortunately been the case recently. The pressure which the lowering of prices has exerted on shops not belonging to our system has had its full effect. A series of bankruptcies has been the result; from the humane standpoint a depressing state of affairs, but one that will lead to the speedy recovery of the retail trade. There are considerable quantities of goods to be bought at extremely low prices from these bankrupt shops. The sick man dies, and the strong man fights, gentlemen!'

Aaron examined his finger-nails. No one seemed to want to say anything. So MacHeath continued:

'An announcement, my dear Aaron, that our sales week was not taking place, would most certainly be undesirable. Just think how the whole of purchasing London has been following our competitive battle! But, of course, a ring composed of the firms represented here could just as well cancel the sales week as let it go on.'

'I see,' said Aaron. 'You would still go on with your sales week if we came to no agreement? But I thought that the warehouses of the C.P.B. were momentarily exhausted?'

'So they were,' explained MacHeath willingly, 'but I have just bought several consignments – from Chreston. They were somewhat more expensive than those supplied by the C.P.B., but not so dear as those on the ordinary market.'

'In a ring such as you suggest,' said Aaron, 'you, as president of the C.P.B., would have an exceptional position, MacHeath?'

'Shall we say – exceptional responsibilities!' answered Mac-Heath agreeably.

'Well, what do you think?' asked Aaron, turning to the gentlemen of the Commercial Bank.

Henry Opper looked at his brother and said sharply:

'I'll tell you what I think. For my part, I propose that we have nothing at all to do with Mr MacHeath. And I will now ask you to leave the room with us.'

He stood up.

Aaron looked at him unhappily.

'But why?' he said plaintively, remaining seated. 'Listen to what he has got to say.'

Henry Opper looked at him a moment longer with cold disdain. Then he turned without a word, nodded shortly, and left the room, followed by his classically-minded brother.

Aaron stared hard at each of those present.

'My friend has really no sense of humour. There's no doubt about that. I remain here because I *have* a sense of humour, and for business friends to know that of one another is a step in the right direction. I cannot go away if my firm is faced with ruin,' he concluded angrily.

Since no one spoke, he went on:

'A question which might become acute, is the following: can we do without the financial assistance of the Commercial Bank?'

For the first time that afternoon, Peachum took a hand in the discussion.

'I think', he said drily, 'that my son-in-law can reassure you on that point. The Marine Transport Company, which I represent, has luckily suffered no financial loss in the terrible catastrophe which recently overtook one of its ships. So financial loss, at least, was not added to the havoc wrought by loss of life. I may tell you in confidence that a further contract with the Government is to be anticipated. Therefore – at any rate temporarily, until I can start to realize several extensive plans which I have in mind – I am in a position to give my support to a promising young concern such as the A.B.C. Shop Syndicate.'

Aaron bowed in his chair. Then he looked almost dreamily at MacHeath. And he said softly:

'I think I understand, MacHeath. With your fantastically cheap goods from the C.P.B. you involved myself and the Commercial Bank in a desperate price-cutting competition with Chreston, whom you thereby brought to his knees. When he was at the end of his resources and had drawn on the money of the National Credit Bank so as to be able to keep his prices as low as ours, you made the National withdraw his credit. But with us, and with your own shops as well, you cut off the supply of goods from the C.P.B. when the struggle was at its height, and now you are separating me from the Commercial in the same way as you cut Chreston off from the National. It's superb! We must discuss it all over a bottle of '48, eh? But that's enough of business! From what I see, most of us here are hoping to attend the memorial service this afternoon. In which case we must go now. Anyhow, we cannot settle any more details today.'

The others were in complete agreement. The A.B.C. Syndicate, under the management of Mr MacHeath, was a *fait accompli*.

Polly and Fanny, who had been waiting in the next room, had had an entertaining conversation.

Fanny had told Polly, with much laughter, about an amusing episode at the trial.

After the acquittal, several B. shop owners and their wives had taken part in the search for MacHeath. Fanny had followed behind them and listened to what they said. They were all wanting to shake him by the hand.

And they were all cursing Walley, for he had apparently irritated them.

'It's obvious that this Walley had some dirty reason for doing it,' they said angrily.

Fanny told Polly that the alibi, which had pleased them so much because it had freed MacHeath, had been the very meeting of the C.P.B. which had decided on the stoppage of deliveries and, therefore, their ruin.

Polly laughed very much and they went on to discuss the coming autumn fashions. When the conference ended, they had already invited each other to their homes. Polly was a little nervous, for her father was seeing Mac for the first time today.

She saw her husband come out of the conference room with her father. They were walking side by side in silence. Both deep in thought.

They drove to the cathedral in four cabs. Polly sat alone with her husband in one. She held his hand. For their love had triumphed over all obstacles.

During the conference in the National Credit Bank, the fog had become, if possible, still thicker. The cabs advanced at a crawl. At several of the cross-roads discussions arose between the cabbies as to which direction they were to take.

In the second coach sat Peachum, Fanny, and Bloomsbury. The latter spoke enthusiastically of the talents of his friend MacHeath.

'He's a tremendous worker,' he said reverently. 'He's always working. He never thinks of himself, only of his business. He scarcely ever rests; at midday he only stops to swallow a few mouthfuls of food. Really, the only peace he gets is in prison.'

Then Fanny discussed with Mr Peachum the prices of shops in Hampstead.

They were soon quarrelling, and Fanny said, laughing and looking sideways at Peachum, that he knew she always spoke the truth.

Peachum smiled laboriously.

He was quite grey in the face and looked old. He was afraid. Looking out into the fog, he saw vague forms, groups of men with boards bearing horrible slogans which he himself had devised.

'This fog is a piece of luck,' he thought, leaning back. 'But it may clear any minute. And what then? Of course, I live on threats. But this time I've threatened a little too much. It may cost me my neck. The police are my only hope; but will they be successful? They, too, have to march in the fog. They don't know what they've got to face; they've never seen the placards which are advancing on them. Oh God!'

Grooch was driving with Chreston and Aaron. The latter still had his secretary with him.

Aaron had formed a high opinion of MacHeath. He now admitted to himself that when he had heard in court that MacHeath was behind the C.P.B., he had immediately made up his mind to give him a key position in the new syndicate.

The cabbies seemed not quite certain as to whether they were on the right road. Several times they pulled up and shouted to one another from their boxes. And once, they all turned round.

Then they stopped some passers-by, who, however, were equally ignorant of their whereabouts.

A policeman gave them directions, and they hurried their horses into a trot, as though they now knew the way for certain.

MacHeath shouted several times from inside:

'To St Paul's Cathedral!'

But then Grooch and Aaron got out and went across the road and reported that they could already see open fields, at least on one side.

The cabbies held a parley. They counted up the number of places where there were open fields on one side of the road. Since they could come to no agreement, they drove on. Hawthorne said gloomily to Miller (the One and Half Centuries were driving in the last cab):

'No one knows where they are now!'

After a further half an hour's driving MacHeath lost patience and said roughly to Polly:

'We're going to get out at the next corner and go into the nearest house. We can't go on like this.'

And he actually did get out, and with him all the others.

The first building they came to had a high wall and seemed to be fairly large, although it was impossible to distinguish anything clearly in the fog. The wall ran for a long way, and for some time they were unable to find the door.

When they did find it, they saw that they were standing in front of the Old Bailey.

They turned round laughing and climbed into the cabs again. It was now clear that they had gone completely astray.

It was pure chance that they met a second policeman who, when he heard that the company had tickets for St Paul's, guided the cabbies round a corner whence they only had to drive straight ahead to reach their destination. They arrived more than an hour late.

There was scarcely anyone to be seen outside the cathedral – except begging soldiers.

Peachum looked out of his cab and stared incredulously at the doors.

Dozens of his people stood there, wet through and miserable.

He took one of them aside and learned that Beery had not reached the meeting-place in time. But the demonstration had not taken place. Early in the morning a regular rebellion had broken out among the men. They had thrown their posters away and refused, on a day so auspicious for trade, to be kept away from work by having to carry placards.

'Blood is thicker than water,' one of them said.

'It's much better not to attract the attention of the police. Today the public are prepared to be generous so that the poor soldiers shan't be discouraged from giving their legs and arms for the greatness and glory of England. And we're supposed to be accusing complete strangers in the Government of trying to betray us! What about our business? Tomorrow, wounded soldiers will be handed over to the police; today, they are being fêted. One doesn't get a shipwreck every day. We can just as well demonstrate against corruption in times of depression.'

Thus reasoning, the demonstration had broken up before it had even begun.

The beggars were well distributed among the adjacent streets. But the fog was a great hindrance to their work. Again and

343

again, instead of approaching the relatives of the victims, they found themselves soliciting from the numerous representatives of the Government.

Peachum entered the cathedral, considerably relieved.

The place was still half empty. The great high columns were wrapped in black cloth. Beneath the pulpit lay enormous wreaths.

The service had not yet begun.

Not even the military escort had arrived. Half blinded in the fog, the company of guards had groped their way through Chelsea and had at last arrived at the Thames. They had almost fallen in.

Cursing, they marched back again. They were supposed to be guarding their drowned comrades from the excesses of the mob.

When they finally arrived, the clergy were still missing. They had lost their way in the gloom and had wandered into Smith-field Market. The bishop, who had the funeral oration in his pocket, had become confused while searching for a porter and had run, in desperation, down one of the narrow passages through which the animals are driven to slaughter. He was sitting in an empty sheep-pen, when some porters ultimately discovered him.

After the arrival of the clergy, the service in posthumous honour of the victims of the *Optimist* began.

The representatives of the Government were all there. Mac-Heath saw Brown sitting beside a high official whose picture he had often seen in the weekly papers. He was glad that Brown looked so inaccessible to the man-in-the-street, and was proud of him.

The man beside Brown was Hale. Peachum discovered him immediately. Brown's cab had run into Hale's in the fog. So, hoping that between the two of them they could find the right direction, they had driven the rest of the way together.

The pews for the general public were still only half full. The relatives of the victims had not been expected to be very numerous, but hundreds who had husbands and sons in the field were unable to arrive in time.

They wandered about in the streets, asking at every street

corner, and even at houses and shops, where the memorial service was taking place.

After an introductory voluntary on the organ, which set the tone of the proceedings, the bishop, still trembling from his adventure in the slaughter-house, delivered his sermon. He had taken as his text the parable of the nobleman and the pounds.

He first read the parable from the Gospel according to St Luke, which begins with the words:

A certain nobleman went into a far country to receive for himself a kingdom, and to return.

The man gave each of his servants a pound, with the command that they were to make use of the money until he returned. When he came back, one servant had gained ten pounds. The nobleman gave him authority over ten cities. The second had gained five pounds and received authority over five cities. But the third had gained nothing at all. So the nobleman took his pound away and gave it to the man who had gained ten pounds. Unto everyone that hath shall be given, he said, and from him that hath not, even that which he hath shall be taken away from him.

That was the parable, and the bishop based his sermon on it.

'*My friends,*' he began, '*the terrible disaster which overwhelmed the transport,* Optimist, *in the Channel has aroused a wave of* patriotism *in our land. It is as though the affliction which has been visited upon our country has opened the eyes of the people to England's mission – a mission which the nation had all but forgotten when, on the morning of last Thursday, the readers of newspapers found beside their breakfast plates the awful announcement of the disaster which had overtaken England.*

'*What do I mean now, when I say: their eyes were opened? My friends, all events in life – and life is made up of events – have a* front *and a* back. *There is a foreground to every occurrence, even to such as the catastrophe to our* Optimist; *and there is a background. And there are people who see the front but do not see the back. Although the background is, in reality, the more important; only he who sees it, sees life.*

'*And what, my friends, I ask you now, is the* background *to this catastrophe which has hit us so hard?*'

The bishop leaned back until he was standing upright. With a cool, clear gaze he surveyed the congregation below him; the representatives of the Government, the officials of the Admiralty with Hale at their head, and the business men, and the relatives of those at the front.

'*My friends,*' continued the bishop after this inspection, '*the lord in our parable is a strict lord. He demands his money back with interest and compound interest. The servant who only returns him one pound is cast into outer darkness where there is wailing and gnashing of teeth. Yes, my friends, God, who is the Lord in the parable, is our Lord, and He is a strict Lord and demands His interest. But, my friends, He is also a righteous Lord. He does not demand the same interest from each of His servants. He takes ten pounds from the one and five pounds from the other. He takes what He gets. Only the one pound of the third servant, the lazy, ungrateful, unfaithful servant, does He reject. The man has failed. And from him shall be taken away even that which he hath, namely the pound, the initial capital, which each has received. The deep meaning of this parable is expressed in that astonishing sentence: "To every man according to his means."*

'*I would like to interpolate here a short digression on the meaning of the word "Pound". There are, in the Holy Scriptures, two versions of the parable of which we are speaking. In the one, pounds are mentioned, in the other, talents. Talents – that means two things: firstly, a large silver coin of ancient Greece, and secondly, a mental faculty. That seems to me a beautiful allegory. Faculties are money, accomplishment is wealth. – But all this is by the way.*

'*My friends, everywhere we go on earth we meet with in*equality. *Every man enters the world as a tiny bundle, naked and unashamed. In this condition he differs in no way from any other suckling. But after a time, differences begin to show. One man remains on a lower rung; another climbs upwards towards success. He is cleverer than his fellow men, he is more industrious, more thrifty, more energetic, he surpasses the other in everything he does. And he will become more prosperous,* more powerful, more respected, than the other. The inequality becomes self-evident. How then does God regard this?

'Does He also value men differently according to their different levels? Does He love a man with superior capabilities more than another who is more modestly gifted? No, my friends, God does not. He divides the rewards among His servants, ten cities to the one, five cities to the other, according to what they have accomplished. Beyond that, He recognizes no difference. Beyond that, He loves all His servants equally. And that, my friends, is the meaning of equality before God!

'My friends, this parable of the pounds shows us how we must regard the loss of our soldiers in the Optimist.

'Our land has great men whose accomplishments are truly wonderful. Our statesmen stand day and night on the bridge of the ship of State. Our generals, bending over their maps, evolve plans and stratagems. We here in the pulpit, the chosen servants of God, do our part by strengthening the hearts of our fellow men. And our soldiers embark on the ships. And sink with them – if such be God's inscrutable will. We return our pound with interest. So do they. But altogether we are helping our country continually to increase the pound which God has entrusted to it, so that, when we are ultimately called before the Heavenly throne, we can point to our country and say: Thou hast given us statesmen, generals, merchants, soldiers, and see, oh Lord, here is what we have made out of them!

'If we thus consider everything that happens, the good with the bad, then we no longer see the foreground of a national disaster such as the sinking of the Optimist, as do those people whose senses are wholly earthbound. Then, the scales fall from our eyes and we see the background – and when we see this, we realize that our soldiers and sailors, although they never reached the foe, have yet not died in vain. Then we realize that the ship which sank in the impenetrable fog was not unjustified in bearing the proud name of Optimist. For its optimism, my friends, consists in the supreme hope that its fate will be rightly interpreted by the nation. Then, even from this ship that was destined to sink, we have gained something: it has paid interest and compound interest, oh Lord!'

After the service, Mr Peachum and Mr and Mrs MacHeath, together with the gentlemen of the National Credit Bank and those of the A.B.C. Syndicate, all retired to a nearby restaurant to give personal considerations their due after having disposed of all business ones. Mr and Mrs MacHeath stood in the middle of a cross-fire of complimentary speeches and congratulations.

Aaron spoke first:

'Ladies and Gentlemen,' he began, *'today is an important milestone in the history of England's retail trade. Today, the leadership of a great retailing syndicate was taken over by a man whom we all, during these past few months, must have recognized as a leading light in our profession. From tomorrow onwards, he will put at the disposal of our common interest his undivided attention, his remarkable business ability, his unflagging energy, and, above all, that skill in handling men which we have come to know and to value. The public will shortly be convinced of this new power behind the scenes. No longer will we merchants dissipate our strength in fruitless competition; henceforth, we shall be fighting a common fight together. We have all just heard the wonderful words of the bishop when he spoke of the parable of the pound. We may be sure that our new board of directors, with Mr MacHeath at the helm, will extract from the pound which our world-wide organization represents, every penny that is humanly obtainable.'*

Mr J. J. Peachum made a remarkable suggestion in his speech.

'I will not pretend', he said, *'that I have always been so enthusiastically in favour of my daughter's marriage to Mr MacHeath. In fact, I was not really convinced that my daughter had chosen rightly until I took a glance at the business activities of my son-in-law. I saw then that it was one of his principles to serve the lower classes. This immediately struck a corresponding chord in myself. Most people think comparatively little about the lower classes; and that is very wrong. They may be less cultured than we, coarser in their ways, even rough; they may have but a vague idea of that necessity which ordains that all men, whether high or low, must live together in harmony if the whole world is not to sink down to the brutish conditions in which they only too often exist: but none of that can alter the fact that they deserve recognition. I would like to make a prac-*

348

tical suggestion now: you, gentlemen, and you, my dear son-in-law, sell razor-blades and clocks, household utensils, and heaven knows what. But a man cannot live on such things alone. He is not satisfied if he is shaved and knows what the time is. You must go further. You must sell him culture. *I mean books, cheap novels, things which do not portray life as a uniform grey but paint it in brighter colours; things which will show to the ordinary man a finer world, which will acquaint him with the better customs of the higher levels of society and with the admirable way of living of the socially elect. I am not thinking of the profits – they might possibly be considerable – I am thinking of humanity which would thereby be rendered a great service. In short, give them a little excitement.'*

After Mr Aaron had thanked Mr Peachum in the name of the A.B.C. Shop Syndicate for his suggestion, old Hawthorne got up and jokingly related a small episode which had occurred in the last few months.

'At this point I will not deny', he said good-humouredly, *'that it was a definite, purely personal experience which persuaded us of the National Credit Bank to do everything in our power to put an end to the murderous competition among the great chain shops. This experience was a visit to the bank by Mrs MacHeath, who sits among us here. She said nothing about business. She spoke only of private matters. But her words moved us so – for even elderly people have a heart – that we could not do otherwise than agree to visit her much abused husband, who lay innocent in a prison cell. And it was with him that all further discussions of amalgamation took place. It was not – and I would like to emphasize this, however old-fashioned it may sound – it was not business acumen which found a way out of the difficult situation. It was – love.'*

When Polly stood up she looked more like a lovely ripe peach than ever. She made the following little speech:

'Although it's not popular when we ladies make a speech, because men don't like us trespassing on their preserves, I would just like to say how very happy I am that I always followed my own feelings and never wavered in my love for my husband. Of course, we women can never think so clearly as the lords of creation, *but you can see from my case that true love*

can also be quite successful. But it must be strong enough and one must never mind if people look a little askance at one. The clever plans which our men work out may often be quite useful; but we of the weaker sex are sometimes more successful – just because of love, however silly it may seem at the time. Why, I can remember how more than once, Mac, that cold business man, threw everything away, risked his whole career, in order not to lose me on whom he had set his heart. Isn't that so, Mac?'

And lastly, MacHeath spoke:

'My dear wife, my dear father-in-law, my friends! On the whole, I am satisfied with the conclusion which we reached today after so many misunderstandings. I make no secret of it: I come from the lower classes. I have not always sat at tables like this, and rarely with such admirable people. I began my activities in a small way, in other surroundings. But, for the most part, my interests have always remained the same. A man's success is generally ascribed either to his ambition or to some complicated scheme. I freely admit that I never had a great scheme. I only wanted to keep out of the poor-house. My maxim has always been: the sick man dies and the strong man fights. And after all, it is only people like myself who get to the top. Should there be anyone now at the top who will not endorse this motto, he'll soon find himself at the bottom. I am in complete agreement with my friend Aaron when he says that the business world always has need of men of my stamp. Other people cannot make the smallest profit out of the pound which providence has placed in their hands. I will make no prophecies, but I believe that our new syndicate will do its duty. One thing is clear: however low the prices may be at present, they cannot remain so. I close with the motto: Ever upwards! per aspera ad astra! And: Never look back!'

During these last sentences of Mr MacHeath's, the company had grown suddenly serious. All felt that he had here touched upon a fundamental problem.

Pensively, they emptied their glasses.

THE POUND OF THE POOR

But those who have no pennies
O, what do they do, pray?
Lie down and get themselves buried
While the world goes its way?

O no, for we'd have no pounds, then,
If they were allowed to do that!
For without their toiling and moiling
We'd none of us grow fat.

(NURSERY RHYME)

The Dream of the Soldier Fewkoombey

FEWKOOMBEY, too, had been in St Paul's. Since his attack on the broker, he had only appeared once at the house in Old Oak Street. And Beery had immediately thrown him out.

He had gone to St Paul's because he was hoping to be able to speak to Mr Peachum there. He knew Peachum had had something to do with the *Optimist*. But of course he never got near him. So he sat down in the church, which at least was heated, and listened to the sermon about the pounds.

After that he wandered round the docks; without a home, without friends, skulking from the police. His state grew worse and worse. He knew nothing of the result of the Mary Sawyer case, for he never read the newspapers.

On a cold November morning there was some excitement in front of a baker's shop in West India Road.

A small boy snatched a loaf of bread from the counter and ran out of the door. The people in the shop raised a cry, at which the passers-by outside took up the pursuit of the thief. He ran hard, as hard as his little legs could carry him, but he did not get far. At a street corner a man stuck out a leg in front of him. He fell on the pavement, was caught, led back to the shop, and shortly afterwards taken away by the police.

The people dispersed, grumbling.

Amongst those who had chased the boy was a ragged man of uncertain age. When the child had been handed over to the police, he went away towards the docks. He knew a place there where he could spend the night.

To be precise, he was the man who had stuck out the leg over which the boy had tripped. The action had been purely mechanical.

When he arrived beneath his bridge, he drew a decaying morsel out of his pocket, unwrapped the paper round it, and ate it slowly. Then he took off the remains of a shoe which he still dragged round on one foot, lifted up a certain stone, pulled out two newspapers from beneath it, sat down, spread the newspapers over his legs, rested his head on both hands and on his coat which he had removed, and curled up as tightly as possible. Then he went to sleep. And he dreamed:

After the years of misery came the day of triumph.

The masses arose; shook off at last their tormentors; with a single ablution rid themselves of their comforters – perhaps the most terrible of their enemies; finally gave up all hope, and won the victory. Everything was changed. Vulgarity lost its glory, usefulness attained renown, stupidity lost its privileges, brutality was no longer the key to success. Not the first nor the second, but the third or the fourth, had been delaying the great *Day of Judgement*.

Everyone knows what that is. This day of judgement has continually been discussed; since time beyond memory the world has been talking about it; every nation and race has imagined it in elaborate detail. Some people tried to postpone it until the end of all time, but this attempt at procrastination had become suspect; at any rate, the nations could not wait so long. There could be no question of the judgement day coming at the end of all life, because, after all, it was to be a prelude to life. Before this great judgement had taken place, there could naturally be no talk of real life.

Now it took place.

The dreamer was the judge. Of course, he only gained this position after a bitter struggle, for there had been a monstrous crowd of candidates, screaming and fighting like madmen for the privilege. But because no one can stop a dreamer from getting what he wants, our friend became the judge of the greatest arraignment of all times, of the only really essential, comprehensive, and just tribunal that has ever existed.

He was to judge not only the living, but also the dead; all who had in any way wronged the poor and defenceless, either by word or by deed.

The task of the soldier Fewkoombey, who was now the supreme judge, was a colossal one. He estimated the duration of the proceedings at several hundred years. For all who had ever lived on earth were to be allowed to voice their plaints.

After lengthy reflection, which itself lasted for months, the judge decided to start with a man who, according to a bishop's sermon at a memorial service for drowned soldiers, had invented a parable which had been used in pulpits for two thousand years. In the view of the supreme judge, this constituted an especial crime.

The proceedings took place in a yard, in which, curiously enough, there was washing hung out to dry, and in the presence of fourteen dogs who sat in a kennel and listened to everything that was said. They had not been fed, and were not to be fed until judgement had been passed.

The accused was led forward by two beggars.

He was a tradesman or an artisan, as could be seen from his cheap but neat clothes and his celluloid collar.

On the judge's table lay a knife and a letter written in ink to which was attached a printed document.

The proceedings were opened by the judge asking the accused whether he knew how far-reaching were the effects of his talking, in fact of all talking.

The accused answered: yes, he was known everywhere as a religious teacher.

His answer, like everything else said, was written down by a gigantic beggar, a Mr Smithy, who was well known to the supreme judge for his accuracy as a recorder. He had once been extraordinarily accurate in recording the earnings of his employee Fewkoombey when the latter had taken up begging.

The second question of the supreme judge was: whether the accused pleaded guilty to having misrepresented facts in his parable and to having circulated such misrepresentations.

The accused excitedly refuted such allegations.

With industry and suitable management, so he said, it was quite possible to obtain five or even ten pounds from one pound.

When asked *what sort of* management, he could only repeat: just by ordinary, suitable management.

Being further pressed by the judge, he admitted that he took no interest in practical matters and details. So he knew very little about such things.

The supreme judge stared at him fixedly to discover whether this were the truth. Then he banged on the table so that the rusty knife and the letter flew into the air. But he said nothing. He went on and asked:

'You are supposed to have said that not only some people but *everybody*, receives his or her pound. I would point out to you that this is the crucial point of the prosecution.'

The accused admitted to having said such things. He only seemed astonished that this should be the crux of the matter.

'Then tell us,' continued the judge calmly, 'who told you that every man on earth received such a pound, which then increases to five or even ten pounds?'

'Everyone says so,' answered the accused slowly, because he was still wondering why this should be the crux of the matter.

'Then we will summon those who told you this, and question them,' announced the judge sternly.

He rang a luncheon bell and from behind the washing came a number of people, all similarly clothed and wearing celluloid collars like the accused, in fact they were acquaintances of his, friends of his youth, neighbours, teachers, and masters, even relations.

They stood in front of the judge's table and were cross-questioned.

They all said that they had received a pound. The pound was represented by their understanding, their knowledge of a calling, their industry.

'And did you have anything else?' asked the judge.

Then one admitted that he had owned a carpenter's workshop. This was the father of the accused.

Another had received money from his parents to enable him to attend a school. This was the teacher of the accused.

A third had inherited a grocer's shop. This was a neighbour of the accused.

The judge nodded at each of these statements, as though he had expected just this and nothing else. He looked across at the dogs who were jostling against the iron bars of their kennel, and he laughed at them, without making any sound.

'So there's a great deal that goes with such a pound?' was all that he said. And to the witnesses he said:

'Have you all traded diligently with your pound?'

They all affirmed loudly that they had traded with their pound to the best of their ability; that they had preserved what

356

they had been given, had increased it, and had even brought up children and provided each of them with a pound.

The judge laughed at the dogs again.

Then he once more addressed himself to the accused. He asked him whether he had not met other people, people without the pound such as these witnesses had.

The accused shook his head.

Then the supreme judge rang the luncheon bell again, and from behind the washing appeared other people. They were worse dressed than the previous lot, and they walked more wearily.

'Who are you?' asked the judge. 'And why have you stood apart from the witnesses who are already here?'

It appeared that they were the servants and employees of the others. They would not be so impertinent as to stand beside their masters.

'Do you know the accused?' the judge asked them.

They knew him. He was the man who had often spoken to them. Amongst other things, he had told them that each man receives a pound from God, in the form of his spiritual and physical powers, which he must increase and put to good account. They had heard it from his own mouth.

'So he knows you, too?' questioned the judge.

'Of course,' they answered, and the accused had to admit that he knew them.

'Have you increased your pound?' asked the judge severely.

They shrank back in terror and said: 'No.'

'Did he see that your pound did not increase?'

At this question they did not at first know what they ought to answer. But after a time one of them stepped forward, a little boy, who was the living image of the boy whom the soldier Fewkoombey had tripped up in front of a baker's shop with a leg that was made of wood. He stood bravely in front of the judge and said loudly:

'He must have seen it; for we froze when it was cold, and we starved both before and after we had eaten. Look for yourself and see if we show it or not.'

He stuck two fingers into his mouth and whistled; and out from behind the washing, but wetter far than the wet things drying in the wind, stepped a woman. And the woman was the living image of Mary Sawyer.

The judge leaned forward in his chair, so that he could observe her better.

'I wanted to ask you whether it is cold where you come from, Mary,' he said loudly, 'but I see that the question is unnecessary. I see that it *is* cold where you come from.'

Then he saw that she was tired, so he said to her:

'Sit down, Mary. You have walked too far.'

She looked round for a chair, but there was none there.

The judge rang again. And it snowed out of the air, but only in a thin column, no thicker than the trunk of a medium-sized tree, until a bank of snow was there on which she could sit down. The judge waited until the snow stopped, and then he said:

'It will be a little cold; and when it becomes warm, it will melt, and you will have to stand up again. But there is nothing else I can do.'

And to the witnesses he said:

'The point is proved. So you were cast out into the place where there is wailing and gnashing of teeth?'

'No,' said one of them, growing bold. 'We were never let in.'

The judge gazed pensively at them all. Then he turned again to the accused.

'The case against you looks bad, my man. You must have someone to defend you. But he must be suited to you.'

He rang, and out of the house came a small man with a mean expression on his face.

'Are you the counsel for the defence?' murmured the judge. 'Then stand behind accused.'

When the small man took up his position behind the accused, the latter became pale. He realized that the judge meant ill in giving him this defender.

The supreme judge now explained the situation. The court accepted two of the accused's statements as having been proved true; firstly, that the pounds could be made use of and increased, and secondly, that those who made no use of them were thrown into outer darkness where there was wailing and gnashing of teeth. But the statement that *all* men received a pound was not accepted by the court as proved.

'Mary Sawyer,' began the judge again, 'you signed an agreement with Mr MacHeath. Was there anything in that agreement which provided that no new shops should be started near yours?'

She thought for a moment and then said:

'No.'

'Why did you not notice that that was missing?'

'I don't know, Few.'

The supreme judge rang the bell. From between the washing came a tall man with a crane. This was the former teacher of the suicide.

'You did not teach your pupils to read,' accused the judge. 'How was that?'

The tall man looked sharply at the woman and then said:

'She can read.'

'But not agreements, not agreements!' shouted the judge and became very angry.

The teacher assumed an offended expression.

'My pupils in Whitechapel do not need to read agreements,' he growled. 'They should learn to work, and then they wouldn't need any agreements.'

'What is the meaning of confederacy?' asked the judge quickly.

'Alliance,' answered the teacher astonished. 'What has that got to do with it?'

'Right,' said the judge with satisfaction, 'alliance. And what is the meaning of Attica?'

The teacher kept an obstinate silence.

The supreme judge seemed disappointed, but he went on.

'Did you enjoy a school education?' he said to the accused, who stood there meekly, his head bowed on his breast. And when the man in the celluloid collar nodded, he asked:

'Then what is Attica?'

But the man did not know. The teacher tried to tell him, for it seemed wrong to him that the accused should know so little.

'Yes,' said the judge, 'you don't know much.'

But the little man who was defending him broke in at this and cried:

'He knew enough. He knew enough for us.'

'Of course,' murmured the judge submissively. It was purely mechanical.

When he raised his bell again, a thin man in a waiter's apron stepped up to the judge's table. This was the man who had owned the ale-house before Fewkoombey.

'Can this man write?'

The question was directed at the teacher. The latter looked at the witness, recognized him as his pupil, and nodded with his great head.

'But for me,' said the judge angrily to the witness, 'you never wrote that you only had customers as long as they were building new houses.'

'I couldn't write that,' answered the waiter. 'I hadn't enough money when I bought the place, and I was glad to be able to pay off my debts and become a waiter again.'

'So he couldn't write *that*,' shouted the judge, growing angry again.

But then he controlled himself and said nothing for a time.

While everyone was standing round and waiting for the next question, the judge stood up, walked across to the teacher, and asked him, in a friendly, almost servile voice, what Attica meant. He had not got as far as that in his book because it had been taken away from him. But the teacher only looked at him and gave no answer.

The supreme judge sighed and continued the proceedings.

But he was not quite certain how to go on.

He looked across at the chief witness and saw that she was sewing once more. She was plying her needle, stitch by stitch, although she had no material to sew, because the supply of goods had stopped. So she sewed in the air and no shirt took shape.

'If the supply of goods had not failed,' he said thoughtfully and softly, 'and if the new shop had not been opened, would you then perhaps have made a success of your business?'

'Why not?' she said wearily. 'I had the sewing-girls.'

'That is a crucial point,' said the judge quickly. 'But we are getting no further. I never thought it would be so difficult to get things clear.'

He stood up and went over to the kennel. The dogs whimpered happily, because they thought they were now going to get their meal. But the problem was not yet solved.

The supreme judge looked across the yard. There stood the witnesses for the defence, those who supported the accused, well-fed, well-clothed, with prospects and successes; and opposite them stood the ill-fed, the prematurely aged, the woman, still sewing, sitting on a bank of snow, the boy, with his arm bent as though he were carrying a heavy loaf of bread, but without bread.

When the judge returned to his chair, stumping on his wooden leg, he passed close to the accused. He thought for a moment and then said in an undertone:

'Don't *you* understand it then?'

But the man in the celluloid collar only shrugged his shoulders and could say nothing.

'All this difference,' sighed the judge, 'and no reason! And yet something must be to blame. But what?'

He stood for a moment, indecisively, wondering whether there was really any point in his sitting down in the judge's chair again.

'That's just my ignorance,' he thought. 'I'm too uneducated to find anything out, far too uneducated.'

Suddenly he started. He had remembered the power with which he had been recently invested. He hurried to the table. With a sweeping movement he swung his bell.

From behind the washing, in a long row, stepped the volumes of the *Encyclopaedia Britannica*, twenty-four in number. They walked pompously, they were fat.

They lined up in front of the judge like soldiers, four deep.

'My friends,' began the judge in a respectful tone, 'can you tell me anything about the reason why some of us, the minority, increase their goods and make five or even ten pounds out of one pound, as the Bible commands; while others, the great majority, after a long and hard working life, increase, if anything, only their misery? What, my friends, is this pound of the fortunate, which produces such enormous profits and around which, so I have heard, such a desperate battle rages? Of what does it consist?'

The twenty-four volumes formed a circle and consulted together. Then one of them stepped forward.

'I can give you some information about *capital*,' it said in a loud, coarse, and self-confident voice. 'Money is a thing which produces interest like a cow calves. Be it inherited, be it acquired, whoever has control over it will receive interest from it. Perhaps that will help you.'

The judge turned to Mary Sawyer:

'You had money, too, if I remember correctly. Understand me, I'm not asking you how you came by it, but you had some. That money did not increase.'

'Yes,' she said indifferently, 'I had a little. It was soon gone.'

'It did not calve – you!' said the judge severely.

Then another volume stepped forward.

'I know something about *working-power*,' it said loudly. 'When anyone expends some of his working-power on a thing, that thing becomes more valuable. Stones are not worth much, but a house is, if you understand me.'

'Oh,' said the judge wearily, 'that can't be it. We've all got the power to work. But the thing on which we expend it does not belong to us, or it is a failure. Eh, Mary?'

Several other volumes stepped forward and spoke about *inventions* or *organizing-ability* or *thrift*. But none could explain quite clearly what exactly constitutes the pound of the fortunate.

At last they formed up in a row and numbered off so that the judge could see that none was missing. And there was none missing.

Then the judge told them to withdraw, and he was more worried than before.

He looked again at the chief witness, Mary Sawyer the sempstress.

'Sirius,' he murmured.

He sat down and rang the luncheon-bell.

From behind the washing appeared Sirius. He had five great points and two little feet.

'Have you recently,' asked the supreme judge, 'entered the sign of the Scales?'

Sirius thought for a moment and then replied in the negative.

'If you had entered the sign of the Scales, or any other sign, would that, in your opinion, have threatened danger for Mrs Sawyer's shop?'

Sirius denied this without the slightest hesitation. He seemed very offended.

'So you're not responsible? You've got nothing to do with it? Then it's not luck?'

'What fool said it was?' said Sirius.

The judge dismissed him. With his chin on his breast he sat there and stared morosely in front of him.

There was sudden unrest among the witnesses for the prosecution.

'We must go now,' they said. 'You'll never find the answer. It's just the vast inequality, and the others are cleverer than us.'

'The inequality is very great,' said the counsel for the defence, now taking up the word and pushing his hat on to the back of his neck. 'Between a man with a wooden leg and a blind man without legs there is an enormous difference – which also becomes apparent financially, my dear Fewkoombey.'

The judge listened very attentively. Every word interested him; that was plain to see. And the judge knew that it was plain.

'Call Beery, my business manager,' demanded the counsel for the defence scornfully, 'he is the son of a coal-miner.'

The judge pondered for a moment. Then he rang and Beery appeared.

He admitted, without being asked, that he had a balance at the bank.

'But I've thought of something else,' he boasted. 'The closets with the sloping back-walls were my idea.'

The counsel for the defence supported him:

'He understands how to get something out of people. That's it.'

The witnesses for the prosecution began growling.

'Silence!' the judge reprimanded him.

Then the eye of the supreme judge fell on the things which lay on the table – the knife and the letter. He got up, walked round to the other side of the table, stood there like a witness, and said:

'I received this knife as my pound.'

He stumped hastily back to his chair and said severely:

'That is another crucial point. Mary, what did *you* receive?'
And he showed her the letter so as to influence her answer.

'I received that letter as my pound,' she said, understanding
him; and thereby she helped him a little way further.

'This letter says that you know something about your employer which would send him to prison. That's blackmail, isn't
it?'

'Yes,' she said.

'Yes, that's our pound, that's what our pound looks like,' he
murmured absently. 'But what is theirs?'

He sat there, with his head propped on his hands, and seemed
utterly desperate.

'It gets no clearer,' he moaned. 'These B. shops, these transports! Profits upon profits! Where does it all really come from?
Such wonderful chances, such wars, such inequality! How do
they do it?'

But then he saw Beery standing in front of him, and something occurred to him. He turned to his recorder, who had once
been his employer.

'Smithy,' he asked him, 'if you had been allowed to keep me
that time, would you have got on in the world?'

'Why not?' answered Smithy.

'Then everything is clear,' said the judge, and his voice
trembled with excitement. '*Now* that has proved what your
pound is! Stand up, Mary! Come forward! Smithy, go over to
them!'

And he turned triumphantly to the relatives of the accused:

'*That* is your pound! *We* are your pound! Man is the pound
of man! Whoever has no one to exploit, exploits himself! The
secret is out! You were hiding it from me! *There* is the house
– *where* is the bricklayer? Is he ever really paid for his work?
And this paper! Someone had to make it! Did he receive sufficient for it? And this table here! Is there really nothing owing
to the man who planed the wood? The washing on the line!
the line! and even the tree, which didn't plant itself. The knife
here! Is everything paid for? Fully? Of course not! We must
send round a circular: all who have not been paid fully, please

send in your names and addresses! The history books and the biographies are not enough! Where are the wage lists?'

And turning to the accused he shouted at the top of his voice:

'You are convicted! Nothing but misrepresentation! You have spread lies! Therefore I condemn you! As an accessory! Because you gave people this parable, which is also a pound! Out of which profit can be made! And all who pass it on, all who dare to relate such things, I condemn! To death! And I'll go further: whoever listens to it and dares to refrain from taking immediate steps against it, him also I condemn! And since I, too, have listened to this parable and said nothing, I condemn myself to death!'

And he sat down, bathed in sweat.

A few days later Fewkoombey was arrested. Much to his astonishment he was charged with the murder of Mary Sawyer. He was condemned to death and hanged – amidst the approval of a great multitude of shopkeepers, sewing-girls, wounded soldiers, and beggars.

MORE ABOUT PENGUINS

If you have enjoyed reading this book you may wish to know that *Penguin Book News* appears every month. It is an attractively illustrated magazine containing complete details of the month's new books. A specimen copy will be sent free on request.

Penguin Book News is obtainable from most bookshops; but you may prefer to become a regular subscriber at 3s. for twelve issues. Just write to Dept EP, Penguin Books Ltd, Harmondsworth, Middlesex, enclosing a cheque or postal order, and you will be put on the mailing list.

Another Penguin by Bertolt Brecht is described overleaf.

Note: *Penguin Book News* is not available in the U.S.A., Canada or Australia

PARABLES FOR THE THEATRE

Two Plays by Bertolt Brecht

THE GOOD WOMAN OF SETZUAN
THE CAUCASIAN CHALK CIRCLE

Presented in this Penguin edition in a revised English version by Eric Bentley, these are among the handful of plays generally regarded as the masterpieces of one of the dominating figures in the modern theatre. Both plays are well known from productions in this country, and *The Caucasian Chalk Circle* in particular is an outstanding example of Brecht's epic theatre.

Eric Bentley was a close friend of Brecht and for many years has been one of the most energetic advocates of his work.